Dead Canaries
Don't Sing

Dead Canaries Don't Sing

A *Reigning Cats & Dogs* Mystery

Cynthia Baxter

BANTAM BOOKS

DEAD CANARIES DON'T SING

Published by Bantam Dell
A Division of Random House, Inc.
New York, New York

Bantam Books and the rooster colophon are registered trademarks
of Random House, Inc.

ISBN 0-7394-4124-8

Manufactured in the United States of America

To Mike

Acknowledgments

I would like to thank Faith Hamlin, my eternally optimistic and supportive agent, who held my hand all the way through the writing of this book, as well as her assistant, Kate Darling, for all her clever ideas;

Martha S. Gearhart, D.V.M., who patiently shared her time and expertise, giving me a crash course in the realities of being a veterinarian, along with the entire staff of the Pleasant Valley Animal Hospital in Pleasant Valley, New York, who cheerfully allowed me to eavesdrop on their conversations and get in their way;

Dorothy Hayes, V.M.D., Judy Lombardi, V.M.D., and the staff of the Corner Animal Hospital in Setauket, New York, who also exhibited admirable patience while allowing me to be a "fly on the wall";

Lisa Pulitzer, whose willingness to commiserate about the emotional ups and downs of the writing process was at least as valuable to me as her vast experience as a crime reporter;

Kate Miciak, who so greatly inspired me with her

unflagging encouragement and her tremendous under-standing of both writing and writers, and Caitlin Alexander, whose enthusiasm, insight, and skill with words went such a long way in shaping this book;

And Max, George, Tiger, Petey, Arthur, Snowflake, and all the other wonderful furry and feathered crea-tures who have brightened up my life and served as inspiration for the animal characters in this book.

A Note to Readers

Dead Canaries Don't Sing is a work of fiction, and all names and characters are the product of the author's imagination. Any resemblance to actual events, organizations, or persons, living or dead, is coincidental. Although some real Long Island places and some real people are mentioned, all are used fictitiously.

Dead Canaries
Don't Sing

Chapter 1

"A bird in the hand makes a bit of a mess."
—Anonymous Birdcatcher

If I hadn't forgotten to seal up the package of English muffins, if I hadn't instantly become addicted to *The Crocodile Hunter* the minute it came on the air, if two of the beasts in my possession hadn't developed a Batman-and-Robin complex, that bleak Tuesday in November would have probably turned out to be just another day.

I had a sense it wasn't off to a good start as soon as I opened my eyes and saw my alarm clock. For normal people, 5:45 is their cue to roll over and go back to sleep.

But that's for normal people. For me, those numbers got the same reaction as if somebody casually mentioned they'd put a boa constrictor in my bed.

I let out a cry that sounded like something a terrified animal would make. Then I leaped out of bed and immediately began hopping around the house, trying to keep warm. Chilly mornings are one of the few negatives of living in a stone cottage built back when Andrew Jackson was president. Meanwhile, I struggled to figure out how I would explain to the folks at Atherton Farm why I was so late for my six A.M. appointment to treat one of their horses for what I suspected would be a serious throat condition called strangles.

My two trusty sidekicks, Lou and Max, were already in high gear. Both thought all this shrieking and leaping was a game. Of course, both think just about everything is a game. You'd think that a three-year-old, one-eyed Dalmatian and a two-year-old Westie with a stub for a tail would have developed some sense along the way. But you'd be wrong.

Their reaction was to do some leaping and shrieking of their own, which prompted my parrot, Prometheus, to put in his two cents. From the living room, he squawked, "Crikey! Crikey! *Awk!* Crikey!" doing a perfect imitation of the great Croc Hunter himself. If there was anything more annoying than two dogs who acted as if they'd just overdosed at the espresso machine, it was a Blue and Gold Macaw who affected an Australian accent.

"Give me a break, guys," I pleaded. They were the first real words I'd uttered that frigid morning, one lit by a sun that looked as if it were about as awake as I was.

Predictably, they didn't listen. Prometheus moved on to some of his other favorite phrases. "News at eleven! *Awk!* News at eleven!"

Meanwhile, Max and Lou continued their circus

routine, tumbling over each other like, well, like a couple of puppies as they followed me into the kitchen.

As usual, Catherine the Great lay draped across the rag rug in front of the sink, looking like a siren from the silent movies, even with her nicked ear. The cloud of silky gray cat fur glared at us in a way that revealed exactly what she was thinking. I had to agree. Yes, it would make much more sense if we all just turned around and headed back to bed.

I was about to explain that duty called, but I needed coffee before I could attempt to reason with a cat who *knew* she was superior. So I turned to the coffeepot.

"Damn," I muttered.

That's where my Crocodile Hunter addiction caught up with me. I should have resisted the urge to stay up much too late, watching Steve Irwin play Twister with a seven-foot gator. That way, I would have gotten enough sleep. I would also have remembered to set up the coffee.

Okay, Plan B, I thought, trying to remain calm. The two lords-a-leaping at my feet didn't exactly help me focus. I groped for the tea. As long as I had something caffeinated and an English muffin, my usual way of fueling up just enough to get me out the door . . . And that was when I noticed that the sole surviving muffin was exposed to the air, thanks to an insufficiently zipped Ziploc bag. I didn't even have to touch it to know that during the night the powerful forces of nature had transformed it into a hockey puck.

With no caffeine and no edible English muffin, I had no choice but to turn to Plan C: grabbing breakfast in the outside world.

I tore back into the bedroom and threw on my version of business dress: black jeans, a forest green polo shirt embroidered with "Jessica Popper, D.V.M.," a zippered polyester fleece jacket, and a pair of chukka boots from L.L. Bean. I fastened a ponytail band around my hair, once blond but ever since I'd turned thirty much closer to dirty blond.

On my way out of the bedroom, I glanced into a mirror. A tired-looking woman stared back at me through watery green eyes.

"You go, girl," I sighed.

Max and Lou were already hanging out near the back door. They liked being part of the mobile veterinary services business even more than I did. They got to travel all around Long Island, meet interesting animals and enjoy a fascinating range of smells. And all it took to motivate them were the magic words, "Want to go for a ride?" Who says it's hard to get good help?

As I raced along the quarter-mile driveway that connects my tiny cottage with Minnesauke Lane, I could practically taste Dairy Delight's 99-cent breakfast. A cup of scalding coffee, a toasted muffin dripping with butter . . . and thanks to drive-through, it was all mine without even leaving the driver's seat. It doesn't take much to make me happy.

Of course, the downside was that the detour took me out of the way, making me even later. Fortunately, I knew a short cut to Atherton Farm that led to the back entrance to their forty-four acres. The back road to the barn was more like a dirt path that had been cut into the field, the result of other drivers who, like me, were too lazy or too far behind schedule to drive around to the real entrance.

I gritted my teeth as I bumped along, praying my suspension was faring better than my internal organs. I was just considering turning around and opting for the easier, more sensible route when my van abruptly lurched sideways and stopped dead.

"Great," I told Max and Lou, who'd both been thrown about three feet but didn't seem the least bit perturbed. "Now we're stuck."

As I swung open the door to check the damage, Max and Lou jumped past me. I would have anticipated their escape if I hadn't been so distracted by my traumatized van.

I now had two problems to deal with: my unhappy vehicle and my AWOL animals.

"Max! Lou!" I cried, watching them take off across the field, totally crazed over their newfound freedom. Not surprisingly, they ignored me.

So I turned to the more immediate problem. I checked out my custom-built vehicle, a 26-foot white van with blue letters stenciled on the door:

REIGNING CATS & DOGS

Mobile Veterinary Services
Large and Small Animal
631-555-PETS

The good news was that the tires were all intact. The bad news was that one of them had just dropped into a hole at least a foot deep.

But it wasn't *that* bad. I figured I could dig out the

front of the hole, creating a slope instead of a cliff, and drive the van out.

I was about to start excavating when hysterical barking cut through the silence. I spun around, dropping the shovel.

I know my dogs' barks the way a mother knows her baby's cry. What sounded like nothing but noise to the untrained ear in fact clearly communicated hunger, a need for attention, or a diaper that needed changing. Or danger.

Something was very wrong. The seriousness of Max's and Lou's tone instantly got my adrenaline going.

I spotted them a few hundred yards away. Both stood near a clump of trees at the edge of the field where a dense wooded area began. I could see from their stances that every one of their muscles was tense.

I jogged across the field, the soles of my boots occasionally slipping against the dirt, still wet from the drenching rain we'd had two nights earlier. I was panting when I reached the two dogs and the oddly shaped mound that had caught their interest.

The first thing I saw that was out of the ordinary was a pair of shoes that appeared to have been abandoned in the woods. I didn't know much about men's shoes, especially those fancy wing-tipped jobbies favored by conservatively dressed businessmen. But from what I could tell, this was one expensive pair. As my eyes traveled beyond them, I made out a matching set of legs, two inert protrusions that could have passed for logs if it hadn't been for the high-quality leather at one end.

The fact that I'd stumbled across a partially buried body didn't hit me for a few seconds.

Once it did, my response was to do what any other self-respecting professional woman who had spent four years in college and four years in veterinary school, learning to cope with life and death on a daily basis, would have done.

I shrieked.

Max and Lou instantly stopped barking, no doubt impressed that the leader of their pack was capable of making a sound even more piercing than what they were capable of. Whether I'd simply stunned them or won a new level of respect, I didn't know. And I didn't care.

At the moment, I was too busy struggling to remember what a rational person was supposed to do at a moment like this.

Cell phone. Somehow, the thought cut through my panic.

"Stay!" I told Max and Lou, wanting to mark the precise location of the wing-tipped shoes and the human body that was attached to them.

For once, they actually obeyed. I dashed back to the van, praying I'd taken better care of my Nokia than I had my English muffins. I grabbed it off the driver's seat, yelped with relief when I saw it was still half-charged and dialed 911.

"Officer Johnston, Eighth Precinct. Where's the emergency?"

"Atherton Farm. Brewster's Neck, off Green Fields Road." The shakiness in my voice surprised me. "This is Dr. Jessica Popper. I'm a veterinarian. I came out here on a call and found a dead man in the woods."

"How do you know the person is dead?"

"Not moving, lying half buried in the woods, skin—what I can see of it—ghostly white . . ." *Not exactly a pretty sight,* I was tempted to add, but didn't.

"I'll send an ambulance," Officer Johnston replied, unperturbed. "Tell me exactly where you are."

I gave directions, then ended the call. With the police on the way, I knew I'd done my job. I made a quick call to Skip, the manager of Atherton Farm, explaining that I'd been delayed but would get to the barn as soon as I could. The obvious next step would have been to put the phone away, call my dogs back into the van and wait for help to arrive.

Instead, I stared at the ditch my tire was stuck in and then back at the phone in my hand, thinking. Debating, really. Should I or shouldn't I? Dialing those seven digits, punching in that familiar number that I'd called hundreds of times before, would have been so easy. And not at all questionable, under the circumstances.

Except that even I didn't know my real motivation for calling Nick Burby. Did I really need his help? Or was I merely using the ghastly thing that had just happened as an excuse?

I was about to put my cell phone away when I heard Lou's deep, chesty bark. I snapped my head around and saw him stationed a few feet away from the corpse, glancing down at something in the leaves and yelling his head off. Meanwhile, Max, the digger in the family, was doing his terrier thing. He was working his strong white paws like there was no tomorrow, the dirt flying wildly as he doggedly went after something buried near the body.

"No!" I shouted, moving toward them, worried about what he'd find.

Max shoved his nose into the earth. When he came up, the flash of bright color that contrasted sharply with his white beard sent a shiver through me that was even colder than the early November morning. Even from a few hundred yards away, I knew exactly what it was.

With trembling fingers, I dialed Nick.

• • •

The Norfolk County police arrived with their usual fanfare, sending up splatters of mud as two patrol cars came barreling over the dirt road far more recklessly than they should have. Their red lights flashed and their sirens made those obnoxious beeps that sound like the vehicle in question had too much spicy food the night before.

I stood a safe distance away from the corpse, wanting to seem respectful of death while at the same time serving as a sort of beacon, pointing the way. Max and Lou frolicked at my feet like two little kids. I was glad I'd gotten them away from the fascinating smells of the forest. The last thing I wanted was to disturb a crime scene. Especially this one, since I was already thinking of it as *my* crime scene.

Two uniformed officers climbed out of their cars, hoisting their belts and scowling as if they were already prepared for the worst. Well, they weren't about to be disappointed.

"You the person who called in?" the short, dark-haired one demanded, his New York accent so thick he sounded like a character in a Scorsese film. He wasn't much older than I was, but he already had the tired look and sagging belly of a man firmly planted in middle age.

I nodded.

He peered at me through dull, heavy-lidded eyes that were the same dark brown as his nightstick. "Name?"

"Jessica Popper. Dr. Jessica Popper."

The wheels turned in his head, so slowly I could practically hear them creak.

"Dr. Popper?"

"That's right."

He smirked. "Like the drink?"

"That's Pepper. I'm Popper." *And even though you clearly think you're incredibly clever, this is about the eight millionth time in my life I've had this exchange.*

"Wanna tell me what happened here?"

I glanced at his name tag and learned I was talking to Officer Pascucci. "I came out here early this morning on a call. I'm a veterinarian, and—"

"You're a *what*?"

I peered at Officer Pascucci more closely, trying to decide if he hadn't heard me, hadn't mastered any six-syllable words or was merely toying with me.

"I'm a veterinarian," I repeated patiently. "An animal doctor? I was on my way to make a house call. One of the Athertons' stallions is sick."

He just stared at me. I was really having trouble reading him. Was he not capable of understanding what I was saying—possibly the result of too many hours spent in front of the tube watching arena football and *The Man Show*? Or was he waiting for me to say, "Oh, and on the way, I stopped to drop off a dead body I happened to have with me"?

"My dogs found him," I persisted, trying to hang tough. Pascucci stared me down. "I stopped my van to check the tire, and they raced out before I could grab them. The next thing I knew, they were barking like crazy. That was when I went over there and saw . . ." My voice trailed off lamely.

"These are your dogs?"

I just stared at him. It was *so* tempting to point out that given the fact that we were standing in a deserted field with only two dogs in sight, the odds were astronomical that the gangly one-eyed Dalmatian and the hyperactive, tailless Westie were, indeed, mine.

Instead, I simply replied, "Yes." Then congratulated myself on my outstanding amount of self-control.

"It was actually Max who found the body," I went on. "The furry guy. He's a West Highland White . . ."

Pascucci didn't appear to be listening. He crouched down to examine the witness more carefully.

"What kind of dog did you say this was?" He stuck his hand out, as if he were about to grab Max by the throat to get a better look.

"Hey!" he yelped, pulling it back abruptly and jumping up. "The little bastard tried to bite me!"

"I'm so sorry!" I grabbed the perpetrator and tucked him under my arm like a football, thinking, "Well, what did you expect, approaching an animal like that?" Still, I knew that Max's tendency to snap, at least under pressure, wasn't one of his more endearing qualities. "He only does that when he's excited or scared. I know it's a terrible habit, but I've never been able to break him of it. His original owners weren't exactly the nicest people in the world."

Pascucci's face twisted into an ugly scowl. "You got a license for that mongrel?"

It was probably just as well that the other cop chose that moment to step in. "Why don't you go check out the body, Vince?" he interjected. He was as lanky and fair as his sidekick was stubby and dark. "Officer Nolan," his name tag read. "You know Homicide's gonna want to ask their own questions."

Officer Pascucci shot Nolan a look that told me his surliness wasn't reserved purely for members of the general public. Then he strutted away, positively oozing self-importance as he headed toward the woods.

As soon as he was out of earshot, the second police officer smiled apologetically.

"Sorry about that. I'm afraid Vince has seen too many cop shows. He thinks 'tough' and 'obnoxiously rude' are the same thing."

I put Max back on *terra firma*, then smiled back. If these two are playing good cop, bad cop, I decided, they're doing a pretty good job.

"Besides, you gotta realize what a big deal this is, Dr. Popper. It isn't every day we have a murder up here. Compared to the rest of the Eighth, this area's Disneyland. The worst crimes we ever get up here on the North Shore are little old ladies who lock themselves out of their houses. Maybe the occasional cell phone gets stolen out of somebody's BMW. So for somebody like Pascucci, this is the thrill of a lifetime."

He smiled again. He had a rather nice smile, I noticed, one that lit up his entire face and gave him a boyish look that bordered on charming.

"By the way, I'm Officer Nolan."

"Jessie Popper."

"A veterinarian, huh?"

"That's right. I specialize in mobile veterinary services. In other words, I make house calls."

"Yeah? How'd you get into that?"

I didn't have a chance to answer. A shrieking ambulance careened toward us, trailed by two cars. The isolated dirt road was beginning to look like a parking lot.

"Get ready," Officer Nolan warned me under his breath. "Here comes the big guy."

A well-dressed man with the posture of a four-star general strode toward us, glancing down at the scrubby terrain as if it were peppered with land mines. He struck me as the kind of guy who got his boxer shorts dry cleaned—extra starch, please—and I got the feeling he was more worried about getting his shoes muddy than he was about the unexpected appearance of a corpse in the woods. Still, I decided to give him the benefit of the doubt. The ambulance driver and an EMT followed, lugging medical equipment and looking substantially more anxious about what might be going on here than the man in the suit.

The "big guy," as Officer Nolan had identified him, nodded an acknowledgment at Nolan, then focused on me with pale blue eyes narrowed into slits. "I'm Lieutenant Harned, chief of homicide. You the one who made the call?"

"Yes. I'm Dr. Jessica Popper, and—"

"Tell me exactly what happened."

I elected not to point out that I'd been about to do precisely that when he'd interrupted me. "I operate a mobile veterinary services unit and I came out here on a call at about six-thirty. One of the Athertons' horses is sick. My van stalled, and when I opened the door to check it, my two dogs ran out. They discovered the body over there."

"Exactly what time did you get here?"

The guy was big on exactness, I noted. "I'd say 6:25. Actually, I'm pretty certain of that, because I'd just looked at my watch to see how late I was going to be."

"Did you see anybody else in the area?"

I shook my head.

"Somebody driving away, maybe? Or maybe you passed somebody out on the main road?"

"Not a soul. This area's always quiet, and this early in the morning, it's completely dead." My hand flew to my mouth. "What I mean is—"

Lieutenant Harned frowned. "What about seeing anything unusual? When you went after the dogs, did you notice anything out of the ordinary? A weapon, a footprint . . . anything at all?"

"Well, there was this one thing . . ." I pointed to the spot where the dogs had found the body. From that distance, it was hard to make out the human form half covered by dead leaves. But the flash of bright yellow was unmistakable.

"Max—this one's Max, the Westie, uh, the West Highland terrier—dug up a canary nearby. I'm not sure how deep it was buried—"

"A canary?" Harned repeated the word with suspicion, as if he deeply distrusted my ability to identify such a rare species of bird.

I was debating whether or not to remind him that I was an animal expert when he commanded brusquely, "Give your name, address, and phone number to Officer Nolan here. And don't leave yet. I've got a couple of guys from my unit on the way. They'll want to question you."

As he turned and headed toward the body, I called, "I'd be happy to show you exactly where—"

"We'll handle this from here."

"Isn't there anything I can do?"

"Yes, as a matter of fact." Lieutenant Harned paused long enough to glower back at me. "Put those two mutts on a leash and get 'em out of here. They've already messed up the crime scene enough."

By that point, my blood was boiling so violently I figured there had to be steam coming out of my ears.

What *exactly* were you expecting from the cops? I asked myself. An engraved thank-you note? A proclamation commending your good citizenship?

I answered my own question: How about a little civil treatment?

When I heard another set of tires on the rutted road, my stomach tightened. I didn't know whether to feel relieved or even more agitated over Nick Burby's arrival on the scene.

How long has it been? I wondered, shielding my eyes from the sun with my hand as I watched the black Maxima jerk along the uneven road. Okay, I knew exactly how long it had been. Two months, one week, and four days. A grand total of seventy-one days.

At least you haven't been calculating the hours, I thought.

I tried stepping out of myself, objectively viewing my reaction as I watched Nick climb out of his car. The reasonable part of me felt like shaking me by the shoulders and scolding me over the way my heart got that weird achy feeling. Not good achy; bad achy.

It was the feeling that makes you realize where the term "broken heart" comes from.

I took a few deep breaths. It has to be like this, I told myself firmly. You know perfectly well it's the only way. You made your decision, and it was a good one. The only one. Now, you've got to move on.

I repeated these assurances in my head as I watched Nick stroll across the field, his hands jammed into the front pockets of khaki pants that would have greatly benefited from five minutes with an iron. As he walked toward me, he kept his head down. The lock of dark hair that was always falling into his eyes behaved exactly as predicted. He pretended he was being careful not to stumble. But I knew, deep inside, that he was trying not to look at me.

I was determined to ignore my pounding heart and the adrenaline surging through every cell of my body. In the grand scheme of things, the fact that I had discovered a dead body less than thirty minutes earlier was surely much more important than my lurid past.

I decided to act like a mature adult, focusing on the sticky situation at hand without letting my emotions get in the way, when Nick demanded, "Okay, Jess. What have you gotten yourself involved in now?"

Within a nanosecond, my hackles were up. Here I had swallowed my pride by calling Nick in my time of need, breaking my long silence to humble myself before his years of expertise with crime. And what was his response? He was talking to me the way Ricky used to talk to Lucy.

"I haven't gotten involved in anything," I shot back. "Is it my fault that some . . . some *dead* guy just happened to plant himself directly in my path?"

"Where is he? The dead guy, I mean."

"Over there." I pointed.

"Not exactly in your path, is he?" Nick observed.

"Okay, then. My *dogs'* path."

Nick shook his head, then sighed. "That's what happens when you go looking for trouble."

"I was hardly looking for trouble! I happened to be here for a perfectly legitimate reason. The Athertons called me in a panic, upset because one of their stallions has a dangerously swollen throat and can't stop coughing—"

"Then again, maybe some people are just good at having trouble find them."

I flung my hands in the air. "There's *no* trouble. *Forget* trouble. I'm perfectly fine." At that moment, I regretted having called Nick Burby more than I'd regretted anything I'd ever done in my entire life.

As if he'd read my mind, he asked, "In that case, Jess, why did you call me? It looks like the cops have everything under control."

"My van is stuck in a ditch, and, you know, I guess I thought it might be helpful to have someone here who knows his way around a crime scene. Perhaps in my deranged state I actually imagined that a little moral support might even be forthcoming. Then there's the fact that while I'm finding this whole thing absolutely horrifying, it's also incredibly fascinating, and so I just assumed that you'd be interested, too . . ."

"Actually, to me it's just sad. That poor guy lying over there, whoever he is, just saw his life come to a close. He was probably a good person who just happened to be in the wrong place at the wrong time. But no matter what the circumstances, it's pretty nasty to end up buried in a field."

"He was buried in the woods, not a field. And there was a canary that looked as if its neck had been broken buried right next to him," I announced. I tossed my head arrogantly, wondering if doing so emphasized the golden glints in my hair.

And hating myself for caring.

"A canary—get it?" I went on. "The symbol of 'singing.' Spilling the beans. Telling secrets that aren't meant to be told. That leads me to believe he wasn't exactly a stellar member of the community."

"Jess—"

"And I don't know about you, but the fact that I'm the one who found him, combined with the fact that there was no doubt something fishy going on that led to his untimely and undignified demise, makes me extremely anxious to know who did him in—and why."

Nick cast me a wary look. "Jess, if I were you, I'd answer the questions the nice homicide cops asked me, take a look at the sick horse that brought me here in the first place and then do everything I possibly could to forget all about this."

Before I had a chance to think up a snappy comeback, the cop who was tall, blond, and, I suddenly decided, quite good-looking sauntered over to join us.

"I want to apologize again for Pascucci's rudeness

before," Officer Nolan said. "That's just the way some cops are. It probably has something to do with the bad coffee we're always drinking."

A sense of humor. I liked that.

"Pascucci's here?" Nick glanced at the short, uniformed figure now standing at the mound of dirt and leaves.

"You know him?" I demanded.

"When you're in the private investigation biz, you get to know the local cops. Vince is a pretty good guy."

I glared at Nick, making a statement about the fact that we couldn't seem to agree on anything anymore. *Vince* was most definitely not a pretty good guy. *Vince* was a chauvinistic, obnoxious bore. Then I smiled at Officer Nolan.

"It looks pretty impressive, the way you guys are handling this." I had to stop myself from batting my eyelashes. "I guess you know what you're doing."

"Well, Harned certainly thinks he does."

I laughed loudly, as if Officer Nolan were the funniest, most charming member of the male gender on earth. As I did, I stole a glance at Nick.

Even though I felt unspeakably childish, I was pleased to see he was scowling.

Chapter 2

"Of all the animals, the boy is the most unmanageable."

—Plato

My stomach was still in knots as I drove back home to Joshua's Hollow later that morning after digging out my van and then treating Stormy Weather, the Athertons' stallion, with penicillin for what turned out to be mild *Streptococcus equi* and instructing Skip to continue with three injections a day. The worst part about being in such a state was that I didn't know what was to blame for it: finding an actual murder victim decomposing in the woods or seeing Nick Burby again.

There was one thing I did know. I needed a good strong dose of Betty Vandervoort.

For at least the millionth time, I thanked fate—or my real estate agent—for finding me my cottage. There are three things about it that are unique. Number three on the list is its history. Number two is its beauty. And number one is my landlady, the only person who shares the sprawling property with me.

I dropped Max and Lou at my cottage, knowing they would be welcome at Betty's but not wanting the hassle of keeping them from shattering any valuable antiques. As I trekked toward the Big House, otherwise known as the Tallmadge mansion, I could hear the opening bars of "Everythin's up to date in Kansas City" blaring from inside. I knocked on the front door so hard that my knuckles hurt.

"Jessica! You're just in time!" Betty's sapphire blue eyes twinkled like Christmas tree lights as she threw open the door. "I'm about to give my old audition routine a try. You know, the one that got me into the chorus of *South Pacific*."

I stepped inside a foyer that was as big as my entire cottage. "Don't tell me they're reviving it on Broadway?"

"If they're not, they should. All those ridiculous Andrew Lloyd Whoever monstrosities they're putting on these days! It's a disgrace. There's nothing like the classics when it comes to musical comedy."

With that, Betty shrugged off her pale pink silk kimono. I was about to avert my eyes when I realized that underneath it she was wearing a tap-dancing outfit. At least, that was what I surmised it was. The clingy black scoop-necked top looked like a leotard. Over it, she wore a short crimson skirt. At the end of her long, graceful legs were two old-fashioned tap shoes, tied with fat black bows.

I let out a wolf whistle.

"Surprised it fits?" She struck a pose, meanwhile fluffing her smooth, white hair, carefully styled into a flattering pageboy. "The old legs still look pretty good, don't they?"

I had to admit that they did. Even at her age, Betty Vandervoort didn't have legs; she had *gams*.

As for her age, I estimated it to be seventy-five plus. Although I'd known her for nearly three years, I never could get a straight answer about the year Betty was born. I'd tried to trick her into an admission by casually asking how old she'd been that time she took the gamble of a lifetime, investing an entire summer's earnings as a waitress at the Paper Plate Diner in Altoona, Pennsylvania, in a one-way ticket to New York City.

She hadn't fallen for my ploy. Betty was hard to fool. And today was no exception.

The twinkle in her eyes faded as she studied me more closely.

"Something's wrong." It was a statement, not a question. "You don't need a performance. What you need is a cup of tea. A strong one."

She scooped up her silk robe and headed out of the room, with me trailing after her. It was a long walk, one that took us through an elegant front parlor decorated with gilt-framed mirrors and Victorian couches covered in silk brocade. Next came a dining room featuring a table that could sit fourteen, with a huge crystal vase of long-stemmed white roses at its center. Then a butler's pantry so big a butler could actually live in it.

Finally, we reached the kitchen. As I sat meekly at the table, Betty put the kettle on. She had a firm conviction that water boiled in a microwave didn't taste as good as water from a kettle. She placed an empty

Limoges teacup in front of me with a bit of a flourish, no doubt an unconscious move from the old days at the Paper Plate.

"Now tell me." She sat down and fixed her perfectly made-up eyes on me.

I took a shaky breath. "This morning, I was on my way to see a sick horse at Atherton Farm when Max and Lou found a body in the woods."

"A body?" Betty frowned. "What kind of body? You mean a deer or an opossum—?"

"I mean a human body. A murder victim."

"Murder? In Brewster's Neck?" Betty shook her head, which sent her long gold earrings swaying. "That's the most horrible thing I've ever heard. Who was the victim?"

"I don't know. The cops made me leave before I had a chance to find out."

"You must be in shock!" She pushed back her chair. "I think you need something stronger than tea."

Reaching into one of the upper cabinets, she pulled out a bottle of whiskey. She plunked it on the table, right next to the sugar bowl, and sat back down again. "I want to hear everything."

I told Betty the entire story, all about getting up late and having to rush to get my cup of morning coffee and ending up taking the back road through the horse farm. She listened intently, reacting with subtle facial movements but not saying a word.

When I got to the part about calling the police, I faltered. She raised her eyebrows.

Reluctantly, I said, "I, uh, also called someone else to the scene."

"Who?"

"Just a friend. Somebody with some experience in the area of crime investigation. But he couldn't get any more information out of the police than I could."

She perked up instantly. " 'He'?"

"Betty, it was totally innocent, I assure you. All I wanted was a little professional advice. I figured that, you know, it might be helpful to have him around . . ."

She shook her head disapprovingly and pursed her red lips. "Jessica, when are you going to realize that it would be helpful for you to *always* have Nick Burby around?"

"I didn't come here to talk about Nick." I hoped I sounded more certain about that than I felt. "I came for the comfort of a good friend. For goodness' sake, Betty, I found a dead man in the woods this morning!"

Betty cast me a skeptical look, but said nothing. Instead, she jumped up to retrieve the kettle.

We both remained silent as she made two strong cups of Earl Grey, laced with something a lot more powerful than anything the good Earl had to offer. We each took a few sips before I declared, "I'm going to find out everything I can about this case."

"But you don't even know who the dead man was!"

"I know I'm the one who discovered his body. That links us in some way, doesn't it?"

"If you ask me, you'd be better off putting your time and energy into that Nick of yours. Now *he's* something worth investigating."

I couldn't help but smile at her perseverance. "I've told you that's all over. Nick and I are just—"

"I know, I know. Just good friends." Betty grimaced. "If that's the case, then how come every time you talk about him, your eyes get all sparkly?"

"My eyes do not get all sparkly! I'm just tired. I—I got up much too early this morning."

Betty cocked her head to one side. "At this point, Jessica, I'm old enough to read people pretty well. I'm also old enough to tell them the truth without worrying about them decking me."

"But—"

"What's even more important," she interrupted ruthlessly, "is that when you get to be as old as I am, you see things, things that other people, even younger people with better eyesight, don't see. They're too busy, maybe, or too busy thinking about themselves. But I see what there is between you and Nick."

"I'm not saying that Nick and I weren't . . . *close* at one time."

"Close?" Betty picked up the whiskey bottle and poured another generous dollop into my teacup. "I know I've told you this story at least a hundred times, Jessica, but the first time I laid eyes on my Charles, I knew he was the one for me. I was moonlighting at the Copa, wearing this headdress-thing made out of bananas and pineapple that must have weighed thirty pounds. I was thinking, 'How am I ever going to make it through tonight?' when I looked out at the audience. And there he was, sitting right in front, looking at me and wearing that smile . . ."

Actually, I'd heard this story more like a thousand times. But I never tired of hearing it. Just as I never tired of seeing the look that came over Betty's face as she told it.

This time, however, her expression tightened. "If he hadn't been taken away from me so quickly, back when we were still newlyweds and so crazy in love that we couldn't stand to be away from each other . . ."

She fixed her gaze on me. "The point is that I know what real love is, Jessica. I also know that most people never find it. If you're one of the lucky ones who has, you've got to grab it and appreciate it and do everything you possibly can to hold onto it."

I squirmed, wishing we could go back to talking about something easier, like dead people. It appeared that that wasn't about to happen.

"Jessica, I'm as firm a believer in women being strong and independent as you are," Betty continued. "That whole image of a simpering gal who can't survive without her man never did sit well with me, even back in the days when it was pretty much all we had.

"And I can't help but admire someone like you, who's worked so hard and done so much. But there's a fine line between being independent and being pig-headed. And I believe your determination to run away from Nick falls into the second category. As for this murder investigation business, it sounds to me like it's nothing more than a distraction."

"I think you're reading more into this than there really is," I protested.

"Nonsense. I've seen the two of you together. I've seen the way you look at Nick and the way he looks at you. For heaven's sake, I've practically seen little hearts in your eyes."

"I'm sure there have never been hearts," I insisted. "Besides, even if there was something between Nick and me—and I'm not denying there was—the timing simply wasn't right. I can't help it if he's ready to get married and have kids and walk hand in hand into the sunset, while I still feel that I'm discovering who I really am. Who knows? Maybe I'll never be ready to—"

"Pshaw!" Betty waved her scarlet fingernails in the air as if I were trying to bamboozle her and she was not one to be bamboozled. "Love jitters, that's all it is. We all get 'em."

"Even you and Charles?"

She looked at me slyly, as if she realized she'd been caught. "As a matter of fact, yes. The day Charles and I decided to elope—you know, that day he came to my dressing room right before the show, with ten dozen white roses in his arms?"

I nodded, not reminding her that the last few times I'd heard this story, it had been eight dozen.

"Anyway, I still remember the first thought that flashed through my head when Charles popped the question."

"What will I wear?" I teased her.

Betty whooped. "Are you kidding? That was the least of my worries. Back in those days, Charles and I spent more time out of our clothes than in them. No, I remember thinking, 'Am I sure?' "

I waited, expecting more.

"Of course, I knew the answer instantly. But at least I asked myself the question."

I shot her a look of disbelief. "That's it? That's your love jitters?"

"I didn't say they had to last long. Just that they had to happen."

"Well, Nick Burby is *not* my Charles. And eloping is most definitely not in our future."

"You wouldn't have to elope. You could have a

beautiful wedding right here. We could have the ceremony in the backyard. How about at the edge of the rose garden? We could set up one of those big tents. I love those tents. We could have waiters in tuxedos, passing around trays of caviar. And champagne, in crystal glasses. Even your dogs could come. Can't you picture Max and Lou in black bow ties, working the crowd?"

I had to laugh. The image was just too perfect. Betty was right; Max and Lou would love it. So would everyone else.

Everyone but me, that is. Sure, I could picture the scene she was describing. The only problem was, I couldn't see myself as the bride. At least, not without experiencing a severe anxiety attack.

"Betty, Nick made himself perfectly clear. He gave me the old 'now or never' ultimatum. I couldn't answer 'now,' so it's a moot point. It's time to move on with my life."

"So you say." She sighed and stood up. "Well, you go on resisting and I'll go on hoping. But my advice is still to put your energy into your own life and forget about the dead guy. Now, are you ready to see the tap routine that got me on Broadway?"

• • •

My mood was much better by the time I returned to my cottage. My head was still spinning, but this time it was from Betty's inspiring spirit and spiked tea.

The icing on the cake was coming home to my menagerie. When it came to soothing the spirit, nothing worked better than a little animal love. The rest of the world vanished, at least for a little while, as Max and Lou launched into their usual greeting, acting as if I'd been away for months instead of a measly half hour.

"Hey, you guys," I greeted them, crouching down to their level. "Miss me, doggers? Maxie-Max? How about you, Louie-Lou? Miss me half as much as I missed you?"

In response to my question, Max wagged his stub of a tail so hard his shaggy little butt looked like it was vibrating. He practically climbed up my arm, desperate to slather dog kisses all over my face. A typical terrier, he stopped at nothing to get what he wanted.

My Dalmatian was more cautious. Lou pressed his wet nose against my hand tentatively as if to gently remind me that its primary function was scratching dog ears. He kept peeking at Max, as if wanting to make sure he had his permission to do so. Even though he weighed sixty-six pounds and Max only eighteen, Lou was in the habit of deferring to the smaller dog. His scars from his previous owners went far beyond his missing left eye.

"Oooh, I love you, too, you cute little fuzz balls!" I was glad no one was around to hear me speak in that funny goo-goo voice that was reserved for my animals. I hugged my two canines, scratching necks and ears and bellies. Then I lay down on the floor to make myself an even more convenient target for the inevitable onslaught of dog kisses.

Just then, Cat emerged from the bedroom, where she'd no doubt been curled up on one of my feather pillows. She sauntered over, still looking sleepy. I noticed she was moving particularly slowly today, the damp air no doubt aggravating her arthritis. Still, even aching joints didn't prevent her from brushing against my leg and meowing her hello, pointedly ignoring the dogs. Both of them immediately moved aside to make room for her, having no doubt as to who the *real* head of the household was.

"Hey, Cat," I said in a soothing voice, petting the soft fur of her head and gently running my hand along her back. "How are those old bones of yours, girl? You hanging in there?"

She purred her gratitude. "For what it's worth," I told her, nestling my cheek against her soft gray fur, "nobody likes getting old."

"*Awk!* Who's the pretty boy? Prometheus is the pretty boy!"

It was only fair that everybody get equal time. I brought Cat over to the couch, placing her on the softest pillow. She blinked at me and meowed, her way of protesting against being left on her own. Sometimes I wished I could clone myself. That way, all my pets could have an adoring master at their side every minute of the day.

I headed over to my parrot's cage in the corner of the room, near the window.

"You *are* the pretty boy," I assured Prometheus enthusiastically. He sidled over to me, clearly happy I was home. In typical parrot fashion, he'd assumed from the start that I was his mother. That made him as anxious for affection as the other animals in my menagerie.

I opened the door of his cage and reached in. "Come, Prometheus," I commanded. The elegant bird dutifully stepped on to my finger, using it as a perch.

"There's the pretty birdie," I cooed, smoothing his feathers. He preened proudly, showing off the luminescent blue-green feathers of his body and tail and puffing out his golden chest.

"Welcome home, Jessie. *Awk!* Welcome home!" he said, perfectly imitating the voice and intonation of the person who'd taught him the phrase—me.

"It's nice to see you, too," I said, laughing. "And what's this I've got here? A piece of apple?"

"Apple, *awk*! Prometheus loves apple!"

I watched with my usual delight as he daintily took the chunk of fruit from my hand, holding onto it with one foot while remaining perched on my finger with the other. As he began eating it, I put him back in his cage.

"There you go, boy. Enjoy!"

I felt a rush of delight over the warm greeting I'd received from my menagerie. It's true, I thought. There really *is* no place like home.

"If only life could always be this simple," I mused aloud.

Just then, the blinking red light on my answering machine caught my eye, as if to remind me that that wasn't about to happen. Sighing, I pressed the "Play" button.

"*You—have—one—message.*"

The dogs, seeing a chance to reclaim my attention, came bounding over with their toys, careening into each other as they raced to reach me first. Between them, they'd amassed an impressive collection of playthings that they spent a large part of each day coating with saliva. Today, it was a tennis ball that Lou dropped at my feet, a damp, fuzz-less specimen that had all the bounce of a sponge. Max nudged my leg with his current favorite: a rubbery pink poodle he enjoyed thrashing from side to side as it squeaked for mercy. My two canines stood alert and ready, nearly bursting as they waited for me to fling these objects across the room—a game I lovingly referred to as "Slimytoy." I was bending down to oblige them when I heard, *"Jessie, it's Nick."*

I froze.

"I found out some information about what happened this morning. If you're still interested, give me a call."

I immediately began plotting how I could squeeze a visit to Nick's into the insanely busy day I had ahead of me. It wasn't going to be easy.

But that didn't mean I couldn't manage a few rounds of Slimytoy.

• • •

It just so happened I had an eleven o'clock scheduled at a dog breeder's in Cupsewogue, which was practically on the doorstep of Nick Burby's office. Actually, it was about ten miles away, but at least it was in the same direction. Sort of.

At any rate, I figured that if I kept my shower to five minutes, I'd have enough time to stop in at Nick's before inoculating a new litter of Jack Russells.

"Sorry, guys," I told Max and Lou as I pulled on my chukka boots for the second time that morning. "I'm afraid you'll have to sit this one out."

I didn't tell them about my hidden agenda: wanting to visit Nick unencumbered, without anyone else demanding my attention.

This is not a social call, I reminded myself. I'm taking time out of my busy workday for the good of my crime investigation. Still, I checked the mirror before walking out the door to make sure I didn't look like a woman who'd been raised by wolves.

My stomach tightened as minutes later I drove into the parking lot of a small cluster of offices that looked like quaint little houses. Or they did if you had a vivid imagination. For the most part, Long Island's architecture is far from what you'd call tasteful. The entire length of it had undoubtedly been spectacular from the time the Algonquins clammed along its shores up through the time some of the world's richest individuals—including Vanderbilts, Morgans, Belmonts, and Guggenheims—constructed castlelike mansions on what became known as the Gold Coast. But the building boom that followed World War II crammed the island with cookie-cutter housing developments and strip malls that had less personality than a shoe box.

At least Nick's complex in the charming community of Port Townsend tried. The facades of the brown wooden buildings were mock Tudor, and a few bushes had been planted here and there. The doctors, lawyers, and insurance brokers who shared the space did a pretty good job of keeping it tidy and clean.

Nick's office was located around back. Like the other offices, it was identified by a tasteful sign that read, "Nicholas Burby, P.I."

I didn't bother to knock. I could see through the small window set into the door that the front office was empty. Nick wasn't busy enough or rich enough for a receptionist. Nevertheless, he had made the wood-paneled back room into his office, at least giving the appearance that a secretary could well be part of his operation. He even kept papers and a small vase of dried flowers on the desk to give it a lived-in look.

Through the doorway, I saw his head jerk up when he heard me enter the outer office.

"I thought my message said to call," he greeted me.

I shrugged. "I was in the neighborhood. Mind if I come in?"

His rueful smile said, "Could I stop you if I wanted to?" I ignored it, striding into the small space and plopping down into the chair facing his.

I scanned the big metal desk that separated us. I was immediately struck by two things. One was that he was as disorganized as ever, with papers strewn about in a way that made it hard to believe his claim that he always knew precisely where everything was. The other was that the framed picture of me he used to keep on his desk, right next to the Police Athletic League mug filled with pens, was gone.

"The place hasn't changed much," I commented.

"It's only been a couple of months."

I nodded, not wanting to admit that it felt much longer to me.

"I've only got a few minutes," I said, hoping he wouldn't remind me again that he'd been willing to do this by phone. "So what have you learned?"

"I made a few calls, and I found out who the murder victim was. I figured you'd be interested."

"Of course I'm interested!" Inadvertently, I leaned forward in my seat.

"His name is—was—Tommee Frack. That's T-O-M-M-E-E. He was a big-time PR guy here on the island.

He started his own public relations firm in Pine Meadow about five years ago. He was quite successful, even though he was pretty young. Barely thirty, in fact."

I blinked. "That's it?"

"What else are you looking for? That he was also a bigamist who did a little drug dealing on the side and had recently ticked off the mob?"

"*Really?*"

Nick cast me a dirty look. "Hey, Jess, if you're going to get involved in the murder biz, you'd better stop believing everything everybody tells you. That's rule number one."

"I'll remember that."

"Speaking of which, forget rule number one. In fact, forget this entire thing. I want you to leave this alone."

"What do you mean?"

"You know perfectly well what I mean. I know you. When you and I were together, you were more into the details of every case I investigated than I was. You're not a street-wise homicide cop or a certified private investigator, yet somewhere along the way you decided you're the reincarnation of Nancy Drew."

"I can't be the reincarnation of someone who never really existed," I said crossly. "Nancy Drew was a fictitious character."

"You're being difficult again."

"I'm not difficult!"

"You *can* be difficult," he corrected himself. "And you can be pigheaded. Look, Jess, I know you think this whole thing is very dramatic and romantic and . . . and who knows what else. I mean, it's not every day that someone finds a dead body in the woods. But the fact remains that finding out what happened to Frack isn't a job for a layman."

"Lay *person,*" I muttered.

"It's a job for professionals." Nick leaned back and folded his arms across his chest. "I'm serious, Jess. This could be nasty business."

After an almost imperceptible hesitation, he added, "In fact, that's why I've decided to make a change."

I raised my eyebrows. "Joining the circus?"

"In a sense. I'm applying to law school."

"Law school!" I wouldn't have been more astonished if he had told me that he had just mailed in his application to Clown School, complete with an essay entitled, "What Emmett Kelly Means to Me."

"What's so strange about law school?" He sounded as if I'd hurt his feelings.

"How about the fact that people who go to law school become lawyers? Lawyers are people that nice, reasonable, normal folk make jokes about. Lawyers make a living by taking advantage of other people's misery. Aside from which they wear suits and . . . and drink martinis and drive Mercedes . . ."

"Not all of them. Maybe I'll work for an environmental firm. Or Legal Aid, helping people who don't have any money to defend themselves. Or . . . or . . ."

The ringing of his phone made him jump. An odd reaction, I thought, given the fact that he conducted much of his work by phone.

What was even stranger was that instead of reaching for it, he just stared at it.

"Harassing phone calls?" I suggested. "Telemarketers?"

It kept ringing.

"If you're not going to get that, I will," I offered.

He grabbed the receiver.

"Nick Burby," he said crisply. And then, in a much softer voice, "Oh, *hi*. I thought it might be you."

His tone made my blood run cold. So did the fact that even though he'd turned his face away from me, I could see that his entire expression had changed.

When he laughed softly and said, "That's funny. I was, too," I took my cue.

"Gotta go," I announced, shooting to my feet.

"Wait—Can you hold on a sec?" He glanced up, instantly turning back into the person he'd been thirty seconds earlier. "Jess, I think we need to talk about this a bit more—"

"There's nothing to talk about. There's no law against me nosing around a little. It's not as if I'm about to go breaking and entering this person's house and rifling through his sock drawer to try to find out why somebody wanted him dead."

" 'Nosing around' can be dangerous. Believe me, it's not the way it is in the movies. There are some bad people out there, Jess, and the smartest thing you can do is keep away from them."

"So you keep telling me. I can take care of myself. And maybe I can even find somebody to help me. Like that nice Officer Nolan, for example."

He shook his head, looking annoyingly exasperated. "Look, I have to take this call. But you and I need to continue this discussion before you go off and do something crazy. I mean it, Jess."

"Don't worry about me. I'll be fine."

I strode out of his office, trying to prove with my

erect posture and purposeful step just how capable I really was. At that moment, I was more determined to find out who had murdered Tommee Frack and why than I had ever been about anything in my life.

. . .

As I climbed back into my van, I was trembling with rage. At least, I told myself it was rage that was making my heart pound and my hands shake. The possibility that jealousy might have been responsible was unthinkable.

At any rate, I was glad the rest of my day was booked.

Once I was tooling along the countrified back roads of the North Shore, admiring the smattering of deep red and gold leaves still clinging to the trees, I could feel myself settling comfortably into a familiar rhythm. Driving around in a mobile medical unit suited me much better than being cooped up in some animal clinic. If there's one thing that gives me the heebie-jeebies, it's feeling confined. I can hardly bear to wear turtlenecks, and ordering theater tickets a month in advance has been known to make me break out in hives. So I never failed to appreciate the feeling of freedom that came from visiting my clients and their pets, instead of the other way around.

The wonderful world of technology made it all so easy. Not only did my van have its own generator, running water, heat, and air conditioning; it had everything I needed for performing diagnostic tests, surgery, and dentistry. My shelves were well-stocked with syringes, bandages, antibiotics . . . even doggie treats. True, some of the more complicated procedures required renting a surgery room from another veterinarian, and I frequently used outside laboratories to do some of the testing. But most of the time, I was totally self-contained. And I loved it.

I made it to Cupsewogue just in time for my eleven o'clock appointment to inoculate seven six-week-old Jack Russell terriers against distemper, hepatitis, influenza, and the big killer, parvo. By that time, I'd all but forgotten about the body in the woods. Instead, I focused on the tiny, squirming puppies, which were small enough to cup in my hand. I gave in to the temptation to nuzzle all of them, personally welcoming them to the world.

My next stop was at the home of one of my favorite clients. Like many of my regulars, Alfred Sutter was getting on and didn't drive much anymore. While I'd known Alfred for more than two years, I'd seen him age dramatically since his wife, Evelyn, had died six months earlier.

These days, his black lab, Midnight, was his only companion. Just seeing them together always made me feel good. It was impossible to tell which one adored the other more.

I took a minute to read through Midnight's chart before ringing the doorbell. As I stood on the front step, I noticed that the small house showed signs of neglect. The paint on the shutters was peeling and the late Mrs. Sutter's garden, once her pride and joy, was choked with weeds.

Mr. Sutter's face lit up when he answered the door. "Dr. Popper! How nice to see you!"

Suspecting he'd forgotten our appointment, I prompted, "I'm glad I was able to come by today.

From what you told me on the phone last night, it sounds as if Midnight's leg wound needs to be looked at."

A look of comprehension slowly spread across Mr. Sutter's face. "Oh, sure. Midnight's leg."

As I walked him to the van, I slowed my pace to match his. I could see that Midnight was trying just as hard to be accommodating. He stuck close by his master's side, glancing up every few seconds as if to make sure he wasn't going too fast. I was tempted to reach over and hug the black lab for being so thoughtful.

Inside the van, Mr. Sutter carefully lowered himself into the seat reserved for clients. "How've you been, Dr. Popper?" he asked congenially after he'd settled in.

"Much too busy, but what else is new?" Glancing over to smile at him, I noticed that his well-worn red plaid flannel shirt hung off his bony frame, a sign that he was losing weight.

Mr. Sutter held out both hands hopelessly. "Me, I've got the opposite problem. I got too *much* time."

"I'm sure Midnight keeps you busy," I commented. "He must be good company for you."

"The best." He smiled warmly at the black lab teetering nervously on the examining table. Poor Midnight definitely looked uncomfortable, and I could feel the tension in his muscles.

I felt my usual dismay over causing so much anxiety in an animal, especially an ailing one. I scratched his neck and stroked his ears, trying to relax him. "It's okay, Midnight," I assured him gently. "Nobody's going to hurt you. I just want to take a look at that leg. That's all. You'll be out of here in no time."

"Yep," Mr. Sutter went on, "every morning, me

and Midnight head over to the park for a couple of hours. He loves the exercise. Likes playing with the other dogs, too. He's even got a girlfriend, a white French poodle about one-tenth his size. You should see the two of them together!"

"So you've been steppin' out, huh, Midnight?" I let him lick my hand before I examined his eyes and ears. He wasn't any more relaxed, but at least he seemed resigned to a little poking and prodding. As he looked at me mournfully with wet, woeful brown eyes, it was all I could do to keep from apologizing.

I ran my hands along his spine, checking each vertebra. "It sounds like his activity level is normal. Any change in how much he's eating or drinking, Mr. Sutter? Any vomiting or diarrhea? Coughing? Sneezing?"

"Nope. He's healthier than I am. 'Course, he's a lot younger. A lot smarter, too. He already figured out how to undo the new latch I just put on the back door." Mr. Sutter beamed proudly. "I've started calling him Hound-ini."

"That's a new one," I said, laughing. I moved on to Midnight's left back leg, where I found the wound Mr. Sutter had called me about. "It's okay, Midnight. Whoa. I just need to take a look . . . Mr. Sutter, how did he cut his leg?"

"Must have been something sharp in the park. I didn't notice he'd gotten hurt until I brought him home."

"When was that?"

"Let's see . . . Saturday. Three days ago."

"It's all right, Midnight. We're done." I gave him a final pat, then helped him climb off the table without banging his wounded leg. He couldn't move fast enough, and his powerful paws skittered across the stainless steel. I was at least as relieved as he was that he'd gotten through his ordeal. I often felt frustrated that I couldn't simply explain to my patients that all I wanted to do was help them.

I turned to Mr. Sutter. "Can you get hold of one of those mist bottles, the kind you spray plants with?"

He nodded. "My wife had one. You know Evvie and her plants! I swear, she used to act like they were her grandchildren—" He stopped suddenly, taking a moment to compose himself. This time, it was him I wanted to reach over and hug. "Anyway, I'm sure it's still around somewhere."

I nodded. "I'd like you to clean it out really well, then fill it with peroxide and spray Midnight's wound three times a day. The spray won't hurt him because he's already healing and peroxide doesn't sting old wounds. He needs antibiotics, and I'm also going to give you one of those big cones to put around his neck. If we want that wound to close up, it's really important to keep Midnight from licking it."

"He won't like any of this, but he'll do what I tell him. He's a good dog." Mr. Sutter reached down and stroked his head lovingly. "Aren't you, boy? You're a *real* good dog, Midnight."

Midnight wagged his tail and gazed up at him, saying everything he needed to say with his body language.

Later, as I sat alone in my van, updating Midnight's chart, I remembered that the reason I'd gone into veterinary medicine in the first place was that I wanted to take care of animals. But it hadn't taken me long to learn that taking care of their owners was just as important.

I made a few more house calls, then checked the voice mail on my cell phone. I called back the three clients who'd left messages, making appointments with two and assuring the third that the antibiotics I'd given his beagle needed more than twenty-four hours to have an effect. Then I headed out east for acupuncture treatments on a sixteen-year-old collie with debilitating arthritis.

It was nearly six by the time I veered onto the Long Island Expressway for the trip home. Even though my brain was fogged by fatigue, I found myself brooding about the animals I'd seen that day. Midnight, in particular. I hoped his leg healed quickly—and that he remained healthy for a very long time. Mr. Sutter would be lost without him. Of course, the reverse was also true.

While all the day's patients were still very much on my mind, there was one animal in particular that kept popping into the forefront: the canary buried next to Tommee Frack.

Whatever the murder victim's faults might have been, I was pretty certain the bird had nothing to do with it. Yet he, too, had been a victim of the horrific crime I had uncovered that morning. He had been killed in cold blood, his neck broken as if someone had maliciously snapped his tiny, fragile body in two. Then he was unceremoniously hauled away by the police as Exhibit A.

As for the reason behind the crime, I remained completely in the dark. The situation reminded me of a dog or cat that presented with symptoms which didn't readily point to any particular ailment. The next step was to dig deeper: doing tests, asking questions, struggling to fit the pieces together to come up with a diagnosis and a treatment. In other words, launching a full-scale investigation.

If I could do it with animals, I figured, there was no reason why I shouldn't be able to use the same process to find out who had been responsible for Frack's murder.

And it didn't take a certified P.I. to know where to start.

Chapter 3

"Handsome cats and fat dung heaps are the sign of a good farmer."

—French Proverb

As I pulled my red VW Beetle into the parking lot of the Mangione Brothers Funeral Home in Ni-amogue at nine A.M. two days later, my mouth dropped open. Literally. Tommee Frack's wake had drawn a star-studded crowd. There were so many limousines lined up that I felt as if I'd come to Long Island's version of Oscar night.

I already had an inkling that Nick hadn't been ex-aggerating when he'd told me that Tommee Frack had been successful. The day after I discovered his body, the headline "PR MOGUL FOUND DEAD!!!" was splashed across the front page of *Newsday,* the only newspaper that covers all of Long Island. Below was a picture of a man I'd last seen covered with dirt and leaves—Tommee Frack, his smile as wide as a little kid's and at least as innocent.

I'd opened the newspaper and found that page three was completely dedicated to him. Pictures of a short, pudgy man wearing a pleased grin dotted the page: Frack with the New York State governor, Frack with the Norfolk County executive, Frack with Julia Roberts. My heart raced as I began to read.

> In what Norfolk County police are labeling one of the most tragic occurrences in the area's recent history, the body of public relations mogul Tommee Frack was discovered in a wooded area in the countrified yet chic Brewster's Neck section of Seaponak.
>
> Frack's body was found near Atherton Farm, a horse farm and riding facility. Medical Examiner Richard Stokes has not yet released information on the cause of death. Frack was thirty years old.
>
> The body was discovered by local veterinarian Jessica Pepper as she chased her three dogs, who were running loose. Pepper, who called police on a cell phone, has not been linked to the murder at this time.

"Great," I muttered. "Three strikes, you're out. First of all, that's Popper, with an 'o.' No relation to the fizzy stuff. Second, that was two dogs, not three. Third, thanks for making it sound like there's at least a chance your friendly local vet might be a cold-blooded killer."

Still, I read on.

> According to friends and family, Tommee Frack began his enormously successful public relations

career while still a student at Caumsett High School. After graduating from Brookside College in Edgewood, he became an assistant account executive at The Babcock Group in Apaucuck. Within three years, his creative abilities, combined with what former Norfolk County Executive Eugene Guilford, a longtime friend, referred to as Frack's "outstanding people skills," catapulted him to the position of senior vice president.

After making a name for himself with The Babcock Group, Frack left to start his own firm. Tommee Frack & Associates, which he founded three years ago, represented a wide range of clients, including private companies, not-for-profits, and organizations such as the police union, the Norfolk County PBA.

Guilford stated, "Tommee Frack had an uncanny ability to read people. Just from speaking with someone for a few minutes, he instinctively knew what truly mattered to that individual. He had a sixth sense about where that particular person wanted to be next year and in five years. Tommee was truly an asset to Long Island. He will be sorely missed."

"Tommee Frack was exceptionally versatile," commented Joseph DeFeo, president of Pomonok Properties. "He had an understanding of so many different fields. He was comfortable with just about very aspect of government, business, and community service. And he really knew what made the media tick. He was a master at bringing people together, be it the presidents of companies, powerful community leaders, or even members of opposing political parties."

That same sentiment was echoed by the president of a community hospital.

"The range of clients that Tommee served during his successful career as the head of his own public relations firm demonstrated just how versatile he was," noted Gary Tarniff of St. Luke's Hospital in Woodhull. "Frack was unique in that he recognized the common bonds that tie us all together. Perhaps his greatest contribution was uniting Long Islanders, finding ways for us to help us help each other in our shared efforts to make this the greatest place in the world to live and to work."

Wow, I thought. Mother Teresa with a cell phone.

The standing-room-only crowd inside the funeral parlor served as proof that the captains of government and commerce who had been quoted in the *Newsday* article weren't the only ones who revered the late Tommee Frack. I wasn't exactly what you'd call a newshound, but even I read the paper and watched the local news often enough to recognize many of the saddened faces around me.

Gene Guilford, the ex-county executive who had deified Tommee Frack in the newspaper, was there, glancing around and adjusting his tie nervously as if he, and not the dead guy, was today's main attraction. Just about every other politician I could think of was there, too, representing every level of government. I identified the current county executive, our state assemblyman, three Norfolk County legislators, and all five members of the town council. I even spotted the commissioner of highways, who I recognized from the posters that had decorated every telephone pole in the county before the last election.

But those were just the politicos, people I assumed had bothered to put on their suits and ties because they recognized this occasion as a valuable photo op. I also saw businessmen whose faces were familiar, Long Island's corporate bigwigs, like the head of a big computer company and the CEO of a major insurance company. As for the media, I saw so many of the reporters I was used to watching on TV that I wondered who was covering that day's car accidents on the Long Island Expressway. There were quite a few men in uniform in attendance, as well, all looking dutifully somber. I even noticed Officer Pascucci standing in back, checking out the scene and, not surprisingly, wearing a malevolent expression.

All in all, it was an impressive showing. As I shuffled toward the rows of wooden chairs that faced the open casket, I had to admit that I was kind of enjoying being in the midst of such a high-profile event. That is, until I spotted one more familiar face.

"What's the matter, Nick? Don't tell me even you're starting to find Tommee Frack's murder intriguing."

"Actually, Jess," he said, without missing a beat, "you're the reason I'm here."

"*Moi?* Should I be flattered?"

"Let's just say that after our conversation the other day, I had a feeling you'd show up today. And I wanted to make sure you didn't do anything stupid."

"Were you afraid that I'd leap up in the middle of the eulogy and yell, 'Would the real murderer please stand up'?"

"Something like that."

It took every ounce of self-control I possessed not to growl at him.

"Well, since you've taken it upon yourself to baby-sit me, you might as well make yourself useful. I recognize a lot of these people—the highway commissioner, the president of Kel-Tech Computers—but maybe you can fill me in on who some of these other movers and shakers are."

He sighed, then reluctantly pointed. "That's Daniel Sharpe, the police commissioner. And that's Jerry Siegel, chairman of the board of Norfolk Imaging. Over there is Ralph Pereira, head of Channel 14 News. And I'm pretty sure that guy over there is on the town's zoning board."

"Golly, gee," I said breathlessly. "Is there anybody Frack didn't know?"

Nick shrugged. "That's PR, I guess. From what little I understand, it sounds as if knowing the right people is the key to success. Jess, I hope you're not planning to do what I think you're planning to do." He must have noticed me eyeing the crowd hungrily.

"Which is—?"

"Go up to complete strangers and start asking a bunch of inappropriate questions."

"People do chat with each other at wakes, don't they?" I asked indignantly. "I think it's called being polite."

Before he could get another word in, I said, "You know, I think I'll pop into the ladies room before this thing gets started." I wrinkled my nose. "Too much coffee."

I moved away, no easy feat in that crowd. But I got

far enough so that Nick couldn't see what I was doing—or try to stop me.

I looked around, wondering how to go about meeting and greeting in a situation like this. It was like being at a school dance, desperately searching for some guy who was standing by himself so you could ask him to dance without anyone seeing you do so.

And then I spotted my victim, standing alone and looking decidedly awkward. Between his military-style haircut and his eyeglasses, so thick it was a miracle he could hold his head up, he had the look of someone very intelligent, not to mention important. Not a single wrinkle defiled his gray suit, his immaculate white shirt, or his dignified Harvard tie. Even his shoes gleamed, with not a speck of dirt or even a scuff mark daring to mar their shiny black surface.

I mustered up all my bravery and sidled up to him.

"Tragic, isn't it?" I began conversationally. "That such a terrible thing should happen to someone so young?"

He peered at me, his eyes blurs behind the bullet-proof lenses. "Terrible," he repeated in a voice that was at least an octave higher than I'd expected.

"I'm completely in shock," I prattled on. "I mean, when I read about this in the newspaper, I was just beside myself."

This time, all I got was a nod. It was increasingly apparent that my interviewing technique needed work.

I decided I had to be a little more creative. "I mean, Tommee was so . . . so . . ."

"Greedy?"

I blinked. "Actually, that wasn't the word I was looking for."

Of course, I didn't add that I had no idea what word I was looking for. But I was pleased to have learned something about Frack, who was still pretty much an unknown quantity to me.

"Let's face it," the man volunteered glumly. "The guy did nothing but work. He barely slept. He's the guy who invented the phrase 'twenty-four/seven.' "

I'd often thought I'd like to find myself alone in a dark alley with whoever had invented that phrase. But I had a feeling that Tommee Frack, for all his accomplishments, couldn't really be credited with that one.

"Did you know him well?" I ventured.

The man snorted. "Let's just say I saw a side of him that very few people got to see."

"What do you mean?"

My curiosity was piqued. Was I speaking with Tommee Frack's bookie? His psychiatrist? His proctologist?

His answer was kind of a letdown.

"I am—I *was*—his accountant."

Figures, I thought. Of all the people at the funeral who could provide me with an inside look at Tommee Frack and what might have brought about his demise, I have the bad luck to pick out the biggest dead end in the room.

"How . . . fascinating."

He snorted again. I realized that what sounded to me like a colt who thought I was getting a little personal during a physical was actually this accountant's laugh.

"Accountancy is an underrated field," he informed me indignantly. His voice had gotten even higher, moving dangerously into the squeaky range. "Most people don't realize just how exciting it can be."

"Gee, I never really thought about it." At least that part was honest. "But I'm curious: why do you think Tommee was greedy? I mean, as opposed to simply . . . successful?"

"Because his highest priority wasn't servicing his clients. It was collecting their checks."

Better and better. A mourner who had a grievance against the dead man. "I have to admit I'm at kind of a disadvantage here," I said meekly. "I don't know much about public relations."

"Not much to know. A client hires a PR firm in order to get his name in the news as often as possible. And the way the PR firm accomplishes that is by employing account executives who get on the phone and pitch the media."

" 'Pitch the media'?"

He looked at me oddly.

"I'm a veterinarian," I offered as my apology.

"The account executive calls the editors of magazines and newspapers, as well as the producers of TV and radio shows, and basically tries to sell them an idea over the phone. You know, like, 'My client, John Smith, just gave a million dollars to such-and-such charity.' Or invented a new product or hired a new vice president or whatever. And if the account exec is doing his job, that story ends up on the six o'clock news or on page two."

"I see. So what was Tommee Frack doing that made him, you know, greedy?"

"Pitching the media is time-consuming. You figure most account executives would probably handle six, maybe eight clients, tops. Even that's pushing it. But Tommee liked to keep his costs down. He had only three or four account execs at a time, but he was billing over sixty clients."

"Sixty clients! Wow, he *was* successful!"

"Except I never understood how he could possibly service all those clients with such a small staff. You'd think they would have felt shortchanged and taken their business somewhere else. Instead, they stayed with him, year after year."

"Maybe he was just good with people."

"Well, it's true that he did have a way with people. At least, when he wanted to." The accountant smirked. "Or maybe I should say, when there was something he wanted from them."

It occurred to me that this hardly seemed like the kind of conversation one should be having at a wake. Then I reminded myself that I wasn't here to mourn Tommee, but to sneak around and find out all the dirt I could about him.

But there was no more time to speak ill of the dead. A minister was making his way toward a wooden dais placed in front of Tommee, who lay in front of the room in pretty much the same position he'd been in when I'd first come across him.

"I guess we'd better sit down," I said. "But I enjoyed talking to you, Mr.—"

"Havemeyer. Jonathan Havemeyer, CPA." He reached into his pocket and pulled out a business card. I glanced at it politely, then stuck it in my purse.

By the time I looked up again, Tommee Frack's

cranky accountant had wandered off toward one of the middle rows. I headed to the back of the room, where I figured I'd get the best overview of the proceedings.

I'd just found myself a comfortable spot, with a wall to lean on and a towering potted plant to hide behind, when I felt someone else's presence. I glanced up, intending to offer to share my space. Instead, I did a double take.

"Officer Nolan! How nice to see you again!"

"Hey, call me Jimmy. And it's Jessie, isn't it?"

I felt ridiculously pleased that he remembered.

"I hope you've been keeping out of trouble." He grinned, that same spectacular smile that had impressed me the last time we'd met. "No more dead bodies?"

"Not a one."

"Good. Murder is something to steer clear of. Trust me."

"I guess you should know."

"Are you kidding? One of these days, you and I should sit down over a couple of beers so I can tell you about some of the things I've seen."

I had to admit that didn't sound like a bad idea. And my curiosity over Tommee Frack had nothing to do with it.

"Jesus H. Christmas. Will you look at all these people?" Officer Nolan—Jimmy—commented.

I raised my eyebrows, surprised by such an odd phrase—especially coming from a cop. "I guess Frack was a pretty important guy."

"What about you? What are you doing here?"

I shrugged. "I guess it's kind of weird, but I feel a

sort of kinship with Tommee Frack, even though I never met the guy. I guess I'm hoping that coming to his wake will give me a sense of closure."

"I hear you."

"And you?"

"I've gotten involved in the investigation a little bit, so I figured it wouldn't hurt to come to his wake."

Before I had a chance to ask any more questions, the minister tapped on the microphone. I wouldn't have expected such a high-tech touch to be appropriate at a wake, but in this case, it was a good idea: there were so many people packed into the room that it would have been impossible to hear without a speaker system.

"Family, friends, business associates of Tommee Frack," he began when the noise died down. "While all of us in this room knew Tommee for many different reasons, today we are all united by a common bond: mourning the loss of this committed, involved, caring man . . ."

I was already growing bored. I looked around the room, not knowing what I expected to see. Somebody grinning diabolically, maybe, or giggling to himself in a corner.

Instead, I saw a bunch of business-types, men and women in suits. Nothing too interesting there. Sitting in front, I noticed an older couple clinging desperately to one another. Tommee's parents, no doubt.

The minister droned on and on. I was beginning to wonder if I was wasting my time when a shrill voice from the hallway cut through the minister's sugary words.

"You mean they started without me? They couldn't wait five minutes?"

I glanced toward the doorway. So did everybody else in the room.

We weren't disappointed. A pretty young woman—more young than pretty—flounced inside, looking annoyed.

But the expression on her face was the least of her inappropriateness. She was dressed in black, all right, but her dress was cut so low on top and so high on the bottom that she could have been wearing a dish towel. The result was enough leg and enough boob to stun even the minister, who halted mid-sentence.

Something else separated her from all the other mourners. Strutting alongside her was a black-and-white Tibetan Terrier, a twenty-pound version of an Old English Sheepdog. The breed is a bit of a rarity, even in my circles. The black-and-whites are particularly high maintenance, requiring two different shampoos, one for the black fur and one for the white. These days, most busy families prefer the wash-and-wear varieties of house pets.

The minister remained silent as everyone in the room watched the woman with the living, breathing fashion accessory prance toward the front of the room on heels so high and so spiky that I feared for the carpet. When she reached the first row, the one reserved for family, she wiggled her way into a seat, displacing several coats in the process. Someone—possibly, but not definitely the Tibetan Terrier—let out a little yelp.

"Goodness, who's that?" I whispered to Officer Nolan.

"Barbara Delmonico," he whispered back. "Tommee's fiancée."

So, I thought with satisfaction, good old Tommee wasn't such a stuffy businessman, after all. There was another side to him, a side that, from the looks of things, was still rooted in his adolescence. In fact, I'd be willing to bet he had a poster of Pamela Anderson hanging in his bedroom.

As my attention turned back to the ceremony, one mover and shaker after another stood up to extoll Tommee Frack's virtues. I was tempted to yell out, "If Tommee was such a great guy, how come somebody wanted him dead?" Instead, I continued studying the crowd, not knowing what I was looking for but naively certain I'd know it when I saw it.

And then I noticed the sobbing woman.

She stood hunched over in the opposite corner of the room, next to the doorway, her shoulders heaving violently. Unlike most of the other mourners, who looked like they had charge accounts at Bloomingdale's and Today's Man, she was more of a Wal-Mart type. Her dress, dark blue with more ruffles than anyone over the age of six has a right to wear, had a tired look. She was barely five feet tall, yet round enough that she could have benefited from a bigger size. Her nondescript brown hair was worn straight down, as if it had never been introduced to the concept of a stylish cut. And yet, I could see that she was fairly pretty, even though her face was half-hidden by the clump of tissues she kept pressing against her eyes.

Something else struck me. Whoever she was, she was the only person at Tommee Frack's funeral who was crying. Even his fiancée seemed more irritated than grief-stricken.

I tensed up like a retriever about to dive into a lake as I watched her head out of the room. "I'll be right back," I told Officer Nolan, figuring he'd assume I was going to the bathroom.

Actually, it turned out to be precisely where I was going. As I turned the corner, I saw the crying woman pushing the door labeled "ladies."

Inside, I found a pleasant sitting room with flowered wallpaper, mirrors, and upholstered benches. The perfect place for collecting oneself.

The woman had sunk onto one of the benches and appeared to be trying to do just that. She wasn't having much luck.

Impulsively, I sat down beside her and slipped my arm around her shoulders.

"It's so sad, isn't it?" I asked gently. "He was so young, and so involved. There were so many people who cared about him."

"None of them cared about him the way I did." She spat out the words.

"Are you related?"

"I used to be. As a matter of fact, I used to be his wife. I'm Merrilee Frack."

I patted her shoulder. While my attempts at comforting her until this point had been sincere, I now realized I'd stumbled upon a gold mine.

"It must make you feel great that so many people turned out for Tommee's funeral," I soothed her. "He was such a vital part of the community—"

"I hate those people!" She swiped at her eyes with her ball of wet tissues. What was still left of her eye makeup became even more smeared, the blues and greens swirling together like the colors of Monet's water lilies. "They're responsible." She spat out the words venomously.

"Responsible . . . for his death?"

"Everything! His death, the stupid way he led his life . . . I wish they would all just go home. Especially her. How dare she show up here? That . . . that *whore*!"

Not knowing what to say to that, I indulged in a little more patting. Then I stood and reached for Merrilee's hand.

"Come on," I said briskly, using the same tone I use with puppies who aren't grasping the basics of good behavior. "Let's get your face washed. A little cold water will make you feel much better."

"I bet I look a mess," she wailed, trailing after me obediently.

When we reached the sink, she gasped. "Oh, my God! I actually appeared in public looking like this? Tommee would have *died*!"

And then, to my astonishment, she started laughing. At first, I was afraid she'd lapsed into hysteria. But then I realized her laughter was sincere. This was precisely the relief she needed.

Splashing water on a paper towel, I said, "First of all, let's get some of that makeup off."

"I can do it." Merrilee focused on her reflection, scrubbing at the streaks of color. "You're right. This cold water does feel good. And maybe it'll stop my eyes from looking so red."

I pulled a comb out of my purse for Step B. She took it from me gratefully.

"I especially don't want *her* to see me looking like this," she mumbled.

I knew exactly who she meant.

Within just a few minutes, she looked composed enough to face the world.

"Okay, now take a few deep breaths," I instructed. "Come on, I'll breathe with you."

"I took a yoga class once." She sounded childlike. "It didn't really do anything for me. And whenever we had to stand on one leg, I was the only one in the class who kept falling over."

"I've never had much luck with it, either," I admitted. "I guess I'm always in too much of a hurry to be a yoga-type."

Merrilee smiled gratefully. "It was really nice of you to do this. I'm not used to having anybody take care of me."

"We all need taking care of sometimes."

"Were you and Tommee friends? Or business associates?"

The moment I'd been dreading. "Well . . . neither. I—"

"You're not in public relations?"

"Actually, I'm a vet—"

Her face lit up. "Oh, I'm so glad to meet you! And thank you for taking such good care of Dobie and Maynard!"

I didn't bother to correct her. My mind was clicking as I said carefully, "Dobie and Maynard. I just love those names. From the old *Dobie Gillis* TV show, right?"

"What else would you name a Doberman but Dobie?" Merrilee giggled. "That was my idea. Naming the other one after Maynard G. Krebs was Tommee's. Imagine, a Doberman pinscher named after a beatnik!" She hesitated, then added, "That was back when Tommee still had a sense of humor. Before he started taking himself so seriously. Before he decided our life together wasn't good enough. That *I* wasn't good enough."

Merrilee's face crumpled again as she relived the pain of rejection. Anxious to distract her, I asked, "So—how are Dobie and Maynard doing?"

"Not too well, actually. They're with me now, you know. Of course, I'm thrilled to have them back. I mean, they were Tommee's dogs, but I got real attached to them. And then I lost them in the settlement. At the time, giving them up seemed like a good deal. I got a bunch of money and Tommee got the dogs. But for the past three years, not a day has passed that I haven't missed them so much I could hardly stand it."

I wondered if she meant only the Dobermans, or if Tommee was included in there, too.

"But they're not doing so good. They haven't eaten a bite since I got them back. They just lie by the door, resting their noses on their paws. They're waiting for Tommee to come home." Her eyes filled with tears. "The poor guys. They don't know *what* happened. They were completely devoted to him. Tommee was the center of their lives for as long as they can remember, and they just don't know what to do with themselves without him."

She brightened. "Hey, maybe you could check them out. Make sure they're okay."

"I'd be happy to."

"That's great! When can I bring them in?"

"You don't have to. I have a mobile unit. I'll come right to your house."

"Oh, could you? That would make things so much easier! I just have a little Hyundai, and believe me, driving around with those two monsters in the backseat is no picnic."

One hundred and sixty canine pounds would definitely test the limits of a Hyundai. "How about later today?" I asked. "Around eleven?"

She looked over my shoulder as I jotted down her name, address, and phone number in the small address book I retrieved from my purse.

"You spelled my name wrong," she pointed out. "That's okay. Everybody does. It's M-E-R-R-I-L-E-E."

"Interesting," I observed. "Just like Tommee."

"That's where he got the idea. Of changing the spelling of his name, I mean. He was just 'Tommy' before that. But he wanted his name to be different. Something people would remember."

The cloudy look came over her face again. "You see, him and me, we really were good together. I inspired him. We had a terrific future together. It's just that, well, in the end, he didn't see it that way."

"Something like that must be awfully hard to forgive."

Merrilee cast me a steely look. "It's something I've never gotten over."

The contrast between her ruffled dress and the naked vehemence of her tone left me feeling chilled.

As I made my way back to my original vantage point, the eulogies were coming to a close. People were getting restless, shifting in their seats and sneaking glances at their watches. These were busy people, I thought, and now that they'd paid their respects, it was time to move on with the rest of their day.

Before taking off myself, I turned to Officer Nolan. "It was nice to see you again, Officer—"

"Jimmy," he corrected me with a grin.

"Jimmy." Flirtatiously, I added, "And who knows? Maybe I'll take you up on your offer one of these days."

He looked confused.

"Hearing all your war stories? Over a couple of beers?"

Before he could respond, I felt someone grab my arm.

"Jessie, I know what you're doing," that same somebody hissed in my ear, "and I'm warning you that you're playing with fire."

"Will you excuse me?" I asked Jimmy sweetly.

"Sure," he replied cheerfully. "I've got to get going anyway. See you around, Jess."

The second he was out of earshot, I turned back to Nick.

"This is *such* a sad occasion," I told him calmly. "A terrible loss to Long Island's business community, not to mention those who truly loved Tommee—"

"I saw you flirting with that cop. And I know exactly what you're doing. You're kissing up to him so you can horn in on the investigation. I'm telling you, it's not a smart idea."

Nick was beginning to remind me of my parrot Prometheus, the way he kept saying the same thing over and over again until you just itched to throw a sheet over his cage.

"You've made your point," I told him.

He glared at me. Then he sighed. "Look, Jess, why don't you just stick to what you know? You'll be much safer setting bones and removing hair balls than playing detective."

I smiled at him sweetly. Then, with the same lady-like grace and dignity, I stuck out my tongue.

Chapter 4

"An empty house is like a stray dog or a body from which life has departed."

—Samuel Butler

Fifty-four Heather Court was one of five identical houses dotting the edge of a perfectly round cul-de-sac, like the numbers on a clock. Yet despite their architectural similarities, each of the modest ranch houses had been customized by the residents who owned and loved them.

I had a feeling I would have been able to pick out Merrilee Frack's home even without a street address. The touches at number 54 were all variations on Merrilee's favorite theme: cuteness. Inside the white picket fence was one of those wooden cutouts showing the backside of a woman bending over to pull weeds. A straw hat hung on the front door, with long satin ribbons in pastel colors dangling from it. White ruffled curtains framed the windows, which had flower boxes decorated with hearts along the bottom.

Something about its desperate attempts at cheerfulness made me sad. This house clearly belonged to a woman who longed for a real home. But from what I'd seen so far, I knew that Merrilee's dream house was missing a very important ingredient.

As I climbed out of my van, the front door flew open. The movement sent the ribbons on the straw hat flying like streamers. Then two massive Dobermans emerged, their powerful chests heaving and their long legs eager to run. Only the sheer determination of the tiny woman at the other end of their leashes held them back.

"Thanks again for coming," Merrilee called to me as they dragged her down the driveway. She'd changed into jeans and a lavender sweater, and she wore a matching lavender plastic barrette in her hair. The contrast between her soft, almost girlish look and the two mighty beasts she managed to keep in check was startling.

"Sit!" she commanded. Two sleek, muscular butts hit the ground so fast you'd have thought they belonged to United States Marines.

"Sorry they're so rambunctious," Merrilee said. "Like I told you, they just don't know what to do with themselves now that Tommee is—well, you know."

She cast me a meaningful look. I instantly understood that we weren't to use the D-word in front of the dogs.

"Bring them inside the van and I'll check them out," I offered. Just from eyeballing them, both dogs looked pretty healthy to me. I suspected that my initial diagnosis would prove correct: that they were simply going through some grieving of their own.

Merrilee came into my van and watched as I did the usual tests, exhibiting the same anxiety most pet owners show as I touch and prod their little bundles of fur. Sure enough, there was nothing wrong with Dobie and Maynard that time, the great healer, wouldn't correct.

"They're beautiful animals," I told Merrilee, admiringly running one hand along Maynard's sleek fur as he eased himself off the examining table. "And they're fine, at least physically. As for their emotional state, it's probably going to take them a while to get used to the fact that Tommee is gone."

Merrilee's eyes filled with tears. "That's true for all of us."

"I'm sure they're also responding to your grief. They can sense that you're upset, and that contributes to their state. If you can, try what's called 'the jolly treatment.' Act cheerful around them, play happy music, do your best to act as if there's nothing wrong.

"In the meantime, don't worry about them not eating. They're both strong, healthy animals. It won't hurt them to go without food for a few days. It shouldn't be long before they're back to normal." I reached down to stroke Dobie's silky head, and was rewarded with a long, wet tongue slurping my wrist. "If you don't see any change in another week, call me. We can always do blood tests at that point to make sure everything's all right."

"Thank you so much, Dr. Popper." She smiled tremulously. "Hey, would you like to come in for a few minutes? I could make coffee. If you have time, I mean—"

"I'd love coffee. In fact, every day about this time, I *need* coffee."

"Good." Shyly, she added, "Frankly, I'd be really grateful for the company. This hasn't exactly been my best day." She gathered up Dobie and Maynard's leashes. "Why don't you go ahead in? I'll put these guys in the backyard. They could use a little fresh air."

As I wandered unattended into Merrilee's house, I saw that the inside was consistent with the outside. Cute touches abounded, ranging from appliquéd throw pillows with a daisy design on the living room couch to a shelf lined with Precious Moments statuettes. Every square inch of clutter was absolutely immaculate. Somehow, the house had the feeling of being stuck in a state of readiness, like a model home. It was as if everything in there was untouched, waiting to be used.

I did a double take when I saw the large picture prominently displayed in the front hallway. The blown-up photograph in an elaborate gilt frame showed Merrilee and Tommee side by side, their arms around each other as they stood beneath a canopy of pink roses. Merrilee, engulfed by a puffy white cloud of a dress, looked as if this was the happiest day of her life. Next to her stood a red-haired, freckled, pudgy Tommee Frack, looking as if he couldn't wait to get out of his tight tuxedo.

When Merrilee came in behind me and caught me gawking at the king-size wedding picture, she sighed.

"I know; it's beautiful, isn't it? So was everything about that day. It was absolutely perfect."

"You both look so . . . young."

"We *were* young. I was twenty-one, and Tommee had just turned twenty-two."

"How long had you two known each other?"

"We met in high school. Tommee and I were high school sweethearts from the ninth grade on. You know, the kind of kids that are always holding hands in the hall and making out in front of their lockers? Junior Prom, Senior Prom, the whole nine yards . . . Then we both went to college here on the Island. I went to the state university, because my parents didn't have the money for a private school. But Tommee's folks sent him to Brookside College. They didn't have much money, either, but somehow they found a way. They doted on Tommee."

"Did he win a scholarship?"

She shook her head. "Tommee was brilliant, but not in a school-type way. I mean, his grades weren't anything to write home about. He was people-smart. He could talk anybody into anything, you know? He could take any situation, anything at all, and make people see things the way he wanted them to see them.

"It even worked with teachers. He'd talk them into giving him a few extra points, or dropping the lowest test grade. That kind of thing. And because of it, everybody knew who he was. They didn't necessarily like him, but they *knew* him. It was like this special talent Tommee had. You know, always finding a way to be at the center of things."

I was watching her face as she reminisced. With a shock, I realized she had stars in her eyes. It was the same look Betty accused me of having whenever I was around Nick.

She really loved him, I thought. I hastily amended

that statement. She really *loves* him. Even now. He's the one she never got over. The one who broke her heart.

"Is there a bathroom I can use?" I asked abruptly. I didn't really have to go, but I was anxious for an excuse to look at the rest of the house. It was funny, the way going to the ladies room was turning out to be a terrific investigative technique. It literally opened doors.

"Sure. Right upstairs. End of the hall. And I'll get that coffee started."

As I walked down the second-floor hallway, I glanced into each bedroom. The first room on the left was the master bedroom. Merrilee had decorated it all in white lace. Next to the bed, I noticed a framed close-up of Tommee.

Amazing, I thought. The first face she sees in the morning and the last face she sees before she goes to sleep at night.

But it was the next room that totally floored me.

It was much smaller, probably meant to be a study or a guest room. And it did contain a desk with an outdated-looking computer and a sofa.

Otherwise, it looked like an altar to Tommee Frack.

Business-style letters had been framed and hung, congratulatory notes from politicians praising Tommee for his valuable contribution to Long Island's economy, and thank-you letters from satisfied clients. I skimmed a letter from George Babcock, President of The Babcock Group, printed on thick, expensive-looking stationery embossed with gold. It was a job offer, dated eight years earlier. Using ridiculously flowery wording, Babcock welcomed Tommee Frack to his firm and said he was looking forward to a long and prosperous association.

But that was just the beginning. Framed articles from *Newsday,* the Long Island Weekly section of the Sunday *New York Times,* and what looked like weeklies from all over the Island covered the walls. Every one of them was about Tommee.

I stepped into the room, so astonished that I forgot to worry about being found out. "PR Genius Starts Own Firm," one headline trumpeted. "Wunderkind Turns Entrepreneur," screamed another.

They weren't all about the young public relations star opening up his own public relations shop. There were also pictures of Tommee with every politician and every celebrity who had ever set foot on Long Island. The governor, the past governor, and no fewer than three U.S. presidents and seven presidential candidates. There was Tommee with every member of the town council, and there he was with most of the Norfolk County legislators.

He also posed with a number of celebrities who were Long Island natives, actors and sports figures who had probably returned from Hollywood to visit their relatives who still lived here. Tommee and Jerry Seinfeld. Tommee and Eddie Murphy. Tommee and Rosie O'Donnell. Tommee and basketball legend Julius Erving, a.k.a., Dr. J.

Then there were photos taken with the Hamptons crowd, the summer people who regularly came out to the East End to recreate the social scene they'd left behind in the city, only this time with a beachy backdrop. Tommee with Christie Brinkley, Steven Spielberg, Peter Jennings, Dr. Atkins, Betsey Johnson.

Even Martha Stewart stood stiffly beside Tommee, looking tortured as she let him pose with his arm around her.

Charity events, fund-raisers, the world-famous Hampton Classic horse show. Whatever the occasion, it seemed that if important people were there, so was Tommee.

"Pretty amazing, huh?"

I jumped at the sound of Merrilee's voice. But she didn't sound at all irritated that I'd been distracted on my way to the loo. In fact, she sounded as if she completely understood my amazement.

"Like I told you, he had an awesome talent. People *liked* Tommee. They trusted him. They just wanted to be around him."

"And he obviously put a lot of effort into being at the center of things." I glanced at the walls of photos, wondering what the guy had paid for tuxedo rentals every year. "A person has to, if he's that ambitious. But I suppose that kind of drive is what comes of growing up without having a lot of money."

"Money?" Merrilee looked bewildered. "But it was never about money. Not really. I mean, sure he liked what he could buy with all the money he made. You know how boys are with their toys. And Tommee was even more extreme than most. Everything had to be the best. Dinners at the most expensive restaurants. The biggest suites at the best hotels. Silk shirts and handmade suits he got on his weekend trips to Hong Kong. He even drove a Rolls. I think it was only leased, but the point was that he had to have it all."

"But if his ambition wasn't about money, what was behind it?"

"Tommee was star-struck, back from the very beginning. He was always attracted to people other people considered important."

"You mean he was a social climber?"

"No, he just liked to be around people who had distinguished themselves in some way," she said happily. "Like in high school? After a football game, he'd always make a point of sneaking into the locker room so he could hang out with the winning team. If our team lost, he'd go out partying with the guys from our school's rival. After a school play, he'd wangle his way into the cast party, even though he'd had nothing to do with putting on the production."

"Sounds like he was kind of a hanger-on. Didn't the other kids find that annoying?"

"Are you kidding? They loved it! Tommee was always fawning all over them, telling them how great they were. In fact, that's how he got started in the public relations business."

"Really? How fascinating!" Nancy Drew herself couldn't have done better.

"When we were still in high school—I think he was, like, a junior—Tommee started getting kids' names in the local paper. Like if somebody won some poetry award or scored the winning point in a basketball game, Tommee would offer to call the newspaper and get some reporter to come over and take their picture. He was really good at it. He could talk anybody into anything."

"Did these kids pay him?"

"He didn't expect to be paid. All he wanted was

their gratitude—and a way of being close to them. Here, let me show you. Take a look at our yearbook."

Proudly she held up the blue and white cover for me to see. It was embossed with the name, *The Caumsett Commemorative.*

"You can practically open to any page and you'll see Tommee standing next to some kid who'd just done something special."

To demonstrate, she flipped the book open. Sure enough: There was a photograph of the varsity soccer team carousing after a victory. Tommee—looking younger and thinner—hovered in the background, wearing a pleased expression.

"This is the Debating Team, the time they won the Norfolk County Championship." Six serious-looking students posed in front of lockers, standing at attention for the camera. Lurking a few feet behind was Tommee.

Frankly, I found the whole thing kind of creepy. But Merrilee had that starry look in her eyes again. "He was so terrific with people. Tommee really had a special, special talent. And it took him exactly where he wanted to go."

I jumped as she slammed the book shut. "I still can't believe he didn't want to take me with him." Her voice had become hard.

After a few seconds, I broke the heavy silence that had fallen over the room. "It sounds like you've never gotten over him," I said gently.

Staring straight ahead, as if she'd forgotten I was in the room, Merrilee said, "To this day I believe I'm the only person who ever truly loved him."

My heart was pounding. I knew I was treading in dangerous territory, but I couldn't help myself.

"It must have been extremely hard, then, seeing him with other women." I spoke softly and slowly, the way I talk to animals who are behaving erratically because they've been abused. "When you heard he was going to marry Barbara Delmonico—"

"That bimbo!" Merrilee snarled. "She was only after his money. I mean, did you get a *look* at her? Showing up at his funeral dressed like some hooker, dragging that stupid dog along with her . . . She never loved Tommee. It was the *money* she loved!"

Her shoulders slumped. "You know, I always thought he'd come back to me. Even after all this time, I never stopped believing that one of these days, he'd come to his senses and realize that all those other women were just a waste of time. That *I'm* the one who truly loves him."

I put my arm around her. I always seemed to be doing that. "I wish I'd had a chance to know him better."

She shook her head, and tears rolled down her cheeks. "If you really want to know about Tommee, talk to the people who knew him as a businessman," she said angrily. "His job was his life. In the end, that was what he really cared about."

"I'm sorry to be asking you all these questions. I can see it's difficult for you to talk about him. Besides, I'm sure the police have bothered you enough."

"The police? They haven't been around. Although now that you mention it, you'd think they'd be a little more anxious to find out who killed my husband. He certainly knocked himself out for the Norfolk PBA,

getting good press for the cops, working his butt off
day and night—"

"You know," I interrupted, "I think we're both
ready for that coffee now. Would you like me to help?"

"I can manage." She swiped at her face, smearing
her makeup once again.

I followed a few paces behind, sensing she needed
a chance to pull herself together. As we neared her
kitchen, I braced myself for more domestic cuteness,
something along the lines of checked curtains or
maybe a rooster theme. But I wasn't prepared for
what I saw hanging in the kitchen window.

A birdcage. With three canaries.

"Yes, more pets," Merrilee said, in response to my
involuntary gasp. "Tommee and I got those before we
got Dobie and Maynard. We decided to start small.
You know, to practice being pet owners?"

I swallowed. "So you went out and bought three
canaries?"

"Six. We started with six."

"What happened to the others?"

"Oh, you know how it is with birds. They're always dying."

She sighed, her eyes glazing over as she stared at
the trio of bright yellow birds, bobbing and chirping
in their prison.

"It's funny," she said, her voice suddenly thick
with emotion. "I can't look at them without thinking
of Tommee. I remember the day we got them like it
was yesterday. We were so happy, and the birds were
so pretty . . ."

Her voice trailed off. That heavy silence hovered in
the room again for a few seconds.

And then she turned to face me, forcing a smile. "How do you take your coffee? Milk or sugar or both?"

. . .

My brain was swimming with caffeine and suspicion as I made my way back down Merrilee's driveway. Knowing that I might have just sat at a coldhearted killer's kitchen table, discussing the merits of the Home and Garden channel and commiserating about how bad Long Island's traffic was getting, left me with a dazed feeling I expected would stick with me for a very long time.

"Excuse me! *Excuse me!* Hell-o-o-o!"

I glanced up and saw a woman in a pair of turquoise sweats and a faded yellow Bon Jovi T-shirt rushing toward me from the house next door. Despite her casual outfit, her hair looked as if it had just baked in a dryer for an hour after being wrapped tightly around plastic rollers. Given the airy bubble on top and the swirls on both cheeks that looked dangerously like spit curls, I wondered if Frenchie from *Grease* was her hairdresser.

Cradled in her arms was a fat orange cat. Even though he looked as if the color of his fur had come from the same bottle as her hair, I suspected his was natural. Not only did the animal look like Garfield; his body language communicated the fact that he also shared the cartoon cat's point of view: this feline clearly ruled the world.

The woman was out of breath by the time she reached me. Up close, I saw that the arched eyebrows that made her look continually surprised were simply drawn on. Her pussycat, meanwhile, had a look on his face that clearly indicated he didn't exactly relish being treated like a baton in a relay race.

"I don't have an appointment," she said in a gravelly voice that told me cigarettes constituted one of her four basic food groups, "but d'ya think ya could look at my cat anyway?"

This kind of thing happens to me a lot. People see my van parked outside someone's house and assume that the kind of mobile services I offer are just like the ice-cream man's.

I rarely have the heart to turn anyone away, even when I have another appointment to rush off to. Today, given the fact that I was still trying to comprehend what made Merrilee Frack tick, how could I help pouncing on the opportunity to talk to one of her neighbors?

"Sure," I told her. "I'm Dr. Popper."

"Joan Devlin. And this here is Caesar."

I learned long ago not to ask for the stories behind the names. In most cases, the explanation takes longer than the examination.

Instead, I reached over and fondled Caesar's ears. "What's the matter, fellah? Not feeling so hot?"

His owner answered for him. They always do.

"It's his ear. He keeps scratchin' at it. And it's got this yellowish goo coming out of it. I think maybe he's got an infection or something."

"Poor guy! We'll have to take care of that right away. Come on, Caesar. Let's have a look."

Inside the van, I stroked Caesar's back to let him know I was trying to help. I put him on the examining table, then handed Joan a clipboard with an information form to fill out. She started writing, but glanced up every few seconds to watch as I took out my otoscope and examined her cat's ear.

"You're okay, Caesar. No one's going to hurt you . . . Any changes in eating or drinking habits?" I asked. "Any vomiting or diarrhea? Coughing or sneezing?"

"No, he's been fine, except for the ear thing." Anxiously, she added, "Y'see anything in there?"

"His eardrum is intact. That's good. Now I'll just take a sample of this discharge and put it under the scope . . . There you go, Caesar. You're a real trouper."

As I peered through my microscope, Joan said in an oddly casual tone, "I noticed ya just came out of Merrilee's house."

So I wasn't the only one who was incurably nosy. "That's right."

"Everything okay in there?"

"Oh, sure. The dogs are both fine. They just need a little time to—"

"I wasn't talking about the dogs. I meant Merrilee."

Her bluntness caught me off-guard. "I guess you heard about her ex-husband?"

"Sure. The whole neighborhood's talking about it."

"Everyone must be pretty upset."

"Upset?" She sounded surprised.

"Wait. We're talking about Tommee Frack, right? And the fact that he, um, recently passed away—"

"You mean the fact that he was murdered." Joan shrugged. "Sure, it's a shock. I mean, it's kind of weird, seeing the face of the guy ya lived next door to for years plastered all over the front page of *News-*

day. But to tell you the truth, nobody around here is exactly cryin' their eyes out."

Even though I was still absorbed in peering down a microscope, my posture must have registered my astonishment.

"Look," she went on, "I know the newspapers and the TV coverage are full of what a great guy Tommee Frack was. Successful businessman, entrepreneur, friend of the community, blah, blah, blah. But everybody in this neighborhood knew the guy for years. And we could see for ourselves what the bastard did to poor Merrilee."

"I thought Merrilee adored him."

"Oh, she did! That was the problem. She was much too forgiving about the way he carried on."

"What do you mean, 'carried on'? What was he doing?"

She laughed. It was the kind of laugh that made it clear that what she was about to say wasn't the least bit funny. "You kiddin'? Even when Tommee and Merrilee were still married, the guy had more women than Hugh Hefner. Hard to believe, isn't it? I mean, just look at him. You've seen his picture, right?"

I'd seen more than that, but I didn't feel like pointing out that I had been the one to find what was left of the PR mogul moldering in the woods.

"Looks aren't everything," I pointed out. "From what I've heard, he could be incredibly charming."

"Charming? That's a laugh! He was the biggest oaf you've ever met! I mean, sure, there was kind of a sweet quality to the guy. But he was basically the most socially awkward person you can imagine. You just knew, when you met him, that he'd been the school nerd. Y'know, the fat kid who never got picked for teams or invited to parties."

I thought of the Who's Who I'd seen on Merrilee's wall, along with Joan's insistence that Tommee was busily tom-catting around Centerview, and was more puzzled than ever. "Then why did women find him so attractive?"

"Three guesses." Joan rolled her eyes. "Look, the guy liked to spend money on the ladies. He was no dummy. He knew what it took, that there's a certain kind of woman who'll hang out with a guy just because he's loaded. He was always buyin' them gifts, takin' 'em out to the fanciest restaurants in the city, even on weekend trips. Anything to get laid."

"Maybe this was late in the marriage?" I suggested. "After things had already started falling apart for him and Merrilee?"

Joan shook her head. "It was no secret that Tommee was runnin' around almost from the time him and Merrilee first got married. In fact, it wasn't long after they bought the house that Eddie and me started noticing the hours he kept. Eddie was workin' really late in those days, moonlightin' as a bartender. We'd just bought our house, and we were a little strapped . . . Anyway, Eddie would come home at three, four in the morning. Even if I wasn't actually waitin' up for him, I found it hard to fall asleep until he came home, y'know? So I'd sit in the living room with the TV on, which also gave me a first-rate view of the Fracks' driveway."

"And Tommee was a night owl?"

"That's an understatement! It got so Eddie and me

used to kid around about who'd come in later the night before, him or Tommee."

"It's possible that Tommee was working late, though, isn't it?"

"Hah! You obviously never heard the screamin' matches him and Merrilee used to have."

It was difficult to picture Merrilee screaming at anyone, much less the man she adored.

"You mean she would accuse him of seeing other women?"

"More like he'd rub her face in it. I remember him yelling stuff like, 'You push me into the arms of other women because of the sloppy way you keep the house.' Or he was always tellin' her she was too fat. Like he was one to talk!"

She shook her head angrily. "He was really some piece of work, that guy. Everybody in the neighborhood knew what was goin' on. And the day after one of these big blowout fights at three o'clock in the morning, you'd see Merrilee out by herself, her eyes all red as she walked those two dogs. And they were *his* dogs, too. Completely devoted to him. But she was the one who walked them every morning and every night, carryin' that stupid pooper-scooper thing around."

"I guess poor Merrilee had a lot to be angry about." I didn't mean it as a leading statement; I was just thinking out loud.

"Ya'd think so. Instead, she worshipped him. You saw the inside of her house, didn't you? She's got so many pictures of him all over the place you'd think they were still married. *Happily* married, which of course they never really were."

As I pulled off my rubber gloves, she finally refocused on Caesar. "So how's my little putty-tat?"

"Caesar's fine," I told her. "It's just a simple bacterial infection. I'll give you an ear cleanser that'll get rid of it. But keep an eye on him. If he keeps getting ear infections, he might need blood work or X-rays to figure out why. He might even need surgery."

I gave Joan a quick lesson in the delicate art of putting medicine inside a cat's ear, showing her how to massage it to spread around the liquid.

"Then clean his ears with some mineral oil," I instructed her as I demonstrated. "Just soak a cotton ball in it, clean the outside of the ear canal and the inside of his ear like this . . ."

"He doesn't like it." Joan bit her lip.

"Cats never do. I have a feeling most people wouldn't be crazy about having something cold running into their ear, either."

"I guess you're right," she admitted reluctantly, still wearing a pained expression.

"There. We're done." Stroking the car's soft fur, I added, "You were a great patient, Caesar. A real credit to your namesake." I handed him back to Joan. I don't know which of them looked more relieved.

After we settled the bill, Joan took a business card, informing me that I was now officially Caesar Devlin's veterinarian. Then she nuzzled her cat's furry little face, cooing, "Come on, Caesar. Let's go home. You've had a very tryin' day."

Once I was alone again, I sat down in the driver's seat and made notes in the chart I'd just created for Caesar. Then I pulled out the spiral notebook I used to keep track of details like how many miles I drove each day and the cost of the fast-food lunches I grabbed on the way to calls in remote places. When you run your own business, every tax deduction counts.

But my trusty little log book was about to take on an additional role. I suddenly found myself swamped with information about the life, loves, and business dealings of Tommee Frack, and I needed a way to organize all of it. I realized that keeping track of what I learned, when I learned it, who I learned it from, and what the implications might be was of critical importance in putting together the pieces of this puzzle.

I realized something else, too. Although I was making some progress and already starting to develop a few theories of my own, I needed help.

From a professional.

Chapter 5

"Romance, like the rabbit at the dog track, is the elusive, fake, and never attained reward which, for the benefit and amusement of our masters, keeps us running and thinking in safe circles."

—Beverly Jones

As I drove away from Merrilee's house, a black Jeep that had been parked halfway down the street during my visit began to move. I slowed, waiting for it to go ahead. Instead, it stopped to let me leave the cul-de-sac first.

I waved a thank you, surprised by what struck me as an unusually considerate act. Long Island drivers aren't exactly known for their politeness. But as I drove by, I saw that the driver had turned his face away.

I headed toward Port Townsend, my mind clicking away, plotting a strategy. Merrilee had suggested talking to people who knew Tommee from his public relations business. I agreed with her off-handed comment: chatting with them *was* an excellent way of getting to know the dead man better. As for coming up with a *reason* for them to talk to me, that was a trifle more complicated. But I had some ideas about that, too.

I'd forgotten about the Jeep until I came to a busy corner, one at which I needed to make a turn. Glancing into my rearview mirror, I saw that it was right behind me. It struck me as an odd coincidence that one of Merrilee's neighbors happened to follow the same convoluted route I'd just taken.

But it wasn't until I made a risky left turn, rushing in front of the oncoming traffic with a little less leeway than I liked, that the "coincidence" began to seem like something more. The black Jeep stuck to my tail, causing the driver of the car we both raced in front of to punch his horn furiously.

"Is this guy following me?" I murmured. I was squinting at the rearview mirror, trying to get a better look at him. But he'd dropped back and was far enough away that I couldn't see him well. The fact that the driver—definitely male—wore a baseball hat and sunglasses made it even harder.

"This is a busy road," I told myself after driving another half mile or so. "A lot of people drive on it."

Just for the heck of it, I pulled into a Dairy Barn. I figured I could always use an extra dozen eggs, and this seemed as good a time as any to stock up. Besides, a straightforward confrontation with reality might help cure my paranoia.

Ten minutes later, when I pulled back onto the highway, the Jeep was behind me again. Yet I remained unwilling to accept the ridiculous notion that I was actually being followed. I decided I had simply seen too many James Bond movies. "It's probably not even the same car," I muttered to myself.

By the time I turned into the parking lot of Nick's Olde English office complex and watched the Jeep drive on, I was convinced I'd imagined the whole thing—even if the vehicle in question did have tinted windows.

"No more caffeine for you today, young lady," I told myself firmly. "Not when you're already starting to see things that aren't there."

I decided to focus on something really cloak-and-dagger: solving the mystery of how to convince Nick Burby that it really did make sense for me to try to identify Tommee Frack's killer.

His greeting was less than encouraging.

"You again." As I stepped into his office, he glanced up from a thick paperback the size of the Norfolk County phone book. His expression instantly shifted from engrossed to exasperated.

"Like a bad penny," I assured him. "Mind if I sit down?"

Instead of waiting for an answer, I sat.

"So what have you been up to?" I asked casually.

"Not much. Studying for the LSAT." He held up the paperback. It was a review book for the Law School Admission Test, crammed with advice on how to read pie diagrams and figure out the best title for a story.

I nobly resisted the temptation to launch into another speech about the evils of the law profession. Instead, I offered, "Let me know if you need any help. I'm really good with flash cards."

Before he could make a snappy comeback that

would take us in a direction I didn't want to go, I said, "By the way, I've been meaning to ask how Leilani is doing."

"She's doing fine."

"Does she miss me?"

"It's kind of hard to tell."

"Tell her I said hello."

"I'll give her your regards. But somehow I get the feeling you didn't come here to talk about Leilani."

"Ah. Very perceptive. No wonder you're in the P.I. business."

"Now you're flattering me. I'm starting to get nervous."

"Actually, I wanted your opinion on a couple of things. I also have a business proposition."

He narrowed his eyes. "I liked it better when we were talking about the weather."

"We haven't talked about the weather."

"I meant that metaphorically. You know, the LSAT, Leilani, the easy stuff."

"Forget easy. I have something much more interesting to tell you."

"Now I'm really getting nervous."

I leaned forward in my chair. "I think Merrilee Frack may have murdered her ex-husband."

I expected silence. I expected a cynical look. I didn't expect him to laugh out loud.

"You're joking, right? I don't really know the woman, of course, but from what I saw at the wake, she didn't look as if she could hurt a fly—if you'll excuse the cliché."

"Maybe not a fly. But what about a man she's madly in love with—a man she's been absolutely crazy about almost her entire life—that she's just learned is about to marry somebody else?"

"The jealous lover." Nick thought for about a tenth of a second, then shook his head. "Somehow, it doesn't fit."

"Why not?" I asked indignantly. "I found out she's still waiting for Tommee to come back to her. Even though they've been divorced for three years, and even though he cheated on her constantly when they were married, she still loves him. She's convinced—or at least she was up until recently—that it was only a question of time until he saw the light and realized she was the love of his life. It's totally conceivable that learning that Tommee was about to marry Barbara Delmonico was enough to push Merrilee over the edge."

His look of silent skepticism spurred me on. "You should see her house, Nick! It's filled with pictures of Tommee. She even has this, this altar, practically, in her spare bedroom. And as if *that* wasn't freaky enough, she has a cageful of canaries in her kitchen—"

"Wait a minute. You were in her *house*?"

I nodded.

He exploded. "Are you insane? What the hell do you think you're doing, Jess? You actually went *into* Merrilee Frack's house?"

I sat back in my chair. The force of his reaction had practically catapulted me backward.

"What's wrong with that?" I countered.

"You can't just ring people's doorbells and start prying into their lives!"

"Why not?"

"Because one of them might be a murderer!"

"Well, it's not as if I just walked up to her front door out of the blue. She invited me over."

Coldly, he said, "Do you mind if I ask why?"

"To check on her dogs. They're named Dobie and Maynard. Which sounds weird, unless you know that they're Dobermans. Get it? Dobie the Doberman? And Maynard, well—"

"I get it, Jess. Go on."

"Anyway, apparently Tommee bought the dogs when they were still married, and when he and Merrilee divorced, he kept them. But now that he's dead, they're back with Merrilee. She was worried because they weren't eating. It's not uncommon, actually. A lot of times, even when a dog's owner just goes away on vacation, he—"

"So you just volunteered to play doctor with her dogs."

"No." I was getting impatient. "She asked me to."

"Because you happened to mention to her that you were a vet?"

"It's a little more complicated than that."

Nick raised his eyebrows.

"She kind of assumed I was *already* their vet. She thought that was why I was at the wake in the first place. You know, that Tommee and I had a professional relationship."

"So she made that faulty assumption, and you didn't bother to correct her."

"Are you kidding? It was like a gift!"

Nick was scowling. "What if she really is the murderer, Jess?"

"But isn't that the whole point of a murder investigation? Talking to suspects, one of whom is likely to be the actual murderer?"

"Yes, of course it is. But this is not a game of Clue, for heaven's sake. Whoever killed Tommee Frack is dangerous, remember? Which is why I keep telling you the investigation should be left to the professionals."

"As a matter of fact, I've come to realize you're absolutely right." I reached into my purse and took out my checkbook. "How much?"

"How much for what?"

"For your retainer. How much is required to hire you?"

He sighed. "I'm not for hire, Jessie."

"You're a private investigator, aren't you? Isn't that the whole idea? People pay you to investigate whatever they want investigated?"

"If I choose to accept the assignment."

"How often do you turn something down? I mean, don't you pretty much take anything that comes along?"

"No-o-o," he replied, looking offended. "Just last month, for example, this gorilla of a guy came into my office, offering to pay me whatever it took to find his wife. But I had this uneasy feeling that his wife really didn't want him to find her. So I told him I was booked."

"Can't say I blame you, in that instance. But this isn't exactly the same situation."

"No, Jessie. You're right. This is a bad idea for an entirely different reason. Put your checkbook away."

I did exactly that. Then I stood up.

"Well, then, I guess I'll have to go somewhere else for help."

"You're going to pay somebody else, somebody

you don't even know, to investigate the murder of somebody else you don't know?"

"Let's just say I have other options. And I'm about to take advantage of them."

"Oh, no. You're not planning on doing what I think you're doing. Not that cop, for heaven's sake, the one you were falling over at the wake—"

"'Bye, Nick." Sarcastically, I added, "Have a nice day."

Tossing my head in what I hoped was a haughty manner, I stalked out of the office.

"Jess, come back. Hey, let's talk about this!"

Ignoring Nick Burby gave me the biggest rush I'd experienced all week.

"Damn you, Nick Burby!" I cried once I was safe inside my own four walls. "Damn you, damn you, damn you!"

The good feeling I'd derived from my little Bette Davis act in Nick's office was already long gone. Instead, I found myself angry and frustrated.

I flopped into the soft, upholstered chair next to the couch, pulling Cat into my lap and nuzzling her fur. Lou immediately came over and rested his head on my thigh. He gazed up at me mournfully as if to say, "Isn't there *anything* I can do?"

Max tried a different tack. He pushed Lou's favorite tennis ball around with his nose, glancing at me every few seconds to see if I found it as irresistible as he did.

I fondled Lou's ears distractedly, anxious to let him know him how much I appreciated his concern. As for Max's suggestion that play therapy was the answer, I gave the tennis ball a half-hearted toss, then sank back into my ruminations.

Was I in such a black mood because of Nick Burby's refusal to take me seriously? Or was it just Nick Burby, *period*?

"Thanks, you guys," I told my sidekicks as I jumped up and headed for the phone, "but this calls for *human* intervention."

I dialed the Eighth Precinct.

"Officer Nolan, please." I hoped my voice could be heard over the jackhammer pounding of my heart.

I told myself he was probably out on the streets of Norfolk County, arresting bad guys. So I was shocked when he picked up.

"Oh, *hi*!" I said, immediately embarrassed that I sounded like I was sixteen. "I didn't think you'd actually be there—"

"Who is this?" he asked crisply.

"Jessie Popper. Tommee Frack, remember?"

"Oh, sure, Jessie." Now *his* voice had a teenaged twinge. I could feel my cheeks getting warmer. "How y'doing? Keeping out of trouble?"

"I'm trying. Actually, I was calling for kind of a different reason. I, uh, was wondering if you'd like to come over for dinner Saturday night. At my house, I mean. Well, it's really only a cottage—"

"Dinner sounds great."

This was turning out to be easier than I'd expected. I felt strangely giddy even as I plummeted into a state of acute anxiety. "Okay, then let me give you my address."

"I already know where you live."

"You do?"

"You gave it to me the day you went hiking into the woods and tripped over more than you bargained for. Remember? For the police report?"

"That's right." Just Say No to Paranoia, Jessica. "Okay, so I guess I'll see you Saturday night."

"Aren't you forgetting something?" Jimmy asked.

"Uh—"

"What time?"

Okay, I wasn't as good at this as I wanted to be, I thought, after Jimmy and I had worked out the details and said goodbye. Still, it had been a while since I'd invited a man to dinner. In fact, it had been a while since I'd called one on the phone, too, unless you counted worried pet owners, male relatives, and Nick.

I suddenly longed for a little female companionship.

This time, as I neared the Big House, I didn't hear any Broadway show tunes. But when Betty flung open the door, her eyes glittered and her cheeks were flushed. A stretchy one-piece jumpsuit in a leopard skin print clung to her svelte frame, showing off her dancer's body. Her earrings were also *faux* leopard skin, two fluffy clumps the size of ping pong balls that dangled at least three inches below each ear. As for her thick *faux* eyelashes, I assumed they were an antidote to the gray November day. The same went for the red high heels.

"Jessica! You're *just* the person I wanted to talk to!"

"Another dance recital?"

"Even better. I have an important decision to make and I need your help."

She pulled me into the front parlor where at least a

dozen slick travel brochures were strewn across the silk-covered Victorian sofa. Colorful photographs of calm, blue seas and white sand beaches were interspersed with pictures of majestic lions and tigers, staring out from behind dense foliage.

"I simply cannot decide where to go in January," Betty said with an exasperated sigh. "On the one hand, the South Pacific is calling to me. Tahiti, Moorea, Bora Bora . . . lounging on the beach, surrounded by handsome men in loincloths fanning me with palm fronds . . . Can you believe I haven't been to Polynesia since that USO tour in the early fifties?

"On the other hand, I haven't gone on safari in ages. Jessica, there's nothing like watching the giraffes and the elephants run wild and free!" She threw her arms out dramatically, making her leopard skin earrings swing wildly. "Of course, the last time I was in Kenya, one of those elephants charged our tent and nearly trampled us to death. It was one of the most exciting moments of my life."

I sank into a chair. "I envy you, Betty. You've led the kind of life most people only dream about!"

"To me, the world is a magnificent smorgasbord, stretching before us with an infinite number of wonderful things to choose from. I've certainly done a lot of things I never could have imagined back when I was still living in Altoona.

"Then again," she went on, her tone becoming wistful, "there are some things I always assumed would be part of my life that never came my way. Things most people take for granted, like the feeling of being truly cherished, of being the most important person in someone else's life . . ."

"What about Charles?" I protested. "You two had something so special!"

"What we had was a honeymoon. Two short years. I barely got to know him."

"But you loved him."

"I absolutely adored him. But I never had the chance to *grow* with him. We never weathered the hardships life dishes out or learned to put up with each other's flaws, along with the virtues." Shaking her head, she smiled sadly. "I wouldn't trade my experiences for anything. But I never stopped wishing I could share them with someone who *really* mattered."

Even though we went on to discuss the pros and cons of lying on a tropical beach versus stalking rhinos with a camera, Betty's words stuck with me. I'd heard her stories about her passionate love affair with Charles more times than I could count. Yet she rarely let me see how much losing him had hurt her.

I couldn't help feeling she was sending me a message. But at the moment, it was one I was in no mood to hear. Not with my breakup with Nick, and the reasons behind it, still an open wound—and the topic of independence versus living happily ever after with Prince Charming too damn hot.

I'd spent my entire life working my butt off, making sure I'd get to the place I so desperately wanted to be. In high school, I'd stuffed my schedule with as many classes as I could, even sacrificing lunch period in order to squeeze in an extra lab science. In college, I spent a lot more Saturday nights studying than partying, wanting to make sure I'd ace Monday morning's exam. As for vet school, it had been nothing short of grueling: four more years of pressure and exams and all-nighters, fueled by caffeine and determination.

But I'd never considered doing things differently. Not only did I love both animals and science, so that the idea of combining them into a career seemed like heaven on earth, but being independent, getting myself into a position where I never had to rely on anyone else for *anything*—emotional support included—was at least as important. I had no intention of ending up like my parents, trapped in a life that made them absolutely miserable. My father, working as a middle manager at an electronics firm, hating his job and taking it out on everyone around him, yet insisting that in the abstract, at least, family was sacred. My mother, bitter about being stuck in an unsatisfying marriage but having neither the education nor the self-confidence to even imagine a different life.

I found the prospect of compromising the independence I'd knocked myself out to earn nothing short of terrifying.

"So what do you think, Jessica?" Betty finally demanded, her sapphire blue eyes bright with expectation.

A wave of exhaustion came over me as I surveyed the glossy booklets covering the couch. "I'm sorry, Betty," I said with a sigh, "but I'm afraid I just don't know."

The look on her face told me she was perfectly aware that I wasn't only talking about her vacation plans.

· · ·

As soon as I got home, I plopped down in front of my computer. I didn't want to think about Nick. I didn't even want to think about Jimmy Nolan. Instead, I intended to focus on a man who didn't either make my blood boil with rage or my heart flutter with anxiety.

I logged on to my favorite search engine, then typed in the key words, "Tommee Frack & Associates." My melancholy reverie disappeared when Cat padded over. I pulled her into my lap, then watched as she climbed up onto the computer keyboard. I couldn't help but smile as she pranced over the keys, intending to make herself the center of my attention but sending my computer into a frenzy.

"We'll have to get you a keyboard with paw-sized keys," I told her, laughing as I maneuvered her down into my lap. The commotion we were making set Prometheus off. He launched into a hardy rendition of "Yo-ho-ho-*oh, the pirate's life for me!*" A souvenir of Nick, whose boyhood passion for the book *Treasure Island* had inspired him to teach my bird the entire song one night, after deciding to dress up as Captain Kidd the very next time we were invited to a costume party.

I pushed the memory away, giving Cat a quick kiss and retyping my request. My computer spent an unusually long time thinking. While I waited, I fondled the softest ears in the entire galaxy, taking care to avoid the nick, which had never stopped being sensitive. Finally, a stark screen with the discouraging words "Can't Find Website" popped up.

"Hmm," I muttered. "Somebody over there is on the ball."

I needed something more general. I tried the key words, "Long Island Business."

Within a few seconds, I discovered there was a website called libusinessbeat.com. When I clicked on it, it turned out to be the site of a weekly publication.

I scanned the home page, learning that *Long Island Business Beat* claimed to be the only magazine that completely covered Long Island's business scene. "Works for me," I said, typing in the words, "Tommee Frack & Associates."

"Yes!" I cried when a dozen different entries came up on the screen. Cat's ears perked up at my excitement.

Merrilee Frack had told me that if I wanted to understand Tommee, I should talk to his business associates—and that included his employees. And the numerous short pieces from the magazine's weekly "People on the Move" column gave me the names of the people who had joined his firm over the past three years, along with their changes in title and responsibilities. It also contained short write-ups of the people who had left Tommee Frack & Associates, presumably to work at other firms.

I jotted down the names, along with the companies at which they currently worked. I also wrote down any other personal information that was listed, like what town they resided in. I knew, of course, that I couldn't very well just call these strangers up and start asking them questions about the now-deceased PR mogul whose name happened to be on their résumé. Nick had been right about that.

But he had also underestimated me. Even though

the man had shared my bed for over three years, he clearly had no idea just how devious I could be.

To prove my point, I dashed off a quick E-mail to Vanda Jackson, a friend of mine who worked in the New York State Department of Agriculture and Markets in Albany. She'd been a great source of help to me in the past, and I was optimistic about her willingness to help me out now.

I clicked "Send," muttering, "Nick Burby isn't the only one with friends in high places."

•   •   •

I logged off, listened to my voice mail and responded to half a dozen messages left by clients. I also followed up with several others whose animals I'd treated in the past couple of days. Midnight, I was glad to learn, was on the mend—and Mr. Sutter happily reported that he'd made a friend of his own at the park, a retired electrician who was teaching him how to play chess. My last call was to Skip, the manager at Atherton Farm, who reported that Stormy Weather's fever had broken and the stallion was doing much better. By the time my dogs and I got on the road, I'd completely reshifted my focus to the afternoon of house calls that lay ahead.

I always enjoyed visiting Winifred Mack, the quintessential cat lady. In addition to the seven living, breathing cats sprawled across her doorstep, along her windowsills, and in her flowerbeds, every corner of her house was decorated with pictures, figurines, pillows, and mugs with a feline motif. She even had a stained glass cat hanging in her front window.

"Hell-o, Dr. Popper," Winifred sang as she entered

the van. Her abundant form was draped in a flowing purple caftan, and her jet black hair, lit up with dramatic streaks of gray, was piled in a loose knot on top of her head. An ankh, the Egyptian symbol of life, dangled from a long gold chain hanging around her neck, while another necklace linked silver charms I recognized as symbols for all twelve signs of the zodiac. Her prodigious chest also served as the backdrop for at least half a dozen strings of colorful beads.

In her arms, she cradled James, a Himalayan-Persian cross with one of the most gorgeous coats of thick, smoky-gray fur I'd ever seen. "Thank you for coming so quickly," Winifred continued in her lilting voice. "You know I never call unless there's a real problem. And something's just not right with James."

"It never hurts to check." I focused on the cat in her arms. "Hey, James! How's my favorite pussycat today?" I scratched him under the chin with one finger and was rewarded with deep, satisfied purring. "You said he's limping?"

"He was lame on Sunday, but then he seemed just fine. But today is Thursday, and he won't walk at all. You can see that his front leg is swollen.

"They talk to me, you know," she confided, lowering her voice. "Oh, not the way you and I are talking. I'm not *that* looney. But my cats and I have a way of communicating. And James tells me he's in great pain."

You didn't need a psychic connection to see that was true. The cat's entire body was swollen. I already had a theory about the cause.

"Let's put him on the examining table." I picked

him up gently, taking special care not to cause him any more pain than he was already putting up with. "What's up, James?" I asked him in a soothing voice. "Your mommy's very worried about you. You haven't been fighting, have you?"

When I touched his spine, he let out a howl. Max and Lou, lying side by side in a small patch of sunlight near the front of the van, both pricked up their ears. Even I cringed, regretting that I'd hurt him and wishing I could explain that it was part of trying to make him better. At least he didn't hold it against me. He was surprisingly cooperative about letting me take his temperature. It was high. A healthy cat's temperature is 101, and James's was 104.5 degrees.

"I think James has an abscess," I told the anxious Winifred.

"Oh, dear," she whimpered, her hands so fidgety that the dozen or so thin silver bracelets running up her forearm jangled. "That sounds serious."

"It needs to be treated right away."

"Whatever you say, Dr. Popper. I know cats' souls, but their bodies are totally mysterious to me."

"I'm going to anesthetize James. I'll need you to hold him while I inject him with a sedative-analgesic cocktail. It'll keep him from feeling any pain."

Winifred winced as I stuck the needle into the cat's thigh. I never liked causing my patients pain—and hurting their owners, even vicariously, was just as unnerving. But my initial suspicion proved correct. When I lay his limp body on the table and shaved off the fur on his leg, I found two punctures.

"Another cat bit him," I explained, showing her the wound. "Are there any strays in the area? Or do you think he might have been fighting with one of your other cats?"

"I have noticed a big tomcat hanging around . . ."

I opened the puncture holes with a hemostat, gently, thankful that James couldn't feel a thing. Thank God for the wonders of modern veterinary medicine. "I'm going to sew this piece of rubber tubing in place to drain out the pus," I told Winifred, "plus give him a shot of penicillin. I'll leave you with a two-week supply of pills, too. If he's been fighting, he should be given a booster shot for leukemia and feline AIDS when his fever is gone. In the meantime, keep him isolated from your other cats. I'd like to do a blood test to see if he's been infected with either."

"Whatever you think, Dr. Popper." She fluttered around me nervously. "You know I only want the best for my cats. They're my *family*."

After I'd revived James by injecting an antidote to the sedative, I had to fight off Winifred's insistence that I come inside for green tea and a "nice long visit" with her cats. I still had several appointments ahead of me.

Still, I was glad to be keeping busy. In the back of my mind, the plans I'd made with Jimmy for Saturday night loomed ahead of me. An intimate dinner for two was one of those things that had seemed like a good idea when I'd first decided to do it, but was beginning to feel like more than I could handle.

• • •

It's not a date, I reminded myself as I wrestled with a mascara wand while leaning over the bathroom sink the following Saturday evening at three minutes to seven. At least, not *exactly*.

To be honest, I wasn't sure what it was. I had to admit that I was more than a little attracted to Jimmy Nolan. Or I thought I was. My interest in him could have been rooted mainly in the fact that he seemed interested in me. That made him the first male to pay me any special attention since my breakup with Nick—unless you counted a hormonally challenged English bulldog named Abner who'd instantly developed an obsession with my leg.

Then again, there was surely more to be gained from an evening with Jimmy Nolan than the pleasure of male company. Officer Nolan was my link to my crime investigation.

Which, of course, led to another entirely different set of motives, both conscious and unconscious.

No matter what motivations Dr. Freud might have been able to uncover, I realized that I hadn't been this nervous over an evening with a gentleman caller since—well, since my first date with Nick.

When I heard an authoritative knock at the door, I jumped, sending my basket of cosmetics flying. Max and Lou, who'd been lounging beside me, immediately skittered across the slippery bathroom floor with all the dignity of a couple of Looney Tunes characters. Lou started barking. Max grabbed my blush brush, probably mistaking it for a small rodent on a stick.

Why can't I have a normal life? I wondered, chasing after them as they dashed toward the front door.

"Get down! Get *down*!" I commanded as somehow I managed to push them aside just enough to wedge the door open.

On the other side stood Officer Jimmy Nolan, dressed in jeans and a beat-up leather bomber jacket. Grinning, he thrust a bouquet of wildflowers at me.

"I thought of bringing wine, but I figured you were probably one of those organized types who'd already taken care of it."

"Do I look organized?" I lunged for Lou's collar. The leggy Dalmatian was all paws and slobber as he greeted the stranger who'd shown up on our doorstep, acting as if the two of them were long-lost friends.

"Some watch dog you got there."

Max, meanwhile, dropped my blush brush and started barking his head off.

"I'm obviously in good hands here," I said. "Definitely better than a security system."

"*Awk!* Get down, Lou! Get down! *Awk!*" Prometheus shrieked as Cat slunk into the room, suspiciously sniffing the air around the stranger who was causing all this commotion before sticking up her nose and taking refuge under the couch.

"Jeez, you've got a parrot, too? And a cat? This place is like a zoo! I guess you must really love animals."

"Most of the time." I shot Max a dirty look. In typical terrier fashion, he pretended not to notice.

I had no choice but to exile my two hyperactive roommates to the bedroom. As for Cat, I just hoped she wouldn't use my dinner guest's leg as a scratching post.

As Jimmy sank into a chair, I said brightly, "Okay. The monsters are safely behind bars." I pointedly ignored Max's indignant barks and Lou's pathetic whimpers. "What would you like to drink? I've got wine, beer, Coke, diet and regular, orange juice . . ."

"A beer sounds great."

"That's right." I smiled. "You promised to tell me some of your war stories over beer."

"Yeah, well, not tonight." He leaned back in his chair. "It's my night off."

I tried not to let on how disappointed I was over his reluctance to talk shop. Instead, I grabbed a Corona out of the fridge and poured myself a glass of wine. I'd try him again later, after I'd had a chance to ply him with Mexican beer and honey-mustard chicken.

"Interesting house you've got here," he said conversationally as I sat down on the couch.

"Thanks. It started out as a caretaker's cottage."

"Yeah, I noticed the mansion on the property. That's some house. Who owns it?"

"A woman named Betty Vandervoort. It's funny; even though she's at least forty years older than I am, we've become the best of friends. Anyway, she and her husband bought it when they were newlyweds, something like fifty years ago. But it was originally owned by the grandson of Major Benjamin Tallmadge."

Jimmy frowned. "Should I know who that is?"

"Sorry. Sometimes I forget that not everybody's a local-history buff. Tallmadge was the head of the Culper Spy Ring, which was based right around here during the Revolutionary War. The spy ring kept track of the British military's movements."

"Wow."

I loved that he was impressed. And I loved telling the story.

"You know, Long Island is the only place in America that was ever occupied, back when we were fighting the British. The occupation lasted seven years. And the Culper Spy Ring played a really important role in the colonists' victory. A woman named Anna Smith Strong used to hang a black petticoat on her clothesline as a way of communicating that one ring member, a sea captain named Caleb Brewster, was in town. The number of handkerchiefs she hung indicated which of six landing spots Brewster had docked his boat at."

"Cool."

"After the Revolution, Washington came to eastern Long Island to meet the members of the spy ring. Anyway, Tallmadge's grandson really prospered. He owned several mills in the area, and he made enough money to build this place. And now I'm benefiting by living in his caretaker's cottage."

"But it sounds like you spend a lot of time in that amazing vehicle you've got out there."

For a moment, I thought he was referring to my little red VW. Then I realized he meant my other pride and joy, my mobile services van.

"A complete clinic on wheels," I told him proudly. "Everything a vet could possibly need. Hot and cold running water, X-ray processor . . . I can even perform surgery in it."

"I'll keep that in mind, in case I ever need my appendix out." He took a swig of beer from his bottle. "So what made you decide to become an animal doctor?"

"According to family lore, I was always an animal doctor. One of my mother's favorite stories—one I always found horribly embarrassing, of course—was that when I was really tiny, I used to play with my stuffed animals by wrapping their paws in toilet paper and making them lie in this wooden bed my father made me. Then, a few years later, I started bringing home butterflies and crawly things in jars so I could 'make them better.' I even set up a little hospital next to my father's workbench. I always felt it was my duty to take care of creatures that couldn't take care of themselves. I guess it never occurred to me to do anything else."

"So you studied hard, got straight A's in college and went on to four more years of vet school."

"That's pretty much it."

"And what about the van? Is it yours? Or do you work for some big organization that owns it?"

"Nope, it's just me. I named my business 'Reigning Cats and Dogs' to make it memorable, but it's really just Jessica Popper, D.V.M."

"If you don't mind me asking, how did you ever afford something like that?"

I hesitated, swallowing hard. As always, my throat had instantly tightened up.

"I bought the van with my inheritance."

"Holy cow! You're an heiress?" Jimmy joked.

"Not exactly. My parents were killed in a car accident a few years ago."

"Oh, jeez." His expression had already tensed. "God, I'm sorry. I had no idea."

"I know you didn't. It's okay."

"What happened? I mean, if you don't mind talking about it."

"I don't mind." And I didn't, at least not if I could take enough deep breaths to keep tears from falling.

"They were driving home from an evening out with friends. It wasn't even that late. It had been raining, and the roads were a little slippery. . . . Anyway, my father—he was driving—ran a stop sign. And they plowed right into a truck."

"Was alcohol involved?" Jimmy sounded very cop-like.

"No. It wasn't that late, either. I mean, it's not as if my father was falling asleep. My theory is that he and my mother were arguing. They did that a lot. He probably just wasn't paying attention."

I didn't bother to explain that, true or not, this was the scene I'd played over and over in my head so many times that I'd almost come to believe that I'd seen it happen. I desperately needed to understand what had gone on that night, and to me, this scenario made perfect sense.

"My parents spent more time arguing than just about anything else. They didn't have what you'd call a good marriage." I hesitated. "In fact, I think that's one of the reasons animals became so important to me. Whenever they started up, I'd grab my dog, Muffin, and hide in my room. I used to curl up with him in my arms and just talk to him the whole time, as if I could drown out my parents' yelling that way. Muffin was a good listener. I knew I could always count on him."

"That must have been rough. Especially when you were a kid."

"Well," I said slowly, "it sure didn't make it easy for me to trust. Relationships, I mean. I didn't have a very positive view of what married life was all about while I was growing up. I guess the experience left me kind of gun shy."

Jimmy grimaced. "My folks weren't exactly Ozzie and Harriet, either. I guess nobody's were."

To end the uncomfortable silence that had crashed down upon us, I glanced at my watch. "Everything should be ready in a couple of minutes. I hope you're starving."

We sat down at the small table in the corner of living room that was nearest the kitchen, a family heirloom that doubled as a desk and, on more formal occasions, a dining room table. So far, so good, I decided as I brought out what appeared to be a perfectly respectable dinner. Between the candles I'd lit and Jimmy's bouquet, which I'd stuck in a vase and placed at the center of the table, I gave the impression I actually knew what I was doing.

As soon as Jimmy pronounced my dinner delicious, I said casually, "I've been reading about the Frack case in *Newsday* every day this week. It doesn't sound as if you guys are making much progress."

"They're following all the usual steps. Don't worry; Harned knows what he's doing. Would you mind passing the rice?"

"What about forensic evidence? Have the police turned up any fingerprints? Hairs? Fibers? Anything at all that would provide a clue to who Tommee Frack's killer was?"

"This is really terrific. I never would have guessed you'd be such a good cook."

"I'm not." In response to his look of surprise, I said, "This recipe just happens to work because it requires all of five ingredients—including the chicken.

Do they have any suspects? I mean, Tommee was such a high-profile guy. There must be *somebody* they think had good reason to want him dead. And what about the canary? I haven't read a word about it."

Jimmy looked up from his plate. "How come you're so interested?"

"I suppose because I'm the one who found the body. It's made me wonder why he was murdered. I've been talking to some of the people who knew him, and—"

"You mean you're actually investigating this case? Like you were a cop or something?"

"Not exactly. It's not as if I have any delusions about possessing that kind of expertise, not to mention street smarts." But I did know something about the male ego, at least enough to recognize that I'd come dangerously close to threatening the one in my presence. "I'm just curious, that's all."

"Yeah, well, you know what they say about curiosity killing the cat. You should know all about that, being an animal doctor."

I was about to launch into my usual spiel about how I could take care of myself. But Jimmy wasn't finished.

"My advice, as both a professional and a friend, is to steer clear of this whole mess. Murder is really bad news, Jess. Believe me, it's not something you want to get involved in."

I didn't want to ruin an evening that, so far, seemed to be going surprisingly well. So I merely said, "Okay. In that case, maybe I should settle for you keeping me posted on the investigation. One thing I've been wondering about is—"

"Hey, Jessie? I don't mean to be rude or anything, but I really meant what I said before. About this being my night off."

"But this is a *murder*! Don't you find it fascinating?"

He shrugged. "I don't feel the way you do about my work. I didn't go around playing cop when I was a little kid. To me, it's just a job."

So much for furthering my professional insights into the Frack case.

Yet while Jimmy might not have fit into my master plan, I had to admit that I did enjoy the rest of the evening. True, it felt a little odd to be in the company of an attractive, attentive man who wasn't Nick. But every time I was struck by the strangeness of what I was doing, I reminded myself that an evening like this, enjoying a surprisingly decent meal and laughing and actually having fun, was long overdue.

So I was disappointed when I noticed Jimmy sneaking peeks at his watch.

"I'm sorry, Jess, but I'm going to have to make this an early night. Gotta work tomorrow."

"I understand completely," I said, impressed by his self-discipline.

Then we were standing by the front door. My least favorite part of a first date. That tense couple of minutes that aren't only the most awkward time of the entire evening; they also determine whether the date as a whole will be pronounced a success or a failure.

I still hadn't decided which outcome I'd prefer when Jimmy took a small step toward me, then gently took my face in his hands.

"This was nice," he said in a husky voice I hadn't heard before. "I'm glad you invited me."

"It *was* nice," I agreed. My voice sounded weird, too.

"And Jess? You know what you were saying before, about not finding it easy to trust?"

I nodded.

"I want you to know you can trust me. I'm one of those easy guys. You know, what you see is what you get."

The catch in his voice and the look in his eyes told me he was about to kiss me. I knew I'd been expecting it. I knew I'd even been wanting it. But somehow, now that the moment was here, I knew I couldn't handle it.

So I looked away.

"I'd better let you get out of here," I said with a sunny cheerfulness that sounded ridiculous. "I owe it to the law-abiding citizens of Norfolk County."

"Yeah." I could still feel the warmth of his hands on my cheeks. And then he leaned forward and planted a light kiss on my forehead.

The gesture was as sweet as it was unexpected. It also left me with the impression that no matter what Jimmy Nolan claimed, there was a lot more to him than met the eye.

Chapter 6

"Lettin' the cat outta the bag is a whole lot easier 'n' puttin' it back in."

—Unknown

I could still feel the soft touch of Jimmy's lips on my forehead twenty minutes later as I sprawled across the couch, finishing my wine and trying to decide how I felt about the evening. When I heard a tentative knock at the door, I assumed it was him. I hoped he'd only come back because of a forgotten jacket or some other practical reason, something that wouldn't make any emotional demands on me I clearly wasn't ready to handle.

I was totally unprepared to open the door and find Nick on my doorstep.

"Oh! It's you! I was expecting . . . I wasn't expecting anyone. This late, I mean. It is late, isn't it?"

"Ten-thirty." Nick checked his watch. "Is that too late for me to drop in?"

"It depends on what you're dropping in for." My

defenses were already snapping into place. "If you're here to lecture me again, then yes, it's too late. If you came over to have a civil conversation, then no, it's not."

"No more lectures. I promise."

"In that case . . ."

Before I had a chance to extend a polite invitation to come in, the two monsters descended upon him. In a flash, eight paws were on him, and there were so many wet dog kisses that I was tempted to offer him a raincoat.

"Down, Max!" I commanded. "Lou, get away from him!"

Of course, my attempts at calming them down were pointless. The dogs were so thrilled over seeing Nick again that nothing could distract them. From their level of excitement, you'd have thought Elvis had returned.

"Hey, guys!" Nick crouched down, clearly just as happy to be reunited with them. "How ya' doin', Max? Come here, Lou. How's my boy?"

They lapped up the attention shamelessly, leaping and barking and flailing about like whirling dervishes. I felt like a fifth wheel. I glanced over at Cat, who hadn't budged from the couch. The two of us exchanged a cynical look.

"Okay, guys," I interposed finally. "Calm down. Lou, get *down*."

"Well, at least somebody around here is happy to see me," Nick said pointedly, standing up and brushing wiry white Westie hairs off his trousers.

I wasn't about to touch that one. "Now that you're

completely covered in dog spit, would you like to come in and sit down?"

"Yeah, I could use a minute to recover."

"How about a cup of tea? Would that help? Or a glass of wine?"

"Wine would definitely be more helpful than tea."

I went into the kitchen to pour us each a glass.

"Hey, Prometheus!" I heard him saying. "How's the pretty birdie?"

"*Awk!*" the parrot replied. "Damn you, Nick Burby! *A-awk!* Damn you, damn you!"

I could tell my cheeks were the same color as the merlot I carried as I slunk back into the living room.

"I see my memory lives on," Nick said, laughing.

"I can explain how Prometheus learned that particular phrase . . ."

"No need," he insisted, shaking his head and chuckling. "I'm sure he's had more than one opportunity."

Nick was settled into the stuffed chair and Catherine the Great was settled into his lap. Predictably, she had waited until the dogs had made total fools of themselves before making her own overtures. Now she was purring as contentedly as if our visitor were one hundred sixty-five pounds of catnip. Even though Cat was contemptuous of most two-legged beings, she had decided early on that Nick was in a category all his own.

Max and Lou trotted over, no doubt expecting to plop down on the floor next to Nick. As soon as they got within three feet of his chair, Cat let out such a yowl that both backed off. But even though they begrudgingly found a spot a safe distance away, they kept their adoring eyes glued to him.

Let's face it, I thought. Everybody loves Nick.

I sat down on the couch. My living room was so small that our knees practically touched. I pulled the wooden coffee table closer to us, allegedly to give him a place to put his wineglass, but really to construct a barrier between us.

He took a sip of wine, then set his glass down. Fixing his eyes firmly on mine, he announced unexpectedly, "I'm here to call a truce."

"A truce?" I took a sip of my own wine. More like a gulp, actually. "I didn't know we were fighting."

"We were . . . disagreeing."

"Oh. You mean about whether or not I'm capable of asking a few questions to try to find out who murdered Tommee Frack."

"About whether or not it's safe to . . . Look, let's end this, okay?"

I shrugged. "I never wanted to start in the first place."

"Good." He picked up his glass and settled back in his chair. As he did, his eyes traveled around my tiny home. "The place looks good. Hasn't changed much."

Was it my imagination, I wondered, or did his posture alter slightly as his gaze lit on my dining room table, still set with two plates, two wineglasses, and two candles, now almost burned down to stubs?

I resisted the urge to smile smugly. Instead, I remained mysteriously silent, refusing to answer the unasked question that suddenly hung in the room.

"I guess I should blow those out," I murmured. "Fire hazard and all."

Nick merely nodded. I noticed that he immediately helped himself to a few king-size gulps of wine.

That's one for me, I thought triumphantly as I went over to the table and blew out the candles. But instead of sitting down again, my nervous energy prompted me to start picking up dirty dishes.

"Here, let me help you with that." Nick deposited Cat on the floor, leaped out of his seat, and began scooping up silverware.

"You really don't have to—"

"It's no trouble. Anyway, I came over here tonight because I wanted to make you an offer."

"What kind of offer?" I turned my back to him and headed into the kitchen.

He followed a few paces behind. "I think you'll like this."

There was hardly enough room in the kitchen for one person, much less two. I eased out, taking care not to brush against him.

"So what's this offer?" I asked once we'd sat back down in the living room.

"I've decided to help you."

"Help me with . . . ?"

"The investigation. I've even brought you some information."

He'd just said the magic word. I decided to try keeping my mouth shut. At least long enough to find out exactly what he knew.

"Go on."

"I talked to a friend of mine inside the police force."

I raised my eyebrows expectantly.

"The medical examiner has determined the cause of death. Tommee Frack was struck in the head and died from blunt-force trauma. His assailant hit him three times, using some sort of spherical object about three centimeters in diameter. The police haven't been able to ID the murder weapon."

I nodded, struggling to comprehend the violence of such hatred.

"There's more," he continued. "I also managed to find out what the cops learned from canvassing the neighborhood. No one reported seeing anything unusual the day before you found Frack's body. Just the regular flow of traffic that you'd expect in an area like Brewster's Neck. A few neighbors driving in and out, a UPS truck, a FedEx truck, a cop car cruising the neighborhood, the garbage pick-up, a taxi—"

"A taxi? That sounds interesting. It would be the perfect way for someone who didn't belong in the neighborhood to come and go."

Nick made a face. "And how much do you think you'd have to tip the driver to keep him from mentioning the fact that the luggage you'd put in his trunk consisted of a corpse?"

"It was just a thought."

"Well, to tell you the truth, I had the same thought. I even called the taxi company. Turns out it was just a housekeeper who commutes to her job in a cab."

"So what does this mean? That we should start looking for a murderer with a Brewster's Neck address? Someone local?"

"Not necessarily. The murderer probably drove in with the body in the middle of the night, at a time that no one spotted him."

"Or her," I said distractedly.

He frowned. "Frack's ex again?"

"I'm telling you, Nick. She's still in love with him.

Bizarrely so, in fact. The news that he was marrying somebody else could really have been the last straw for her."

"Well, maybe you're right about not ruling anybody out. At least, not this early in the game."

I jumped up from the couch. "I have to write down this new information. About the cops canvassing the neighborhood, I mean."

"Write it down?"

I retrieved my notebook from my purse. "It's a system I developed for staying organized. I'm writing down every piece of information I have, along with the source. That way, I can go over my notes and look for patterns, clues I might have overlooked, that kind of thing."

I bent my head over the spiral pad, muttering as I recorded the list of vehicles Nick had named.

"UPS, FedEx . . ."

"Don't forget the taxi."

"Got it. You know, this is kind of fun. Having somebody to kick around ideas with, I mean."

I glanced over at Nick, expecting him to agree.

Instead, he grimaced. "I guess I finally had to admit I didn't have any choice."

"Meaning what?"

"Meaning that I realized that whatever I said, no matter how much I warned you about the dangers of what you were proposing, you were going to go ahead and do exactly as you pleased."

"I get it," I said archly. "You decided to protect me from myself."

I stood up, grabbed a few more dishes, and pointedly headed back into the kitchen. Annoyingly enough, Nick insisted upon following me.

"I wish you would stop twisting everything I say and making it into something bad."

I busied myself with stacking dishes. "It doesn't take much twisting, if you ask me."

Without any warning, Nick placed his hands on my shoulders and turned me around so I faced him. Given the size of the room, we now stood eye to eye, so close that our bodies were touching.

"Please, Jess, just hear me out."

His voice had become soft. His eyes had, too. I forced myself to look away, knowing full well the effect that tone of voice and that look could have on me.

"You have some wonderful qualities, Jess. You're remarkably intelligent, you're determined, you're focused . . . you're someone who knows exactly what you want."

He tightened his grip on my shoulders, just the slightest bit. Part of me wanted to shrug him off. But part of me wished he would never, ever let go.

"But those qualities," he went on, "as wonderful as they are, also have the potential to get you into trouble. I want you safe, Jess. If you're going to do this, I figure I might as well do everything I can to make sure you come out of it in one piece."

The intensity of his tone, and of the moment, set off alarms inside my head. When it came to basic survival techniques, I was no fool.

In a syrupy Southern accent, I quipped, "Why, Nicholas Burby, ah didn't know you cared."

"Of course I care, Jess. You must know that," He was still speaking in that soft voice. He rubbed his hands up and down my shoulders in a gentle caressing motion. I could feel myself melting like the candles I'd just put out of their misery. "Look—I know that certain things between us have changed. It breaks my heart, but I'm doing my best to accept it. I wish there was some way I could convince you that you and I aren't your parents. That every couple in the world isn't just replaying their script—and that being with someone doesn't have to mean losing yourself in them." Nick sighed deeply. "I know how you must feel when you're dealing with a dog or a cat who's spent so much of his life being afraid that he's determined never to let anything hurt him, ever again. I guess it's pretty much a losing battle. At least, that's what I'm trying to make myself understand.

"But there are some things that haven't changed, and probably never will—like the fact that no matter what's happened, you're still special to me, Jess." His voice thickened with emotion. "That's just the way it is. And if anything ever happened to you . . ."

I almost exhaled with relief as he was interrupted by Max and Lou barking. But then I immediately tensed. I knew those barks. Someone was on the property.

"It's just the dogs," Nick pointed out.

"There's got to be a reason they're freaking out." I stuck my head out of the doorway and saw they were both standing at the front door: Lou with his nose pressed against it, growling, Max barking his head off.

Sure enough, seconds later I heard a knock. I noticed a look of disappointment cross Nick's face. Or at least I thought that was what it was.

At any rate, I was glad for the interruption. Talk about protecting me from myself.

But then I opened the door and found Betty Vandervoort. The distraught look on her face didn't match the cheerful silk fabric of her flowing kimono, bright oranges and reds depicting fat Buddhas against a background of splashy, exotic-looking flowers.

"What's wrong?" I asked, scooping up Max and grabbing Lou's collar.

"Oh, good," she replied, looking past my shoulder. "Nick is here."

I braced myself for the usual lecture on how the two of us belonged together, made all the more embarrassing by the fact that Nick would actually be present for it. But the annoyance swiftly passed. The expression on my landlady's face told me she was upset about something a lot worse than the sorry state of my love life.

"Jessica, I just got a very strange phone call."

"From whom?"

She shook her head. "Maybe if I had some idea, it wouldn't have been quite as frightening."

"What did the caller say?" Nick asked evenly.

Betty took a deep breath. "He said to tell my nosy next-door neighbor to mind her own business or she'd be very sorry."

It took a few seconds for my initial shock to pass.

"Come in," I insisted once I had regained my composure enough to remember my manners. Besides,

Betty looked as if she needed to sit down even more than I did. Her lipstick, the same electric orange as the kimono's fabric, was actually smeared, and she had considerably more glittery green eyeshadow on one lid than the other.

I freed the dogs and commanded them, "Lie down." Max and Lou reluctantly hit the floor.

I led Betty to my comfortable chair and sat down opposite her. "Tell me again, Betty. Tell me exactly what happened."

"I was standing in the kitchen, about to make myself a cup of herbal tea. It's something I do before I go to bed every night. The phone rang, which I thought was kind of odd, given how late it is. And on a Saturday night, no less.

"Anyway, I picked it up and said hello. At first I didn't hear anything. Just some breathing, so that I knew someone was at the other end of the line. I said hello again. And then this gruff voice, very low and kind of muffled, said, 'Tell your nosy next-door neighbor to mind her own business or she'll be very sorry.' By the time I said, 'Who is this?' he'd hung up."

"He? You're sure it was a male voice?" I asked.

"A hundred percent sure."

"And it wasn't a voice you recognized?"

"No. It was hard to tell, because it sounded as if something was covering his mouth. But I don't believe it was a voice I could place."

"Oh, boy," Nick breathed. He'd been standing a few feet away from the two of us, leaning against the wall with his arms folded across his chest. "Are you okay, Betty?"

She smiled up at him fondly. "I'm fine, Nick. And by the way, it's good to see you."

"Good to see you, too, Betty," he said sincerely. "It's been a while."

"Too long." Her smile faded. "I just wish it weren't something like this that brought us together again."

Both of them turned to me. Their expectant looks worked like a truth serum.

"There's something I guess I should have mentioned before . . . I'm not sure about this, and in fact the more I think about it the more I think I'm just being paranoid—"

"What?" Nick demanded.

"I think that maybe—*maybe*—somebody's been following me. I noticed a black Jeep behind me when I left Merrilee's house, the day of the wake. I took kind of an unusual route from her house to your office, but the car stuck with me the whole way."

"And you didn't think that was worth mentioning?" Nick snapped. "Even when you came into my office on Thursday, admitting that you'd been following Frack's ex-wife around as if you were the Mod Squad or something—"

"I didn't follow Merrilee. She invited me."

"Under false pretenses, since you didn't exactly—"

"Would someone mind telling me what on God's green earth you two are talking about?"

Betty's question shut both Nick and me up.

"Our favorite veterinarian here has taken it upon herself to play Miss Marple."

"With a little help from a professional," I couldn't

resist adding. "Isn't that why you came here tonight? To offer your services?"

Betty flashed me a meaningful look.

"As a private investigator," I added.

"Jessie stumbled across a dead body a few days ago," Nick said, "and for some reason that's impossible for me to understand, she seems to feel it's her responsibility to find the murderer."

"Yes, yes, I know all about that." Betty waved her hand in the air. "And I told her from the start that I thought she should concentrate on more productive things."

"Why are you suddenly talking about me in the third person?" I interjected.

"So you're going to give all this up, Jessica, right?" Betty reached over and took my hand.

"No." I sat up a little straighter. "In fact, I'm going to put even more effort into finding out who killed Tommee Frack. I don't like being threatened. Before, it was kind of like a game. A challenge. But now, it's *personal*."

Betty cast Nick an exasperated look. "We're not going to change her mind," she told him.

He groaned. "I know. Believe me, I know."

"In that case, Nick, I want you to promise me you'll do everything in your power to keep her safe. I want you to follow her around as if you were her shadow and make sure she doesn't do anything that will get her into trouble."

While I didn't doubt that she was truly concerned about me, I also knew Betty well enough to suspect she had an ulterior motive for her request.

"Don't worry," Nick assured Betty. "I'll make sure

she stays safe. Even if I have to follow her around twenty-four hours a day. Even if I have to sleep on her couch."

I couldn't help wondering if he, too, had an ulterior motive.

Chapter 7

"If you play with a cat, you must not mind her scratch."

—Yiddish Proverb

I'll be fine," I promised Nick and Betty as I shooed them out the door twenty minutes later. I appreciated their concern, but at the moment my head was so clouded from fatigue, wine, and drama that all I was interested in was a good night's sleep.

Maybe this whole detecting notion really is insane, I thought before drifting off. I burrowed beneath my cloud of a comforter, warmed by the cat curled up at my shoulder, the Dalmatian crushing my feet, and the Westie glommed onto my thigh. And remembered that life didn't have to be so complicated.

Maybe it was time to forget all about Tommee Frack. Even though I was finding the investigation of his murder the first interesting thing that had come into my life since—well, since Nick had exited from it—maybe the fact that one of my dearest friends was getting creepy phone calls late at night was a good enough reason to call it quits. The prospect of returning to what, in my case, passed for normal life, suddenly had a certain appeal. Like the animals beside me, I could go back to focusing on the things that really mattered: eating, sleeping, and occasionally nestling beside someone in bed.

I still felt the same appreciation for my simple, unencumbered life two days later as Max, Lou, and I piled into the van and headed for my first Monday morning appointment. Lindsay Weinstein was a new client, one I'd spoken to on the phone but never met.

I understood her interest in a mobile veterinarian's services as soon she answered the door. She looked as if she were at least seven months pregnant. Behind her, I could see a pair of twin boys about three years old watching cartoons on television. The living room carpet was littered with tiny plastic cars, puzzle pieces, Legos, Lincoln Logs, and a package of Oreos that looked as if it had exploded. The TV's volume was turned up so high that the sounds of thundering engines and ear-splitting machine-gun fire shook the room. The boys were arguing viciously over a grotesque plastic action figure that looked like something out of a nightmare. Somehow, their behavior didn't quite mesh with their thick golden curls, cherubic features, and innocent blue eyes.

"Mrs. Weinstein?"

"Please call me Lindsay. Thanks *so* much for coming, Dr. Popper. I . . . Boys, will you *please* turn down the TV? I've told you at least a dozen times . . ."

"It's *mine!*" one of the pint-sized angels squealed, completely ignoring his mother's request.

"Anyway," she continued loudly, distractedly pushing back a limp strand of blond hair that had come loose from her ponytail, "I used to go to the vet right here in town, but these days, it's—"

"Give it *back*!" the other boy yelled. "It's *my* turn! *Gimme* that!"

"I'm telling Mom!" his twin brother whined. "Mo-o-o-om!"

"Jason, give Dr. Destroyer to Justin. Let him have a turn. And please, turn that TV down!" She laughed self-consciously. "As I was saying, between having two little ones at home and the fact that I can hardly fit behind a steering wheel, it's next to impossible for me to get out of the house."

"You said on the phone your German Shorthaired Pointer seems to have pulled a muscle?"

"*Mo-o-om!* Jason won't give it to me! Let *go,* you stupid jerk! Mom *said*!"

Lindsay just let out a deep, tired sigh. "What I wouldn't give for a nap right now! Anyway, King's in the kitchen. It's back here."

As we passed the TV, she turned down the volume. I wasn't surprised that little Jason and Justin instantly began to wail.

I found the pointer curled up in his dog bed. As we approached, he wagged his tail halfheartedly but barely lifted his head.

"He's just not himself," Lindsay told me. "He's usually so active—it's like he can't get enough exercise. My husband jogs three miles every morning before work, and King is always right beside him. But lately, he won't run at all."

"Hey, King," I greeted him softly. I slowly extended

my hand, palm out, for him to sniff. He didn't even raise his head. "Mrs. Weinstein, does King spend any time in the woods or open fields?"

"Sure. You're thinking Lyme disease, right? We also thought of that, but he's had his Lyme shot."

"Unfortunately, they're only about eighty-five to ninety percent effective. I'd like to take him into the van and have a look."

As I started out the front door with the dog in tow, I heard a loud crash behind me in the living room. I didn't even turn to see what it was.

When I examined King, I found he had a high fever, as well as swollen lymph nodes behind his knee and ankle. This was one sick animal. Lyme disease was a definite possibility, as was another potentially serious tick-born disease, ehrlichiosis.

I pulled a foil packet out of the Styrofoam ice chest. For a mobile unit like mine, Snap Tests are a godsend, an easy way to check for the organisms that cause Lyme, ehrlichiosis, and heartworm. I drew blood and added a couple of drops to the activator in the package, then poured the mixture into the small plastic device, pressing down until I heard a *snap*.

During the eight minutes it took for the results, I ran my hand over King's smooth brown head and talked to him softly. "You're going to be fine," I assured him in a gentle voice. "You poor thing. I wish I could just make it all go away. . . ." The pointer just looked up at me sadly. Even Max and Lou kept their distance, sensing this was one dog who was in no mood to play.

Given the severity of King's symptoms, I wasn't

surprised that he tested positive for both ehrlichiosis and Lyme.

"Okay, King," I said softly. "Now that we know what's wrong, we'll have you chasing rabbits again in no time."

I found Lindsay hovering near the front door, waiting for me. "Is he okay?" she asked anxiously.

"King tested positive for Lyme, along with another disease dogs get from ticks, ehrlichiosis."

She frowned. "I never heard of that second one. Is it serious?"

"It can be. If it's left untreated, it can cause neurological disorders, kidney disease . . . and in some cases it can even be fatal. Fortunately, we caught it in time."

"That's a relief! King is part of our family! The kids are so attached to him. . . ." A look of alarm suddenly crossed her face. She gasped, placing both hands on her belly protectively. "Oh, my God. It's not contagious, is it?"

"No, you have nothing to worry about. And while King is seriously ill, the treatment is extremely effective. I'm going to put him on an antibiotic, doxycycline, for two weeks for the ehrlichiosis, then a month of amoxicillin for Lyme. I'm also going to give you an antitick collar. . . ."

"Mom, Justin took my cookie! Make him give it back! *Mo-o-o-om!*"

I helped King back into the house and left feeling pleased that I was able to help Lindsay Weinstein's dog. I wondered what it must have been like for animals and their owners in the days before we had access to all the treatments we took for granted these days. As heartbreaking as it was to see a dog as sick as King, I knew that, thanks to the antibiotics, he'd be his usual self in just a few days.

Seeing Lindsay's situation also made me appreciate my own freedom. The thought of being homebound the way she was, even for a short time, made my skin crawl. Little kids are cute, I thought as I drove away, but I'll take a puppy or a kitten any day.

• • •

By the time I returned home late in the afternoon, tired from a long day of back-to-back calls that had me zigzagging all over Norfolk County, I'd all but forgotten about Tommee Frack. A strong hot cup of coffee was a much higher priority.

The blinking light on my answering machine caught my eye as I made a beeline for the kitchen, nearly tripping over Cat, who was crouched on the floor intently watching a dust bunny skip across the room. I pressed the button and kept walking.

The sound of a familiar voice, one I hadn't heard in some time, stopped me in my tracks.

"*Good afternoon,*" a woman said crisply. "*I'm calling for Dr. Jessica Popper. This is Vanda Jackson of the New York State Department of Agriculture and Markets. I've managed to obtain the information you requested. Please call me at your earliest convenience.*" The message ended with a phone number.

Forgetting all about my need for caffeine, I grabbed the receiver and dialed.

"My, my! Aren't we getting formal!" I teased Vanda after she answered her phone with the same businesslike tone.

"It's my work voice," she returned. "When I left you that message, my boss was standing right behind me."

"Hey, this is legitimate business. I assure you that any information you give me will be used in a productive way. I personally guarantee that the taxpayers of New York State will sleep a whole lot better."

"Sounds mysterious. I don't think I want to know any more."

Like me, Vanda was a native Long Islander. But when she was in the ninth grade, her family moved upstate to a suburb of Albany. We'd kept in touch ever since. First we'd written each other long letters on flowered stationery, pouring out every detail of our current crush. Then we became E-mail buddies. Even though we hadn't actually laid eyes on each other in years, I still considered her part of my Active Friend file. It was pure luck that she ended up working in the New York State government office whose functions included handling dog licenses.

"Did you find out anything about those names I gave you?" I asked eagerly.

"A few turned out to be registered dog owners. Why don't I just E-mail all the information?"

"Perfect. And thanks, Vanda. You are such a doll."

"Forget that. Tell me what's going on with you and Nick."

Et tu, Vanda? I was tempted to cry. Maybe I was the victim of a statewide conspiracy, designed to throw me into the arms of one Nick Burby. Not that I could blame her for asking. Nick had been the subject of so many E-mails and phone calls that I suspected he was one topic of conversation I'd never be rid of.

"No news on that front," I told her firmly. "At this point, he and I are just good friends. We talk now and then. That's it."

Up in Albany, Vanda sighed. "It's your decision, Jess. But I can't imagine him not being an important part of your life anymore."

I hung up the phone and logged on to my computer, determined to concentrate on the information Vanda had gotten for me instead of on her well-meaning advice concerning my lack of a love life. As Cat leaped into my lap for her usual ear scratching, I scanned the list of new E-mail messages. Sure enough, there was an E-mail from Vanda.

"Yes!" I breathed after clicking on it. The phone numbers and registration details that she'd sent were exactly what I needed.

I clicked "Print," meanwhile studying the names and phone numbers on the screen. As I did, I remembered an idea that had popped into my mind once or twice in the past couple of days. Something about abandoning the investigation, some wild ruminations about Just Saying No to snooping around.

What could I have been thinking?

Still carrying Cat, I snatched the list out of the printer and headed straight for the coffeepot. My head spun as I worked out a strategy. I now had a whole list of people to question, each of whom could be considered a prime suspect in Tommee Frack's murder.

And I already knew who headed the list.

• • •

A dozen butterflies played tag in my stomach on Tuesday afternoon as I veered off Old Oaks Road and onto the street that led to Barbara Delmonico's home. I've never been very good at telling even white lies, and up until this point, I hadn't had to. True, I'd allowed Merrilee to assume that I'd taken care of her ex-husband's Dobermans, but that was as far as my need for deception had gone.

I'd felt the same nervousness the day before when I first called Barbara.

"Ms. Delmonico?" I began. "My name is Jessica Popper. I'm a veterinarian based in Joshua's Hollow."

At least that much was true. But as I muddled through the next part, I was certain I could feel my nose growing longer.

"A client of mine owns two female Tibetan Terriers. She's interested in breeding them, and she asked me to help her find a possible stud here on the island. I understand you own a male with quite an impressive pedigree . . . Karma Kai Li of Shangri-La Kennels?"

"Oh, yes," Barbara replied enthusiastically. "Karma is a beautiful animal. He's registered with the American Kennel Club and the Tibetan Terrier Club of America."

"Would you consider breeding him?"

"Certainly! I mean, I owe it to all the other people who love the breed the way I do. Karma is exceptional. Everybody tells me so."

As I'd suspected, the way to get to this woman was through her designer dog. But pulling off a charade like that over the phone was one thing. Now, it was time to try it out in person.

Barbara's condominium complex, Edwardian Estates, was a community of luxury town houses designed for the discriminating resident. I knew that because the sign out front told me so. As I drove up to the guard whose job it was to decide who was permitted to enter the gated community, I realized that every one of the dozen or so buildings was identical. They were all outfitted with gabled roofs, oval windows, and other architectural details I'd always associated with the Victorians, rather than the Edwardians.

Somehow, the overall effect reminded me of Disneyland. Everything was too perfect, giving the impression the place was trying just a little too hard. Even the bushes were precisely manicured, as if renegade branches that took it upon themselves to grow faster than the others would not be tolerated here.

Barbara answered the door seconds after I rang the bell.

"Ms. Delmonico?" I said, acting as if I'd never seen her before. "I'm Dr. Popper."

"Come in," she insisted, holding open the door. I was immediately surrounded by a cloud of pungent perfume. "Thank you so much for coming to the house. It's so much more convenient than bringing Karma to your office."

"There's my office, right there." I pointed to my van, parked in the visitors section between a Jaguar and a Lexus. I figured it lent legitimacy to my visit.

Up close, I could see she was a bit older than I'd assumed she was the first time I'd seen her, when she'd made her dramatic entrance at Tommee's funeral. The tiny wrinkles around her eyes added at least a decade to my original estimate of her age.

Barbara gestured toward a sparsely furnished living room. "We can sit in here."

She was dressed in black again, but this time she wore a sleek pantsuit. It looked expensive, even to someone like me, whose fashion sense doesn't go very far beyond knowing not to wear chukka boots to a formal event. Her outfit would have been tasteful if it weren't for the fact that the cream-colored silk blouse she wore with it was open far enough to display a fascinating amount of cleavage. The edge of a lacy crimson bra was also exposed.

Then there were her shoes, four-inch platforms fastened to her feet with rhinestone straps. These were bare enough to reveal three toe rings, as well as part of an ankle tattoo.

"I made us some Deejarling," she said.

I thought I'd misunderstood what she'd said because of the chewing gum in her mouth. Then I realized she was simply mispronouncing "Darjeeling."

"Tea sounds lovely."

"I'll see if the water's boiling."

I watched her disappear into the kitchen. As I debated whether there was enough time to start ransacking drawers and peering under furniture, she stuck her head out of the doorway.

"I forgot to aks you. Do you take lemon or sugar?"

Aks. Her mispronunciation made my ears prick up like Max's when he hears the crinkle of cellophane packaging.

"Sugar, thanks."

She returned moments later, carrying a tray with a silver teapot and two dainty china cups. As she poured, I asked, "How did you get interested in Tibetan Terriers, Ms. Delmonico? It's a fairly rare breed."

"I know." She smiled broadly, as if pleased that I'd

understood that that was the whole point. "I read about them in a magazine. *Town & Country,* I think. Or maybe *The New Yorker.* I've always been a dog lover. My family had dogs while I was growing up."

"Did you grow up on Long Island?"

"Connecticut."

"Really? Where?"

I was just making conversation, but her smile flickered, as if the question unnerved her.

"Uh, northern Connecticut. The New England part. I went to a very prestigious girls' boarding school up there."

She reached into her mouth, removed a wad of gray gum, and stuck it on the Limoges saucer.

I was tempted to ask if that was something she'd learned at boarding school. Instead, I said, "How did you end up on Long Island?"

"I moved to the New York area after I went to college. That was also in New England."

"Oh, really? What school?"

"Vassar."

My eyebrows shot up. I immediately pulled them back into place.

"After graduation, I moved to Manhattan to become a stockbroker. My parents were terribly disappointed, of course. I mean, my father is a surgeon and my mother's a radiologist, and they expected me to follow in their footsteps. But I preferred the world of finance. Anyways, when I lived in the city, I spent most of my weekends out in the Hamptons, so I finally decided it was time to move out here."

There were so many things here that weren't adding up that I wished I'd brought along a calculator. I was reminded of that children's game, "What's wrong with this picture?" The fact that Vassar was located in Poughkeepsie, New York, not even close to New England, was just the beginning. There was also her claim that both her parents were doctors. It didn't jibe with the way she mangled the English language, not to mention her table manners.

Then there was the idea that someone who spent weekends in the ultraposh Hamptons, rubbing elbows with the rich and famous on Long Island's chic East End, would consider a suburban condo complex straight out of Fantasyland the next best thing.

I wished I'd brought along my notebook. I didn't want to forget a single detail.

"But here I am, chatting away and wasting your time when you really came to look at Karma." Barbara stood up. "I'll get him."

Once again, I was dying to poke around. But I could hear her in the kitchen, opening the door of a metal cage.

Oddly enough, that was the only sound I heard. Most pet owners can't resist talking to their animals. I've witnessed many long, one-sided conversations between owners and their pets, everything from gerbils to tropical fish. But Barbara didn't offer so much as a, "There you go, boy."

"This is him," she announced.

She didn't have to. The bundle of fur that came bounding out of the kitchen was impossible to miss.

Karma really was a beautiful example of the breed, which looks like a smaller version of a sheepdog. He shot right over to me, jumping up and placing his oversized paws on my knees, then delivering endless dog kisses to my nose and cheeks as he gazed up at me with dark, liquid eyes fringed with remarkably long eyelashes. I knew those lashes were no accident. They're the breed's best bet for keeping their hair out of their eyes. Nevertheless, they made it impossible not to fall in love with him immediately.

"Well, look at you! Aren't you a beauty?" I greeted him. I ran my fingers through his soft black and white fur, giving him a hard scratching. He twisted his body ecstatically in response, clearly craving more. "Hey, Karma! How's my boy?

"He's absolutely gorgeous," I told Barbara sincerely as Karma plopped down at my feet.

She beamed like a proud parent. "You know, they were originally bred by Tibetan monks in the Himalayas. And here's something else that's interesting: they're not actually terriers. But in England, where they were first introduced to the Western world, they were classified as terriers because of their size."

Barbara Delmonico had clearly done her homework.

"He must be kind of high-maintenance, though." I could feel how thick his fur was as I continued scratching him, this time concentrating on his neck.

"I brush him all the time," Barbara told me earnestly. "I guess you know they have two coats, a soft one underneath and a thick one on top. But it's worth it. You wouldn't believe how many people stop me to tell me how gorgeous he is. And most people have never even heard of the breed. I really get a kick out of telling people about his background. It makes him . . . special."

"They can be shy, you know."

"Not Karma. He's extremely friendly." She sounded oddly defensive.

"And there are some other problems that are inherent in the breed. Genetic diseases, like hip dysplasia, a couple of eye diseases . . . that's why my client wants to be careful about finding the right mate." As do we all, I thought. "Would it be possible to see Karma's medical records?"

"They're right upstairs. Make yourself comfortable and I'll go get them."

I seized advantage of her absence to sneak a closer look at my surroundings. Karma looked on woefully as I roamed around, clearly distressed over having lost his expert scratcher. The few pieces of furniture, as well as the decorative touches, were all of the highest quality. I turned over a decorative blue bowl to confirm that it was Wedgwood. The crystal vase on the mantlepiece was Baccarat.

Even if I hadn't been casing the joint, I wouldn't have missed the only personal item in the room. The photograph of Barbara and Tommee, she in a clingy black evening gown and he in a tux, was prominently displayed in an elaborate frame. I recognized it from the Tiffany catalog I regularly received in the mail, proof that American business doesn't really know as much about each individual's buying habits as they claim.

I hastily put the photograph back when I heard Barbara coming down the stairs.

"Here are the medical records. As you can see, Karma has gotten the best care possible. He's had all his shots and he's never been sick. I never feed him from the table. He gets Science Diet."

I studied the bills, each one spelling out exactly what treatment Karma had received and when. But I was less interested in the thoroughness of Barbara's record-keeping and her pet-care habits than I was in the name of her veterinarian.

Marcus Scruggs, D.V.M.

Not exactly my favorite person in the world, but someone who might be able to supply me with useful information about the woman who'd so very nearly become Tommee Frack's trophy wife.

"Would you mind if I gave Dr. Scruggs a call?" I asked casually.

"Of course not. Aks him whatever you want. I'm sure he'll have only good things to say about Karma."

As I stood up to leave, Barbara grabbed Karma's collar. Now that his usefulness had been exhausted, I suspected he'd be put back in his cage. For a fraction of a second, I entertained the fantasy of kidnapping him and bringing him home with me. Surely Max and Lou could adapt to a new brother, teaching him the intricacies of Slimytoy and the ten best ways to irritate Cat.

Barbara's firm grip on his collar and her stern command—"Sit, Karma!"—snapped me back to reality. Instead, I took advantage of my final moments with her to pretend to notice the photograph in its silver frame for the first time.

"What a nice picture. Is that your husband?"

She froze. For a fraction of second, a peculiar look crossed her face. If I hadn't known better, I'd have interpreted it as distaste.

"My fiancé," she said evenly.

"You two certainly make a lovely couple."

She picked up the photograph, her expression hardening. "There isn't going to be any wedding. He was murdered a little more than a week ago."

"Oh, my!" My hand flew to my mouth. "I thought he looked familiar! That's the man who was found in the woods."

"Tommee Frack."

"You poor thing! I'm so sorry."

"Thank you."

If there was any emotion behind her voice, I certainly couldn't hear it. "He was a very successful businessman, wasn't he?"

"Public relations. Tommee had his own firm, and he knew absolutely everybody. Anyone who matters on Long Island at all used him. To do their PR, I mean. And yes, he was wildly successful."

"I seem to remember reading that."

Interesting that she isn't telling me what a wonderful man Tommee was, I thought. Instead, she's talking about him as if he were as solid an investment as a United States Savings Bond.

"I understand he was also a very caring person," I prompted. "Wasn't he involved in a lot of community activities?"

"He represented a lot of charities, and he did tons of *pro bono* work. Not to mention the fact that he gave one hundred ten percent to every one of his clients."

"You must be devastated. But I'm sure the police are doing everything in their power to find whoever is responsible. Do they have any leads?"

She looked startled. "How would I know?"

"Haven't they talked to you?"

"Why would they? It's not as if I'm a suspect or anything."

I was tempted to point out what to me seemed obvious: that whether she was a suspect or not, as his fiancée, she was surely able to provide valuable information about other people who might be.

Instead, I simply said, "I offer you my deepest sympathies. What a terrible loss."

"It's something I'll never get over."

Barbara sighed deeply. So why didn't she strike me as grief-stricken? I watched her study the photograph still in her hands, her face pulled into a frown. And then, using the hem of her jacket, she rubbed away a tiny smudge on the silver frame before carefully putting it back where it belonged.

•   •   •

As soon as I got into my van, I grabbed my phone.

"Lieutenant Harned, please," I said crisply.

"He's on another call."

"I'll hold. This is Jessica Popper. The person who found Tommee Frack's body?"

It was only a few seconds before I heard, "Harned."

"Hi, Lieutenant. This is Dr. Popper. Remember me from the Frack case?"

"What can I do for you, Dr. Popper?"

"I was calling to check up on the investigation."

"What about it?"

"I was wondering if anybody wanted to interview me further. I mean, I was the one who found the body."

"We already have your statement. We appreciate your interest . . ."

"Is there anything new?"

"Not at this time. I can assure you that we're following all leads . . ."

I was on the verge of saying that if that was the case, then why hadn't Tommee's fiancée and ex-wife made the interview A list? Instead, I decided to keep things friendly.

"Thanks for your time," I said sweetly. "I know you must be *very* busy."

But not knocking yourself out investigating Tommee Frack's murder, I thought. I opened my notebook and jotted down as much as I could remember from the two revealing conversations I'd had so far that day.

Chapter 8

"You gotta have swine to show you where the truffles are."

—Edward Albee

I didn't bother to call before heading straight over to Marcus Scruggs's office. Something about our past interactions told me that no matter how busy he was, he'd manage to squeeze me in.

His office was a trim white house at a busy intersection in Corchaug, a terrible location for a residence but an excellent spot for a medical office. As I got out of my car, I noted that the sign reading "Marcus Scruggs, Doctor of Veterinary Medicine," was perched atop a tall metal pole that protruded high above the parking lot.

Very Marcus, I thought.

But when it came to phallic symbols, even that paled beside his car, a low-slung Corvette parked toward the back. I doubted his male canine patients could resist using it as a urinal.

I took a few steadying breaths before stepping inside the office.

I'd learned early on that Marcus Scruggs and I weren't destined to become close pals. Back in the days when I was applying to Cornell University's College of Veterinary Medicine, the Admissions Department had given me his name as an alumnus who lived locally and might be a good resource, even a mentor, to an aspiring animal doc like me.

I had hoped to visit his hospital and observe him as he treated patients, not to mention pick up a few pointers on practical issues like the odds of me getting accepted and ways of beefing up my application. Instead, he had insisted on meeting me in the lounge of the local Holiday Inn.

At first, I'd tried to keep an open mind. During our first five minutes together, I told myself that the knee pressing against mine under the table was simply the result of not enough space. But the more I asked him about letters of reference and possible essay topics, the more Marcus asked me about my marital status, my favorite mixed drinks, and—no joke—my preference in undergarments. It was like one of those blind dates you quickly figure out was a huge mistake.

I didn't learn much about Cornell that day. But I did learn to keep as far away from Marcus Scruggs as possible. Since then, I'd only run into him occasionally. He zeroed in on me at every convention and seminar we attended. I always made a point of sprinkling the conversation with references to Nick.

Maybe he's changed, I thought, as I gave my name to his receptionist. The fact that she was about eighteen, with masses of very blond hair and a Lycra top that looked as if it had been stretched to its limit, wasn't encouraging.

I sat in the waiting room amidst the usual assortment of animals and the people they owned: two beagles, a Siamese cat, a macaw, and three mixed-breed dogs, what I like to think of as a canine mélange. As soon as he appeared in the doorway—as tall, as blond, and as gawky as ever—I knew he was still the same old Marcus. The instant he saw me, his expression changed from a look of professional friendliness to an unmistakable leer.

"Well, well, well, if it isn't the inimitable Dr. Jessica Popper. I always knew that sooner or later you'd show up on my doorstep, begging for a job. Or maybe even something more . . . intriguing."

I forced myself to smile, even though his eyes were glued to my chest. "Actually, Marcus, I'm here on your doorstep begging for information."

"Hey, I'll take what I can get. Why don't you come into my office? That way, we can be alone."

Oh, goody, I thought. I followed him anyway.

It wasn't until we sat down, he at his desk and me in a chair facing him, that he finally made eye contact. The look in them was more leering than friendly. "So what can I do you for, Popper?"

"I'm trying to get some background information on someone I believe is a client of yours. Her name is Barbara Delmonico."

He pressed his fingers together and stared off into infinity. "Ah, yes," he said profoundly. "Good old Barbara. Interesting woman."

I perked up. "You remember her?"

"Let's just say she's not somebody who's easy to forget. Her friend, either."

"Friend?"

I leaned forward, poised for an earful about Tommee Frack. So I felt a pang of disappointment when he replied, "The two of them were like bookends. Or, if you'll excuse me for being more graphic, like two pages out of *Playboy*. And I'm talking centerfolds, here. High-quality stuff."

"So Barbara's friend was also a woman."

I was trying not to let him rattle me, but his salacious smile turned my stomach. "That's what I'd call an understatement."

He went over to a large file cabinet and opened the top drawer. After rifling through folders, he pulled one out.

"Here you go. Delmonico. And her friend was— let's see, I think her last name began with an *m* . . . *That's* right, Martin." He grabbed a second file. "Claudia Martin."

He opened Barbara's file on his desk. "I remember the first time they came in. It must have been July or August, because they both showed up in shorts that were so short it was like getting an instant anatomy lesson. They were wearing those tiny little halter-top thingies, too."

His glittering eyes made it clear he wasn't suffering as he relived the moment.

"If it was summer, they were probably dressed that way because it was hot," I pointed out.

"But that was what was so weird. They said something about being on their way to work. And they kept looking at their watches, as if they had only minutes to spare. But they both looked like they were heading for the beach."

"Do you remember what was wrong with Barbara's dog?"

"Dog?" He snorted. "That was no dog."

"But Barbara Delmonico owns a male Tibetan Terrier."

"Right. She calls him Karma. Beautiful animal. She still brings him in now and then. But that first time, it wasn't a dog she and her girlfriend brought in for treatment."

"What was it?"

"A boa constrictor."

"Ah," I said noncommittally.

I've always believed that every career has its downside, that no matter how much you love your job, there's bound to be at least one aspect you don't like.

In my case, snakes.

The issue of professional responsibility aside, the mere thought of treating a boa constrictor gives me the creeps. Or, for that matter, even being in the same room with one. And having just spent an afternoon with Barbara, I didn't see her as someone whose personal menagerie was likely to consist of the peculiar combination of cute cuddly animals like Karma and distasteful writhing reptiles like the one Marcus claimed she owned.

Not surprisingly, Marcus didn't tune in to my discomfort. "It was a really nice snake, too," he reminisced. "Close to six feet long. Surprisingly friendly, as if he was used to being around people."

"Are you sure it wasn't Claudia Martin's snake? Is

it possible that Barbara just came along to keep Claudia company?"

"Nope. My records are clear." He poked around one file, then the other. "They each had their own snakes, even though they usually came in together. Lately, though, they've been coming in separately. And even though Claudia still brings her python in every now and then, Barbara's just been coming in with Karma."

"Do you know what happened to Barbara's interest in, uh, reptiles?"

"Nope. Never asked, and she never volunteered anything." The familiar glint was back in his eyes. "Besides, whenever she comes in, I always find myself a little . . . distracted, if you know what I mean."

I knew precisely what he meant, and the thought gave me the willies.

"Claudia Martin sounds like someone who might have some information I need. I don't suppose you'd be willing to give me her address." I desperately hoped I wouldn't have to call upon some of my own feminine charms in order to get what I needed from him.

"For you, Popper, anything." I guess the thought of Barbara and Claudia in hot pants took me out of the running.

He jotted Claudia Martin's name, address, and phone number on a pad printed with an ad for a prescription worming medication. I glanced at it as he handed it to me.

"Route 437?" I read. "In Southaven? Isn't that an industrial area?"

"Got me. That's the address she always used. Hey,

as long as they pay their bills on time, I don't ask questions."

As I tucked the paper into my purse, Marcus leaned back in his chair and crossed his long legs. "So tell me, Popper. What are you doing with yourself these days?"

I cringed at the lecherous smile on his face. "Busy, busy, busy. Never a moment to spare."

"You know what they say about all work and no play."

"Whoever said that wasn't still paying off student loans." I shot to my feet, wanting to make it clear this interlude was definitely over. "Thanks for the information."

"You're not still going out with that investigator guy, are you? What was his name?"

"Nick."

"That's right. Are you still—"

"One more thing. Do you have any idea what was behind Barbara Delmonico's interest in snakes? I've met her, and somehow she didn't impress me as the snake type."

"Well, I do remember thinking that neither of those two ladies seemed to have any real affection for them. You know how reptile lovers can be. It's like a cult. They seem to take pride in being enthusiastic about animals that most people can't even stand to look at. But it didn't seem that Barbara and her pal were really into their snakes. They acted more like they were bringing in a pair of shoes for repair. Struck me as odd."

He shrugged. "I don't know if any of this has been helpful. Or even interesting."

"It's been both. Thanks, Marcus. I really appreciate your help."

"Any time. And Popper? If you and that Nick character ever decide to call it quits, give me a ring, will ya?"

. . .

By the time my meeting with Marcus was over, I wanted nothing more than to go home and take a long scalding shower. The idea of ever being in the presence of a man again, much less going on an actual date, had all the appeal of a root canal.

The company of two devoted canines was infinitely preferable. As I walked into my cottage, Max and Lou charged into their usual routine, literally jumping up and down with glee and then trying to entice me into an invigorating game of Slimytoy. Prometheus was squawking, "Let's go to the tape. *Awk!* Let's go to the tape!" Even Cat deigned a glance in my direction.

"Hel-*lo*, doggies!" I greeted them, getting down on the floor to administer a royal belly-scratching. "How are the best little doggers in the whole wide world?"

Home sweet home, I thought. A home that feels complete, even without a man.

The sound of Jimmy Nolan's voice on my answering machine jolted me back to reality.

"*Hey, Jessie. It's Jimmy. How you doing? I just wanted to tell you I had a nice time the other night and, uh, I hope those flowers are still hanging in there. And, uh, I was wondering if maybe you wanted to do something Saturday night. Go to a movie or grab some dinner, whatever you feel like. Give me a call, will you?"*

"So much for swearing off men," I muttered. "I suppose I shouldn't let a slimeball like Marcus Scruggs determine the course of my life." I decided I'd return Jimmy's call as soon as I was up to it.

At the moment, however, I was still having too much fun playing Girl Detective to let anything distract me. After feeding Prometheus and the dogs, I jotted down some notes from my meeting with Marcus and geared up mentally to enter a world that was so unfamiliar to me that I felt as if I were venturing into the jungle. But instead of waders and mosquito spray, this foreign territory required combed hair, a wool blazer, and lipstick.

It was time to visit Tommee Frack's office.

•   •   •

The second name on the list I'd drawn up with Vanda Jackson's help was Brad O'Reilly. From what I'd learned from the "People On The Move" articles on the *Long Island Business Beat* website, O'Reilly had been Frack's most senior employee. In fact, while many others had apparently come and gone, Brad worked for Frack almost since the beginning.

Loyalty? I wondered as I drove to Pine Meadow the following afternoon, a typical gray, cloudy November day. Or simply inertia?

When I pulled into the parking lot of the office complex that dominated the village's main intersection, I saw that my VW Beetle wasn't the only German car there. Most of the others, however, were either Mercedes or BMWs.

The pricey cars matched the office building's atmosphere of prosperity. Once I passed through its revolving doors, I found myself surrounded by such dense foliage and so many gurgling fountains I felt as if I really were in the jungle. I didn't spot any actual predators, but there were plenty of grim-looking men and women in suits who could have been lawyers.

The names on the roster bore out my theory. In addition to three insurance companies, there were half a dozen law firms, long compilations of names that seemed impossible for anyone to remember.

Tommee Frack & Associates was still listed. As I rode the elevator to the third floor, the butterflies were back in my stomach. This time, I planned to try out a different ploy to get my foot in the door. I just hoped that foot didn't get crushed in the process.

Tommee Frack's office had the same look as the rest of the building, one that declared: Important things go on here. The front was all glass, enabling everyone coming off the elevator to view the company's name emblazoned on the wall behind the reception area. Indeed, it was impossible to miss, given the fact that it was spelled out in foot-high gold letters.

The walls were also decorated, only they were covered with framed newspaper articles like the ones I had seen in Merrilee's house. Here, too, were photographs showing Tommee posing with politicians, sports figures, and movie stars. I noticed a few awards, including "Citizen of the Year" from the Norfolk County Chambers of Commerce and an honorary degree from Norfolk University.

Feigning confidence, I strode up to the receptionist's desk, one of those high counters you have to peek over in order to get anyone's attention. But the person sitting behind the counter didn't look like a reception- ist. He was a well-dressed man in his early thirties, complete with designer tie, monogrammed shirt, and gold cufflinks—all the trappings of success that im- plied he studied GQ religiously. His light brown hair was well cut and neatly styled. Even though he was sitting, I could tell he was impressively large, well over six feet tall. He was good-looking, too, his facial features so well-proportioned that he could have been an anchorman on the six o'clock news.

The expression on his face didn't match his buttoned-up image, however. He looked harried, as if he wasn't really relishing the task of going through the tower of files on the desk before him, a stack of folders he'd clearly pulled out of the empty drawer next to him. On the other side, on the floor, the trash can was filled to overflowing.

"What can I do for you?" he asked.

"I'm looking for Brad O'Reilly."

"You just found him." He flashed me a grin I sus- pected was meant to charm me.

"Mr. O'Reilly, my name is Jessica Popper. I'm a veterinarian, and I'm helping the New York State De- partment of Agriculture and Markets with a survey. We're doing random checks to find out whether dog owners are following up with regular inoculations for their pets."

I suddenly realized that this little white lie had sounded much better in my head than it did when I said it out loud. In a belated attempt at looking offi- cial, I opened the manila folder I'd brought along and rifled through the papers inside.

"Let's see. You own a Rhodesian Ridgeback, right? Female, name of Molly? Born July 15, 1998, registered November 22, same year?"

"That's right."

"Have you kept up with her inoculations?"

By this point, his grin was long gone. Instead, he looked decidedly nervous. I wondered if he had something to hide—maybe even something that had nothing to do with his dog.

"That's the kind of thing my wife always takes care of. But I'm pretty sure she's kept Molly up to date."

"Would you mind giving me the name of the veterinarian you use?"

"Sure. It's Dr. Wyatt. No, Wyman. I think it's Dr. Wyman. He's in Cantiague. Or Quakertown."

I nodded, jotting down notes.

"Maybe you should call my wife," O'Reilly suggested. "I could give you our home number."

"That won't be necessary." I sincerely hoped Mr. O'Reilly got more involved in his children, if he and his wife had any.

I glanced at the gold letters behind him, as if noticing them for the first time. "Tommee Frack," I mused. "That name sounds so familiar. . . ." I frowned, pretending to think. "Isn't he the public relations mogul who was—?"

"That's right. I'm just cleaning out the office before we close it down."

"How tragic. I seem to recall reading that he was phenomenally successful."

"The man was brilliant." Brad said it forcefully. "Absolutely brilliant."

I blinked. It was the rare employee who had nothing

bad to say about his boss, even if it meant breaking the rule about not speaking ill of the dead.

"I've heard he was a real star." I measured my words carefully. "I don't know anything about public relations, and of course I never actually had the pleasure of meeting him, but I guess I don't have a sense of what he did that was so . . . out of the ordinary."

"Tommee Frack was a phenomenal idea man. He was a master at finding a way to make something—anything—newsworthy."

"I guess that's what public relations is all about. . . ."

"Exactly. And Tommee could pitch a story, any story, to the media in a way they just couldn't turn down. Did you know that something like sixty percent of the news you read in the newspaper or hear on TV or the radio is the result of a pitch from some public relations representative? Getting coverage for clients was Tommee's forte. But there was something else he could do that was pure genius," O'Reilly continued, catching fire. "Something nobody else in the business could top. Tommee had an uncanny ability to match people up. His clients, I mean."

"You mean like . . . setting up golf dates?" I wasn't purposely trying to sound stupid. I really had no idea what he was talking about.

"I mean like inventing an award that would give two or even three of his clients terrific exposure. Take Norfolk University's Man or Woman of the Year Awards. Every year, Tommee would put together a huge event, something so big that none of the media could ignore it. He'd even get all the local politicians to show up, since he could always guarantee a photo op. The university was one of his clients, and they'd get great publicity because they'd be giving the award. The winner—let's see, last year it was Kel-Tech Computers, another one of his clients—would look good because the company president would win the award for donating a hundred computers to the elementary school in some underprivileged community. And as if that wasn't enough, Tommee made sure the awards ceremony was always held in the ballroom of Hallsworth Hall, another client, to get *them* coverage."

"You mean that's why awards ceremonies like that are created?" I could feel a little piece of my innocence slipping away. "I always assumed those awards were sincere."

"They *are* sincere!" O'Reilly looked insulted. "The president of Kel-Tech would be getting that award because he truly deserved it for the contribution he'd made to his community. It was a win-win-win situation. You can even add a fourth 'win' for Tommee, because he came out looking like a real hero to three different clients. Wait—add a fifth win for the kids who got the free computers."

All these "wins" were getting a little confusing. I'd had no idea that public relations played such a big role in the grand scheme of things. No wonder Tommee Frack was considered such a player. My corpse had been the King of the Spin Doctors, at least on the Long Island scene.

It also sounded as if he didn't have an enemy in the world. His clients loved him because he was so good at getting their name in the news. His employees loved him because he was such an inspiring role model. Even the media had loved him, because he made their job easier by giving them wonderful, newsworthy events to cover.

I had to remind myself that somebody out there hadn't loved him. That, in fact, somebody had hated Tommee Frack—or feared him or mistrusted him— enough to hit him savagely over the head with a deadly weapon.

"Sounds like a fascinating guy," I said enthusiastically. "It really makes you wonder who could have possibly wanted him dead."

"You want to know what I think?" O'Reilly asked.

More than he knew. "Sure," I replied casually. "What's your theory?"

"That it was random. A robbery gone wrong. A carjacking that got screwed up somehow. The thief panicked, killed him, and then did a really bad job of disposing of the body."

"Makes sense."

"It's gotta be. I can't imagine anybody wanting Tommee dead. He was just too important. As a member of his community, I mean. Tommee was more than a business leader. He also helped all kinds of local charities by working for them practically for free."

Brad was beginning to sound like *Newsday,* not to mention the minister who'd delivered the eulogy.

Which brought me back to the personal side of things—in particular, the two women in Tommee's life. I pictured Merrilee, still waiting for her ex to come home to her, then learning that her fantasy of reconciliation was about to crash and burn. Then Barbara, who seemed more irritated with Tommee than in love with him.

"I just hope the police figure out who's responsible," I said. "It sounds as if Tommee's death was a tremendous loss to a lot of people."

Now that Brad O'Reailly was convinced he and I were on the same side, it was time for me to ask a favor.

"By the way, do you have a bathroom I could use?" I smiled apologetically. "I'm on the road all day."

"Right in back." He gestured with his chin. "Just down that hall, on the left."

I walked as slowly as I dared, taking in my surroundings as I did so. Peering through open doors, I saw that no one else was in the office suite. Just Brad, who had, indeed, turned out to be motivated by loyalty, from what I could tell. He was the only one who stayed behind to clean up the office, to sort out what Tommee had left behind.

As I continued along the hallway, I didn't notice anything out of the ordinary. A water cooler, a Xerox machine, a shredder . . .

A shredder.

After checking behind me to see if Brad was watching, I slipped into the small room in which it sat, along with an impressive cache of office supplies. It was on a counter, set up so that the shredded paper emptied into a large cardboard box.

The box was filled to overflowing.

Standard procedure? I wondered. Does a public relations firm really have *that* many secrets?

Or was the ability to keep secrets one of the reasons for Tommee Frack's extraordinary success?

It's time to go back to the beginning, I decided after

I thanked Brad O'Reilly for his time and rode down in the elevator. If I was ever going to understand what made Tommee Frack tick—and if I was ever going to figure out what stopped the ticking—I needed to know the man who had given him his start.

Chapter 9

"If you pick up a starving dog and make him prosperous, he will not bite you. This is the principal difference between a dog and a man."

—Mark Twain

Given the splendor of Tommee Frack & Associates, I expected the offices of The Babcock Group to be just as grand. I was becoming quite well versed in the world of public relations, and the main lesson I'd learned was that appearance was what mattered most.

So I was surprised to find that the Apaucuck address I'd been given by Babcock's chirpy receptionist belonged to a two-story red brick office building with all the charm of a warehouse. I dashed inside, cringing as the first drops of an icy winter rain started to fall. Checking the roster, I discovered that most of the other tenants were doctors. That accounted for the large number of people using walkers and sniping at their spouses—one of the many reasons I prefer working with patients whose vocabulary doesn't extend beyond "arf" and "meow."

The Babcock Group was in the basement.

I flashed back to the company's elegant stationery hanging on Merrilee's wall. The letter George Babcock had written, welcoming Tommee to his firm, had been on thick cream-colored paper that positively reeked of success. Then there was the company's name. "The Babcock Group" conjured up knowledgeable men and women in designer suits, making important decisions—a Long Island version of *L.A. Law*.

I headed down a flight of stairs, figuring I should leave the lone elevator to those who really needed it. The walls were badly in need of a paint job, and the scuff marks and stray bits of paper gave me the impression that the cleaning staff didn't exactly make the stairwells a priority. I hoped they did better with the examining rooms.

The Babcock Group's receptionist was even more of a shock. Maybe I'd seen too many movies, but I was braced for a mannequin with perfect hair, perfect makeup, and perfect nails. Instead, the very young woman sitting at the front desk looked as if she were just filling time until her punk rock band had its first hit.

Her black hair was cut short and gelled into spikes, the points in front dyed a lovely shade of cobalt blue. Her nails were perfect, but they happened to be black. And she wore no makeup at all, unless the silver eyebrow ring counted.

"Hi," she greeted me cheerfully. "You looking for George?"

I nodded.

"Dr. Popper, right?"

"That's right." Maybe it wasn't such a bad thing that *Newsday* got my name wrong. At least I was less recognizable to anyone who might be following the story of Tommee Frack's murder—including his murderer.

"I'll tell him you're here."

I used my few moments alone in the 10-by-10-foot space that served as a reception area to case the joint. The place was in chaos. There were cardboard boxes everywhere, stuffed with files. Thick books with titles like *New York Publicity Outlets* and *Bacon's Business Media Directory* were piled up unceremoniously. Either George Babcock was moving or he needed a crash course in Feng Shui.

"George'll be right out," the blue-haired one informed me when she returned.

The phone rang, and she answered with the same chirpy voice.

"The Babcock Group. Uh-huh, uh-huh . . . Actually, we don't represent them anymore. Gee, I guess it's been a few weeks now." In a slightly harsher tone, she added, "No, I *don't* know who represents them now."

I glanced at her, wondering if I should say something consoling. It was then I noticed the photograph on her desk. The same young woman grinned at the camera, as did her companion, a young man whose hair was at least as spiky and whose face was decorated with substantially more silver.

But it was the third figure in the photograph that caught my eye. His hair was kind of spiky, too, but not any more than that of any other wire-haired terrier.

Ah, I thought. A dog lover. Even better, a *terrier* lover.

I filed that fact away.

A few moments later, a small, wiry man with a thick blond mustache and a rumpled suit came rushing out from the back.

"Dr. Popper? I'm George Babcock. Thanks for coming in."

He pumped my hand a few times, then dropped it as abruptly as he had grabbed it. "Sorry for the mess. We're in the middle of a move." *We'reinthemiddle- ofamove.* I immediately pegged him as a classic Type A personality. "Of course, this place was always just temporary. One of those emergency situations where I had to grab whatever I could find. But we'll be in our new offices soon enough. Can I offer you some coffee? Belle, get Dr. Popper some coffee."

"I'm fine," I assured her. I'd only been in George Babcock's presence for seconds, but I was already on the verge of swearing off caffeine entirely. Turning to him, I inquired, "Where are you moving to?"

"Oh, a much bigger space. Much bigger. Fact of the matter is, we're growing so fast, we need a place three times this size. I'm about to bring some more people on board, just to keep up."

I noticed that Belle's eyes grew wide and her eyebrows shot up near her hairline, ornaments and all. When she saw me looking at her, she turned away, suddenly absorbed by her computer.

"But come in, come in, Dr. Popper. We're both busy people, so let's get right down to business."

His office was small, windowless, and as desperately in need of a fresh coat of paint as the stairwell. But George Babcock seemed oblivious to all of it. He plunked down in the wheezing chair behind his desk, motioned for me to sit in the only other chair in the room, and clasped his hands together in front of him, as if he needed to do so in order to keep them still.

"I understand you're interested in getting some publicity for you and your business."

"That's right."

"Why don't we start with you telling me about yourself and what you're looking for in a public relations outfit."

I took a deep breath. "Well, as I mentioned on the phone, I'm a veterinarian. I have a mobile services unit—a clinic on wheels, basically—that treats animals all over Long Island. It's called Reigning Cats & Dogs."

"Cute. I like that." George's head bobbed up and down. "Short, catchy, clever. Go on."

"My practice is primarily small animal, meaning dogs and cats and the other usual house pets. But I do some large animal, as well. Here on Long Island, that means horses. Riding schools, private horse owners, that kind of thing. I also treat exotics, which is a little unusual. Tropical birds, lizards, turtles, pets that aren't your usual garden variety."

More nodding, even harder than before. "Good, good. This is all very good."

I tried not to buy into his enthusiasm, reminding myself this was the sales pitch he fed everybody. Even so, I could feel my head swelling, at least a little.

"Anyway, when I started the business, I expected

that by this point, my practice would have grown a lot more than it has. I'd like to have a couple of assistants, more clients, maybe even a second van. I figured the best way to expand was by getting my name out there, but I didn't really know how to begin.

"Then, a few weeks ago, I was at a conference, and some of the other veterinarians were talking about how beneficial it had been for them to hire a public relations firm. You know, someone to get their name in the paper, maybe set up a few lectures at local libraries, that kind of thing."

"You're exactly right." George's nodding had accelerated to an alarming pace. "I can see you're a very smart girl, Jessie. May I call you Jessie?"

I believe you already have, I thought.

"Actually, I prefer Dr. Popper, if you don't mind. It's more professional."

"Dr. Popper, then. Anyway, given the current economy," he went on, "keeping your name in front of people—in a positive way, of course—has never been more crucial. If you want your business to grow, you must become a household name. There's advertising, of course, but we all know how expensive that is."

I nodded.

"But what's even more important is the question, Why should you pay an arm and a leg to be in a newspaper or on television when your PR firm can get you there for *free*?" His cheeks were flushed and the look in his eyes bordered on maniacal. "Did you know that more than half of what's presented to you as news is actually the result of a PR pitch?"

Actually, I did. I really was becoming a PR expert.

"That's what public relations is all about," George

continued. "The name of the game is taking who you are and what you do and turning it into *news*. Not only does that mean you're getting your name out there without any charge besides the modest fee you pay your PR firm every month; it also means you're being positioned as somebody the media *respects*. You're an expert. An authority. You're instantly someone who can be trusted. After all, the general public has seen you on TV! You've been in their living room, thanks to the six o'clock news. Or you've been in their car, your voice dropping pearls of wisdom on CBS radio. They've seen your picture in the paper. They've heard you at their community center, lecturing to an enraptured audience about the most effective ways of treating cats for ticks and fleas. All of a sudden, you're not just a name in the Yellow Pages. You're *somebody*!"

Yes! Yes! I was tempted to cry. Instead, I reluctantly clung to my composure by reminding myself that I hadn't really come here in the hopes that George Babcock could turn me into a household name like Lysol.

"It all makes sense to me," I told him. "Except for one thing. It's not as if I'm a celebrity. I'm not selling records or movie tickets or thrillers. I'm just an animal doctor."

"Let me show you something." Leaping out of his chair, George pulled a video labeled "Dr. Westoff" off a shelf. He inserted it into the VCR sitting on top of the television in one corner and commanded, "Check this out. Then tell me what you think."

For the next five minutes, I watched a good-looking plastic surgeon do one television interview after another, discussing the pros and cons of manipulating fat, wrinkles, cellulite, and half a dozen other unseemly side products of being human. He was enthusiastic, cheerful, and authoritative, exactly the person I'd want rearranging my body parts if I ever chose to do so.

George was right. Seeing him on television shows that were familiar to me did make Dr. Westoff look like an expert. Now I understood the true alchemy of public relations. With the right connections, anybody could be made to look good.

"Of course, Dr. Westoff deals with an entirely different aspect of the medical profession," George said as he hit "Eject." "But that doesn't mean we couldn't try to get you coverage like that. Does this kind of thing look like it could be of value to you?"

"Definitely."

"Frankly, I see a lot of opportunity here. You present yourself well, you're obviously intelligent, you're attractive . . . I think I could do a lot for you. Have you ever thought about a weekly television spot? Channel 14, maybe, on Saturday mornings? Or how about a one-minute spot once a day? Something like, 'Pet Care Fact of the Day'?"

Right, I thought. We could call it "Sound Bites."

"It's certainly something to think about . . ."

"Why don't you take a few days to do just that?" George Babcock suggested. "In the meantime," he went on, "whenever you watch TV or listen to the radio or read articles in newspapers and magazines, think about what you saw here today. When you see a segment on the news about a discovery at some hospital, think about the fact that the reason it's on TV is that the hospital's PR department contacted the media. When you see a story about the head of some charity getting an award, think PR. When a rock star has a new CD out or a movie star has a new film, they're suddenly all over the media. How do you think that happened? I'll tell you how: their PR people have been faxing press releases and making phone calls, that's how."

"I had no idea PR played such a big role in everyone's life," I confessed. "But you're right; I do need a chance to digest it all."

I stood up to leave. It was time for me to focus on the real reason I'd sat through George Babcock's sales pitch.

"You know, I keep hearing about somebody else who was in public relations here on Long Island," I said casually. "That man who was murdered. Tommee Frack."

A spasm creased George's face.

"Did you know him?" I pressed. "I mean, it's such a small world—"

"Yeah, I knew him," he said, suddenly sullen. "In fact, I gave him his start in the PR business."

"*Really?*" Boy, I was getting good at this.

"Yup. I was the fool who offered him his first job, right after he graduated from Brookside College."

"But that doesn't sound foolish! From what I've read, it sounds as if Frack was a genius."

"A genius at screwing people," he shot back bitterly.

The same crazed glint I'd glimpsed earlier was back in his eyes. But this time, it had nothing to do with the thrill of getting a client on television to chat about sucking out love handles.

"Look, the guy did a real number on me. After I trained him—taught him everything he knew, in fact—he walked."

"You mean he went to work for a competitor?" I asked, even though I already knew Tommee Frack's history.

"He left to start his own PR firm," George replied. "Problem was, he took half my clients with him."

This time, my surprise was sincere. "How awful! That must have been quite a blow."

"Damn right. And most of my clients were new to public relations. I was the one who'd spent hours convincing them that they could benefit from hiring a PR agency.

"Dr. Westoff is the perfect example. You sound like you're pretty savvy, Dr. Popper. But Westoff started out as just a guy I played golf with. He didn't know PR from a hole in the ground—no pun intended. I worked on him for months, educating him about the realities of building his practice by getting his name out there. Actually, Westoff's one of the few who stuck with me."

"But if Tommee was just starting his own firm, what could he possibly have offered your clients? I mean, you clearly had more experience and more contacts, not to mention a better track record."

George's facial muscles tightened into an expression I couldn't quite read. "That's something you and I will never really know," he said darkly.

"But it's all ancient history, isn't it? Didn't Tommee Frack start his company years ago?"

"Yes, but he never stopped stealing my clients."

"I don't know anything about this, of course . . . but would it be that unusual for a client to switch agencies every few years? You know, to try working with someone else to see if the results were better?"

George smiled coldly. "You clearly don't know much about Tommee Frack."

No, but I'm learning, I was tempted to say. *And I want to learn even more.*

"Competing fairly in the business environment is one thing," George told me. "Resorting to immoral behavior is something else entirely."

"You make it sound as if Tommee was doing something really unethical," I said, "if not out and out illegal."

If looks could kill, the expression on George Babcock's face would have been registered with the police. "Why don't you ask Joey DeFeo?"

Joey DeFeo. Joey DeFeo. The name sounded familiar . . .

"Who is—?"

"You know, I think we've talked about Frack enough," George said curtly. "I've already said more than I should. He's gone now, so why don't we just let bygones be bygones?"

"You're right. Besides," I couldn't resist saying, "I'm sure you've already been through all this with the police."

"The police?" George looked puzzled. "What would the police want with me? They have no reason to think I had anything to do with what happened to Tommee."

But before I had a chance to explore that further, George Babcock was back to business. "Here's my card, and here's our brochure. Why don't you give me a call after you've had a chance to think about what you saw here today, Dr. Popper? Better yet, I'll follow up with you in a few days."

He walked me as far as the reception area. Or to be more exact, half-walked and half-ran. Before I'd even made it out the door, he'd grabbed a sheet of paper out of the fax machine and started reading it, already focused on the next order of business.

Once I was back in my car, I lingered in the parking lot. I made some notes, but I also kept my eye on the entrance of the building. A light rain had begun to fall, making it a little hard to see. Then again, Belle was hard to miss.

When I saw her emerge, I checked my watch. Three minutes past twelve. I watched in my rearview mirror as she went to her car, a white Honda. I waited until she got in before turning the key in my ignition.

I followed her out of the lot, memorizing her license plate and taking mental notes on the car's other distinctive characteristics, including the *Mean People Suck* bumper sticker and the shattered left taillight.

She didn't appear to notice me, which was just as well. It would make phase two that much easier.

• • •

As I drove home along Niamogue Highway, I was convinced that George Babcock had murdered Tommee Frack.

It's got to be him, I reasoned. George had every motive in the world to hate Tommee. He'd taught him everything he needed to know, and Tommee paid him back by swiping half his clients. And as if that weren't bad enough, Tommee wouldn't let up, even after his business had become far, far more successful than George's. It makes perfect sense.

The rain grew heavier: I turned my windshield wipers to Frenetic and they could still barely keep up. As if that weren't bad enough, a light fog had swept in. Long Island drivers are notoriously bad in rotten weather, and I decided I'd be safer sticking to less traveled roads. I turned north on Selah's Path. As I expected, there wasn't nearly as much traffic. I ambled along at a much slower—and safer—speed.

I continued replaying my conversation with George in my head, glancing in the rearview mirror every once in a while and noting with relief that the car behind me had the sense to keep a good distance away. Braking hard on these rain-slick roads would be treacherous.

It wasn't until I came to a red light and the car eased up behind me that I realized it was a black Jeep.

My heartbeat ratcheted up considerably. I peered into the rearview, trying to see the driver. With the fog and the pelting rain, all I could make out was that the driver wore a baseball cap.

He was also wearing sunglasses, although the sun clearly had no intention of putting in an appearance.

"Damn!" I muttered.

It took me a few seconds to realize I was gripping the steering wheel so tightly that the muscles in my hands ached. For some reason, that was my wake-up call.

"Okay, buddy," I breathed. "Let's see if I'm just being paranoid. Especially since the VW doesn't exactly advertise my identity the way my van does. Fasten your seat belt, because you're about to take the grand tour of Long Island's scenic North Shore."

Instead of heading east, I raced through the light as it turned from green to yellow. The Jeep followed. I headed north on a road I couldn't remember having ever been on. I made a right turn, then two quick lefts. The Jeep stuck right behind me, always a safe distance away. I made three more turns and headed north. The vehicle clung to me like a black shadow.

How dare he? I thought. Not only is this guy following me; he's not even good at it.

Suddenly, numbness washed over me.

Oh, my God. He *wants* me to know he's following me! Maybe he really is tailing me to see where I go and who I talk to. But what really matters to him is making sure I *know* I'm being watched.

And now he knows that I know.

I didn't like feeling as if I'd walked—driven—right into a trap. I pulled into the next driveway and braked hard. It was time to turn the tables and follow *him*. But by the time I backed out, he'd sped off.

As I entered the driveway that led to my cottage, I had just decided not to say anything about this to Nick the next time I saw him. That decision fizzled when I saw his car parked in Betty's driveway, right in front of the Big House.

"What's he doing here?" I cried, pulling up right behind him and dashing out into the rain. My heart pounded so furiously I felt dizzy.

I ran around to the back door, which I knew Betty usually kept unlocked during the day. The beating rain ran down my neck in icy rivulets and plastered

wet strands of hair around my face. Without bothering to knock, I stormed inside.

"Nick?" I demanded. "What are you doing here?
Is Betty all right?"

I stopped cold at the sight of the two of them sitting placidly at the kitchen table. Porcelain cups of
tea steamed in front of them.

"Oops! Sorry."

"There's nothing to be sorry about," Betty insisted
gaily. "This is actually a lovely surprise."

"Paranoia is a good thing," Nick chimed in obnoxiously. "Especially when your hobby is poking
around into murders."

"I didn't mean to interrupt. It's just that I got nervous when I saw Nick's car. I was afraid that . . ."

"Betty did her dance routine for me," Nick told
me. "One thing's for sure: the girl's still got it."

"Oh, you flatterer, you!" Betty batted her eyelashes at him. I could see that the two of them had
been flirting wildly.

"Maybe I should leave you two alone. I wouldn't
want to be in the way."

"You might as well pull up a chair," he said cheerfully. "Betty's already made it clear that she won't have
me."

"I told him I'm saving him for someone who really
deserves him." Betty winked at me.

Before I could defend myself, she jumped to her
feet. "Let me make you some tea, Jessica. And you
look like you could use a towel."

"Actually, we were just talking about you," Nick
said as I reluctantly joined him at the table.

"Somehow that doesn't surprise me." Had they

been bemoaning my pathological fear of commitment or commiserating over my foolhardy insistence on playing Hercule Poirot? Probably both.

"Have you been staying out of trouble, young lady?" Nick's tone was joking, but the look in his eyes was dead earnest.

"Of course," I returned indignantly. Still, I looked down, pretending to find the pattern on Betty's flowered tablecloth fascinating.

Nick—damn him—noticed. "Jessie? Is everything okay?"

"Everything's fine."

"Jess?"

"Oh, all right. It's possible—maybe even probable—that I was followed again."

So much tension filled the room it was as if someone had turned it on with a switch.

"When?" Nick demanded tersely. "Just now?"

I nodded.

"Where were you? And where were you coming from?"

"This morning, I met with a man named George Babcock. He has a PR firm in Apaucuck. He's the guy who gave Tommee Frack his start. And I found out that Tommee thanked him by stealing half his clients and nearly destroying his business. Anyway, as I was driving home, the black Jeep I saw the other day followed me."

"Are you sure?" Betty was frowning as she handed me the fluffy hand towel she'd retrieved from a drawer. "Between the fog and the rain . . ."

"I'm sure. Not only was the car the same, so was

the driver. He was wearing a baseball cap and sunglasses."

"If only you'd gotten the license number." Nick didn't even try to hide his exasperation. "I've got a friend who could trace it for me. Then, we'd be able to find out who—"

"B-L-D," I said, wiping rain off my forehead.

"Excuse me?"

"B-L-D. The first three letters of his license plate. I couldn't make out the numbers, but I got that much."

Nick grinned. "Good work, kiddo. Now you're acting like a pro."

I wished his words of praise didn't make me feel so warm and fuzzy.

"But there's something really strange about this, Nick," I mused.

"The whole thing is strange, Jessica," Betty interjected, setting a cup of Earl Grey in front of me. "Which is why I wish you'd forget all about this sleuthing nonsense and spend your time—"

"Yes?" I smiled innocently, unable to resist the temptation to put her on the spot and make her squirm. "What do you think would be a better use of my time, Betty?"

I should have known she wouldn't back down. She looked me right in the eye and said, "You'd be better off asking Nick that question."

He was watching us both warily. "What's strange, Jess?"

"The way this whole thing is being done. I mean, I'm sure the guy who's following me *wants* me to know he's following me."

"Happens all the time," Nick said. "It's a form of

intimidation. In fact, there's even a name for it in the PI biz. When someone doesn't want you to know he's following you, it's called 'stalking.' When someone does want you to know, it's called 'tailgating.' "

"Surely it's more troubling when they want you to know?" Betty said thoughtfully. "Jessica, this man, whoever he is, is clearly sending you a message—the same message he was sending when he made that awful phone call to me Saturday night. Assuming it was the same person, of course."

Up until that point, I hadn't made the connection. I instantly felt a pang of guilt. "Oh, Betty! I'm so sorry for having dragged you into this."

"Believe me, Jessica, it's not me I'm worried about."

"I know," I assured her gently, touched by her concern. "I'll be more careful. I promise."

Two cups of tea later, Nick stood up to go. He reached for Betty's hand.

"Thank you for the tea, and thank you for the dance recital. And most of all, thank you for the superb company."

"Ah, Nick," Betty sighed. "If only you were a few decades older. . . ."

"I keep telling you, Betty. Superficial things like age don't matter. It's what's in your heart that counts." He kissed her hand and turned. "Come on, Jess. I'll walk you out. At least *I* had the good sense to bring an umbrella."

"Thanks for visiting Betty," I said once we had reached our cars. We stood shoulder to shoulder, huddled under his bright red umbrella. "It was nice of you to look in on her."

"Actually, it wasn't Betty who brought me here. I'm doing a little stalking of my own."

"You were *spying* on me?"

"Calm down, Jessie. I was *checking* on you. I promised Betty I would, remember?"

"I really can handle this, you know. No matter what you and Betty think."

"Let me put it this way: You worry about Betty, right?"

"Of course I do! She's someone I care about."

"And I worry about you. Face it, Jess. The people who care about you are going to elbow their way into your life. I suggest you get used to it."

He leaned over and planted a swift kiss on my cheek.

"Keep the umbrella," he said gruffly. "I've got others."

I stood in the chilly downpour, watching him climb into his car and drive away. Even though Nick had kissed me more times that I could count, at times with so much passion that it took my breath away, the brush of his lips against my skin had sent a shiver through me that had nothing to do with the cold, rain-swept November day.

Chapter 10

"There may be more than one way to skin a cat,
but you only get one try per cat."

—Unknown

There was only one antidote to the state of mind Nick's kiss had put me in. As soon as I walked into the house and went through the welcome-home ritual with my furry housemates, I called Jimmy Nolan.

"He-e-ey! It's the doggie doctor!" he greeted me. "Save any lives lately?"

He sounded happy to hear from me. Really happy. And I could tell he was trying his best to be charming. As we made plans to get together that weekend, a little voice inside my head kept asking me what I thought I was doing.

You're confused enough! The voice scolded. *Why drag someone else into this?*

I never came up with an answer. But as I hung up the phone with a date for Saturday night, I decided that dead men were definitely a lot easier to deal with than the living variety.

. . .

I was still holding onto that thought two days later as I drove back to Apaucuck, home of The Babcock Group. This time, I brought along my posse. Both deputies were extremely cooperative, expressing their canine enthusiasm for having been invited along by coating all the car windows liberally with nose slime.

The parking lot was so crowded that it took me a few minutes to locate Belle's little Honda. I finally found it way in back, parked near a small concrete divider covered in dirt and a few dying blades of grass. Perfect.

I pulled into the nearest empty space. Seventeen minutes later, just before noon, I turned to my two pals.

"Okay, you guys. You're on. I'm not asking you to take on anything you can't handle. Just do what you do best."

Out in the lot, the two of them romped around as if they'd been unexpectedly released from twenty years in prison. The instant they spotted the grassy corner of the parking lot, they knew precisely what to do with it. So far, so good.

I wandered along beside them as they sniffed every square inch of the ground as diligently as if they were rooting for truffles. The moment I saw Belle emerge from the building, I bent to Westie level.

"Okay, Max," I instructed. "Be *cute*."

Belle spotted me right away, her attention undoubtedly drawn by the incongruity of a woman walking two frisky dogs in an office building's parking lot.

"Dr. Popper?"

I glanced up, feigning surprise.

"Hey! Hi!" I called as she strode toward me. Her black leather jacket was covered with silver studs that were the perfect complement to her eyebrow ring. She also wore a colorful knitted cap, a strange design with oversized ear flaps that could only have been considered fashionable in the Himalayas. "It's Belle, isn't it?"

"Belinda, actually. But everybody calls me Belle."

Just as I'd anticipated, she crouched down right in front of Max. The little con man never let on that he was my shill. Instead, he jumped up and rested his paws on her knees, then proceeded to nuzzle her face in that irresistible way West Highland Whites have mastered.

"O-o-oh, you are so *cute*!" she told him, as if he didn't already know. "He's a Westie, right?"

"Yup. Don't tell me you're a terrier fan."

"Are you kidding? My boyfriend has a wirehair! I *love* terriers. They're just the sweetest little doggies . . ."

As she gave Max an expert head-and-neck scratching that showed she did, indeed, know her way around a terrier, Lou nosed his way in. He wasn't about to miss out on any attention, especially now that he knew he'd found a pushover.

"What are their names?" she asked me eagerly.

"The Westie is Max. And this guy's Lou."

"What happened to Max's tail? And what's the matter with the Dalmatian's eye?"

"Let's just say that their previous owners weren't dog lovers the way you and I are."

"Oh, you poor little doggies," she crooned, then proceeded to lavish enough love and affection on both of them to make up for at least some of the trials of their puppy days.

"Are you here to see George?" Belle asked, glancing up at me.

"Actually, I have a gynecologist's appointment." Grimacing, I gestured vaguely toward the building. Belle nodded sympathetically. As I hoped, the mere mention of gynecology resulted in instant female bonding. "I had to bring my dogs because they have haircut appointments this afternoon. Max's fur gets so matted when I let it go too long."

"Aren't terriers the worst?" Belle rolled her eyes. "Last summer, Pete and I had Dudley *completely* shaved."

"What about you?" I asked casually. "Going to lunch?"

"Yeah. By the time noon comes around, I'm desperate to get out of there. So even if I bring a yogurt or something, I go sit in a park for an hour. Sometimes, if the weather's bad, I sit in my car. Anything to get away from that office."

"Mr. Babcock does seem a little intense," I ventured. "I got the feeling he's probably not the easiest person in the world to work for."

"Are you kidding? George is a madman! Have you ever seen anybody that hyper in your life? I'm just working for him until January, when Pete finishes school. Then him and me and Dudley are packing up and moving to Montana."

"Montana! What's there?"

Belle shrugged. "It's just someplace different. We want to get away from our parents and everything that's familiar and start experiencing life." Looking at me shyly, she asked, "Is it okay if I pick Max up?"

"He'll love it."

She scooped him up and hugged him like a teddy bear. Max was more than happy to cooperate, especially since belly scratching was now involved.

"I guess you won't miss working at The Babcock Group when you go to Montana," I commented.

"That place is *so* not me. I mean, everything about it is phony. Even the name is a joke. 'The Babcock Group'? Give me a break! A 'group' has to have more than one person in it. But George is it. He's the group!"

"He must have had a larger organization at some point. I know of at least one person who worked for him."

"Tommee Frack, right?"

"How did you know?"

"I heard you and George talking the other day. But I already know all about him." She shook her head. "George sure hated his guts."

"So I gathered. But it sounds as if he had good reason."

Belle shrugged. "I guess. I didn't work for George then—I've only been here about five months—but I know there's a whole file cabinet full of paperwork for ex-clients. And most of them left at the same time as this Frack guy. He swiped them when he stopped working for George and started his own company."

And here I'd thought that wasn't supposed to be common knowledge.

Belle continued, "George gave me the job of going through all his old files, supposedly to clean them out. But it was pretty much just busy work. I've had a lot of time on my hands since I started working here. There hasn't been much going on.

"But the last straw was just a couple of weeks ago. I swear, I've never seen George so bent out of shape. I was afraid he was going to have a heart attack or something."

"How awful! What happened?"

"He found out Frack had stolen one of his oldest clients."

My heartbeat accelerated. "Do you remember the name?"

"Sure. Pomonok Properties."

A lightbulb went on in my head. Of course! *That* was why Joey DeFeo's name had sounded so familiar when Babcock mentioned him. DeFeo, the president of the land development company, had been one of the people quoted in Tommee's *Newsday* obituary. I mentally kicked myself for taking so long to make the connection.

"Anyway, George went on and on, ranting about loyalty and ethics and how Tommee was ruining him with his unscrup—unsoup—"

"Unscrupulousness?"

Belle grinned. "I can never say that word. But George sure can. Anyway, he was in this total rage. I'd never seen him like that before. It was kind of scary."

"I'm surprised you're still working for him."

She nuzzled Max, who rewarded her with doggie kisses. "I keep telling myself it doesn't matter, since Pete and I are leaving soon. To tell you the truth, I've been worried about getting fired, since George's business is falling apart. I just need to hold on to this job until January so we can save up some money. If I lost it, it'd be really hard to find something else, with the holidays coming and all." She shrugged. "George keeps telling me things are going to get better. And I guess he really believes it. For the last few days, he's been acting weird. Kind of . . . I don't know, *happy*. I mean, George is always wired. But lately he's been acting positively . . . like he's high or something. And he keeps going on and on about all these new clients he's gonna get."

"Has he mentioned any names?" I inquired innocently.

"No. I don't even know if he's telling the truth or just fooling himself. He keeps telling me that things are really going to go crazy, that his whole business is on the verge of exploding. That's why he's moving to a bigger office."

"How long has he been planning this move?"

"Since, like, last week."

Interesting timing, I thought.

I tried a different tack. "You know, this is turning out to be a bigger decision than I thought. I want to hire a public relations professional to help my career, and it's a huge investment for me. I mean, I'm not some mega company with a big budget. I'm just one person. And I'm not convinced that George is the guy to go with. Given all his ups and downs, I'm beginning to wonder if he's any good at what he does. . . ."

"He used to be good," Belle said thoughtfully. "Maybe even the best in the business, at least here on the island. But that was all before that Frack guy came along. At least, that's the impression I've gotten from working here. But if what George is saying is true, maybe he really is about to get back on his feet again. I don't know why, but he sounds like he expects a huge turnaround."

I'd gotten what I wanted from Belle. There would be extra treats for Max and Lou, pages of notes and questions recorded in my trusty notebook, and lots to think about.

"I guess I should go in," I told her. "Even though my gynecologist always keeps me waiting for hours, I always make a point of getting there on time."

Her eyes widened. "Yeah, they always do that, don't they? What's that about?"

"Beats me. But it was nice talking to you, Belle."

"Nice talking to you, too."

She placed the ball of wriggling white fur gently on the ground. She started to turn away, then reconsidered.

"You won't say anything to George, will you?" she asked anxiously. "About me planning to leave soon?"

"Of course not. Your secret is safe with me. And I hope you won't say anything to him about me having doubts about his abilities."

"Yeah, right. Like me and George have ever had a heart-to-heart talk."

It was true that George Babcock hadn't impressed me as someone who put a lot of effort into establishing close personal relationships with the people around him. From what I'd seen, the man was utterly driven. His entire life was his business.

The question was, was his business something he'd been willing to kill for?

• • •

I pretended to fuss with the dogs, waiting until Belle drove off and disappeared from view. Once it was safe to leave, I corralled Max and Lou back into the van, thanked them profusely for not blowing my cover, passed around a few Milk Bones and headed home.

Every time I talk to someone who was involved with the late Tommee Frack, I'm convinced he or she had sufficient reason to murder him, I mused as I drove. For a guy who was such a well-loved pillar of the community, Tommee sure created a lot of ill will.

My head was spinning with all the information I still had to sort out: the things I'd been told, the things I hadn't been told, the subtle and the not-too-subtle nuances I'd picked up everywhere I went. The canaries in Merrilee Frack's kitchen, the mala-propisms in Barbara Delmonico's vocabulary, the sudden optimism in George Babcock's business future. . . .

I definitely needed help.

From Nick.

Nonsense. I could do this on my own.

"Are you busy?" I demanded a half hour later, after dialing his number the instant I got home. I balanced the phone in the crook of my shoulder as I took a squawking Prometheus out of his cage, perched on my finger.

"Hello, Jessie," Nick replied. "I'm fine. Thanks for asking. And how are you today?"

"Nick, I am so overloaded—"

"*Awk!* Damn you, Nick Burby!" Prometheus interrupted, cued by hearing Nick's name.

"Same to you, Prometheus!" Nick shot back, chuckling.

"Sorry about that. Anyway, I'm so overloaded with everything I've learned about Frack, not to mention all the questions that are still unanswered, that I feel like I'm going to burst. Which brings me back to my original question. . . ."

"Who's the pretty boy?" my parrot squawked.

"I know the answer to that one," Nick replied. "*Prometheus* is the pretty boy."

This was turning out to be a lot more difficult than I'd anticipated. "Thanks for answering my bird's question. Now, maybe you'll answer mine: Are you completely swamped? Or do you have an hour to spare—soon? Like tonight? I've got so much I want to tell you."

He sighed in my ear. "Yes, I'm busy. The LSATs are on Saturday, and I've been obsessing over this review book. And in about ten minutes, I have to stake out an office building so I can follow a married father of three. His wife suspects that after work, instead of going to the gym, he goes to a gay bar. But I guess I can spare an hour. A change of focus would probably be good for me. Want to come over around seven, seven-thirty?"

"Your office, right?"

"No. Come to my apartment."

Seeing Nick at his office had been one thing. Going to his apartment was a much bigger challenge. For three years, I'd spent nearly as much time in his four spacious rooms on the second floor of a sprawling Victorian house in Port Townsend as I'd spent at my own cottage. His place was the scene of too many memories—dinners cooked for ourselves and for our friends, Christmas Eves spent sipping mulled cider and singing along to the schmaltziest carols we could find, laughing and arguing and making love—that I didn't know if I was ready to go back there. Or if I'd ever be.

But Nick was doing me a favor, so I was hardly in a position to argue. "Your place at seven," I repeated.

"I'll be there."

"Oh, boy," I said to Prometheus after I'd hung up. "I hope I know what I'm doing."

"*Awk!*" he squawked. "Damn you, Nick Burby!"

"My sentiments exactly," I muttered.

• • •

As I walked around to the back of Nick's house that evening, taking the route I'd followed hundreds of times before, I held my notebook tightly against my chest, reminding myself I was here on a mission. While he had played many different roles in my life, including lover, best friend, and confidante, tonight I was merely calling upon his expertise as a private investigator. Nothing more. Nothing.

I rang the doorbell. Without waiting, I went inside and headed up the stairs. "Nick?" I called as I neared the top. "Anybody home?"

He opened the door, filling the stairwell with Led Zeppelin. Hardly surprising: he was the ultimate classic-rock freak. The throbbing bass and eerie vocals of "Stairway to Heaven" may belong to the world, but I always thought of them as Nick Burby's personal possessions.

I could feel that damn ache starting in my heart.

"I guess I should turn this down," he said as I came inside.

"Or off." In response to his look of surprise, I said, "I'm here to work, remember?"

"Right." He lowered the stereo, then turned back to me. "Where do you want to sit? You know the options."

"Here in the living room is fine." I hoped my cheeks were only pink, not bright red. I was beginning to believe this whole visit was a mistake.

But it was too late for second thoughts. I plopped down in a chair and opened my notebook. I allowed myself only a quick glance around, taking in the Aerosmith poster and the Van Gogh calendar. Nick's books were still piled up on a makeshift bookshelf made from cinder blocks and wood, Shakespeare mixed in with Beckett, Faulkner next to Vonnegut.

I also saw Leilani in her tank, the chameleon's tiny feet curled gracefully around a branch as she stared at me with one eye. I looked away.

I cleared my throat. "Okay. This shouldn't take too long. Up to this point, I've spoken to—let's see, six people who were close to Tommee Frack. That includes his accountant, Jonathan Havemeyer, who I met at the funeral. The way I see it, so far we've got three suspects."

Nick sat down on the sagging couch he'd saved from demolition by hauling it home from someone's curb. Our knees were nearly touching. "And they are . . . ?"

"The first is Merrilee, the furious ex-wife who's still smitten with him and who just learned he was about to marry someone else. The fact that she and

Tommee kept canaries is another reason she's made my top ten list."

"I already know your theory about the ex-wife."

"The second is George Babcock. He gave Tommee his start, and Tommee repaid him by stealing half his clients and starting his own PR firm. As if that weren't bad enough, he continued stealing his clients—as recently as a few weeks ago. The latest was Pomonok Properties, one of Babcock's oldest clients. And on top of that, his secretary claims that since last week, starting right about the time Tommee was murdered, George has been acting—and I quote—'high.'"

"Right . . ."

"And number three is Barbara Delmonico, Tommee's fiancée. I haven't yet figured out what her motive would have been. Even if she was just marrying the guy for his money, she'd be ruining her chances for a lifetime meal ticket if she—"

The shrill ring of the doorbell interrupted me. A shock wave ran through me as I imagined the worst.

"Expecting someone?" I asked coolly.

"As a matter of fact, I am. I'll be right back."

As he made a dash for the door, I braced myself for the possibility that I was about to come face to face with the new object of Nick's affection, the individual whose phone call the other day had reduced him to a teenager in the throes of puppy love. I glanced over at Leilani for strength, but I could already feel my defenses snapping into place.

They drooped considerably when he returned, accompanied only by a large brown paper bag.

"Takeout." He held up the bag. "Chinese."

When I just stared without replying, he added, "It

was always your favorite. I figured that hadn't changed."

If he's ordered spring rolls and Garlic Triple Crown, I thought, *it's all over.*

"I got Garlic Triple Crown and a couple of spring rolls. I hope that's okay."

It was the culinary version of presenting me with a dozen roses.

"I didn't know we'd be having dinner together," I protested feebly.

"A *working* dinner." He began unpacking the bag. "Unless you've already got plans . . ."

"No. No plans." I couldn't help adding, "I guess you don't have any plans, either."

"No. I'm free all night. I mean, all evening. Uh, until tomorrow."

It would have been the perfect time to ask about the woman I'd heard him talking to on the phone. During the silence that followed, I could have casually inquired, "So how's your social life?" or even, "Tell me about the great new woman you're seeing."

But while part of me was dying to know, another part—a much more sensible part, I'm sure—wanted as few details as possible. It wasn't my business. Nick's love life didn't matter to me. My relationship with him was something I'd put behind me.

"Anyway, I still haven't figured Barbara Delmonico out," I said firmly. "Whenever I try to focus on what she's all about, I see a big question mark. On the one hand—"

"Chopsticks?"

"Sure." I reached for the chopsticks, taking care not to make bodily contact. Boy, this was turning out to be difficult. "On the one hand, she's playing the role of the heartbroken fiancée whose one chance for happiness has been snatched away. On the other hand—"

"Tea?"

"I get the feeling she's not who she . . . What?"

"I'll make tea, if you like." He held up the tea bag he'd just pulled out of the bag.

Another one of my favorites.

"Yes, tea. That'd be great. As I was saying, Barbara the fiancée strikes me as someone who's trying very hard to be something she's not. If I had a dollar for every lie she told me, I'd be sitting in a hot tub right now—in the Caribbean. I get the feeling her relationship with Tommee was part of some desperate attempt at upward mobility."

Unwrapping my chopsticks, I mused, "There's something about her that just feels *wrong*. My gut tells me she could have killed him, even though my head hasn't been able to figure out why she would have wanted Tommee dead—"

Suddenly Nick stood up.

"Where are you going?" I asked.

"To make the tea."

I flopped back in my chair, not even trying to hide my exasperation.

"*What?*" he asked innocently. "You said you *wanted* tea."

"I did. I do. But I'm trying to focus on the investigation and—and I feel like I'm talking to a brick wall! I thought you'd agreed to play Starsky to my Hutch."

"Within reason. I figured I could make a few calls, help you piece together bits of information . . . But frankly, Jess, if you're going to go traipsing around Norfolk County, interrogating people like the guy whose business Frack destroyed and his nutty ex-wife and his—"

"None of them have any idea I'm investigating Frack's murder."

"Says *you*."

"You don't think I'm capable of doing this, do you?" Fury was forming a knot in my stomach.

"On the contrary. You seem to be doing a terrific job."

"So what's the problem?"

"The problem," he responded evenly, "is that this insane thing you're insisting on doing has got me worried sick."

The word "insane" made my blood boil. "Maybe this wasn't such a good idea. Me coming over here tonight, I mean."

"Look, why don't we take a break and eat?"

"I don't see what—"

"The food's here, it's getting cold, and there's no point in letting it go to waste."

"Fine."

We sat in silence, shoveling in shrimp. Then, just as the knot in my stomach was beginning to loosen, Nick asked, "So how did you do it?"

"Do what?"

"Get Frack's fiancée to talk to you."

"I saw a photograph of Tommee and Barbara on a table in her apartment, so I asked about it. The rest was easy."

"No, before that. How did you get into her house? How did you find out where she lived?"

I hesitated. I knew Nick would disapprove of my methods. At the same time, I couldn't help being proud of my ingenuity.

"I have a friend who got me Barbara's address, based on her dog's registration."

"And you just knocked on this woman's door and introduced yourself?"

"Not exactly." I hated the defensiveness I heard in my voice. "I called her first and told her I had a client who wanted to mate her female Tibetan Terriers. I said I was looking for a stud."

"Whoa. Now *there's* an opening even *I* would find difficult to turn down."

He laughed, a welcome sound. I couldn't resist taking advantage of the cease-fire. "You know, Nick, there's something that's been bothering me. I've been tracking down all these people who knew Tommee, people who seem like the obvious people to talk to, and it doesn't seem as if the police have been interviewing any of them."

"Maybe the people you're talking to aren't telling you everything."

"Could be."

"Or maybe the police just haven't gotten to them yet."

"Come to think of it," I mused, "the police haven't asked me any more questions, either. Just the statement I made at the crime scene. Don't you think that's odd?"

"A little. Then again, you didn't even know the dead guy. You were just the person who happened to find his body."

"That's true. . . . Nick, is there any chance you

could ask your pal Officer Pascucci what's going on?"

"Vince? I don't know him that well. Besides, I'd rather save him for a really big favor." He paused. "Hey, Jess?"

The softness of his voice surprised me.

"Aside from being worried about you day and night, I think you're doing an incredible job."

I eyed him suspiciously, bracing for the "but." If he was going to tell me one more time that I had no business poking around in this murder—

"I mean it, Jess. I'm really impressed with all the information you gathered, not to mention the clever ways you got it."

His compliment caught me completely off guard. I focused my attention on devouring a spring roll with an enthusiasm that was reminiscent of the canine branch of my family.

"Can I ask you something?" I asked.

"Shoot."

"Who do *you* think murdered Tommee? Based on what I've found out so far."

He was silent for a few moments. Deciding whether or not to indulge me, I guessed.

"From what you've told me," he said, "I think all three of your suspects are possibilities, although I agree that you don't know enough about Ms. Delmonico to figure out what her motive could have been."

"What would *you* do? If you were investigating this case, I mean."

He looked at me warily. "If it were me, I'd keep going. Talk to more people. Find out why George

Babcock is so cheerful all of a sudden. Get more information about what was really going on between Barbara and Tommee. But I'd never forget for a minute that—"

"That's exactly what I've been thinking," I interrupted. "I need to track down some of Tommee's other employees. There's got to be at least one who didn't think Tommee was a prince. As for Barbara's relationship with Tommee, maybe her snake-loving pal Claudia Martin knows something. I'm going to look her up."

"At least let me go with you," Nick pleaded.

"I think this calls for a woman-to-woman approach. Less intimidating."

He shook his head disapprovingly. But at least he refrained from putting his two cents in.

When the Chinese food was gone, I knew it was time for me to go. As I stood up to leave, I noticed the fat LSAT review book lying on the couch, half-hidden by a pillow. The Eagles were on in the background, singing "Take It to the Limit."

"Hey, Nick?"

"Hmm?"

"Why law school?"

"It's not as if becoming a private investigator was ever my career goal. The only reason I fell into it was that there weren't many options. I remember looking for a job after college and being astounded that potential employers weren't falling over themselves to grab someone who'd gotten an A on his honors thesis on Edgar Allan Poe." With a shrug, he added, "Anyway, I need a change."

I impulsively asked the question that had been nagging at me ever since I'd learned about Nick's decision to take his life down a totally different path.

"Deciding that your life needed a major overhaul didn't have anything to do with me, did it?"

"Maybe."

Not the answer I'd been hoping for.

"Don't tell me that"—I searched for the right words—"what happened with us precipitated some kind of midlife crisis."

"I like to think I'm too young for midlife, but sure, our breakup precipitated a crisis. I'd be lying if I told you otherwise."

"You know, Nick, we never really talked about . . . all that."

"I don't think we need to, Jess. I know how you feel, and that's all there is to it."

All the emotions of our dreadful trip to Hawaii came rushing back. For me, our week in paradise had seemed like a chance to sleep late, snorkel, and drink mai-tais while watching the sun go down together. I thought that adopting Leilani, an injured female Jackson's chameleon we found on the low limb of a banyan tree, would be the biggest surprise of the trip. It never occurred to me that in addition to packing a pair of rubber fins and a blue Speedo I teased him about mercilessly, Nick had also packed an engagement ring.

Maybe if I'd had an inkling of what was on his mind, I would have handled things more gracefully. Instead, his unexpected proposal—made on our final evening there, delivered shyly on Kaanapali Beach at sunset—threw me into a state of utter panic. I'd responded by stomping clumsily all over his feelings.

What should have been the most romantic moment in both our lives turned into one of the most excruciating.

We flew home in silence, enduring a twelve-hour flight and an endless layover in San Francisco. After we returned, we spoke only a few more times. Most of our conversations dealt with logistics, like who would get to keep Leilani.

And all of our conversations were short.

We never had the one we needed most. Or maybe it simply wasn't possible. Nick felt so hurt and I felt so threatened and confused and angry at him, not only for taking away my lover but also for depriving me of my best friend, that maybe there was no way for either of us to talk about what was really going on with us.

We had been so good at loving each other. I guess it shouldn't have surprised me that we also turned out to be good at causing each other pain.

"It's late," I said. "I should get going."

He nodded, the two of us silently agreeing to pretend that was the only reason I was hurrying out the door.

As I stepped outside, I was surprised by the frigid air that assaulted me. It was one of the first bitterly cold nights we'd had so far.

Winter really is coming, I thought. In fact, it's here.

I pulled up the collar of my jacket, hurried to my car and drove home.

Alone.

Chapter 11

"If cats could talk, they wouldn't."

—Nan Porter

By the next morning, I was more than ready to throw myself into another round of interviewing. I told myself it was because of Nick's begrudging encouragement. For the moment, at least, that sounded like as good a reason as any.

My day was booked with back-to-back appointments that ran into the middle of the afternoon, but I had time for two quick phone calls before heading out. I settled on the couch with Cat in my lap, Max chewing a mangled piece of rawhide at my feet, Lou standing guard at the front door, and Prometheus happily devouring a slice of orange—the best way to keep him quiet. First, I dialed the number Marcus Scruggs had given me for Barbara Delmonico's pal, the woman who shared with the murder victim's fiancée both a love of snakes and a love of hot pants.

"Four-seven-oh-oh," a male voice answered gruffly.

Not exactly what I'd been expecting. I'd just assumed Marcus had given me Claudia Martin's home phone number, and I'd anticipated the usual uncomplicated "Hello." "I'm, uh, trying to get in touch with Claudia Martin."

"Nobody's here now. But she should be in later, like around two, two-thirty."

"And you're still at 1055 Route 437?" I spoke quickly, sensing he was about to hang up on me.

"Been here seventeen years."

Odd conversation to have with a husband or roommate, I thought. But I didn't dwell on it. Instead, I made my second call of the morning, hoping to find out why the official murder investigation was proceeding so slowly.

I was put through the usual rigamarole before finally getting through to Harned. I kept myself from growling as I waited "on hold" by tossing Max's slime-covered rawhide across the room a few hundred times. Somehow, he never tired of chasing after it and bringing it back for one more action-packed round.

"I'm just calling to check in, Lieutenant," I began cheerfully. "I haven't heard anything more about the case on the news—"

"It's an ongoing investigation," the lieutenant interrupted. "We're looking at everybody. I can assure you, Dr. Popper, our detectives are following all leads."

"You know, I was wondering—"

"Thanks for your interest, but I've got another call."

And the line went dead.

I held the phone in my hand for a few seconds, flabbergasted over our conversation. If you could call it that.

. . .

I was still steaming over Harned's rude refusal to take me seriously as Max and Lou and I pulled up in front of a small, run-down house in West Munchogue a half hour later. The two of them started skittering around the front seat, already itching to get out. I looked to them for inspiration, telling myself to stop brooding and get over it. After all, this was no mind-set for tackling my first house call of the day—especially given who it was.

Victor Fazio had been a client for almost a year, ever since his motorcycle accident had left him wheelchair-bound. I always got the feeling he didn't like taking advice from a woman. Or maybe his anger was more generalized and I was just too sensitive.

As soon as I opened the door, Max and Lou shot outside, oblivious to the brisk autumn air that had me zipping up my fuzzy fleece jacket and pulling on my gloves. As I set up the ramp outside the entrance to the van, they romped around playfully on the stubby brown grass that constituted Victor Fazio's front lawn. Before heading toward the front door, I called them over and fastened leashes on their collars. I wanted to be sure they remained on their best behavior. I reminded myself to do the same.

"How are you today, Mr. Fazio?" I greeted him as the three of us stood on his front step, using the same hearty tone I always adopted when I expected a less-than-warm reception.

"Considering that my cat is sick, I'd say I'm doing pretty well," he grumbled. He barely glanced at me, instead keeping his head low so that his long stringy hair formed a curtain that half-covered his face.

"Let's bring him into the van and I'll check him out. Harley, right?"

"Yeah." He laughed coldly. "Crummy choice for a name, don't you think?"

I scooped up Harley, then moved aside to let Mr. Fazio go out to the van ahead of me. Even though there was a definite chill in the air, he didn't bother to put on a jacket. *Real men don't need coats,* I thought wryly. As I followed, I was treated to a first-rate view of his spectacularly muscular bare arms. They rippled impressively as he wheeled himself along the ramp outside his house, along the short walkway, and up the ramp that led into my van. His biceps, the size of cantaloupes, each sported a large, dark blue tattoo: on the right, a malevolent-looking eagle, poised to strike as he hovered in front of an unfurling American flag; on the left, the logo of the Harley-Davidson Motor Company.

I stroked Harley as I walked, trying to calm him. But the sleek black cat kept trying to jump down. He clearly didn't like being held, and I suspected he wasn't used to affection. The best strategy, I decided, was an examination that was as fast and matter-of-fact as possible.

Back in the van, I set Harley on the exam table as I read through his chart. He sniffed the metal surface and immediately jumped down and started slinking toward the door.

"Okay, Harley, back up on the table," I said cheerfully. The four-year-old cat had never had any real health problems. "Mr. Fazio, when you called you said you'd noticed a yellow discharge around his anus?"

"Yeah, it squirted out from a couple of spots. And he keeps . . . cleaning himself, if you know what I mean."

"Does the discharge smell?"

He looked at me as if I'd just asked the dumbest question in the world. "You really figure I stuck my nose down there?"

I decided to let it pass. "Have you noticed him rubbing his behind on the carpet? Is he eating and drinking the same as usual? Any problems with urinating or defecating?"

"Look, like I said, I noticed this yellow goo around his butt." Crossly, he added, "You're the doctor, not me."

I resisted the urge to say something equally obnoxious. "His anal glands are probably ruptured," I said, palpating the cat and finding everything else in order. "They get infected sometimes."

By that point, Harley and I had reached an understanding. I was all business, asking nothing of him but his cooperation. He continued to glare at me, but let me do whatever I needed to do without protesting. I found myself missing Cat, who, for all her airs, had a sweetness and vulnerability that were sorely lacking in this animal. I vowed to bring her a treat the first chance I got, some catnip or her favorite indulgence in the world: chicken livers.

I took Harley's temperature, which was normal: 101 degrees on the nose. Then I pulled on a pair of rubber gloves and did a rectal exam.

"Glad I don't have your job," Mr. Fazio observed, scowling. "Sticking your fingers up animals' butts all day . . ."

I had to laugh. I'd never thought of my chosen career in those terms.

"Actually, I really enjoy what I do. It's pretty rewarding to treat sick animals and make them well again."

"Sounds like I'm not gonna have to go out and get a new cat."

"Harley's going to be just fine. I'll give him an injection of amoxicillin, and I'll leave you with pills. Make sure you put them in his food so they don't upset his stomach. I'd also like you to hold a warm, wet washcloth on the infected area for five to ten minutes, twice a day. I'll stop by and take another look at him in a week or so."

"I'm not going anywhere," Mr. Fazio replied glumly. "So how much is this gonna cost me?"

After I left Mr. Fazio and Harley to enjoy each other's enchanting company and got back into my van, I definitely needed a short hug break. "Come here, you guys," I instructed Max and Lou. "Who are the best doggies in the world? *Who are the best doggies?*"

They climbed all over to me in response, covering my face with wet dog kisses and testing the resiliency of my internal organs with a total of eight paws, jabbing at me with the force of a pneumatic drill. I wouldn't have had it any other way.

As I drove away, I congratulated myself on how polite I'd been with both Lieutenant Harned and Mr. Fazio. I decided I deserved a few hours off later that day, after I'd finished the morning's calls.

• • •

It was just after two when I headed for Route 437.

"This can't be right," I muttered as I drove along the four-lane highway, peering at the numbers and trying to find 1055.

I knew the road was mostly industrial, the home of office buildings and warehouses and, down around this part of the island, Long Island Airport. But I had assumed that a condo complex or maybe some garden apartments were wedged in somewhere.

I was even more puzzled when at last I spotted the sign sporting a big "1-0-5-5." Right below it was the silhouette of a woman, a cartoonish figure who looked like she'd undergone extensive and overly enthusiastic plastic surgery.

"SILK 'N' SATIN LOUNGE," the sign read. And underneath, in smaller letters, "EXOTIC DANCERS FROM ROUND THE WORLD."

I pulled into the lot, deciding this was as good a place as any to figure out where I'd gone wrong. The few cars that were parked in the nearly empty lot were pretty run-down, cheap models that probably hadn't looked that great even when they were first purchased. There was one exception, however: a sleek black Porsche. I decided it had to belong to the lounge's owner, especially when I saw that the license plate read, "HOTGIRLZ."

"You'll have to wait in the van," I told Max and Lou. "I don't think you're old enough for this place—even in dog years."

The sky was clear and the sun was shining, making for a bright November afternoon. I pushed open the heavy wooden door of the lounge and instantly confronted nearly total darkness.

Don't these people pay their electric bill? I wondered.

Inside, I hesitated. I breathed in stale air that reeked of beer and sweat and something that smelled suspiciously like urine. I'd stay just long enough to find someone who could explain to me where the real 1055 Route 437 was hiding.

As soon as my eyes adjusted, I realized I was in the real 1055 Route 437.

Hanging in the front entrance of the club were large color photographs of some of the hot girlz who worked there. One, completely nude except for what looked like a large postage stamp covering her nether regions, was wrapped around a pole that ran from the floor to the ceiling. She possessed both hair and breasts that would have put Dolly Parton to shame.

A second woman, who also looked as if she did her clothes shopping at the post office, straddled a large inflatable object that I guessed had originally been designed to simulate a hot dog. Her eyes were squeezed shut and her expression was one of devout ecstasy, as if nothing came even close to the feeling of polyurethane against one's thighs.

But it was the third photograph that convinced me.

A woman wearing eye makeup so thick she could have qualified for a heavy-metal rock band stared defiantly into the camera. She, too, had a prop, but hers wound around her neck, twisted across her stomach, and ended up between her legs. The python wore the same in-your-face expression as his dance partner.

"Something I can help you with?"

I whirled around, expecting to see a burnt-out six-tyish sleazeball chomping on a cigar. Instead, the man who'd approached me was about twenty-five. He was dressed in tight-fitting jeans and a T-shirt that looked as if it had been dry cleaned, and he was clearly no stranger to hair gel.

"I'm looking for Claudia Martin."

"Too bad." He was looking me up and down. "I was hoping you were here for a job."

"Thanks, I already have a job. Is Claudia here?"

"You mean Peaches."

"Excuse me?"

"Around here, we call her Peaches. As in Peaches N. Cream. Y'know, her stage name."

"Is, uh, Peaches around?"

"You're in luck. She just came in to pick up her check."

He continued looking at me in a way that really gave me the creeps. I had a feeling he was trying to picture how I'd look with my legs wrapped around something long, hard, and one hundred percent synthetic.

"Could you please tell her I'd like to talk to her?"

"Tell her yourself. She's in back."

With his thumb, he gestured inside. Peering in that direction, I saw a wooden platform shaped like a half-circle, jutting out into a small room crammed with tiny tables. On one side of the makeshift stage, there was a curtained doorway.

"Go ahead," he urged. "Nobody's gonna bite you. Unless you want—"

"Thanks," I said hastily.

You never know where life will take you, I reminded myself as I walked gingerly through the Silk 'N' Satin Lounge, afraid of what I might step in. The air was thick with something I couldn't identify. Testosterone, maybe.

Even though I would have preferred not to touch anything, I had no choice but to push aside the curtain, which turned out to be black velvet. I found myself in a narrow hallway. Through the doorway to my left, I could see a metal desk covered with papers. The business office, no doubt, the heart and soul of the operation, if an operation like this possessed either. A second door, to my right, was decorated with a flimsy star cut out of aluminum foil.

"Claudia?" I called. My voice sounded annoyingly high-pitched.

"Whaddya want?" a voice even higher than mine called back.

My heart pounded as I swung open the dressing room door. I was imagining all kinds of bizarre scenarios involving G-strings, inflatable objects, and body positions out of the Kama Sutra.

So I was startled to find an ordinary-looking woman perched on a stool, writing in a checkbook register.

She glanced up. "You looking for me?"

Claudia Martin was dressed in gray sweatpants

and a sweater I'd recently seen at Old Navy. Her hair, dyed the same light blond as Barbara's, was pulled up in a haphazard knot and held in place with a plastic clip. Her face had an unexpectedly fresh look, as if she'd just washed it. But even without the Halloween makeup, I recognized her as the woman in the photograph out front, the one dressed in a python and very little else.

"Ms. Martin, I'm Dr. Jessica Popper. I'm a veterinarian, and I'm working with Dr. Scruggs—"

"Oh, sure. Doc Scruggs is the best. He's cute, too. But I'm sure you've noticed."

I forced a smile. "Anyway, he asked me to stop in and make sure that everything was okay. With your snake, I mean. It's been a while since you've brought him in."

Claudia shook her head. "Isn't he just the sweetest guy in the world? You tell him everything is just fine. Jasper and Clarence are both doing terrific. But that is *so* like Doc Scruggs to be concerned. One time, when I'd only had Jasper, like, a couple of weeks, his eyes got all cloudy. I totally freaked. I figured I wouldn't even be able to go on that night, because it was making him so cranky. Pythons sure get fussy when they're not feeling so great. Anyway, Doc Scruggs saw him right away. He explained to me that he was just shedding. I felt, like, a zillion times better. I brought Jasper on stage with me and he did just great."

Beaming like a proud mother, she gestured across the room. "Isn't he the cutest little python you've ever seen?"

I took in the dressing room, a cramped, windowless space with a Formica counter, a blurred mirror, and a few hooks. The counter was littered with makeup and beauty products, a can of glitter hair spray, boxes of temporary tattoos, and a huge stack of false eyelashes. Limp bits of fabric, not one of them larger than a washcloth, dangled from the hooks. Some were shiny, some decorated with sequins or feathers. Most were nearly transparent.

Pushed into one corner was an enormous glass tank. Inside, two snakes were wrapped around each other as if they were the best of friends.

"Jasper and Clarence," I observed. "Are they, uh, both yours?"

"They are now. One of them belonged to a friend of mine, but she's out of the business." Claudia rolled her eyes. "She's moved on to bigger and better things."

Time for the $64,000 question.

"That friend wasn't Barbara Delmonico, was it?"

"Sure was," Claudia replied matter-of-factly. "She was good, too. You can't imagine what that girl could do with a boa constrictor."

I was certain I couldn't, and frankly, I preferred it that way. But what was more exciting was the fact that my suspicions were correct: Tommee Frack's fiancée wasn't even close to what she claimed to be.

"So I guess she's not really an ex-stockbroker whose parents are both doctors."

"Hah! You actually believed that? Well, don't feel bad. So did just about everybody else she fed that line of crap to—pardon my French." Claudia shrugged. "But I don't hold it against her. I mean, it's not as if Bubbles and me are exactly in a line of work you go around bragging about."

"Bubbles?"

"That was Barb's name around here. Bubbles LaRue, the way I'm Peaches N. Cream. You know, it's like we all gotta pretend we're these sex queens or something. Paul's really into that. You met Paul coming in, probably. He guards the door like a Doberman."

I nodded. "Paul and I met. So when, exactly, was Barbara—Bubbles—uh, an exotic dancer?"

"She did it for a couple years. Started around the same time I did. I guess that's why we became such pals. Both the new kids on the block, you know? That's how we got stuck with snake duty. Nobody else wanted it."

"I can understand that."

"Oh, it isn't dancing with them that's the problem. The snakes are really kind of nice, once you get to know them. They have their quirks, of course, but if you treat them good, they generally treat you good right back. No, what I'm talking about is the expense. El Cheapo out there makes us take care of our own props. That means we get stuck taking them to the vet and even feeding them. And you don't want to know what they eat."

I happened to know quite well. I'd fed quite a few living, breathing dinners to reptiles in my day. It was not my favorite part of the job.

Still, at the moment, my job was looking pretty darned good.

"It's worth it, though," Claudia continued cheerfully. "I mean, even though I got seniority now, I stuck with snake dancing. The guys go absolutely nuts over my act, especially when I do this thing where . . . Well, it's kind of hard to explain, without actually showing you. But believe me, the tips I get are incredible." She grinned. "Sure beats working at Starbucks."

"Did Barbara specialize in snake dancing, too?"

"At first, yeah. But then she got creative, experimenting with a lot of different animals. I guess she liked the challenge. When you work with something alive, you never really know how it's gonna go. It gives you lots of room to improvise, so it keeps the job interesting. She tried all kinds of animals: lizards, birds, you name it."

Birds. "Did she ever work with . . . oh, I don't know, canaries?"

"Yeah, she gave it a try. It didn't work out real well, though. Birds kept flying off in the middle of her act. It got real expensive, 'cuz she kept having to replace them. And Paul got pissed about the mess they made, if you know what I mean." She grimaced.

"If Barbara was so good, why did she give it up?"

"Let's just say a great opportunity came along. Meaning she finally snagged herself a rich guy." Claudia brightened. "Y'know, now that I'm thinking back, it was the canaries that first brought them together."

I had to struggle to maintain a neutral expression. "Really?"

"One night, Barb was doing her thing with the canaries, and one of those birds just flew right at this guy who was sitting way in back. I guess he was trying to keep a low profile. A lot of our customers do. Anyway, the stupid bird flew by, and the guy actually grabbed it! At the end of the show, he brought it backstage. Y'know, to return it to Barb? And they ended up going out that night."

She shrugged. "That was the beginning. The story they would've told their grandchildren, I guess. Of course, everything's changed, now that Barb's Mr. Right is six feet under. She's right back where she started."

"Have you and Barbara lost touch?"

"More like she decided to lose touch with me. I haven't seen her since the day she showed up here with a rock the size of a golf ball on her finger. Going on and on about the caviar and champagne they were serving at the wedding, and how these celebrities and political hotshots were coming . . . The way she carried on, you would've thought she won the lottery.

"Just like that, I wasn't good enough for her. Not when she started planning her wedding at Hallsworth Hall and her honeymoon in Cancún and her life as a trophy wife. I even made a joke—well, kind of a joke—about me being her maid of honor. You should have seen the look on her face. It was like I'd just said something so awful it made her gag." She sighed. "Maybe if I was a better friend, I'd have been happy for her. But Barb really changed after she started hanging out with that guy. It was like she decided that her goal in life was to become an entirely different person. She started reading magazines like *Vogue,* always carrying one around like it was the Bible or something. She studied it, you know? Like she was trying to educate herself about what real class was."

With only minimal results, I was sorely tempted to comment.

"Next thing you know, she stopped getting her

hair cut around here. Instead, she went into Manhattan, even though it cost tons more. And she had her makeup done at one of those places models go so she could learn how the pros do it."

"There's nothing wrong with trying to look good," I pointed out.

"But that was just the beginning. She did things like . . . like going to the opera. Guess she figured it'd impress Tommee and all his high-fallutin' business pals. Can you imagine? Bubbles at the *opera*?"

Claudia sighed again. "Of course, in the end, it didn't work out at all the way she expected. With him being murdered and all."

"Tough break," I commiserated. "Losing your fiancé like that."

"More like losing your meal ticket." Claudia laughed coldly. "Barb thought she had it made. If they'd had the ceremony a little sooner, she'd have inherited every dime that guy had."

"That is bad timing," I agreed, thinking, *So much for my theory about Barbara Delmonico killing him for his money.*

"Well, it was real nice talking to you." Claudia hopped off her stool. "If you don't mind, I gotta get to the bank before it closes. I got a two-year-old son, and you wouldn't believe how much having a kid costs. Between the diapers and the baby food and the toys . . . Hey, give Doc Scruggs a kiss for me, will ya? The guy is such a sweetie."

I was still haunted by the idea of carrying out Claudia's request as I groped my way out of the Silk 'N' Satin Lounge. I'd almost made it to the door when I heard Paul, the Doberman owner of the lounge, somewhere behind me in the shadows.

"Hey, I wasn't kidding before," he called. "You ever need a job, you come back and see me. I'm sure we could work something out."

• • •

Barbara Delmonico had turned out to be a dead end. True, she wasn't at all what she was trying to convince the rest of the world she was. But her buddy Claudia was right. Without a marriage certificate that awarded her the official title of Wife, Barbara had nothing to gain from Tommee Frack's death. But was the dead canary buried next to Tommee's body nevertheless a reference to the act that had brought them together?

Still, between Barbara's lack of a motive and Nick's insistence that Merrilee Frack didn't have what it took to be a cold-blooded killer, Tommee's personal life wasn't yielding many clues as to what got him killed and buried beneath dead leaves. I decided it was time to really concentrate on Tommee's business life.

Before I left the Silk 'N' Satin parking lot, I pulled out my notebook. I picked out my next victim by checking the list of former employees I'd put together from the *Long Island Business Beat* website, then cross-referenced with Vanda's list of registered dog owners.

Wade Moscowitz was interesting for two reasons. One was that he'd only worked for Tommee Frack for four months. The other was that when he left Tommee's firm, Wade appeared to have left public relations completely. And the entire business world, too, from what I could tell. The fact that he was never again mentioned in *Long Island Business Beat,* not in the "People On The Move" section or anywhere else, left me wondering what might have happened to him.

Wade lived in Hawkins, a beachy North Shore town that had first been developed as a summer community during the 1920s. As I pulled up in front of his house, I saw that it was like most of the others in that it looked as if it had started out as a vacation bungalow but over the generations evolved into a nicely kept home.

Max and Lou scampered in the grass as I rang the bell twice, then knocked. Nothing. Together, the three of us circled the house. I found a back door and knocked again, but there was still no response.

I was trying to drag the dogs back away from examining every inch of Wade Moscowitz's yard with their noses when I heard somebody call.

"Hey, are you really a vet?"

As the dogs evaded my grasp, I turned and saw a teenaged boy, probably fourteen or fifteen, hugging a skateboard and watching me. His faded Ozzy Osbourne T-shirt was about two sizes too big, his khaki cargo pants at least four. He made up for all that extra fabric by wearing his dark blond hair in a buzz cut.

"I really am." I was glad to have some company on this quiet road that ran to the beach. Not another soul was around.

"Cool. So you, like, take care of cats and dogs in there?"

"Yup. And sometimes rabbits and hamsters and even horses."

His eyes widened. "You can fit a horse in there?"

"Actually, I usually treat the horses right in their barns. But I can bring everything I need along with me." I'd forgotten how badly teenagers needed to be treated like human beings, instead of incompetent children. "What about you? Do you have any pets?"

"Naw. My mom's allergic to, like, everything."

Max and Lou came bounding over, clearly excited over the prospect of someone new to sniff. Once they reached us, Lou held back. But Max, as usual, was Mr. Personality. He jumped up on the boy's leg, assuming that love and affection were on the schedule. But the boy clearly wasn't used to animals, and Max must have startled him with his rambunctiousness. He instinctively reached for the dog's head, trying to push him away.

Max reacted instinctively, too—by opening his jaws.

To me, the scene practically unfolded in slow-motion. I grabbed Max just in time, pulling him away before he had a chance to bite.

"Hey, what was that about?" the boy cried.

"Sorry. My Westie has a bad habit of biting when he feels threatened. You okay?"

"Yeah." The boy eyed Max warily.

I got the feeling he was about to hightail it out of there. "By the way," I asked quickly, "I'm looking for the guy who lives here, Wade Moscowitz. I don't suppose you know him?"

"You should try the place where he works."

"Where's that?"

"Dream Catcher."

I shrugged. "Don't know it."

"It's right in Port Townsend. You know, that hippie store that sells New Age stuff?"

I wasn't sure we were talking about the same Mr. Moscowitz.

"He's there, like, all the time."

"Thanks. I'll check it out."

"Good luck. Later."

As I watched him skate off, I found myself wishing for the simpler days of youth. Then remembered, with a pang, that, romanticizing aside, the simpler days of youth hadn't been that much simpler. At least, not for me.

I appreciated my young friend's helpfulness, especially since we hadn't all been on our best behavior, but I was sure we'd somehow gotten our wires crossed. Although my Mr. Moscowitz had only been part of Tommee's public relations world for a few months, I couldn't envision selling Birkenstocks and frangipani incense as the next rung on anyone's career ladder.

An entire orchestra of wind chimes jingled and jangled as I pushed open the door of Dream Catcher, a tiny shop on one of the back streets of downtown Port Townsend. I was immediately assaulted by the scent of sandalwood and the hypnotic sounds of Enya.

I suddenly found myself in the mood for a massage. But I had more stressful business to attend to.

I picked my way through the displays of candles, inspirational books, and, yes, Birkenstocks, glad that my destructive pets were safely resting in the van. I passed a young woman in an Indian print skirt, with long wisps of golden hair falling around the shoulders of her peasant blouse. She looked up from the hemp shirts she was folding and offered me a vapid grin.

As I neared the counter, the fiftyish man standing behind it, sporting a colorful tie-dyed T-shirt and a silver ponytail, smiled soothingly. "How are you today?"

"Fine, thanks. I'm looking for Wade Moscowitz."

"That's me."

I studied his tall lean frame, gaunt face, and intense hazel eyes, trying to picture him in a suit and tie. I still wasn't convinced I had the right person. But I geared up to deliver the same line I'd fed Brad O'Reilly. Maybe it would be easier the second time around.

"My name is Dr. Popper. I'm a veterinarian, and I'm working with the State of New York. We're surveying dog owners to see if they've been following up with inoculations for their pets."

"You're referring to Sugar?"

I set my manila folder on the counter, next to a display of herb-scented massage oils, and opened it. "That's right. Sugar. A boxer born on February 12, 1989, and registered on July 28 that same year—"

"You've got a lot of information in there."

"As I said, I'm working with the state."

"I guess the state doesn't record death dates."

I blinked. "Excuse me?"

"Sugar died almost a year ago. She was hit by a car."

I blinked. My excuse for questioning him had just flown out the window.

"So why don't you tell me why you're really here?" His voice was tinged with impatience.

"I already told you. I'm here on behalf of the State of New York—"

"Since when does the State of New York have a budget that allows for random checks of dog owners?

The government can't even keep track of convicted felons."

I'd been found out.

"Okay. I'm not here about your boxer. I was just looking for an excuse to talk to you."

"What makes me so special?"

"You used to work for Tommee Frack."

Wade Moscowitz suddenly looked very interested. "You a cop?"

"Not exactly."

"Private investigator?"

"Well . . . no."

"Do I have to spend the rest of the afternoon guessing?"

"I'm a veterinarian—"

"So we're back to that, are we?"

"No, I really am a veterinarian. See? There's my van, parked right outside. But I'm also the person who found Tommee Frack's body in the woods at Atherton Farm."

Wade studied me skeptically, then glanced at Sister Goldenhair. "Why don't we go in back and talk?" he suggested to me.

I was expecting a crowded storage room packed with hammocks woven in Third World countries. Instead, the back room contained a comfortable-looking futon couch and a molded plastic chair shaped like a large hand.

I opted for the hand.

"So you're the vet who found Tommee," Wade said, settling onto the futon. "I read about it in the paper." He frowned. "Seems to me it was a different name, though.

For some reason, I'm remembering something about soda."

"That's because they got my name wrong, along with a couple of other key facts." I could see no reason to go into the Popper/Pepper problem that had haunted me even before I'd earned the title "Dr."

"I still don't understand why you're here."

"I've never found a dead body before," I replied. "Stumbling across Tommee Frack got me interested in trying to find out who murdered him. It also got me interested in who he was. I'm trying to learn everything I can about him."

"I see. So this is kind of like your hobby."

I was about to make some scathing comment about there being no need to make fun of my new-found avocation when he added unexpectedly, "Not a bad hobby at all. Especially since our Tommee was a very interesting guy."

"Do you have any theories?" I asked, encouraged. "About anyone who might have wanted him dead, I mean?"

"Compiling a list would take me more time than I'm willing to spare."

Wade made a sound that was somewhere between a laugh and a snort. It didn't strike me as the kind of sound someone who was truly centered would make. But I was finding that while Wade Moscowitz looked the part of a purveyor of inner peace, several other dimensions were undoubtedly lurking beneath the blinding red, yellow, and blue swirls covering his chest.

"Here I thought he was such an upstanding, well-loved pillar of the community," I persisted. "From what I've read in the papers, the man didn't have an enemy in the world."

"You believe that?"

"Well . . . I've been talking to some of the people who knew him—and finding that Tommee had a few skeletons in his closet."

"Do tell."

"His ex-wife, for one. And his fiancée, Barbara Delmonico. Did you know that she—well, let's just say I found out that she's not exactly what she wants us to believe she is." I hoped that impressing him with how much I'd already learned would motivate him to fill in the blanks. "Then there's George Babcock . . ."

"You're a very bright girl. Maybe even too bright. And I see that you've been working very hard. Who else have you talked to, if you don't mind me asking?"

"I talked to Brad O'Reilly—"

"You mean Mini-Me."

"Excuse me?"

"Mini-Me? From the Austin Powers movies?"

"You mean a pint-size version of someone else, right? A clone?"

Of course, in the movies, the original version was Dr. Evil, a man who tried hard to live up to his name. It was difficult picturing Tommee in that role: his chubby face and his innocent grin conspired to make him look more like a cherub than a villain.

Wade smiled. "Don't mind me. I got a weird sense of humor. So tell me, what did our good friend Brad have to say? What was his theory about Frack's murder?"

"That it was a random killing. Maybe a carjacking gone wrong."

"Yes," Wade said drily. "Brad would come up with something like that."

"Brad thinks the world of Tommee. He said he was brilliant. A real genius."

"He wasn't the only one who felt that way."

"He did make it sound like Tommee was pretty incredible at what he did. Brad told me the thing that made him so successful was his ability to match people up."

"Is that what he said?"

"Yes. Something about setting up awards ceremonies designed to make just about everybody on Long Island look good."

I waited for him to comment but he merely watched me, his face expressionless. Only his eyes betrayed him. The intensity I saw in them gave me the uncomfortable feeling that this was a man who felt a great deal—and felt it passionately.

"What about you?" I stared back with the same intensity. "You must know a lot about Tommee."

"You mean, who do I think killed him?"

"I mean, do you *know* who killed him?"

"No, I don't. And that's an honest answer."

I wasn't sure I believed him.

"And if you knew, you wouldn't tell me anyway, would you?"

He laughed. "I wish Sugar was still alive. I'd definitely want her vet to be somebody as smart as you. As for this little Jessica Fletcher thing you've got going, I'm afraid I won't be able to help you."

"So you don't know anything."

He shrugged. I was convinced the real answer was that he knew too much.

"But I will give you a piece of advice."

My heart pounded as I waited for Wade Moscowitz to reveal some obscure clue known only to insiders like him, a piece of the puzzle that, when added to all the other pieces I was collecting, would lead me to Tommee Frack's killer.

"My advice, Dr. Popper, is to stay as far away from this as you can. It's no coincidence that our friend Tommee was in PR, a field that was expressly created to make things look much better than they really are. If you're as bright as you seem, you'll forget all about this and go back to taking care of kittens—or whatever it is you do."

I knew his words of wisdom were meant to frighten me. Instead, all they did was annoy me. They sounded too much like the words I'd been hearing from Nick Burby ever since I'd gotten involved in Frack's murder.

Maybe I'm contrary by nature, but having some man tell me I'm treading in water that's too deep always makes me want to swim with the sharks.

I even came up with a name for it. Nick Burby Syndrome.

I had one more question to ask.

"Why did you leave? Public relations, I mean. Was it the whole profession? Or just Tommee?"

The hard look in Wade Moscowitz's eyes didn't match his easygoing smile. "Just remember what I told you."

Chapter 12

"No matter how much the cats fight, there always seem to be plenty of kittens."

—Abraham Lincoln

Even though my determination to press on with my investigation remained as strong as ever, my meeting with Wade Moscowitz left me feeling distinctly unsettled. He was clearly someone who knew Tommee well—not only the man, but also the kinds of things he'd been into.

I still had no idea what they could possibly have been. But from the looks of things, Wade's experience at Tommee Frack & Associates had driven him as far to the other end of the spectrum as possible.

I felt as if I were trying to process too much bewildering information, and by the time Saturday night rolled around, I was ready for a night on the town. I spent a solid hour primping, fussing endlessly with my hair and deliberating over which of two sweaters to wear. I even smeared on the mud pack I'd bought months earlier after perusing *Glamour* at my dentist's office and failing a quiz called, "Are You Your Own Best Friend?" Cat sat on the edge of the tub with a look that said I should have tried harder.

"What do you think?" I demanded, planting myself in front of Max and Lou for a second opinion. "Am I gorgeous? Or at least presentable?"

Lou wagged his tail halfheartedly, as if he desperately wanted to give the right answer but had no idea what I was talking about.

Max—the cagey thing—chose to interpret my attention as an invitation to play Slimytoy. He scooped up his beloved hot pink poodle and swung it enticingly.

"That's what I get for asking dogs for fashion advice," I grumbled.

They both looked so disappointed that I felt bad for having put them on the spot.

"Aw, come here, you guys. You know I love you both, even though you don't know Liz Claiborne from Lassie." I got down on my hands and knees for a little roughhousing. A few dog hairs on my part-cashmere sweater wouldn't hurt.

My primping received a much more positive reaction from Jimmy when he arrived ten minutes later. Unfortunately, by the time we reached the bar he'd chosen for our night on the town, the rain that had merely been an annoying drizzle all day had escalated into a torrential downpour. Not only did I end up with wet feet from a puddle I hadn't noticed as I raced through the parking lot, my hair looked as flat as when I'd gotten out of the shower.

I refused to let any of it get me down. Wellington's

was the kind of place I liked: wooden booths high enough to create the illusion of privacy, music low enough to make conversation possible, and a simple menu that spelled out exactly what you'd be getting.

If only I wasn't so nervous. This dating thing was harder than I remembered. I seemed to recall that it was supposed to be fun. Instead, as I worked on my beer while waiting for Jimmy to come back from the men's room, I felt like I was interviewing for a job— one I really wasn't qualified for.

"Sorry about that." As he neared the table, he flashed me the grin I found so irresistible. A smile like that would make it easy to forgive a lot more than a quick trip to the bathroom.

He slid into the booth opposite me. The table shook as he crashed his knee against the wooden leg.

"Jesus H. Christmas! I can't believe I did that." Sheepishly, he added, "Guess I'm a little nervous."

Having Jimmy admit that he was nervous, too, suddenly made the whole thing a lot easier.

Of course, the beer helped, too. I glanced down and saw it was almost gone.

"We should probably order," I said. "If I keep drinking on an empty stomach, you'll end up having to carry me out of here."

"Oh, yeah? I could think of worse things."

I turned my head slightly and looked at him through narrowed eyes. "I bet."

Oh, my God, I thought. I'm *flirting*.

At Jimmy's insistence, the waitress brought two more beers. At my insistence, she also brought a huge plate of buffalo wings.

I nibbled a minuscule shred of meat drenched in

bleu cheese dressing, trying to counteract the effects of the alcohol. If there was any chance of learning anything about the Frack murder tonight, I'd better do it sooner, rather than later. The way things were going, there was no telling what later would look like.

"What's going on with the Frack case?" I asked conversationally. "Anything new?"

Jimmy frowned. "It's my night off, remember? And like I told you, this stuff isn't all that interesting to me. It's just a job." He shrugged. "Besides, I thought you'd decided to take what I told you to heart. About not getting involved with this murder. I wasn't kidding when I said it's something that should be left to the police."

"From what I've seen, the police aren't all that interested."

When he started to protest, I said, "Just indulge me a little. I've got a few simple questions."

I would have added, "Pretty please," if I'd thought it would have helped. Instead, I took Jimmy's silence as permission to continue.

"For one thing, I'm still waiting to read in the paper that they found some clue that points to his killer. I figured they'd find a hair or something and do a DNA analysis."

With another shrug, Jimmy replied, "Maybe somebody committed the perfect crime. It does happen, you know."

"Not very often."

"True. And you're right about the physical evidence usually turning out to be conclusive. You must have heard the basic rule of forensics: Wherever you go, you take something with you and you leave something behind."

I shook my head.

"Like tonight, for example? When you and I leave this booth, we'll have left some evidence of us having been here behind. We'll both have lost a few hairs, we'll leave fibers from our clothes, and this floor will be covered with our shoe prints. You know, no two pairs of shoes leave the same prints, even if they started out as the exact same shoe. People walk differently and their weight is distributed differently, so after you've been wearing a pair of shoes for even a short period of time, you've already created a unique set of prints."

"I guess the rain that night obscured any footprints that were left out at Atherton Farm," I mused.

"Frack's body being left outdoors does make things a little harder. For one thing, he'd been there for hours. There's another expression: The longer you wait, the colder the trail. Being out in the elements can make it harder to find clues. The wind blows stuff away, he's got dead leaves all over him, stuff like that.

"The other side of the coin is that when you and I leave here, we'll take something with us. Like if you checked the bottom of your shoes tonight, you might find a couple of grains of dirt that contain the fertilizer the owner of this place uses around his property. Or a piece of gravel from the parking lot. Something that could prove you'd been here."

Despite his claim that he didn't like discussing business on his night off, I got the feeling Jimmy was more interested in police work than he was letting on.

"Let me show you something." I said impulsively, reaching into my purse.

I opened my spiral notebook and laid it in front of him. "I've been keeping detailed notes. Every time I talk to somebody who knows something about Frack, I write down what I learn in this book. This way, I not only have a record of everything I've learned; I also know who told me and when."

"Gee, you're really serious about this, aren't you?" He wore an expression of amazement as he turned over page after page of my notebook, glancing at the newspaper clippings I'd stapled in along with the detailed listing of facts written beneath the source, the date, and in some cases, the implications. On several pages, words like *SUSPECT!!* or *LYING?* were scrawled across the page and underlined. "I had no idea you'd covered this much ground. Boy, you've talked to everybody, haven't you? I see you even got the business card of Frack's accountant."

"Jonathan Havemeyer. I met him at the wake."

"Geez, you got everything right here. Names, dates, and serial numbers. Sooner or later, you're gonna crack this case, aren't you? Probably months ahead of Harned and his squad."

I beamed, wondering if the pride I felt was making me glow.

He continued turning the pages of my notebook. "Wow, Frack's ex-wife, his fiancée . . ." He looked up at me and grinned. "Anything about me in here?"

"Sorry," I replied with a laugh. "I'm saving that for my personal diary." Inwardly, I groaned. I was flirting again.

He raised his eyebrows. "I'd *much* rather read that."

"Oh, no, you don't." I cocked my head to one side. "A murder investigation is one thing. My inner thoughts and feelings are something else entirely."

"Which is why you should forget all about that crime stuff. Concentrate on the living. I guarantee you'll have more fun."

"Think so?"

"I know so. In fact," Jimmy continued in a husky voice, sliding the notebook back to me, "how about if later on, you let me show you something that's really worth writing about in your diary?"

I gulped, unable to come up with the words to respond to an offer like that.

"Do you like cars?" he asked.

So much for my warped mind.

"Uh, yeah, I suppose so . . ."

"I've got a couple that'll blow you away. Classics. Real collectors' items. I've got them stored in a garage in Westfield. If you like, I'll take you over to see them later."

Suddenly my head snapped up. Something over at the bar had caught my attention. I could feel the color drain from my face.

Nick.

As he headed across the bar, toward the dining room, he looked like he was auditioning for a cowboy movie. And I would have bet my autoclave that he was wearing hair gel or some other product designed to make his hair behave.

And then I noticed the woman right behind him.

"My pride and joy is a '55 Thunderbird. Mint. It's

pink, believe it or not. The other one's a '65 Porsche 550 Spyder, the same model James Dean was driving when he was killed. And I'm about to get another one . . ."

Suddenly, Jimmy stopped. He'd finally noticed that my eyes and my attention were elsewhere.

"Everything okay?"

"Um, yeah. I just . . ."

The correct ending for that sentence was, "I just made the unforgivable mistake of making eye contact with the one person in the world I would like to have hidden from." But it was too late to explain, not to mention too late to do anything about it.

Nick's expression changed the instant he saw me. The cool confidence of a handsome young stud out on the town, with his filly in tow, vanished. Suddenly, instead of looking like he was trying out for a western, he looked like he was auditioning for a horror movie.

A look of total confusion followed. I knew he was debating whether to ignore me or come over and say hello. Personally, I voted for A.

Predictably, he chose B.

"Well, look who's here!" he said with false cheerfulness. He was Cowboy Joe again as he headed over to our table. His friend followed, looking a little confused herself.

I glanced over at Jimmy, wondering what he thought of all this. But he didn't have a clue about the awkwardness of the situation unfolding before him. As far as he knew, Nick was just a neighbor or a pet owner who just happened to have the same taste in night life we did.

"Hello, Nick." Involuntarily, I tossed my head, suddenly the picture of womanly self-assurance. "What a surprise!"

He glanced at Jimmy. "Surprise is definitely the word."

"Uh, this is Officer Jimmy Nolan. Jimmy, Nick Burby."

The two men shook hands, studying each other as they did so. I'd seen that look many times before—most recently on the Animal Channel when two male penguins were checking each other out to see which one looked bigger, stronger, and more capable of winning a fight if a question arose about who owned that particular ice floe.

"Yeah, we met," Nick said. "At Atherton Farm. Tommee Frack?"

"Now I remember. You were at the wake, too, right?"

"That's right. Terrible thing."

"Awful."

We all turned our focus to Nick's date, whose Good Sport look was starting to fade.

"Oh, sorry," Nick said belatedly. "Everybody, this is Tiffany Fisk. Tiffany, this is Jimmy and this is Jessie."

Jimmy and Jessie. Way off the cuteness scale.

But *Tiffany*? Geez.

She, too, deserved a place in the Cuteness Hall of Fame. Her perky smile, her pearly pink lipstick, and her bare midriff, peeking coyly from between the top of her tight jeans and her even tighter nylon shirt, also placed her in good stead. Of course, the thick, glossy chestnut-brown hair hanging to her waist didn't hurt, either.

You're just jealous, I told myself. My inner voice sounded cranky. Even so, I had to admit she was actually kind of pretty. If you like the thin, graceful type with the extraordinary cheekbones of a supermodel.

"Well," Nick said heartily, "I guess we'll go hang out at the bar. I had no idea this place would be so crowded. Do you believe there's a twenty-minute wait for a table?"

"Hey, sit with us!" Jimmy insisted. "At least while you're waiting."

"No!" I cried, without thinking. The other three turned to stare at me.

"I mean, I'm sure they'd rather be, you know, just the two of them—"

"Right," Nick piped up quickly. "Thanks for the invitation, but we'll just—"

"Don't be silly." Jimmy had already slid across his seat, making room for another butt. I suspected the butt he was hoping for was Tiffany's. "The bar is so jammed you'll never get a seat."

I looked at Nick pleadingly, begging him to come up with a stronger counterargument. But unexpectedly, it was Tiffany who took charge.

"I'd rather wait here." She positively flowed into the booth beside Jimmy. "This is much more comfortable."

Nick cast me a forlorn look.

"Guess I'd better move over, too," I muttered lamely.

Nick sat down next to me. Even though my hip practically merged with the wall, we had no choice except to sit arm to arm and thigh to thigh. I tried crossing my legs to create a little more room, but the table was too low.

"Do you think you could move over?" Nick asked through a clenched jaw.

"Not without sitting in the parking lot," I snarled back. "Remember, this wasn't my idea."

"So how do you and Nicky know each other?" Tiffany flicked her hair off her shoulder in that way I thought only movie stars and other women who were paid enormous amounts of money to look good had mastered.

"*Nicky* and I met about three years ago." He refused to look at me. "Yes, Nicky and I go *way* back. In fact, Nicky is one of the—"

"We should probably order a drink," he interrupted. "I'll try to flag down our waitress—"

"Are you a private investigator, too?" Tiffany persisted. Her eyes were the tawny color of a lioness's.

"No. Actually, I'm a veterinarian."

She nodded approvingly. "I adore animals myself. I'm one of those people who's always had, oh, like, three cats and two dogs at a time. I don't even know where they come from. They just seem to find me."

"I'm not much for pets," Jimmy interjected. He smiled at Tiffany in a way that told me he was enjoying himself. And in the process, losing a few points in my book. "My work schedule is too irregular. It wouldn't be fair to the animal."

"What line of work are you in?" Tiffany looked absolutely enthralled, as if she were inquiring about one of life's greatest mysteries.

"I'm a cop."

"Wow! That is *totally* cool."

"Norfolk County P. D. That's me." He took a sip of his beer, clearly basking in the admiration of the little lady at his side.

"What about you, Tiffany?" Since we were all identifying ourselves by our line of work, I figured there was no reason we should let her off the hook. I was imagining all kinds of answers that suited my need to feel superior: supermarket checkout girl, manicurist, examiner for the Internal Revenue Service . . .

"I'm an attorney," she replied, dashing my hopes. "An associate with Givens, Doyle, Peet, and White."

"Ah," I said, reaching for my beer. "Then you'll be able to give Nick *lots* of pointers."

Tiffany giggled. "I already have."

I glanced over at Nick, intending to cast him a meaningful look. But he was clearly so pathetically uncomfortable that I actually felt sorry for him.

"In fact," Tiffany told me, "we were up practically all night last Friday. We started around nine, and by the time we finished, it was, like, four o'clock in the morning."

"Poor Nicky," I crooned.

"It was worth it," Tiffany assured me cheerfully. "I think all that cramming really helped Nicky with the LSAT. He took it today. Don't you agree, Nicky?"

"I think I did okay."

"Well, that's certainly good news," I said brightly.

The waitress finally acknowledged our existence, and Nick and Tiffany each ordered a drink. I hoped the conversation would move on to something neutral.

Instead, as soon as the waitress left, Tiffany said, "You still haven't told me how you two know each other." I'll give her one thing: she was persistent.

"Nick—Nicky—was investigating a dogfight ring that was based in Corchaug," I replied. "Pit bulls. I'd treated some of the dogs, and somehow he got hold of my name."

And he came to what was then my office to interview me, and we ended up going out to dinner, then making plans for the following evening . . .

"Wow. And you kept in touch ever since."

"You could say that," I said lightly.

"You two are waiting for a table, right?" said a voice from nowhere. "It's ready. I'll bring your drinks over there."

Our waitress clearly had no idea what a relief her sudden reappearance was. I was tempted to tip her a twenty.

Tiffany actually looked disappointed. "It was fun talking to you two. Enjoy the rest of your evening."

"You, too." I even managed to smile as she and Nick stood to leave. "Nice meeting you, Tiffany. And, uh, it was great seeing you again, Nicky."

"Right." I thought I could detect real agony in his eyes as he cast me a parting glance. But what the source of that agony was, I couldn't be sure.

"Seems like a nice guy," Jimmy commented after they left. "Her, too."

"Yeah," I agreed sullenly. "Very nice. The two of them should be very happy together. Lawyers deserve each other."

"Yeah, well, I'd much rather talk about us. And what we're going to do later." He leaned forward so that our noses were only inches away above the remaining buffalo wings.

I jerked back, hitting my head on the back of the booth.

"Yeow!" I yelped, sounding just like Cat.

"Hey, are you okay?"

"I'm fine." I rubbed the back of my skull, wishing the bar wasn't so crowded that asking for ice would have been a waste of time. "Sometimes I'm such a klutz—"

"Here, let's see if this helps." Jimmy reached across the table and began massaging my neck. I had to admit, it felt good. His hands were strong, and he knew exactly what to do. In fact, it felt great.

"That's okay," I said hastily. "I'm feeling better already."

"You sure?" He frowned. "Maybe we should get out of here. I could take you home—"

"No, I'm fine. Really."

I managed to get through dinner, even though, across the crowded bar, I could see Nick and Tiffany cuddling together in their booth, yukking it up. At least she was. To watch her, you'd have thought she was having a cheeseburger with Robin Williams.

As for Nick, he looked miserable. Probably because he didn't like having me along on his hot date as a chaperone.

Finally, mercifully, dinner was over. When Jimmy and I headed out the back door of the bar and found ourselves in an icy downpour, I broke the bad news.

"If you don't mind, I'd like to postpone the car thing."

"You're kidding!"

"I don't know if it was that second beer or banging my head, but I've got a killer headache . . ."

"Then why don't we just go back to your place? You can take something for your headache. In twenty minutes, it'll be gone."

"Thanks, but I just don't feel up to it." I really did feel lousy. The part about the headache was true, too.

"But it's not even eleven o'clock yet!" He added, "And I'm not on duty tomorrow. I can stay as late as you want."

I knew what he meant. And I realized that, given my mood, I didn't feel like having him stay late at all.

. . .

"Sorry about the change of plans," I said as we pulled up in front of my cottage fifteen minutes later. It was at least the hundredth time I'd apologized since we'd left the bar.

"That's okay." He said the words, but I could tell by his tone that it wasn't really okay at all. "You take care of yourself."

"You don't have to walk me in," I said. "It's pouring," I added, as if he hadn't noticed the blinding fury of drops pelting the windshield.

As I opened the car door, Jimmy sat studying me. I figured he was considering whether or not to kiss me good night. I guess I looked pretty terrible, because he just took my hand, gave it a quick squeeze, then let it go.

I really am turning into a wet blanket, I thought miserably, dashing through the rain to my front door. I can't even go on a normal date with a normal guy.

Nick Burby has ruined me for the entire male gender.

• • •

I was still cursing Nick as I lay on the couch with Cat curled up on my chest, the two of us watching *Saturday Night Live*. Max and Lou snoozed on the floor, lying beside us like two mismatched throw rugs.

Damn him, I thought, distractedly stroking Cat's soft gray fur. Why is that stupid man always getting in my way?

But instead of being angry, I was overcome with an emotion that was much more confusing. And that stupid pain in my heart was back.

At least the throbbing in my head was beginning to fade, thanks to the wonders of Advil. I could feel my muscles relaxing, and my eyelids were starting to droop.

The sound of a soft knock at the door made me jump. Cat leaped off my chest with an enraged, "Meow!"

Max, vegged out on the floor beside me, glanced up, for once only mildly interested in who the interloper might be. Lou, meanwhile, dragged himself over to the door, uttering halfhearted *woof-woof* sounds.

And then his tail went into fourth gear, a clue that whoever had come to call was somebody on his A list.

"Who is it?" I called.

"It's me. Nick."

"At *midnight*?"

I tried to sound irritated, but deep inside I knew it wasn't Nick I was trying to fool. My heart fluttered like a Victorian maiden's as I unlocked the door.

He stood on my doorstep, illuminated only by the sickly light of the single bulb overhead. He looked pretty pathetic. His hair was slicked down, and big fat raindrops slid down his face. His jacket was splattered with wet splotches, except for the shoulders, which were soaked.

Under one arm he carried a cardboard box.

"It's Leilani," he said. "Something's wrong."

"Oh, my God!" I cried. "Bring her in!"

The dogs had started up, but through some miracle they actually responded when I ordered them in no uncertain terms to behave. Something in my tone of voice must have warned them I was serious.

As Nick set the box on the table near the kitchen, I stepped into the bathroom to grab a towel. When I returned, he had unfolded the flaps that had been keeping Leilani out of the rain and Cat was trying to sneak a look inside the box.

I peered at the sweet, funny little Jackson's chameleon we'd adopted in Hawaii. One of her eyes was closed and bulging out.

"What do you think it is?" Nick asked anxiously.

I tossed the towel on the chair, then picked up the lizard and studied her. "She probably got something in her eye. A dust particle, most likely. I'll take her in the kitchen and mist it with some water. That should wash it out."

"That's *all*? I was afraid it was something serious."

"No worse than you or me getting something in our eye."

"So she's not going to die?"

"Not unless somebody runs over her."

He didn't laugh. In fact, he looked so traumatized

that I was tempted to reach over and squeeze his shoulder as a show of support.

"What about you?" I asked as he followed me into the kitchen.

"What *about* me?"

"You don't look very good. Didn't you have fun tonight with Miss America?" The tenderness I'd felt for Nick only moments earlier evaporated. I focused it on the chameleon instead, spraying her eye and feeling relieved when she opened it and began swirling it around.

"It's not what you think," Nick said, watching Leilani closely.

"How do you know what I think?"

"Because I know you. Believe me, Tiffany is just somebody who's been helping me study for the LSAT."

I snorted. "Right. Don't tell me—you two are just good friends."

"Look, it's over, okay?"

"I get it. She dumped you tonight."

"Not that it's any of your business, but no. As a matter of fact, she practically jumped on me as soon as we walked into her house."

I stalked back to the living room and put Leilani in her box. Cat was still sniffing around. "I'm sure that was terrible for you."

"As a matter of fact, it was."

"Why, for heaven's sake?" I demanded, swinging around to face him. "Even though she has a name that belongs on a jewelry store instead of a birth certificate, she's not bad looking, if you happen to like the type that looks like she spends two hours in front of the mirror just to—"

"Because it's you I want, damn it!"

His words stopped me cold. I gaped at him, experiencing one of those rare moments in my life when I was actually speechless.

"It's not as if you don't already know that, Jess."

"I thought you'd gotten over . . . us. That you'd moved on."

"I've sure been trying. But to be perfectly honest, I haven't exactly done a great job."

My head was spinning so hard I probably couldn't have put together a sentence, even if I'd known what I wanted the point of it to be.

Nick must have interpreted my silence as horror. I watched his face crumple.

"Look," he said brusquely, "I'd better go."

"It's pouring rain out there."

"It's not going to get any better."

"At least let me dry you off."

I grabbed the towel off the chair and held it up. But instead of letting me pat his hair, he took hold of my arm and pulled me close.

"Maybe I'm crazy," he said softly, "but I get the feeling you still like having me around. At least a little."

His warm breath brushed my cheek. The sensation made me dizzy.

"Yes," I admitted. "At least a little."

"Maybe a lot?"

I hesitated. "A lot."

The familiarity of his mouth on mine, the way my hand fit so perfectly against the curve of his neck, the feeling of his arms closing around me . . . it reminded me of being back in a place I'd missed terribly and couldn't quite believe I'd returned to.

"What do you want, Jess?" he asked. "Is this the part where you decide this is all a mistake? Or is this the part where you tell me you really don't want me to leave?"

I don't want you to leave, I thought. *But that doesn't mean I'm certain your staying isn't a mistake.*

I was still listening to both voices in my head, trying to decide which one to go along with, when something outside the window caught my attention. Big, white flakes were drifting downward against the backdrop of the jet black sky.

"It's snowing!" I cried.

"Wow! Look at that!"

The two of us stood in silence, still clinging to each other as we watched the first snowfall of the season sneak up on us when it thought everyone was asleep.

"What do you think?" Nick asked quietly. "Could this be a sign that we should snuggle together under the covers and keep each other safe and warm?"

"I bet the snow is making the roads slippery."

"It's pretty cold out there, too. They're probably icing up."

"And the heat in this place isn't that great . . ."

"I remember." He laughed softly. "All good reasons for me to stay. But I won't—unless you can come up with the only one that matters."

"I want you to stay."

"That's the one."

Our lovemaking was as sweet as it had always been. Our bodies moved together as if we were recreating a dance we'd come to know so well that it was as natural as breathing. Being with Nick felt like an oasis in the midst of the insanity going on in the rest of our lives.

So did simply lying next to him, my head cradled inside the curve of his shoulder.

This feels good, I thought as I drifted off to sleep. This feels right.

It definitely beat sleeping with my menagerie.

Chapter 13

"The early bird may get the worm, but the second mouse gets the cheese."

—Unknown

It wasn't until the next morning that the full magnitude of what had happened crashed down on me. There's something about sunlight that makes things seem an awful lot clearer then they do in the moonlight—or amidst the season's first snowfall.

"I guess we need to talk about last night." I wrapped my hands firmly around my mug of coffee, hoping its comforting warmth would fend off the very real threat of an anxiety attack.

Nick frowned. "Uh-oh. That doesn't sound good."

"I don't want you to take it as a sign that I've, you know, come around to your way of thinking. The whole happily-ever-after bit."

I wasn't surprised to see the muscles in his face tense. But the words needed to be said. There was no other way.

"So for you, last night was just a one-night stand."

"Kind of a cold way of putting it, isn't it?"

"It's cold, all right," he returned.

"I just don't want you to mislead you. I think . . . last time, we got our signals crossed."

He sighed impatiently. "Terrific. The trauma of Jessica Popper's less-than-perfect childhood raises its ugly head once again."

Anger rose up inside of me like a bad case of indigestion. "Thank you, Dr. Freud. Look, if I wanted to be psychoanalyzed, I'd—"

"That didn't come out right." Nick hesitated. The air around us felt unnaturally still. "Jess, I love you. I want you in my life. But this thing you have about holding on to your self-sufficiency as if it's some kind of . . . of *life raft* or something is getting to be too much, even for me. I won't let myself be jerked around emotionally at every turn."

I was suddenly finding it hard to talk. "Maybe you're right. Maybe we should just chalk last night up to bad judgment. On both our parts."

I didn't want to be without him. But he was absolutely right: unless I could make the commitment he was entitled to, unless I could let go of my own independence or fear or whatever it was that kept holding me apart from him, it wasn't fair for me to keep pulling him back.

Nick didn't deserve to be jerked around emotionally. And as strange as it may have sounded, I cared about him too much to do that to him.

That didn't keep my heart from feeling as if it was being crushed in a vise as I watched him pull on his jacket and pick up the box that was Leilani's temporary home. I was surprised to see that Cat was still sitting guard over her, and Nick gave her a quick pat on the head. Even the dogs were strangely subdued. Lou picked up his tennis ball, then immediately dropped it. Max lay on the floor, his eyes moving back and forth between us.

As Nick opened the door, I could see that the snow was already melting, and only a few white patches remained.

"Thanks for taking care of Leilani," he said.

And he was gone.

. . .

Must be allergies, I told myself, blinking hard to stop the stinging in my eyes.

Max and Lou frolicked beside me joyfully as we stepped outside into a brisk, sunny morning. With Nick gone, the cottage seemed absurdly empty, and I couldn't bring myself to stay inside another minute. A long walk was precisely what I needed to clear my head.

I'd only been outside for a few seconds when I suddenly got the eerie feeling I wasn't walking alone.

Nick? I jerked my head up, already feeling my heartbeat accelerate.

It was almost as bad. Max and Lou were bounding toward Betty, who was shuffling toward me through the heavy, wet leaves. She was encased in a fake fur coat that covered her from her neck to her knees, the "fur" dyed a shade of lime green that bore no resemblance to any living creature outside a Dr. Seuss book. Still, with the high, black patent leather boots, it worked.

" 'Morning, Betty." I shielded my eyes with my hand, hoping she wouldn't notice the guilty look I was certain was on my face.

"Looks like a *very* good morning to me," she said. Her blue eyes glittered as brightly as the silver eyeshadow that she somehow made appear tasteful.

"You're out early," I observed, sticking my hands deep inside the pockets of my fleece jacket.

"Just doing some raking."

"Personally, I've always found that using a rake is extremely helpful when raking."

She bent over to return my dogs' enthusiastic greeting. "All right, so I was spying."

Inwardly, I groaned. I knew what was coming.

"And I saw a familiar face around here," she continued.

"Did you also see the scowl on that familiar face?"

"Oh, dear. And here I just assumed from the looks of things that you two had made up."

"Leilani—the chameleon Nick and I got in Hawaii—had a problem with her eye." I could feel my cheeks reddening. "He brought her over so I could treat it."

"I see. I suppose that explains why he was here so early in the morning."

I left that one alone. In fact, I thought I was getting off easy.

But then Betty said, "He's still deeply in love with you, Jessica. And you're still—"

"The only reason he came over was that he was worried about Leilani!"

A heavy silence followed. I was only able to tolerate

it for a few seconds. "So, are you still debating between Africa and the South Pacific?"

"As a matter of fact, I've made my decision." Betty looked at me oddly. "What about you, Jessica? Have you made yours?"

. . .

I spent the rest of the day keeping maniacally busy. I filled my refrigerator with food and my drawers with freshly washed clothes. I weeded through the mountain of junk mail that was threatening to require a room of its own. I checked in with some of my clients by phone, learning that Winifred Mack's cat, James, was well enough to prowl the neighborhood again and that the Weinsteins' Pointer, King, was engaged in an energetic game of Frisbee with Justin and Jason at the moment. It was all a welcome reminder that I had more important things going on than my tumultuous social life.

One of them, I reminded myself early the next morning, was the successful recovery of the Athertons' stallion. I'd been monitoring Stormy Weather's progress regularly, checking in with Skip every couple of days. While he'd been the Athertons' manager for more than five years, Skip had spent nearly four decades in the company of horses, and I figured he knew as much about them as anyone I'd ever worked with. He'd certainly encountered just about every common horse disease in the book. But I still needed to examine Stormy Weather to determine if he was ready to be taken off penicillin.

As I drove along Green Fields Road, I felt a fluttering of nervousness. Without thinking, I'd taken the back road to Atherton Farm. I'd be driving past the spot that loomed large in my mind as The Scene of the Crime.

I expected that the entire area would be cordoned off with yellow crime-scene tape. Maybe a patrol car would be posted there around the clock.

Even so, I had a perfectly legitimate reason for being on the Athertons' property. And if worse came to worst, I was prepared to mention names. In particular, the name Officer James Nolan.

I was prepared for anything except what I found.

Nothing. Absolutely nothing.

Not a scrap of yellow plastic tape, not a single police officer, not even a Do Not Disturb sign.

I pulled my van over, this time carefully avoiding the pothole that had started all this trouble in the first place. I jumped out and headed toward the edge of the woods.

I stepped carefully so I wouldn't disturb anything. But all too soon, I saw there was no need to bother.

Not only was there no sign that only thirteen days earlier, a corpse and a dead canary had been lying in that very spot. The leaves, crusted with a few lingering patches of snow, looked as if they'd been raked over, so that not a trace of what the murderer might have left behind could be retrieved.

I was hardly an expert on murder investigations. But from what I'd learned from Nick, not to mention from the movies, I'd been certain that someone being murdered and half-buried in the woods deserved a little more attention.

The fact that the someone in question wasn't just anybody made me even more suspicious. Tommee

Frack had been well-respected, widely known, a pillar of the community. He was also highly connected—and, if Wade Moscowitz were to be believed, a major player.

My hands were shaking as I pulled up to the Athertons' house. But by this point, it was anger, not shock, that made them tremble. I pulled out my cell phone.

"Homicide," a deep male voice answered.

"I'm trying to reach Lieutenant Harned."

"Harned's on another call."

"Tell him it's Dr. Jessica Popper. From the Tommee Frack case."

"Lieutenant Harned," I heard a few seconds later. There was an edge to his voice I didn't remember hearing before.

"Lieutenant, this is Dr. Popper. I was making a house call at Atherton Farm this morning, and I happened to drive by the crime scene. I noticed the site isn't marked off. Is that usual procedure? It's only been a couple of weeks . . ."

"Yes, young lady, it is usual procedure. Once all the evidence has been gathered, we open up a crime scene as quickly as possible. That doesn't mean we're not still doing everything possible to find the killer."

"So your investigation's still ongoing?"

"An investigation is never closed until the case has been solved."

"But shouldn't the crime scene be more . . . protected? Shouldn't the investigation be more active? You could have missed something. Some clue, some piece of evidence—"

"A detective has been assigned to the case. But you've got to understand that he's got other cases to deal with." I heard him talking to someone else in a low voice. And then, he said something like, "Let me get rid of this."

"Look," the lieutenant said, not bothering to hide his impatience as he got back on the line, "this is not like TV, where everything gets wrapped up in sixty minutes. It's different in real life."

I wasn't about to let him off the hook that easily. "Lieutenant, did you know that Tommee and his ex-wife, Merrilee, kept canaries, and that she never let go of the idea that one day he was going to come back to her? And did you know that he met his fiancée back when she was an exotic dancer who used canaries in her act?"

There was icy silence at the other end of the line.

"Besides," I pressed, "no one's ever gotten back to me. I'm the one who found his body, for goodness' sake! No one ever contacted me again!"

"We already have your statement."

"But it's true of everyone I've spoken to! Not one of them has been approached by the police. It's made me wonder if you cops are doing anything about this investigation at all!"

"What do you mean, *everyone* you've spoken to?"

Something in his tone warned me to be very careful of what I said next.

"I've had a few conversations with people who knew Tommee Frack. That's all."

"Maybe you just haven't been talking to the right people."

Now it was my turn to be silent. It wasn't that I agreed with him, and it wasn't that I couldn't think of anything to say.

It was that something about the way this conversation was going was setting off alarms in my head.

"Listen, Dr. Popper." Harned's voice was brittle. "Interfering with police business is a serious offense, one you could be prosecuted for. I strongly suggest you stop bothering people and leave this investigation to us."

His tone told me that, at least for now, I'd better let him believe I was doing exactly that.

· · ·

I sat in the van for a minute or two, trying to digest what I'd just heard.

From the way the newspapers presented it, Tommee Frack's murder was one of the biggest things that had happened on Long Island in anyone's memory. It was up there with Amy Fisher and Joey Buttafuoco, not to mention both the trial and the funeral of John Gotti.

Yet Lieutenant Harned practically made it sound as if it had been dumped on a back burner.

It made absolutely no sense.

I stared at my cell phone. I was dying to call Nick. I wanted to repeat the conversation I'd had with Harned. I wanted Nick's opinion on whether the lieutenant had been telling the truth about this being the way all murder investigations were handled.

Of course, I couldn't call Nick. I had to start getting used to not thinking about Nick at all.

Ruminating in my van would accomplish nothing. I climbed out, figuring I'd make a quick social call before heading over to the barn to check on Stormy Weather. With all the suspicions and questions that were running through my brain, taking the time to make small talk was bound to do me good.

I peered through the window as I knocked on the back door. I could see the Athertons sitting at their kitchen table, sipping coffee over a blue-and-white checked tablecloth. They looked like they were posing for Norman Rockwell: Violet with her delicate wisps of white hair and her withered, fragile hands; Oliver with his tall, spindly frame folded into his chair, his face gaunt yet still heroic.

Violet came to the door, her mug in her hand. "Jessie! What a nice surprise!"

"Actually, Skip's expecting me. I'm following up on Stormy Weather's throat infection. I thought I'd stop off to say hello before heading over to the stable."

"Do you have time for a cup of coffee?"

The aroma was seductive. "A quick one."

As Violet set a mug down in front of me, she studied me more closely. "You look shaken, dear. Is everything all right?"

"It's just being back here again, I guess. After what happened last time."

Violet shuddered. "I know. It's horrible, isn't it? I haven't been able to think about anything else ever since it happened. Imagine, a murder victim, right here on our property. And I'm sure it was even more traumatic for you, since you're the one who found him." She placed her hand on her husband's arm. "Don't you think that must have been upsetting for Jessie, dear?"

"What's that?" Ollie asked. He looked surprised, as if he'd only just realized that a conversation was going on around him.

"He refuses to wear his hearing aid," Violet confided. "He's afraid it'll make him look old. I keep telling him he *is* old.

"Jessie found that dead man on our property two weeks ago, remember?" she shouted at Ollie.

"Terrible, terrible." Ollie shook his head. "Is there more coffee, Vi?"

Violet cast me a conspiratorial look as she brought his cup to the counter for a refill. "Thank goodness we have Skip to run the farm."

"Have the police been here?" I asked Violet.

"The police?" She frowned. "Why, you saw them yourself, didn't you? The day you found the body?"

"No, I mean have they come around to question you since that day?"

She looked confused for a few seconds. "No. Unless they came when Ollie was here by himself. Of course, I hardly ever leave him alone these days. I'm just not sure he can manage. In fact, I don't think he's been on his own since then."

"Atherton Farm has been in our family for generations," Ollie began, speaking slowly. From what I could tell, he didn't appear to be talking to anyone in particular. "My great-great grandfather bought this land right after the Civil War. . . ."

"Oh, Ollie, I'm sure Jessie's already heard all this."

He scowled. "How do you know that?"

"Because you tell the same story to everybody who walks in here!"

"I bet she hasn't seen the pictures."

"What pictures?" I asked politely.

"What pictures? The pictures of the farm, of course!"

"Jessie doesn't want to see those boring old pictures," Violet insisted.

"I'll go get 'em. I think I remember where they are."

He shuffled off, leaving the coffee his wife had just put in front of him untouched.

Violet shook her head. "He's getting worse. I can't even trust him to go to the supermarket. I send him for milk and lettuce, and he comes home with heavy cream and a head of cabbage. And the way he goes on and on about this farm and his great-great grandfather." She sighed. "To think that the old fool nearly lost it. If our daughter hadn't been here that time. I don't know what would've happened."

"Nearly lost Atherton Farm?" I was sure I'd misunderstood.

"Nearly had it stolen out from under him, is more like it. 'Course, Ollie doesn't see it that way. I still worry that that man will come back some time when neither me or Gwennie are here and trick Ollie into signing something."

"Somebody is trying to trick you out of your land?"

"Oh, they're offering a fair price. I'll give them that. At least, it sounds like a lot of money to me. A crazy amount, in fact. Only where on earth would we go if we sold this place? Ollie and me, we've been on this land practically our whole lives. He grew up here, for heaven's sake. Why he would even let somebody like that in the door is beyond me."

She glanced around, as if checking to make sure her husband wasn't listening. " 'Course, he's doing that kind of thing more and more these days. He doesn't have the sense he used to have. His hearing's going, but that's just part of it. It's his mind I worry about. And his judgment."

"Who was this man, Violet?"

"Oh, I don't remember his name. Some young fella in a suit. Looked important. At first, I figured he was selling something. I wasn't even going to let him in, but Ollie got to the door before I did. Next thing I know, he's sitting on the couch with these legal papers spread out all over the coffee table. Soon as Gwennie figured out what was going on, she threw that young man out on his ear!"

"When was this?"

"Let me think . . . It was just after Gwennie got here, and she came the weekend after we changed the clocks. I guess that makes it some time at the beginning of November."

"Right before the body turned up in your woods. . . ."

"Now that you mention it, yes. A week or so earlier, I suppose. I hadn't put the two things together in my mind, but I think you're right. You don't think they're connected, do you?"

"I honestly don't know." It could have been a coincidence, of course. The Athertons owned one of the few remote wooded areas around, making it an obvious place to drop off a corpse.

Then again, when it came to trying to hide the body, the murderer hadn't exactly knocked himself out.

"Violet, do you think you can remember the man's name and where he was from? It's really important."

She waved her hand in the air. "Goodness, I can't even remember what I had for dinner last night!"

"Did he tell you the name of his company?"

"Like I say, I can't—"

"Did he leave anything behind? A contract for you to look over? Or maybe a business card?"

"A card!" She brightened. "Yes, he did leave a card. I was so mad about the way he came barging in here that I was going to throw it away. But Ollie saves everything. That's another thing he's been doing lately. He won't throw a thing out. Every plastic bag, every piece of mail—"

"Can I see the card?"

"Well, now." Violet frowned. "I'd have to remember where he put it."

"It's *really* important."

"Maybe in the junk drawer . . . That's as good a place as any to look."

"I'm sorry to put you through so much trouble," I told her. "It's just that I really need to know who's interested in buying your land."

Violet didn't seem to hear me. "I'll never find it," she grumbled. "That old man's got so much junk in there. The other day I went looking for a coupon I remembered seeing. Seventy-five cents off Clorox. I don't think the store brand works nearly as good, even though Gwennie's always telling me they're the same. And do you know what I found in there? The cardboard from a ten-pack of triple-A batteries. Can you imagine? He was even saving that."

I stood close by, watching as she rifled through what she referred to as her junk drawer. It was well named, and Ollie's fondness for packaging was only part of the problem. I saw fliers from chimney-cleaning services, unopened credit card offers, and even an advertisement for Sears' Back to School sale.

"I don't know where it is," she insisted. "There's so much stuff in here. I wish that one of these days he'd just—"

"Is that it?" A small white business card protruded from a pile of coupons.

"Could be."

I picked it up and studied it, never letting on that my heart was pounding furiously.

Andrew Karp, it read. *Vice President of Acquisitions, Pomonok Properties.*

Seeing the name sent a chill through me. Pomonok Properties, one of George Babcock's oldest clients— until Tommee Frack stole it away. The firm's president, Joseph DeFeo, had been quoted in Tommee's *Newsday* obituary, singing his praises.

"Is that what you wanted?" Violet looked exasperated.

"Yes. Thank you. Would you mind if I kept this?"

"Take it. Get it out of here. Far as I'm concerned, it's one less piece of paper. Besides, I don't want Ollie getting it into his head that he should call that man. These days, I never know what he's going to do, the old goat."

We both looked up at the sound of footsteps shuffling across the linoleum. I hoped he hadn't heard her.

He didn't seem to. He held a stack of photographs out to me.

"Here they are. This is Gwennie, when she was growing up. Her high school graduation, her sweet sixteen, they're all here."

"Finish your coffee," Violet told him. I noticed

that this time, she spoke much more gently. "Jessie doesn't have time for that right now. She has to go look at Stormy Weather."

"What's this about the weather? It's not going to storm. Look outside. The sun is shining!"

The look Violet cast me was somewhere between desperate and heartbroken.

Chapter 14

"A bird is known by his feathers."
—Yiddish Proverb

It was time to learn more about Pomonok Properties. The company's name was coming up too many
times, and in too many different contexts, for me to
ignore.

But first, I had more practical matters to attend to.
I put aside all thoughts of Tommee Frack as I stopped
in at the Athertons' barn to determine whether
Stormy Weather was well enough to be taken off medication. As I looked him over, Skip stood near the wall
of the barn with his hands jammed into the pockets of
his loose, ill-fitting jeans, giving me space but clearly
interested in what was going on. His weatherworn
face was pulled into a serious expression, but I was
pretty sure I saw admiration in his eyes.

"There you go, boy," I said soothingly, stroking
the stallion's nose after I'd finished the examination.

His temperature was normal, the swelling in his throat had gone down...he was good to go. "You're doing just fine. We can take you off the antibiotics. I bet you feel a heck of a lot better, right?"

He nuzzled me in response. The feeling of his warm, hot breath on my neck made me laugh.

Skip shook his head. Grinning, he said, "You sure are a softy."

"About some things, anyway." I patted Stormy Weather's neck affectionately. "You're *definitely* back to your old self, aren't you? Wait—what's this?" I reached into my pocket. "An apple? And look, it has your name on it!"

I held out the apple, the biggest Delicious I'd been able to find, within the stallion's reach. He nuzzled me again before nibbling at it. The unexpected gesture made me wonder if, somehow, he understood that I'd had something to do with healing his excruciating sore throat.

"Feels good to be able to swallow again, doesn't it?" I murmured.

"He doesn't understand a word you're saying, you know," Skip teased.

"I don't know about that," I countered. "I think he understands plenty."

"Maybe you're right. Sure looks like he knows who his friends are."

After Skip and I spent a few minutes discussing Stormy Weather's recuperation, I went straight home, basking in a true sense of accomplishment. But I quickly shifted my focus. With my gray feline computer buddy on my lap, I logged on to the *Long Island*

Business Beat website, then held my breath as I typed in the words "Pomonok Properties" under "Search."

"Whoa!" I cried, astounded at how often it was mentioned.

Cat merely blinked. I scratched her neck and ears distractedly, clicking on to one article after another. All of them recounted success stories. Pomonok Properties to Build Long Island's Largest Office Complex. Pomonok Properties Breathes New Life into Failing Strip Mall. Zoning Change Results in New Industrial Park for Pomonok Properties.

When I came across a piece entitled "Joseph DeFeo of Pomonok Properties Named Man of the Year," I smiled knowingly. Sure enough; in addition to giving Pomonok Properties super publicity, the article applauded the Chamber of Commerce for bestowing this great honor, the Somerset Gardens Catering Facility for sponsoring the event, and the Police Officers Choir for providing the entertainment. They all came out looking like heroes.

Still, I was frustrated. All I was getting from *Long Island Business Beat* was glowing reports. Greedily I read about the valuable contribution the firm made to Long Island's economy, the sorely needed improvements it made to the dilapidated malls it renovated, the public service it provided by building luxury condominiums for young professionals in need of gourmet kitchens and recessed lighting.

The whole thing reminded me of everything I had read and heard about Tommee Frack.

None of this was news, I realized. It was *all* public relations.

At least I have a name that gives me a place to

start, I thought. Joseph DeFeo. Man of the Year. He knew both Tommee and George Babcock, and his company was certainly a force on Long Island.

I wondered if he had a dog registered with the State of New York. But I quickly decided that instead of going the sneaky route, I'd head right into the belly of the beast. It was time to take my wool blazer out of the closet again.

•   •   •

Pomonok Properties' headquarters was an eight-story office complex in Island Terrace, right off the Long Island Expressway. The building was covered in mirrors, giving it an impenetrable look.

That image didn't help much in the confidence department as I rode the elevator to the top floor. When I stepped off, I found myself surrounded by huge windows. Beyond was a panorama of Long Island—or at least its businesses. Office buildings and shopping centers stretched out as far as I could see, a crazy quilt of commerce. And Pomonok Properties stood at its very heart.

I pushed through the pair of glass doors that opened into a reception area. There I was confronted by an entire wall of glossy color photographs of apartment complexes, commercial buildings, and shopping centers. All were spiffed up to look their enticing best. The garden apartments had freshly painted shutters, the lawns were lush green and freshly mowed. None of the office buildings had a single car in the lot, making them look more like architectural models than actual workplaces. Even the shopping centers looked like illustrations in a children's book, rows of carefully maintained shops that sold only attractive things like flowers and ice cream and fresh produce in bright Crayola colors.

On the opposite wall, in the same three-dimensional letters that decorated the Tommy Frack & Associates office, was what I took to be Pomonok Properties' slogan: *Building a Better, Brighter Long Island!*

I stepped right up to the receptionist. "Excuse me. I was wondering if I might speak with Mr. DeFeo."

"He's in a meeting. Do you have an appointment?"

"I'm afraid not. But I only need five minutes," I added hastily.

She was unimpressed. I tried another tack. "George Babcock suggested I drop by," I improvised.

A spark of interest flared in her dull eyes. "Can I ask what this is about?"

"I really need to speak with Mr. DeFeo directly."

She kept her eyes on me as she picked up the phone. "Jane? There's a woman here to talk with Joey. No, no appointment. But she said George Babcock sent her."

Holding the phone away from her ear, she said to me, "I didn't get your name."

"Jessica Popper."

"You're not a lawyer, are you?"

I had to stop myself from laughing. "No."

She spoke into the phone again. "She said she only needs a few minutes with him. Sure, I'll hold."

Another minute passed before she said, "Thanks, Jane. I'll tell her to wait."

I stood in the reception area, admiring the architectural wonders that constituted Pomonok Properties and a better, brighter Long Island. Finally, a gaunt woman whose navy blue suit had the crisp look of a military uniform emerged from behind a door.

"You can come with me." She turned, walking off without waiting to see if I followed commands well. Then, abruptly, she stopped and faced me. "George Babcock sent you?"

I nodded.

"Really." I couldn't tell if she sounded impressed or incredulous.

She led me into a huge corner office with windows that covered two sides. The other walls were decorated with photographs. These were much more artful than the pictures in the reception area. One showed a strip mall in the snow, kind of a modern-day Currier and Ives. Another showed an office building at night, its windows glowing like stars.

But there were other photographs, as well. I found these much more interesting. Appearing in all of them was the same man, with thick black eyebrows and an exceptionally large stomach. I assumed he was De-Feo. As for the other people in the photographs, I recognized most of them from Tommee's funeral.

What really caught my attention, however, were the two photos that featured Tommee Frack. In one, he stood with Joe DeFeo on his left and the zoning board member I'd seen at the funeral on his right. The second showed Tommee, Joey, the highway commissioner, and Gene Guilford, the former Norfolk County executive.

Tommee, posing with Joey and a bunch of other "players." Yet hadn't George Babcock said that Tommee Frack & Associates had become Pomonok Properties' public relations firm only quite recently?

I sat in one of the available chairs, choosing a seat that put the photographs behind me. Almost immediately, the man with the stomach and the eyebrows strode in. Up close, I saw that it wasn't only his eyebrows that gave him that distinctive Neanderthal look. His five o'clock shadow was so heavy it would no doubt need a lawn mower to remove—and it was barely three o'clock. But it was his eyes that were the most disconcerting. They were such a deep shade of brown they appeared almost black. Yet the darkness I saw in them had nothing to do with their color.

"I don't usually meet with someone without an appointment," Joe DeFeo declared in a gruff voice.

"Thanks for seeing me," I replied politely. I leaned forward in my seat. "I just need a minute or two—"

"I never got your name."

"Dr. Jessica Popper."

He barely seemed to be listening as he lowered his massive form into a swivel chair that screeched in protest. He sat in silence for what felt like a very long time, squinting at me across the massive desk that dominated the spacious room and drumming on the desk nervously. A trio of rings adorned his stubby fingers: a thick platinum wedding band, a chunky gold college ring with a massive red stone, and a monstrous diamond pinky ring that dwarfed them both. "Did I understand this right? Babcock sent you to see me?"

"He didn't *send* me, exactly. He just mentioned that you two had worked together for a long time—that he'd handled public relations for your company—and I thought you'd be a good reference. I'm very interested in hiring a firm, and—"

"*Babcock* suggested you talk to me?" Joe DeFeo didn't look as if he believed me.

"Well, yes." First rule of sleuthing: When in doubt, lie. "George told me you were one of his first clients."

"What else did he say?"

So far, he was the one asking all the questions. Things weren't proceeding quite the way I'd planned.

"That you'd worked together for a very long time and that he'd done a lot for your firm. As I started to tell you, I'm a veterinarian, and I'm about to hire a public relations firm. I met with George the other day, and I'm still trying to decide if he's the person to go with. So I thought that speaking with some of his other clients might help me get a better feel for what he really does. For his clients, I mean."

DeFeo's eyebrows twitched infinitesimally. "Are you aware that Babcock isn't handling my PR anymore? Did he tell you that?"

"Yes, he did mention you'd had a . . . parting of the ways. Which made me even more anxious to talk to you. You see, hiring a public relations firm is a big step for me. I'm not a big company. I'm just one person—"

"Did he tell you who we went with instead?"

I thought desperately, wondering how much to divulge. I decided to play it safe. "He didn't have to. I'd read that Pomonok Properties was a client of Tommee Frack & Associates."

He studied me thoughtfully. I studied him back, wearing the most innocent expression I could muster. "Maybe you can tell me something about the difference between Tommee Frack and George Babcock. Since you had experience with both, I mean."

His eyes shifted away from mine. "Well, of course I

hardly knew Tommee. I—that is, Pomonok Properties had just signed on with him when that terrible thing happened."

I was glad the photographs of Joe and Tommee were behind me. Otherwise, my natural instinct would surely have been to glance over at them. Maybe Joe DeFeo's company hadn't officially been Tommee Frack's client for long. But from the looks of things, the two of them had been buddies for quite some time.

There was no reason for him to know I'd picked up on that.

"Look, I really don't have time for this," he said curtly. "The only reason I agreed to see you was because I was curious about what Babcock was up to. All I can tell you is that when it comes to public relations, The Babcock Group is fine. George does a perfectly good job. I changed firms because I thought maybe Tommee could do an even better job. I felt it was time to try something different—from a business perspective, I mean. Of course, that's all water under the bridge now."

He stood up. Our meeting was over.

"Give George my regards, will you? Tell him I wish him the best."

As I walked out, I snuck one last glance at the photographs. They said so much more than the little I'd been able to pry out of Joe DeFeo, and I wanted to imprint them in my brain.

I'd come looking for answers, but all I'd come up with was more questions. From all indications, there was a great deal more to Tommee's business than just getting coverage in *Long Island Business Beat* and on

Channel 14. Tommee seemed to have been in the middle of everything—business, government, the media.

What his role was, I had yet to learn. And I couldn't shake the feeling that I wouldn't be able to find his killer until I had a better understanding of what he was up to.

Fortunately, I still had a couple of tricks up my sleeve.

. . .

I was glad I'd had the foresight to hold on to the business card Jonathan Havemeyer, CPA, had given me at Tommee's funeral. At the time, I'd thought Havemeyer was one of the least interesting people I had ever met. Now, I wondered if he had the potential to be one of the most useful.

Even before I left Pomonok Properties' parking lot, I pulled out my cell phone and dialed the number at the bottom of the card I'd stapled into my notebook. He answered on the second ring.

"Havemeyer." I'd forgotten how high-pitched his voice was. If I hadn't known better, I'd have thought I was talking to a teenaged girl.

"Mr. Havemeyer, my name is Jessica Popper. You probably don't remember me, but we met at—"

"Frack's funeral. Of course I remember you."

"You do?"

"I remember everyone I meet."

"I'm impressed. You must have a good mind, not to mention an excellent eye for detail."

Actually, I found it kind of creepy.

"So you probably also remember that I'm a veterinarian," I continued. "I have a mobile services unit that treats animals all over Norfolk County. Anyway, you gave me your business card on that terribly sad day—"

"I remember."

"And I suddenly find myself in need of an accountant. The person I was using is moving to another state. I was wondering if you and I could get together to talk . . . maybe even later today?"

To my delight, he agreed.

The rest of the morning was filled with house calls. As I periodically checked my voice mail, I found more messages from clients and scheduled additional appointments throughout the day. But I made sure I left enough time to rush home and shower before hopping into my VW and scurrying to my late afternoon meeting with Tommee Frack's former accountant.

At five minutes past four, I sat opposite Jonathan Havemeyer. He ran his one-man operation out of a complex like Nick's, a cluster of small buildings occupied by other small businesses: a pediatric dentist, an architect, two lawyers who apparently specialized in estate planning. Havemeyer's office, like the man himself, was strictly no-nonsense. White walls, gray carpeting, the requisite framed diplomas and certifications behind him. His personal life—assuming he had one—was clearly not invited to encroach upon his professional life. No photographs, no homemade paperweights, not even a decorative pencil mug.

As for the man himself, he was just as buttoned up as last time. He looked like someone who routinely had his entire being cleaned and pressed.

"It's nice to see you again," I began politely. "And under much happier circumstances, I might add."

He peered at me through the thick lenses of his eye-glasses. They made his eyes so blurry I was having trouble focusing on them. "What can I do for you, Dr. Popper?"

So much for chitchat.

"As I mentioned on the phone, I'm looking for an accountant . . ."

We spent the next thirty-six minutes talking about my billing procedure, my experience with bad debt, my estimated tax payments—in short, the kinds of things I generally tried to think about as little as possible in my day-to-day life. While I had to admit it wasn't the most scintillating conversation I'd ever had, Jonathan Havemeyer clearly knew his stuff.

Still, I hadn't really come here to discuss my bottom line.

"I'm sure you'd do a wonderful job," I said as a way of wrapping up the business portion of our meeting. "But I'll be talking to a few people before making a final decision. The relationship between a small-business person and an accountant is extremely personal. I want to be certain I choose the right person."

"Of course. Why don't you give me a call once you decide?"

"I'll do that. Thanks for your time. I appreciate it, especially since I can see how busy you are." I motioned toward the pile of envelopes on his desk, the only clutter in an otherwise meticulous room. "Especially if you get that much mail every day."

"Interestingly, most of it's for our friend Tommee."

I shook my head to show I didn't understand.

"Payments. Remember I told you that I was amazed at how many clients Tommee had?"

"I remember."

"They're still paying him. The checks keep coming in, even now." He picked up the pile. "The odd thing is that Tommee is making as much money dead as when he was alive."

"Maybe some of his clients haven't heard."

"Oh, they've heard. I saw most of them at his funeral." He smirked. "They all know he's dead. They just don't seem to know that means they don't have to pay him anymore."

"Maybe it's some kind of time-lag thing," I suggested. "A paperwork glitch in Accounts Payable."

Havemeyer eyed the stack in his hand warily. "I suppose all this money will just be passed along to Babcock."

I sat up straighter. "George Babcock? What does he have to do with this?"

"Do you know George?"

"Yes. I mean, we've met. In addition to shopping for a new accountant, I've also been exploring the possibility of hiring a public relations firm. I met with George last week."

"You'd better hire him now, while you still have the chance." Jonathan smiled coldly. "Babcock's about to get more business than he can handle."

"I don't understand."

"I went to the reading of Tommee's will three days ago. His lawyer said he'd just revised it in October. He also said Tommee had made some dramatic changes, including leaving his entire business to George."

"But—why—how—?"

"There's no reason for you to know this, of course, but Babcock gave Tommee his start. Then Tommee started his own PR firm, one that competed directly with George's. He even walked off with half of George's clients."

"How do you know all this?"

"I used to be Babcock's accountant."

Small world, I thought, still dizzy over having learned that George—who had every reason to hate Tommee—had inherited his business. In fact, it's turning out to be smaller than I ever imagined.

"According to the will," Jonathan went on, "Tommee had a change of heart. He said in it that he wanted to make amends. That was why he left his greatest asset, his business, to George."

"I'm curious: When did you stop working for Babcock and start working for Tommee?"

"Right after Tommee left The Babcock Group." Sounding suddenly defensive, he continued, "Tommee offered me three times what Babcock was paying me! There was no way I could turn down an offer like that!"

"Of course not. Who could blame you?"

He didn't acknowledge my words of support. "Besides, it was an exciting time for Tommee. Overnight, he went from being a mere employee of The Babcock Group to becoming the center of the universe, at least in terms of Long Island business. Within weeks, he started picking up even more accounts in addition to the ones he'd had at the start. It was absolutely phenomenal."

"More accounts? Like . . . five or six?"

"Like twenty or thirty. Good ones, too. Local government, even. He started doing PR for the town. They have their own internal public relations department, but Tommee did extra work for them. Setting up press conferences, arranging special events, you name it. And he'd barely been in business a month when he picked up the Norfolk County PBA, the police union, as a client.

"But the bulk of his business was always private companies, everything from that fancy catering place Hallsworth Hall to big land develpers. Charities, too. Not-for-profits, but still huge, powerful organizations. A lot of the work was supposed to be pro bono. At least that's what he wanted people to believe. But I knew the truth—that those clients were sending in fat checks every month, too.

"Tommee was everywhere. Every high-profile event, every restaurant opening, all the chic events out on the East End like the Hampton Classic Horse Show and the annual Long Island Feeds Long Island fund-raiser.

"From day one, the money just kept rolling in. That's always the bottom line, isn't it? Money? Even though Tommee loved being the center of attention, hobnobbing with movie stars and CEOs, even being Mr. Popular pales beside having a fat bank account."

Everything Jonathan Havemeyer was telling me was consistent with what I'd heard from everyone else I'd spoken to, not to mention the photographs I'd seen on the walls of Pomonok Properties. Tommee Frack *was* everywhere.

And I still didn't understand why.

"Wow. What a success story," I gushed. Fishing for some insight, I added, "But I guess he deserved it. Everyone says he was an incredibly talented man."

"For Tommee, it was a dream come true. It's like he had a fairy godmother or something."

"But it sounds as if it all happened so fast," I mused. "And so easily. What was his secret? How did he do it?"

Havemeyer shrugged. "Who knows? Don't ask me; I'm just the accountant. For all I know, he made a deal with the devil."

I nodded. Maybe he had. Had it killed him? "And now, it's all going to George Babcock. In the end, he's the one who benefited most from his protégé's success."

And perhaps the one who had the most to gain from Tommee Frack's untimely death, I wondered.

"George certainly hit the jackpot," Havemeyer agreed. "Now that he's getting sixty new clients, he'll have to get bigger offices, hire more people, and start thinking on a whole new scale." More to himself than to me, he mused, "I wonder if he needs a new accountant."

I pretended I hadn't heard. I stood and was about to say goodbye when I thought of something else.

"What about you, Mr. Havemeyer? Did Tommee leave you anything in his will? It sounds as if you were with him from the very beginning."

"Yes, I was." His tone became strained. "In fact, he used to say to me, 'Jonathan, I never could have done it without you. I'm good at shaking hands and making people feel important, but the sad truth is that I don't know the first thing about how to run a business.' And it was completely true. The man couldn't have balanced a checkbook if his life depended on it. He really couldn't have done it without me."

"So what did he leave you?"

In response, he opened his top drawer and took out what looked like a pen. Gold-plated, but a pen, nonetheless.

"A pen?" I asked, confused.

"That's right." He stared at it as if he couldn't quite believe it himself. "But not just any pen. His favorite pen. In his will, he said he valued my loyalty as much as my ability, and he hoped I'd remember him every time I used this pen."

He tossed the pen back in the drawer. "He got that right."

I was still replaying the words of our conversation as I left Jonathan Havemeyer's office.

I remembered that after talking to Babcock's receptionist, Belle, about what really went on at The Babcock Group, I'd asked myself if George Babcock's business was something he was willing to kill for.

I was convinced I had the answer.

• • •

It was already dark by the time I came out of Havemeyer's office. As I headed toward my red Beetle, parked right outside, I noticed something white stuck under my windshield wiper.

A parking ticket? I thought, instantly outraged over what I was sure was some overly zealous cop's mistake.

When I got closer, I saw it was the wrong shape. Probably a takeout menu from a local Chinese restaurant, or maybe an ad for a car wash. My scruffy VW was certainly a likely candidate.

But when I grabbed it, I saw it was an envelope, the

kind that comes with a greeting card. It was sealed, with no writing on it.

A secret admirer? I wondered if someone—like, oh, maybe Nick Burby—had thought it would be cute to communicate this way. I glanced around the dimly lit lot. There were no signs of life, and I didn't see his black Maxima anywhere. If Nick was behind this, he was lying low.

I got into my car, holding the envelope with both hands. All the raw emotions that had been dredged up that morning as I watched Nick walk away were suddenly back. I dreaded reading whatever was inside. If it *was* from Nick, it could only be one of two things: a desperate plea for us to get back together . . . or a complete kiss-off.

I didn't know which would be worse.

I was tempted to toss it out, sight unseen. But I've never had much willpower. Even though I figured this was one of those no-win situations, that whatever was inside was bound to throw me into a state of emotional turmoil, I couldn't resist opening it.

When I slid my finger under the flap and tore it open, I was hit with a wave of disappointment. Empty. There was no note in the envelope.

I peered inside, utterly bewildered. I didn't stay that way for long.

Lying at the bottom was a single yellow canary feather.

Chapter 15

"A forest bird never wants a cage."

—Unknown

My first instinct was to lock the car doors. Then, with the metallic taste of fear in my mouth, I turned the key in the ignition and hightailed it out of the parking lot.

As I drove home, I nervously checked my rearview mirror every few seconds to see if the black Jeep was following me. There was no sign of it. And when I reached Joshua's Hollow and turned onto Minnesauke Lane, mine was the only car on the road.

I glanced nervously from side to side as I scurried from my car to the cottage. From what I could tell, the only thing out there was the stillness of the dark November night.

But once I made it safely inside, my fear turned to anger. I resented the fact that George Babcock or whoever was behind these cheap scare tactics thought he could control me. The person who was going to the trouble of tailgating me and leaving nasty surprises on my windshield clearly wanted me to mind my own business. But the more he tried to frighten me away, the more determined I became to uncover the truth about the murder.

I did my best to discourage my canine entourage's usual welcome home party and ignored the socks Max had dragged out of my laundry pile and strewn across the furniture and throw rugs. Instead, I barreled past Max and Lou and made a beeline for my bedroom. I put the envelope containing the canary feather in the top dresser drawer. I'd just closed it when I heard Max's sharp bark. I stiffened, instantly on alert for the sound of an intruder.

When I stuck my head out the doorway, I saw both dogs hovering near the refrigerator. And realized my Westie was just reminding me it was dinnertime.

"Good going," I chided myself. "See how cool, calm, and collected you are?"

I picked up Max and cradled him in my arms, sorry I'd blown him off. Even more, I was suddenly in desperate need of a terrier hug. Of course, the usual shower of dog kisses was part of the deal. I didn't mind. They were more soothing than aloe. Naturally Lou joined in, slurping my hand as if it was a popsicle.

Then Cat slunk over, announcing her presence with a loud meow. I picked her up, too, relishing the feel of her soft fur against my skin. She and Max eyed each other warily, but at least for a little while, my household enjoyed a rare state of peace and togetherness reminiscent of the Age of Aquarius. Even Prometheus chimed in, squawking, "*Awk!* I don't talk to telemarketers. Please don't call again. *Awk!*"

For a few moments, I actually felt better. It was just my animals and me, the rest of the world be damned.

On my way into the kitchen, I noticed the blinking light on my phone machine and pressed "Play."

"*Hey, Jess. It's me, Jimmy. Thought I'd stop over tonight about eight to see if you're around. I can't wait to show you the two loves of my life.*" He chuckled. "*My cars, that is. You won't be disappointed. I promise.*"

A welcome distraction, albeit the human variety. I decided not to mention the feather to Jimmy when he dropped by that night. Even though I had no intention of letting cheap scare tactics stand in my way, I wasn't up for another lecture.

After serving up three bowls of dinner and replenishing the birdseed in my parrot's dish, I recognized that this rare moment of relative silence while the animals ate afforded me the perfect opportunity to concentrate. Plopping down on the couch, I opened my notebook and jotted down everything I remembered from the conversations I'd had that day: Violet Atherton, Joey DeFeo at Pomonok Properties, Jonathan Havemeyer, CPA . . . and of course my telephone call to Lieutenant Harned, not that there had been much to it.

At that point, I'd had enough of the nasty business of murder, at least for the moment. The time had come to put my efforts into something more pleasant. By the time eight o'clock rolled around, I'd showered, put on my favorite sweater and my best pair of pants, and pulled my hair back with a plastic geegaw I'd bought months earlier but never had the confidence to wear in public. I'd promised myself that I was going to forget all about Frack and his friends, lovers, and enemies for the next few hours. I was going to have some pure, unadulterated fun.

Jimmy was right on time. As soon as his car pulled into the driveway, Lou began barking his head off. Max tried to burrow through the front door with his powerful paws, as determined as if he were attacking a badger's hideaway. Cat simply looked at me and blinked. If I hadn't known any better, I would have thought I saw her shaking her head disapprovingly at their antics.

"Who needs a doorbell?" I asked them. I kissed Cat's silky head and gave each of my puppies a quick hug. Then I dashed out, calling, "Wish me luck, guys!" before slamming the door.

"I'm really glad you decided to go out with me tonight." Jimmy grinned at me across the front seat as we drove south along Governor's Road toward Westfield, a town in the middle of Long Island. "Kind of surprised, too."

"Surprised? Why?"

He glanced at me. "Last time, by the end of the night, you acted like you couldn't get away from me fast enough."

"That's not true! I mean, maybe that's what you thought, but that's not how I felt."

"Don't tell me you *really* had a headache."

"As a matter of fact, I did."

And a Nick Burby-ache.

I was debating whether or not to tell Jimmy the real reason for my hot-and-cold behavior that night at Wellington's when he said, "Anyway, I was kind of nervous about calling you again. I didn't know what kind of reaction I'd get."

"Well, I'm here." I smiled at him. "And very happy to be here, I might add."

"I guess you must *really* like classic cars."

I laughed. "I guess that must be it."

When we turned onto a street lined with dilapidated warehouses and used-car part yards, with not a streetlight anywhere as far as the eye could see, however, I felt a flutter of anxiety. Something about being alone at night in dark alleys, I guess. Even if I was driving with a cop.

"Are we going the right way?" I asked nervously.

"Sorry. Guess I should have explained. I keep my cars locked up safe. The place where I live doesn't have a two-car garage, and besides, I park this car there. So I rent space from a guy."

We turned onto an even smaller street. On one side was a plumbing supply shop, its huge sign boasting about its exceptional selection of valves. On the other stood another nondescript building. Only a few windows were cut into the gray cinder block. In addition to being high up enough to keep anyone from seeing in or out, they were crusted with what looked like decades of grime. Jimmy pulled into the tiny lot.

"Not exactly picturesque," I commented.

"It's just a place to store my cars. Wait 'til you see what's inside. You're gonna love this."

I followed him across the lot to a door, tucked away at the back. Jimmy took a ring of keys out of his pocket and fiddled with the lock, muttering. It wasn't surprising that he was having such a hard time. He wasn't getting much help from the single bulb right above the door, which couldn't have been more than 15 watts.

I was wishing I'd opted for a movie instead when he finally got the door open. Even in the semidarkness, I saw his face brighten like it was Christmas morning.

"You won't regret this. I promise."

He flicked on a light. The way he was carrying on, I expected something magical.

Instead, I saw two cars, blanketed in the beige pads movers use.

"Here they are. The two loves of my life."

"Oh. Very nice."

"No, wait," he said passionately. "You haven't had a chance to see these beauties yet. Here, I'll show you."

He pulled off the blankets, exposing what, to me, still looked like . . . two cars. Two funky, oddly shaped cars, at least compared to what I saw on the Long Island Expressway every day, but two cars nonetheless. The pink one looked like something out of *Grease*. And the black one, the sports car, looked like, well, a sports car.

"Aren't they great? One of the things I like best about them is that they're so different. I mean, the Thunderbird is a fifties classic. And did I tell you that this one, the Porsche, is the exact same model that—?"

"James Dean died in. Right."

I was about to try explaining politely that I'm not really a vehicle person when Jimmy folded his arms across his chest and looked at me expectantly. "So what do you think?"

"I think they're fabulous. They're just . . . incredible."

I'd said the right thing. He beamed.

"Yeah. I never thought I'd be lucky enough to have anything like these two beauties. But I'm afraid I can't take you out for a drive in either of them tonight. I'm still waiting for a part for the T-bird. And the Spyder—see that crumpled back fender? I want to bang it out before I take it out on the road. Guess I'm kind of a perfectionist."

"That's too bad." Actually, now that I was here, it might actually be fun to go for a spin. The pink one was definitely a car in which someone would "take a spin." As for the other one, I was getting attached to the James Dean idea. Maybe it would be interesting, putting myself in the actor's place, imagining what it was like as he drove down that lonely California road that turned out not to be so lonely when another car unexpectedly appeared from out of nowhere.

"I'm working on both of them at once. I mean, I knew they needed work when I got them. That's the fun part. I spend whatever free time I get playing around with them." He pointed to the back area of the garage. "See? This is where I keep all my tools. Whenever I can, I try to get original tools from those two eras. It's neat, working on fifties car with fifties tools."

I politely admired Jimmy's collection of wrenches and crowbars, some hanging on the wall, some stored in cardboard boxes.

"I'm a lucky man." Jimmy stood, his hands on his hips, radiant as he admired his fleet. "I'm thrilled that I'm about to get another car, but I haven't figured out yet where I'm gonna keep it. I haven't decided what to get, either. I'm looking at a few different ones that I found on the Web . . ."

I was starting to get really bored with this. I didn't want to look like a poor sport, but now that I'd seen them, I'd had my weekly dose of automobile appreciation. I was also getting hungry. And it was cold.

"Well, thanks for bringing me here," I said. "So where should we go for dinner?"

A look of surprise crossed his face, as if he were astonished I wasn't enjoying basking in the glory of a dirty garage filled with old cars just as much as he was. Then he grinned.

"Sorry. I know; I get carried away. Sometimes I forget that everybody doesn't love cars as much as I do."

"It's nice that you have something you care about so much," I commented once we were driving away from the seedier side of Westfield. "Classic cars are a real passion with you, aren't they?"

His hobby was easier to romanticize now that I was no longer standing in an unheated building, pretending to admire hubcaps. Still, I really was impressed by the fact that there was something in Jimmy's life he was so enthusiastic about. It made him seem so much more alive than a lot of the people I knew.

"Yeah, I guess so. How about you? What gets you excited?"

By now, I knew enough to recognize a simple sentence for what it was. At least, where Jimmy Nolan was concerned. For some reason, his question made me think of Marcus Scruggs. That, in turn, made me think about Barbara Delmonico, Claudia Martin, and Tommee Frack.

"For now, it's this murder investigation."

The pleasant, easygoing mood that had been buoying us both up suddenly took a nosedive.

"Jesus H. Christmas, you're not still messing around with that, are you?" Jimmy stared straight ahead at the road, his expression stony. "Jess, you gotta listen to me. I'm a cop. I know what's out there. You have no idea of the risk you're taking by getting involved in something like this. Just keep out, okay? Read my lips."

I tried telling myself he was concerned only for my safety. But I was irritated by the tone of his voice and his air of superiority. Even more, I was furious over his implication that I couldn't take care of myself.

Most of all, I was glad I hadn't told him about the canary feather on my windshield, not to mention Betty's threatening phone call or the games of Follow the Leader a black Jeep had been playing with me.

We rode in silence for a minute or two. And then, in a voice that sounded much more like the one I was used to, he said, "Listen, I'm sorry." He grinned sheepishly. "I didn't mean to sound so much like my father."

"It's okay," I mumbled.

"In fact, why don't you tell me what you've found out? Got any suspects?"

It was hard to stay angry at Jimmy. "I think I figured out who killed Tommee Frack."

"Yeah?" He glanced over. "Who?"

"George Babcock."

"Who's that?"

"The PR guy who gave Tommee his start. I just found out Tommee left his entire business to him. Then again, Tommee had a pretty complicated personal life. At first, I thought his ex-wife killed him. But then I talked to his fiancée, and I started to suspect her, too."

"Yeah? Why her? Wasn't she madly in love with the guy?"

"That's what you'd expect, except that one of her closest friends told me she was really only after his money. But what's even more intriguing is the fact that Barbara Delmonico told me she was the daughter of two doctors and that she went to all these fancy schools and that she was a stockbroker on Wall Street. It turns out not one word is true. When she met Tommee, she was working as an exotic dancer at a sleazy club called the Silk 'N' Satin Lounge."

"Oh, yeah? Never heard of it. You think maybe you could tell me where it is?"

I punched him playfully in the arm.

"The only problem is, I couldn't come up with any reason for her to want him dead. Even if she was after his money—*especially* if she was after his money—she'd have nothing to gain, since they weren't married yet.

"Which brings me back to Babcock. Whether George knew what was in the will or not, he still had good reason to want Tommee dead. If he knew about the will, he had a fortune to gain. If he didn't know, he could still have killed him for revenge. Tommee had very nearly ruined him."

"Wow. Sounds like you got the whole thing figured out."

"Maybe. I'm not completely sure. I'm filling my notebook with all the information I've gathered. I keep thinking that, like you said, if I go through it enough, sooner or later the true story of what happened is going to hit me."

"You know what I think?" Jimmy said. "Based on what you've told me, I mean?"

"What?"

"That the fiancée did it. What's her name? Barbara?"

"Right. Barbara Delmonico. Why do you think she did it?"

"Because she's the one who had the most to hide. Maybe she didn't get any money as a result of Frack being dead. But what if she got something else? Like maybe they'd had a big fight—you know, right before this mega-wedding she's been counting on—and he threatened to tell everybody about her past. Maybe she'd been struggling to move on to something better for years, and here's this rich guy telling her he's going to trash it all. He knew a lot of people, right? What if he started spreading the word that this woman who pretends she's all hoity-toity really started out as a stripper?"

"Exotic dancer," I mumbled.

But Jimmy's speculation got me thinking. It was true that I'd been so focused on the obvious aspects of Barbara's engagement to Tommee that I hadn't bothered to think very far beyond. Now that Jimmy had opened their entire relationship up to question, there were a lot of possible scenarios.

Could she have learned that Tommee was into something bizarre or illegal or otherwise questionable? Was it possible that, like his fiancée, Tommee wasn't what he seemed? Or maybe once they were almost married, he'd let on that he was into some kinky sexual behavior. Maybe he suggested a threesome, and in a fit of rage and jealousy she bludgeoned him to death, then called on someone like Paul, the owner of the Silk 'N' Satin, to help her get rid of the body . . .

Somehow, I found it difficult to imagine Barbara getting upset about unusual sexual behavior. If anything, I could picture her being the one who suggested it in the first place.

But maybe there was something else going on between them. It was such an obvious possibility that I was amazed I hadn't thought of it before.

"I mean, all these business wheelings and dealings are pretty standard stuff," Jimmy was saying. "Everybody knows everybody, the corporate guys and the political guys, and they're all working together to grease each other's palms. That's just the way things work. There's nothing sleazy about it. It's just the old boy network—if you'll excuse the expression. People do business with their friends. They do favors for friends. That's the real world, Jess."

"You're probably right . . ."

"I know I'm right. If I were you, I'd keep looking into this Barbara. Maybe I don't know all the ins and outs of this case, but I've been a cop long enough to have developed kind of a sixth sense about what's going on. And I'd put my money on the fiancée."

•   •   •

This time, when the evening ended, I was careful not to leave Jimmy with any uncertainty about whether or not I intended to go out with him again. After dinner we made out in the car like teenagers.

When I told him I wasn't ready to invite him in for the night, he took it well.

"I need more time," I said when the question of what was next, coming inside or driving home, came up. "I'm just coming out of a very intense relationship. And, well, I'm just not ready."

"Okay." He sounded disappointed enough for me to feel flattered. "But when you *are* ready, you'll let me know, right?"

I grinned. "You'll be the first. Promise."

As I watched him drive away, I realized I meant it.

This one could be a keeper, I thought.

Despite the cars.

• • •

I lay awake in bed for a long time, listening to Max wheeze and Lou snore and running my hand along Cat's silky fur . . . and thinking about Jimmy. Unfortunately, it wasn't his boyish grin, his gentle teasing, or even the impressive way he used his hands and his mouth that kept the adrenaline racing through my bloodstream.

It was his suggestion that there could have been much more going on between Barbara and Tommee than I'd assumed.

I agonized over who might be able to tell me more about their relationship. I needed someone who'd known them both. Maybe even someone who'd been involved in their wedding plans.

The answer came to me at two A.M.

The next morning, I dragged myself out of bed, wishing that somewhere along the line I'd mastered the art of forcing myself to go to sleep. But once I was on the road with Max and Lou, I forgot all about my fatigue. I was too busy treating patients and reassuring their owners. I doled out hairball removers to cat owners and antiulcer medications to horse owners. I discussed the effectiveness of various whitening shampoos with a breeder in Woodhull who felt it was time his French poodles entered the show ring. I trimmed the claws of a rabbit whose owner was afraid of cutting them too close and watching her beloved Thumper bleed to death.

The last appointment of the day, a diabetic cat in nearby Seaponak, was over by three-thirty. I rushed home to shower and slap on lipstick before venturing into uncharted waters.

While I'd dealt with my share of nerves since I began playing sleuth, I wrestled with a different type of demon as I drove along an endless driveway to Hallsworth Hall.

The building itself was spectacular. At the turn of the century, a multimillionaire named James Cullen Hallsworth had commissioned it with the goal of creating the most distinctive mansion on Long Island. He was determined to outshine the ostentatious Gold Coast mansion estates to the west, owned by his contemporaries like Frank Winfield Woolworth and J. P. Morgan.

Hallsworth had been born into poverty, the son of a London chimney sweep. He emigrated to the United States when he was fourteen, began shining shoes on Wall Street and charmed his way into a job at a big investment firm. By the time he was thirty, he was a millionaire, regularly playing croquet with fellow Long

Island residents Teddy Roosevelt and John Philip Sousa.

But when it came to building his house, he wanted to play his own game. So he designed an eccentric fantasy that to many was an architectural nightmare. It combined the best of a variety of architectural styles: Greek columns, Tudor trim, Victorian turrets, even a widow's walk. One more notable element was the bizarre number of chimneys—Hallsworth's personal tribute to his chimney sweep father.

At the time, the mansion had been considered garish. But what was once the epitome of bad taste was now seen as wonderfully idiosyncratic. While I'd heard of it for years, I'd never actually been there. Now that I was up close, I fell in love instantly with its quirkiness.

It was what I found inside that was the problem.

Everywhere I looked, I saw pictures of brides. They smiled into the camera. They smiled at the tuxedoed grooms standing beside them in silent adoration. They smiled at the precious flower girls who clung to their baskets of flowers.

To be sure, events other than weddings also took place at Hallsworth Hall. I noticed a few shots of corporate events, bar mitzvahs, even what looked like an anniversary party for two people who, in my book, deserved a lot more than a couple of platters of shrimp and a champagne fountain for still looking so happy together after what had obviously been decades.

But those events were clearly the exception. While Hallsworth Hall had once stood as a testimony to the American Dream, these days it served as a monument to Marriage.

I was wondering if I should just hightail it out of there before a full-scale anxiety attack set in when an attractive young woman asked pleasantly, "How can I help you?"

"Uh, I'm thinking of getting married," I croaked.

She smiled. "Thinking?"

"Well, no. More than thinking. What I mean is, I'm trying to think of the best way to do it. Have the reception."

"Of course. And it's a very big decision." Another smile. "Almost as big a decision as choosing the right man."

"You probably don't accept walk-ins. Maybe I should go home and call for an appointment . . ." I glanced longingly at the door.

"That's not necessary. In fact, I believe our wedding planner is free right now. Let me see if I can get you in."

She didn't give me a chance to protest. Before you could say, "Here comes the bride," she was on the phone.

"Good news," she informed me as she hung up. "Ms. White can see you now."

I forced a smile. "That *is* good news."

It's for the cause, I reminded myself as I allowed her to shepherd me into a waiting area. You're here to investigate a murder, not choose the color of the tablecloths and matching napkins for the Happiest Day of Your Life.

I wondered if the wedding planner was really named Ms. White or if that was simply a way of fitting her into the bridal theme. The color white was really big here. In addition to the white gowns that were the focus of every photograph, bouquets of fragrant white flowers were enthroned everywhere. A glass case displayed white veils, white satin pillows for the wedding rings, and white garters. Even the china cups next to the complimentary cappuccino machine were a pristine white.

All resemblance to things innocent ended in the person of Ms. White, however. Even though she was barely out of her twenties, Ms. White reminded me of those tough career women in the films of the 1940s, combining the ruthless efficiency of Joan Crawford with the formidable shoulder pads of Rosalind Russell.

It was clearly an image she cultivated. Her tailored navy blue suit was as crisp as her manner. Her hair, an oversized, platinum blond puff that made her look like she was walking—literally—with her head in the clouds, looked solid enough to withstand a tornado.

She stuck out her hand. "I'm Caroline White. And you are . . . ?"

"Jessica Popper." As I shook her hand, I was careful to avoid her bright red fingernails, filed so sharply I was sure they had to be registered with the police.

"Have a seat, Jessica. First of all, congratulations."

It took me a few awkward seconds to figure out what she could possibly be referring to. "Oh. Of course. Yes. Thank you."

"You're about to start planning the most important, most meaningful, most romantic day of your life. It's one that will live on in your heart like nothing else, a reminder of the most important thing we have as human beings here on this earth: Love." Ms. White clasped her hands in front of her and sighed. "Now, what kind of budget are we talking?"

"Uh, I don't know. Modest, I suppose."

"You don't have even a ballpark figure?"

"I'm sorry. I've never done this before."

"No problem. Let's start planning the details and we'll see how it plays out. Have you picked a date yet?"

For the next twenty minutes, I answered relentless questions about my taste in flowers, pasta, music, wine, and ice sculpture. We even tackled the critical flowers-versus-balloons centerpiece issue. I must admit, I put together a pretty nice affair, even though it was all a pipe dream. Just picturing Jimmy Nolan in a tuxedo, leading a conga line with Betty right behind him and me next in line, all decked out in white, burst the bubble so quickly I could practically feel a thin film of soap on my face.

I was wondering how I was ever going to slip Tommee Frack into the conversation when Ms. White said, "I almost forgot to ask. How did you happen to choose Hallsworth Hall?"

"A friend recommended it. In fact, she couldn't say enough about it." I paused for effect. "Barbara Delmonico?"

I had difficulty reading the look that crossed her face.

"Maybe you don't remember her," I persisted. "You must deal with so many brides."

"Oh, I definitely remember her. The Delmonico-Frack wedding."

"So you do remember!"

"Of course. It's so tragic. I'm truly sorry for your friend's loss."

"Thank you. Barbara's devastated, of course. Has

she contacted you about canceling? She's been so grief-stricken, I wouldn't be surprised if—"

"The wedding was already canceled."

"I see. So someone did contact you after Mr. Frack was killed."

"No, before that. The nuptials were canceled before that. Before Mr. Frack's untimely passing."

I blinked. "Excuse me?"

Caroline White looked puzzled. "Barbara didn't tell you? I thought you said you two were friends."

"We *are* friends. Close friends. But no, she didn't say anything. Of course, I haven't seen much of her these last few weeks. I've, uh, been doing quite a bit of traveling."

I was struggling to digest what I was hearing. It wasn't easy acting normal when I felt as if someone had just thrown a bucket of icy water over me. The wedding had been canceled *before* Tommee Frack's murder. Which meant Barbara Delmonico hadn't been his fiancée when he died.

"But now that you've told me," I floundered, "it does explain a lot. Poor Barbara! She has seemed awfully depressed lately. Even before Tommee—several of our mutual friends commented on it to me. Do you happen to know exactly when the wedding was canceled?"

"I can look it up for you."

She pulled the oversized date book that sat at the edge of her tremendous desk toward her. Even though her scarlet fingernails were as long as a mandarin's, she deftly flipped through it, running a single talon down each page before moving on to the next.

"Here we are. November first."

Two days before Tommee's murder.

"They lost the whole deposit. It was a considerable amount of money. But with the wedding scheduled just a few weeks off . . . Well, of course it was too late for me to book another event in that slot. No way, not on such short notice. I'm running a business here, not a club for bleeding hearts."

I doubted anyone would ever think that.

"Still, I felt bad for Ms. Delmonico. When she called to tell me the wedding was off, I mean. Personally, I didn't understand what she saw in Mr. Frack, but if I had a nickel for every time that was true . . .

"Anyway, she wanted everything to be perfect. Every bride does, but I could see how much even the tiniest details mattered to her. She insisted that everything be *classy*. That was exactly the word she kept using."

"I don't suppose she gave a reason? For the cancellation, I mean?"

"To tell you the truth, she was crying so hard, I could barely understand her. But it always boils down to the same thing, doesn't it? The bastard was leaving her at the altar."

She stiffened. "Maybe you shouldn't say anything to her. If she never mentioned it to anyone, not even her closest friends, maybe it was just too—you know, *upsetting*. And now that her fiancé is gone *anyway*—"

"I won't say a word. Promise." I was shaking as I stood up. "You've certainly given me a lot to think about. For my own wedding, I mean. If you don't mind, I'd like to run some of these ideas by my fiancé."

"Of course. What's his name?"

I could have given her any name. But I gave the first one that popped into my head. "Nick Burby."

She wrote it down, damn her.

"Here's my card, Jessica. Call me when you and Nick have worked out the details. And I urge you to think about the balloon archway. It's extremely effective, especially when you combine the white balloons with a pastel color. It can be breathtaking."

"I'm sure. Thanks for your time. I'll be in touch."

Even without a canopy of pastel balloons hovering over me, I could scarcely breathe as I made my way out of Hallsworth Hall to my car. It was already dark, and I walked quickly, constantly looking around to see if anyone was following me. I checked both my windshield and the backseat of my car before getting in, then locked the doors as soon as I was inside.

Yet as I headed home, something other than my newfound wariness of dark, deserted parking lots kept my heart pounding furiously: the tidbit of information I'd just scrounged.

Tommee Frack had canceled his wedding. Just weeks before the big event. After the invitations had been sent out and every last expensive, *classy* detail had been planned, he'd pulled the plug.

Chapter 16

"In a cat's eyes, all things belong to cats."

—English Proverb

I drove straight to Nick's office.

I knew I was taking a chance. Maybe even being unfair. But whatever had happened between us personally, Nick had promised to help me with the murder investigation. As long as we stuck to business, I told myself, we'd be fine.

Just as I expected, he looked surprised to see me. A little nervous, too, as if he weren't sure what to make of my sudden appearance.

"Hello, Jessie." Even the tone of his voice warned me he was keeping his distance. "What brings you here today?"

"I need you."

In response to his look of astonishment, I hastily added, "For the investigation."

Did I just imagine that a look of disappointment crossed his face?

"I think I may have found the murderer, and it would really help me if you were there when I talk to one of the key witnesses. I could use some moral support, not to mention your expertise." I hesitated, then reminded him, "You did say you'd help . . . if nothing else, to save me from myself."

He shrugged, but his eyes had turned cold. "You're right. I'm in."

"Great."

"So?"

"So . . . what?"

"Aren't you leaving something out?"

"Oh. Sorry! Thank you."

"That's not what I meant. I meant, So who's the murderer?"

I took a deep breath. "Nick, I just learned that Tommee canceled his wedding at the beginning of November."

"I see. Tommee backs out of the wedding, and a few days later he shows up dead in the woods."

"Exactly. The more I think about it, the more it seems likely that someone murdered him in a fit of rage. To me, leaving the body dumped in the woods like that says the killing had to be more emotional than calculated. I mean, it was so . . . artless. So sloppy. Whoever murdered Tommee had to be out of their mind because he—or she—had so terribly much to lose. You know I've had my suspicions about Barbara Delmonico almost since the beginning. I just couldn't figure out a motive. Now, we've got one."

"Makes sense to me."

I flashed him a grateful smile. "I want you to come with me to talk to a woman named Claudia Martin. She's one of Barbara's close friends. I believe we can catch her at her place of employment. I promise you're not looking at hard duty."

As we pulled into the parking lot of the Silk 'N' Satin Lounge in Nick's Maxima, I thought the place looked a little less seedy in the darkness of early evening. Then again, the silhouette of the surgically improved woman was outlined in red neon that kept blinking on and off—a special touch I'd been spared the last time I'd visited.

As Nick and I walked inside, I didn't see the owner of the Hot Girlz car anywhere. Instead, a beefy guy who looked like he was moonlighting from the WWF blocked the doorway. From the way he eyed me, I got the feeling women weren't exactly regular customers here at the Silk 'N' Satin.

"Can I help you?" he growled.

"I'm a friend of Claudia—uh, Peaches. She asked me to stop by this evening. We have something important to discuss." I tried to sound authoritative.

"We got a show startin' in a coupla minutes."

"We'll be quick, I promise," I assured him.

"Yeah, well, I'm not supposed to let anybody in."

"But Peaches is expecting us!"

"I realize this is an imposition, barging in like this," Nick interposed. "By the way, I'm Nick Burby." He reached over to shake the hulk's hand. "Listen, we'd really appreciate your help."

"Well . . . aw right. But you gotta be outta there by the time the show starts."

He stepped aside reluctantly to let us pass. As soon

as we were out of earshot, I said, "I think I handled that rather well."

"Right. Although the twenty I slipped him might have helped."

"You didn't have to do that! I was doing just fine without the benefit of bribery!"

"Sometimes bribery is your best bet."

"Maybe that's how *you* operate, but I—"

I never got to finish my sentence. As soon as I pushed back the black velvet curtain, I'd completely lost my audience.

There was no way I could compete with the topless and practically bottomless woman standing in front of us. Her breasts were the size of honeydew melons. I glanced over at Nick. He wasn't trying nearly as hard as I was to look away.

"Nick," I whispered, jabbing him with my elbow, hard. "We're here on business, remember?"

He just made an odd choking sound.

The nearly naked woman cast us an accusing look. "I swear, if I find out who took my mortadella. . . . Either of you guys seen it?"

Nick opened his mouth, as if attempting to reply. No words came out.

I glared at him, then asked politely, "What exactly are you looking for?"

"My mortadella," she repeated impatiently. "It's an Italian sausage. Tonight, I'm doing a tribute to international meats. You know, bratwurst, salami, chorizo, kielbasa? Anyway, after starting with a knockwurst and two dumplings, I was planning to move right on to my mortadella. And now, four minutes before show time, I find out somebody swiped the damn thing! You sure you haven't seen it?"

I shook my head helplessly.

"Great. Just great." She bounced off in disgust. As she turned her back on us, she afforded us a different view. This one appeared to have the same effect on Nick.

"Take deep breaths," I instructed snidely, and pushed ahead.

Two giggling women emerged from the dressing room. One was completely nude except for a large red satin ribbon that was tied around her as if she were a package. In my opinion, she could have used a little wrapping paper.

The other one wore a leopard print G-string and a pith helmet. I did a double take.

"Claudia?"

I wasn't certain the face beneath the shiny red lipstick, glittery emerald eyeshadow, and false eyelashes as thick as fringe belonged to the same woman I'd spoken to six days earlier.

"Oh, hi, Dr. P!" she returned cheerfully. "Nice to see you again!" Without the least bit of self-consciousness, she struck a pose. "How do you like the new outfit? I decided the Alice Cooper thing was getting old. This is a much cleaner look, don't you think?"

I felt she used the term "outfit" a bit loosely, but I simply nodded. "Very nice."

"Do you like it?" she asked Nick.

His answer was written all over his face. I suspected there was other bodily evidence of his approval, but I wasn't about to check.

"Uh, yeah," he muttered. "They're terrific. I mean, it's *terrific*."

She beamed. "Thanks." Glancing back at me, she confided, "I always like to get the male opinion, y'know?"

"Excuse me," the other woman, the gift-wrapped one, said. "I just gotta get through here."

"Oh, sure." I pressed myself against the wall to let her pass. Nick did the same. But the hallway was narrow, and she had no choice but to brush against us as she slithered by.

When I looked up at Nick, his face was as red as her satin ribbon.

"This is Nick Burby," I told Claudia. I figured the polite thing to do was introduce him before he passed out. "He's, uh, a friend. I know your show's about to begin, but I was wondering if you had a minute."

Claudia looked around uncertainly. "I guess. I mean, I usually like to take some time to focus just before I go on. I need to prepare for my performance mentally . . . But, sure, honey. I got a few minutes."

I was relieved when she led us into the dressing room and immediately pulled on a robe. Nick looked a lot better, too. His breathing actually seemed to have returned to normal.

"Look, Claudia—I wasn't completely honest with you the last time we talked," I began. "It's true that I'm a veterinarian, and I really am a friend of Marcus Scruggs, but I wasn't here because of him or the snakes. I came to get information about Barbara Delmonico. Nick is a private investigator. We're trying to find out what we can about the Frack murder."

Even with all that makeup, I saw the color drain from her face.

"Oh, geez." Claudia sank onto the stool, suddenly looking more like a rag doll than a Barbie doll.

"It's better than the police finding out and turning it into something worse than it is," Nick added.

"Think of your little boy," I urged gently. "Why don't you just tell us what you know about Barbara and Tommee?"

"I guess I don't have much of a choice, do I?" She cast each of us a long, woeful look, then took a deep breath. "Okay. When I told you last time that Barb and I weren't friends anymore, that wasn't exactly the truth . . . I mean, we did lose touch for a while. The whole time she was planning her wedding, she didn't want anything to do with me or anybody else from this place. But as soon as her world fell apart, she showed up here again, looking for moral support from her old friends."

"When did you see her again?" I asked.

"It was a Friday. I know that because I'd come to the club in the middle of the afternoon to pick up my paycheck, like I do every week. Barb knew I'd be here around two, since that's the time I always come. See, my son's day care ends at three."

"Was that the Friday before Tommee Frack's murder?" Nick asked.

Claudia looked at us miserably. "Yeah."

"And what exactly did she say?"

"She told me she'd canceled the wedding."

"*She* canceled the wedding?" I yelped.

Claudia nodded. "I'd never seen her so upset. And even though I'd always had the feeling she was only after the guy's dough, I still felt bad for her when I saw how tore up she was. I mean, whether she loved Frack or not, she'd decided that he was the one she wanted."

"Then why did she cancel the wedding?" I asked.

Her eyes darted between Nick and me. "This is the really hard part. But like I said, I guess I better come clean, before somebody figures I've been withholding information or something. Like you said, I got a kid to think of, right?"

"You're being smart," Nick reassured her. "Given what's happened, you have nothing to gain by protecting Barbara. Not if you know something that's important to the investigation."

Claudia hesitated. Then she said softly, "She told me Tommee had been involved in some bad stuff, and she'd just found out that he'd decided to come clean. She—"

"Bad stuff?" I interrupted eagerly. "What kind of bad stuff?"

"I don't know. She didn't tell me that part. What she did tell me was that Tommee was about to turn state's evidence. She said he expected her to stand by him, but she had no intention of doing that."

I had to struggle to keep from reacting.

Claudia didn't seem to notice. "The weird part—and this is so typical of her—is that I got the feeling she didn't really care that he'd been involved in something shady. From the way she talked, I got the impression she'd known about it all along.

"What she was upset about was the fact that he was going to *stop*. He said he was gonna clean up his act, and that meant party time was over. The fancy cars, the wedding with the caviar and the movie stars, the trips to exotic places and everything else she thought she was getting . . . it was over, all of it."

She laughed coldly. "If there was ever any doubt about whether she loved the guy or was after his dough, the things she said to me that day totally clinched it in my mind."

"So Tommee's decision to turn over a new leaf put an end to Barbara's idea of living happily ever after, with nothing to worry about ever again," I mused.

"When you said she was upset," Nick asked, "what exactly did you mean? Depressed? Sad? Hurt?"

"More like angry. Yeah, furious, even. She acted as if she'd been cheated out of something, something she was completely entitled to. She kept talking about how he'd humiliated her. Here everybody thought they were getting married, all these important people were expecting to come to the wedding, and *bam*, he ruins the whole thing by deciding to testify against the people who'd made him rich in the first place."

Claudia bit her lip. "I know what you're thinking. You're thinking, was Barbara mad enough at Tommee for screwing up her chance for a good life to kill him?"

Neither Nick nor I said a word. Instead, we stood in silence, grimly contemplating the very question that Claudia had just put forth.

"This—this is the really hard part." Even though she spoke softly, I could hear the shakiness in her voice. "The last thing she said to me before she left was, 'I'm gonna kill him for what he did to me.' And then, like five days later, I read in the paper that he'd been murdered."

Nick and I looked at each other. I felt a sort of relief.

But at the same time, I was overcome with a terrible sadness.

"Thank you, Claudia." I said it sincerely. "What you told us is extremely important. It was very brave of you to be so honest."

The heavy mood was shattered as a meticulously gelled head appeared in the doorway.

"Hey, Peaches!" my pal Paul barked. "I don't pay you to sit around all night yakking. Don't you have a show to put on?"

Claudia smiled apologetically. "The glamour of a life in the theater . . ."

"Hey! Ya got five minutes!"

He was gone as quickly as he'd appeared.

"Thanks for your time, Claudia," I told her. "And thanks again for being so honest."

"Hey, whatever happens, I hope they're not too hard on Barbara. Sure, she used this poor guy, but it's not like he was born yesterday. Seems to me he got exactly the kind of woman he was looking for. I'm not saying she was right to react the way she did when she found out he decided to come clean. But when you come right down to it, Barb was only looking for a way out of a life like mine."

Claudia dragged herself off the stool, then crouched down in front of the glass tank. As she unhooked the wire netting that served as a cover, she said wearily, "Come on, Clarence. Time to go to work."

• • •

"So what do you think?" Nick asked as we drove away.

"I think we've found ourselves a murderer."

"Looks that way, doesn't it?"

I watched the blinking red silhouette from the Silk 'N' Satin fade from view in my side mirror before saying, "What happens now?"

"I'll give Harned a call tomorrow. That is, if you don't mind me taking over."

"Be my guest. I don't care in the least."

I meant it. Nick had been right. Back at the beginning, he'd warned me that this was a dirty business. I'd had enough of murder investigations. There was nothing glamorous or exciting about putting yourself in the middle of a horrible crime. All it did was expose you to the ugliest sides of human nature.

I felt a guilty rush of joy over the fact that I'd chosen to spend my life primarily in the company of animals, even if most of them did have the bad judgment to cohabitate with humans.

Yet unanswered questions still lurked at the back of my mind. Barbara had been furious with Tommee because he was about to change his lifestyle. But what had that lifestyle been? It had undoubtedly included some wheeling and dealing, which dovetailed nicely with his exceptional talent for wheedling his way into people's good graces. But didn't the fact that he claimed he was about to turn state's evidence imply that whatever Tommee's *modus operandi* was, it wasn't simply "business as usual," as Jimmy had suggested?

I was too burned out to care. As far as I was concerned, this case was closed.

When Nick pulled up in front of my cottage, he put the car into park but kept the engine running.

"Do you want to come in?" I tried my best to sound

casual. "I could make coffee. Or we could open a bottle of wine. You know, to celebrate."

"I should get going. It's late."

"Right. Besides, you must have other things to do."

He rubbed his eyes and sighed. "Look, Jess. Maybe it's time for—"

"I hear the dogs. You should probably go."

He turned to face me. It was too dark to be sure, but I felt certain his expression registered disappointment. "Whatever you want, Jess."

Watching him drive away, I realized that him leaving was the very last thing in the world I wanted. It wouldn't even have been correct to simply say I wanted him to stay. I *longed* for him to stay. Part of me wanted Nick to turn his car around and jump out and take me in his arms, sweeping me off my feet as if he were the hero in some trashy romance novel. . . .

The increasingly frenzied sound of Max's and Lou's barks snapped me back to reality.

"Get a grip, girl," I muttered.

I stomped to my front door and stuck the key in the lock.

I noticed immediately that it turned much too easily.

Did I leave the house open? I wondered. Was I *that* distracted over the idea of confronting Claudia Martin about her friend Barbara Delmonico again?

But it was the sound of a plaintive *meow* that made my blood run cold.

"*Cat?*" I looked down and saw her ambling around the side of the cottage, her body tensed against what I suspected was nearly excruciating pain.

Cat was outside. Yet I *never* let Cat outside.

"What's going on, Cat?" I asked, scooping her up

and cradling her in my arms. "What are you doing out here? Something's very wrong."

I hesitated before stepping inside and switching on a light. The moment I did, my two dogs plunged into their usual Return of the Long Lost Master routine. As reassuring as their behavior was, I still sensed that the cottage felt different.

My heart was pounding so hard I suspected the feline in my arms could feel it. I glanced around wildly, searching for more signs that something was amiss. I sniffed the air like one of my animals, certain I detected a subtle smell that was out of the ordinary. My eyes were immediately drawn to smudge on the rag rug in front of the door, an irregular, dark half-circle that looked like it had been left by a shoe—one much larger than mine.

Somebody had been inside my home.

"Come here, Maxie-Max. Hey, Louie-Lou." My voice sounded edgy as I crouched down to canine level. "Did you have company while I was away? Some guy in a ski mask, maybe? Carrying a big bag over his shoulder?"

If they knew anything, they weren't telling. Max was leaping up and down as if he were spring-loaded, stopping only to grab his hot pink plastic poodle in case anybody was up for a game of Slimytoy. Lou stood a few feet away, barking. Neither of them let on that anything out of the ordinary had happened in my absence. Even Prometheus had nothing to say, for a change.

"You could all throw a wild party while I was out and none of you would ever let on, would you?" I said, sighing with frustration.

I was suddenly struck by a chilling realization: that whoever had broken in might still be here.

I began walking around the house, taking slow, silent steps. Cat was still in my arms and my dogs were at my side. In fact, I'd begun thinking of Max and Lou as my bodyguards. I peered around corners and opened closet doors cautiously, the sound of my own adrenaline-infused blood reverberating in my head as I tried to brace myself for the possibility of coming face to face with an intruder.

"*Awk!* Damn you, damn you!" Prometheus screeched from the living room, sending me jumping into the air at least ten feet. "Damn you! *Awk!*"

"Same to you," I muttered.

As I checked each room, I became more confident that whoever had been here was gone. I surveyed my possessions, anxious to discover if anything was missing. Lou pranced beside me eagerly, probably wondering why it was taking me so long to suggest a romp out back. Max kept slapping my leg with the pink rubber poodle dangling from his jaws.

"I can't play with you guys right now," I told them distractedly. "But I'm sure glad you're here."

I began with my jewelry box. Not exactly the Crown Jewels, but an obvious target for an interloper. I braced myself for something frightening—maybe along the lines of another canary feather. Instead, I found everything in place: the string of pearls I'd gotten for my sixteenth birthday and had yet to wear, the tiny diamond earrings my mother had given me when I graduated from college, even the emerald stick pin that had belonged to my grandmother.

Next I tried my top drawer. My heart was pounding as I pulled it open. The envelope was right where I'd left it, and the delicate yellow feather was still tucked inside. Nothing else appeared to have been moved, either. My practical one hundred percent cotton underwear was still neatly folded, and the pantyhose I kept around for times I was expected to dress like a grown-up were exactly where I'd left them. Even my pitiful cash stash lay untouched.

Next, I looked in the kitchen cabinets and even the refrigerator. Nothing appeared to have been taken . . . and nothing new had been added.

But wasn't the clock near my bed closer to the edge than I was likely to put it? And the drawers weren't all completely closed. The upholstered chair in the living room was placed at a strange angle, as if someone had bumped into it. Minor things, the kind I never would have noticed if it hadn't been for the fact that I'd found Cat outside.

I had to dial the cell phone number three times before I could get my fingers to work right.

"Come on, answer," I growled. "Please, just pick up—Nick? It's me."

"What's wrong?"

"I think somebody broke in while we were out this evening."

"I'll be right there."

"I don't know if that's necessary. I just—"

"I'll be right there!"

I waited impatiently for him to return. The fact that I had four eyewitnesses in front of me only added to my frustration.

"Come on, guys," I pleaded. "Who was here? Was

it a man? A woman? What'd they do? What'd they take?"

All I got was woeful looks, wagging tails, and another invitation to play tug of war with Lou's decrepit tennis ball.

I didn't have to ask Nick any of those questions. I could tell by his worried look that he'd asked them himself as soon as he got my call.

"What's missing?" he demanded above Lou's greeting. "Jewelry? Cash?"

"That's what's so weird, Nick. All my jewelry is still here. It hasn't even been touched." I paused to scoop up Max, who kept dropping the pink poodle at Nick's feet and crouching expectantly, his tail in high gear and his eyes bright with anticipation. "And remember how I always keep a few twenties in my top drawer, just in case? They're still there, too."

"Did you check around? Are you sure there's no one here now?"

Without waiting for an answer, he stormed through the cottage, checking the closets, pulling back the shower curtain, even peering under the bed.

"Whoever it was is gone," he finally reported. "So tell me how you know someone broke in."

I took a deep breath. "After you dropped me off, I found Cat outside."

Nick just stared at me, acting as if I'd just informed him I'd been abducted by aliens.

"That's it? That's the reason you think you've been burglarized?"

"I didn't say I'd been burglarized! At least, not that I know of. But somebody's been in here, Nick!"

"Because your cat was outside," he repeated drily.

"Cat *never* goes outside! You know that! She's strictly an indoor cat. Her arthritis is so bad that there's no way she could ever defend herself—not even against a chipmunk!"

"Maybe she got out on her own," Nick argued. "Like through an open window."

"Do you really think I leave windows open in November?" I countered, totally exasperated. "It's hard enough to keep this place heated! I'm telling you, Nick, the only way Cat could have gotten out is if somebody opened the door!"

I sensed that he was still skeptical. His attitude only fueled my fury—and convinced me even further that I was right.

"There's more," I continued. "Like I'm ninety-nine percent sure the front door was unlocked. I never leave it unlocked, no matter how much of a hurry I'm in. Then there's a bunch of little things. The clock in the bedroom is moved, a chair is in a slightly different spot, there's a footprint here on the carpet—"

"That doesn't look like a footprint. It looks like dirt."

"It *is* dirt, but the point is that it wasn't there before! At least, I don't think it was. Look, whoever was in here tried awfully hard to hide it."

I bit my lip. "I think there's something else you should know."

Nick didn't react as I told him about the canary feather someone had left on my windshield. But when I finished, he pulled off his jacket, then sat down on the couch and started taking off his shoes.

Alarms went off in my head. "What are you doing?"

"I'm staying here tonight. Don't worry. I'll sleep on the couch."

I put Max down and halfheartedly tossed the pink poodle across the room. "Don't you think that's a little . . . dramatic?"

"I promised Betty I'd do whatever was necessary to keep you safe."

"You can't just move in here and sleep on my couch every night!"

"It's just for tonight. Maybe by tomorrow we'll know more than we know right now, and I'll feel better about leaving you alone. But for now, I'm not budging."

I was still trying to come up with a better argument when he stretched across the couch. Folding his arms behind his head, he commented, "Not bad. I'll be comfortable here."

Something about seeing Nick Burby lying on my couch, looking like—well, looking like he *belonged* there, set me off.

"That's a relief," I said crisply. "Especially since you barged in here, deciding you'd stay over without even asking me—"

"First of all, I didn't *barge* in here. You invited me, remember? In fact, you called me on my cell phone when I was already halfway home and dragged me back here."

"I didn't drag you anywhere! I just—"

"Second of all, I made a promise. And I try to keep my promises whenever possible." He wiggled his hips, snuggling down into the upholstery. "Got any Zeppelin CD's?"

"No. You got them all, remember? I got James Taylor and U2."

"How about a blanket?"

"Would you like me to make you some warm milk, too?"

"No, but thanks. That's very thoughtful. You don't mind if I watch TV, do you?"

Max returned with the poodle, trying to entice me into another round by dropping the slimy toy on my foot. "Nick, it's kind of late and I've had a rotten day. I'm beat. I'm going to read a while, then go to sleep."

"I'll keep it down. I know you like it quiet when you're trying to sleep."

I threw up my hands. "Be my guest."

Seething, I retreated to my bedroom. Cat abandoned me, choosing to doze on Nick's chest instead of mine. But Max jumped onto the bed, bringing along a gnarled piece of rawhide that he chomped noisily. Lou stretched out next to him, as usual taking up three-quarters of the bed. At least they stuck by me. When it came to loyalty, there was nothing like the other members of your pack.

"I have to leave the door open," I called to Nick. "Otherwise, all the heat—what there is of it—will stay in the living room and I'll freeze."

"Suit yourself."

As I lay in bed, I could hear the television next door. Every once in a while, Nick laughed or cleared his throat or moved around, causing the couch to creak.

I had to admit, it felt kind of nice, having somebody in the next room.

Having *Nick* in the next room.

I pulled the pillow over my head.

I was wondering whether I would fall asleep that way or suffocate when I heard a soft knock on the door frame.

"Jessie?"

"Mmm?"

"Are you still awake?"

"Yes."

"There's something I wanted to ask you."

"What?"

A long pause followed. "Is it okay if I take a shower?"

"Sure."

"The noise won't bother you? Or the light?"

I noticed he didn't ask me if having him parade around my home practically naked would bother me. I lay on my side, watching Nick walk back and forth between the living room and the bathroom in nothing but a towel.

Damn, I thought furiously. He's doing this on purpose.

I knew I could have turned around. There was nothing to keep me from lying on my other side. I could have closed the door. It wasn't *that* cold.

Realizing that I actually liked having Nick around, hearing his soft, off-key singing in the shower, filled me with resentment.

I was back to lying with the pillow over my head when I heard another knock.

"Hey, Jess?"

"Mmm?"

"Are you awake?"

I sighed loudly, then peeked out. "Yes."

"There's something else I need to ask you."

A really long pause followed. Then Nick said, "Do you think it's dumb for us to sleep in separate rooms?"

I sat up in bed. My heart was thumping and my throat felt thick. But it was the buzzing in my head that made it so hard to think straight.

I wanted to say yes. I wanted it more than I could remember ever wanting anything in my life.

Even if Nick had staged this whole thing, using the break-in as an excuse, I no longer cared. I wanted him here. I loved having him here. The only thing that would have made it better would have been having him right next to me, in my bed.

But I knew there was only one answer to his question.

"Good night, Nick. I've got to get some sleep."

I hugged the pillow tightly against my chest. It was the best way I could think of to protect my heart.

Chapter 17

"Histories are more full of examples of the fidelity of dogs than of friends."

—Alexander Pope

The good news was that we made it through the night, Nick on the couch, me behind a barricade of pillows and puppies.

The bad news was that I didn't exactly sleep well. I tossed and turned until dawn. And Nick's snoring had nothing to do with it.

Instead, I obsessed about Tommee Frack and our conclusion that Barbara Delmonico was guilty. True, she'd confessed to Claudia, telling her in no uncertain terms that she intended to kill him. The timing was perfect, she had powerful motivation, and she certainly had the opportunity.

The problem was, there were too many loose ends.

Like the way Pomonok Properties kept coming up. Not only had the firm left George Babcock to become Tommee's client; Joe DeFeo had already established a relationship with Tommee long before the switch became official. Then there was the fact that at the beginning of November, a representative of the firm had approached the Athertons, trying to buy their land. The Athertons had said no—and a few days later, a dead body had shown up in their backyard.

But there was more. I'd been followed as I drove around Norfolk County, trying to learn as much about Tommee Frack as I could. My next-door neighbor had received a threatening phone call, warning me to mind my own business. I'd found a canary feather tucked conspicuously into my windshield wiper. My home had been broken into, even though whoever had gone to all that trouble clearly hadn't been the least bit interested in my valuables.

Then there was Tommee himself. He'd known everybody. His picture hung in the offices of companies he didn't even represent. Politicians flocked to his funeral. But when you came right down to it, all he was was a PR guy.

Then there were all the others I'd come to suspect, people who were at least as likely as Barbara to want Tommee Frack gone and buried. George Babcock, for example. He had more to gain from Frack's death than anybody, whether he had known what was in Tommee's will or not. If he hadn't known, he could have wanted revenge. If he had known, he could have wanted what he thought was his due.

But there were other suspects, too, like Jonathan Havemeyer, whose loyalty Tommee had never fully appreciated. Even the employees of Tommee Frack & Associates could have had a vendetta against him. Brad O'Reilly, who seemed too good to be true. Wade

Moscowitz, who had fled the public relations field and the entire business world after just a few months' involvement with Tommee and his operation.

Then, of course, there was Merrilee. I couldn't forget the altar to her ex she'd constructed in her spare room. I couldn't forget how intense she was, either. Merrilee was a regular Miss Haversham, quietly raging as she waited for the return of the man everyone else knew would never come back.

Through all my ruminations in the silent darkness that night, I kept hearing Wade Moscowitz's warning.

"My advice, Dr. Popper," he'd said, "is to stay as far away from this as you can."

Of course, Nick had told me the exact same thing. But this was different. Wade knew Tommee and he knew what he'd been involved in.

Wade's warning was still playing in my head when the sun started to come up and I finally drifted off to sleep, too exhausted to think anymore.

When I woke up, I found myself facing another impossible situation. I could already hear Nick moving around in the living room, probably getting dressed. I considered lying low until I heard him leave. But I could hear Max scratching at the back door, his subtle way of telling me he needed to go out. So I pulled on a robe, then banged loudly on the wall before venturing out of my bedroom.

"It's okay," Nick called back. "I'm decent."

As I peered around the corner, the irony of needing to be cautious wasn't wasted on me. I saw that he had his pants on, although he was shirtless and sockless. The sight of him half-clothed—the muscles in his shoulders and back, his taut skin, even the way his khakis dipped down provocatively in front—jolted me awake.

"Sleep okay?" I asked casually.

"I guess so." He caught my eye, then looked away. "All things considered."

I didn't dare ask what he meant. I was too afraid he'd compare this past night with the last time he'd slept here.

"Want some coffee?" I offered halfheartedly.

"No. I'm going. Suddenly, this whole thing seems like a really bad idea."

"You may recall that I wasn't the one who invited you."

"Hey, you're the one who keeps getting into situations where you need my help."

"I don't need your help! I don't need *anybody's* help!"

"I'm sure." He tugged on his shirt. "You're completely self-sufficient, right?"

"You got it."

"You can manage anything that comes up totally on your own. You don't need anyone."

"Exactly."

"And you certainly don't need me."

I didn't have an answer. At least, not a quick, uncomplicated one.

I didn't think I needed Nick. But that didn't mean I'd ever stopped wanting him.

Damn! I raged. Why does everything have to be so convoluted where Nick Burby is concerned?

"You don't have to answer," he said softly. "I already know what you're thinking."

He grabbed his socks, slipped his bare feet into his shoes and headed for the door.

"Wait!" I cried.

He turned. A look of hope flickered across his face.

"Do me a favor, Nick. Don't talk to Harned. Not yet."

"Excuse me?"

"Now that I've had a chance to sleep on it, I'm not so sure Barbara is our murderer."

"*What?*"

"I mean, I know she told Claudia she wanted to kill him, but that doesn't mean she actually went through with it. Besides, there's so much more to Tommee Frack. I realize there's somebody I need to talk to again." I shrugged. "The bottom line is that I need more time."

"Whatever." He cast me a look of complete exasperation, then disappeared out the door.

I could have dwelled on the fact that the house suddenly seemed profoundly empty once again. Instead, I put on a pot of coffee and got into the hottest shower I could bear.

I still had work to do, and for once I wasn't going to let my confusion over Nick stand in my way.

By the time the dogs were walked, all the animals fed, my hair dried, and three cups of coffee consumed, I was a new woman. I was ready for a full day of calls. But I was really looking forward to what I had planned for after my day's calls: a meeting that I hoped would give me some crucial answers.

As I was about to leave, I checked to make sure I had everything I needed. Appointment book, maps, cell phone, notebook . . .

It wasn't there.

I rummaged through my purse, checked every tote bag I owned and looked through the clutter on the table. I couldn't find my notebook anywhere.

I searched the cottage, figuring I might have left it someplace unusual. The table next to my bed, the kitchen counter, the bathroom . . . the notebook wasn't in any of those places. Max and Lou pranced around beside me, barking happily as they made their usual assumption that we were embarking on some exciting new game.

"Not now," I told them. "This is serious."

I checked my car, performing acrobatics in order to get a good look under the seats. Then I ransacked the van. Finally, I went back into the house.

All my clues, all my phone numbers, all the pieces of the puzzle that had consumed me for the past two and a half weeks. All missing.

"*Damn!*" I said aloud, cursing my carelessness.

"*Awk!*" Prometheus chimed in. "Damn you, Nick Burby! Damn you!"

When was the last time I'd seen the notebook? I was positive I hadn't brought it to the Silk 'N' Satin the night before because I'd known I wouldn't have a chance to jot down any notes until I got home. And by then it was late, and when I'd walked in the door I'd discovered that someone had broken in . . .

An unpleasant warmth swept over me. Was it possible that whoever had been in my house had stumbled upon my notebook, realized what it was and taken it?

I told myself I was taking this paranoia thing a bit too far.

It has to be somewhere, I thought. Chances are I'm the one who lost it. Sooner or later, it'll turn up.

These things always do.

• • •

When I walked into Dream Catcher amidst a wind chime fanfare, Wade looked up from the copper bracelets he was patiently arranging in a cardboard display unit. He didn't seem the least bit surprised to see me.

"Dr. Popper. I had a feeling you'd be back."

I glanced around, checking for his sidekick, the girl with the golden locks and the empty smile. From the looks of things, he was alone.

"You have to tell me what you know," I demanded. "Last night, someone broke into my house. I'm sure I'm being followed. I recently found out that just before his murder, Tommee's newest client, Pomonok Properties, tried to buy the Atherton Farm, where his body was dumped, and had the door slammed in their face. Somebody left a canary feather on my car—and when Tommee's body was found, a canary was buried a few feet away. And a couple of weeks ago, my next-door neighbor, a woman in her seventies who wouldn't hurt a fly, got a threatening phone call late one night, warning me to mind my own business."

He looked stricken. "And I take it it's too late for that."

"It's way beyond too late, Wade. I need answers. For all I know, other people's lives are at stake here."

"Let's talk in back," he said. "Summer will be here soon."

It took me a few seconds to realize that Summer was his employee, not a season. I followed him into the room with the chair shaped like a big hand.

He sat down on the futon. "Why don't I tell you a story?"

"A story?"

"A story that may be true . . . or it may be nothing but a story. Let's leave it at that, okay?"

I was catching on. "Okay."

"Once upon a time, there was a man named . . . let's call him Tommee. Ever since he was a little boy, Tommee wanted to be at the center of things. He wasn't accomplished at music or science or even business—and he certainly wasn't what you'd call popular.

"But he discovered he had a special ability. He was what you'd call a people person. He was good at making other people feel important.

"He was also good at getting their names in the paper, because he had a genuine knack for infusing others with the same enthusiasm he felt. This ability endeared these people to him, though they didn't really care about him; they cared about what he could do for them.

"But Tommee had one more talent. He was great at bringing people together, then standing on the sidelines and letting them do what they did best. Making deals, trading favors, networking. Over the years, Tommee's reputation grew. As word got around, more and more people began to notice. People who realized they could benefit from Tommee's very special talents." He hesitated. "People who realized he could do even more for them than get their names on TV or in the newspaper."

"Go on," I prompted, hanging on to every word.

"One day, a few of these people approached Tommee. They made him an offer. They told him they would set him up in business with more clients than he ever dreamed of. All they asked in return was one small favor."

"Which was?" My mouth was so dry I could barely get the question out.

"In addition to providing public relations services, which he loved and was truly good at, he was to act as a middle man. A central point. His role would be to collect money from people and organizations who needed things, then pass that money along to people and organizations who could provide the things they needed. Maybe money can't buy happiness, but it can sure buy a lot of other useful things."

"What kinds of things?"

"All kinds. For example, a generous contribution to the highway department can get the road in front of your restaurant or your condominium complex repaved—or plowed first thing in the morning after a big snowstorm. Regular payments to your friendly police department can ensure that your place of business gets special protection. A few dollars to the health department can make a few code violations go unnoticed. Even not-for-profits stand to benefit, since the government provides funding to various organizations but there's only so much grant money to go around. It's up to government officials to decide who gets it. That holds for private contractors, too. Say a construction company is hoping to get the contract on a new government building. There's a lot of competition out there. Enter, Tommee Frack."

"Payoffs," I said breathlessly.

"Personally, I like the term 'favor broker,' " Wade replied. "Say a land developer wanted to build a strip mall in an area that wasn't zoned for retail space. In that case, what he needed was a zoning change, even if it was the kind of thing the rest of the community would hate. Tommee would take the developer's monthly payment for public relations services and . . . shall we say, pass it along to the zoning board. Voila! The zoning change would be made, and everyone involved would be happy. For the people on the zoning board, it meant a new Jacuzzi or a second Mercedes. For the developer, the money he paid out was nothing compared to what he'd make on his investment.

"And no one would ever be the wiser. Not only was paying a public relations firm a legitimate business expense; it was even tax deductible. Of course, the members of the community might not be thrilled, but they weren't part of the loop. Worrying about them didn't serve either the government or the developer."

"Pomonok Properties." I practically exhaled the words. "They were one of the companies sending monthly checks to Tommee Frack & Associates, even though The Babcock Group was their real public relations firm. That's why Joe DeFeo and Tommee were such good pals, posing for pictures with all those political bigwigs. But why did Pomonok Properties drop Babcock as its PR firm? According to George, they officially became a client of Tommee's a few weeks ago."

"Pomonok had a major project in the works, the biggest they've ever undertaken," Wade told me. "DeFeo's had his eye on Atherton Farm for a long time. It's a prime piece of real estate, forty-plus acres in one of Long Island's most desirable areas. DeFeo had his heart set on building a tremendous complex of luxury town houses there. He hadn't gotten the Athertons to agree, but he'd barely gotten started working on them. Joey is fond of saying he's never met anybody who wouldn't sell if the offer got high enough. As for the town's zoning board, Tommee was sure he'd be able to take care of that end of things, even though the neighbors and the local civic associations were bound to fight the idea tooth and nail. In the end, the government's decision always prevails.

"There was no question that DeFeo would get his way. That was why Frack & Associates existed in the first place, to make sure that the right palms got greased. But for the sake of appearances, it was crucial that Pomonok align themselves with Tommee. Tommee and Joey needed a foolproof reason to be working together. Making Pomonok Properties Tommee's client was ideal."

"I understand that the people who set Tommee up in the first place wanted him gone, once he let on that he was going to spill the beans. But why do you suppose his body was left at Atherton Farm?"

"As a warning, no doubt."

"To the Athertons? In their mind, there was never any link between Pomonok's interest in their property and the body that turned up in their woods."

"No, but I can assure you that there were plenty of others who made the connection instantly. Don't forget; this was a system that had been firmly in place for years. One that worked well for a lot of people, most of them heavy hitters. They were all one big happy family, and they had no intention of changing the status quo. They had to leave Tommee's body somewhere, and the fact that Pomonok Properties was interested in Atherton Farm was pretty well known. So why not really drive home the message to anybody else who might be considering getting in their way?"

I nodded. It all made perfect sense. Chillingly perfect sense. And I now understood the significance of the canary. I'd been correct when I'd pointed out to Nick that canaries were the symbol of "singing." Tommee had been on the verge of singing, all right, and his voice would have been heard loud and clear.

"How did the money move out of Tommee's organization and into the hands of the people granting these 'favors'?" I asked.

"Political contributions, mainly, but of course there's nothing like cold hard cash. I'm sure there was a small army of 'soldiers' who made sure all the transactions proceeded smoothly."

"And how did Tommee get paid?"

"He got a piece of everything that came in. Not only from the 'givers,' like Pomonok Properties, but also from the 'takers,' including the cops and the government. They all made regular payments to Tommee Frack & Associates. The people who set him up took care of the rest. Even Tommee's accountant didn't know what was going on after the money was deposited. Besides, he wasn't close enough to the day-to-day workings of the firm to know what went on. It was all done under the guise of complete legitimacy."

I took a deep breath. "And who were they? Who set Tommee up in business?"

"You didn't hear it here, right?"

I nodded.

"It went straight to the top. Gene Guilford, when he was county executive. A county legislator or two. The commissioner of highways. A guy from the health department who was pretty high up. Even Daniel Sharpe, the police commissioner."

"Sharpe," I breathed. "That explains why the police have been dragging their feet with this. The order had to have come from very high up."

"There were people at the town level, as well," Wade went on, "including some members of the local zoning board. A pretty nice mix, overall. Something for everyone."

"Who else knew?" ·

"Only a select group, those at the very top. People like Joe DeFeo, who were the presidents and CEOs of the companies that were involved. In the case of the cops, it was probably only Sharpe and maybe a few guys close to him. Everybody knew Sharpe handed out special favors, but most people didn't have a clue about how the whole thing worked. Same with the elected officials and the other people in government. The feeling about who needed to know was the fewer, the better."

"Then how come you know all this?"

"All of Tommee's employees knew. We might not have known the details, but we could see that something strange was going on. Don't you think the account executives noticed that there was a tremendous list of clients that the company supposedly represented, yet none of us ever worked on those accounts?"

"So Brad O'Reilly knew."

"I guarantee it." Wade smirked. "Like I said: Mini-Me. But I knew even more than the rest. One day, I was working late, and nobody was left at the office except Tommee and me. We started talking about how successful he'd been in such an incredibly short time. I kept asking questions, trying to piece the whole thing together, and eventually the whole story came out. It was funny, but Tommee seemed relieved to have somebody to talk to about what had been going on for so long. When you come right down to it, he was really a very lonely man. He needed somebody to spill his guts to. I was it."

"But you didn't stick around."

"Nope. As soon as I found out what was going on, I got the hell out of Tommee Frack & Associates. I didn't want any part of it. I ran as fast and as far as I could." He opened his arms. "Dream Catcher was born."

"What about George Babcock? Did you know Tommee left his business to him? He said in his will that he'd had a change of heart."

"Good for George. He deserves it."

"But how will he run the business, now that he's inherited all of Tommee's clients? Will he play the same role Tommee did?"

"I suspect that the clients who choose to stay with George will simply continue getting whatever legitimate public relations services they got with Tommee. Those that weren't interested in PR in the first place will leave, of course."

"Unless the people who set Tommee up extend the same offer to George."

Wade smiled sourly. "Or to someone else, if George doesn't have the stomach for it. But there's another possibility: that the truth about what's been going on comes out. In that case, the payoff system that's been in place for years will come to an end."

I just sat there in the hand chair, my brain spinning as I tried to comprehend the magnitude of what I'd just learned. Wade's "story" certainly made all the pieces fit together. It explained the monumental success of Tommee Frack & Associates, as well as the fact that Tommee was at the heart of nearly everything that went on in the local business and political arenas. It also explained all the big movers and shakers who'd showed up at his funeral, the fat checks that kept coming in after his murder, so many that even Tommee's accountant was astounded, and the huge number of "clients" that didn't jibe with the small number of account executives Tommee had hired to service them.

Then there was the fact that right from the start, Tommee Frack had such an impressive list of clients. And according to Jonathan Havemeyer, that list had expanded almost immediately, growing like a monster in a science fiction movie.

It had been so easy for Tommee. He really had made a deal with the devil.

But at some point, even he had seen that getting everything he wanted—money, success, women, and above all, status—wasn't enough. Somewhere along the line, he'd begun finding it difficult to face himself in the mirror every morning. And he decided he wanted out.

That change of heart very likely cost him his life.

"This wasn't printed in the papers," I told Wade, "but when Tommee's body was found in the woods, a canary was buried nearby."

A look of shock crossed his face. "How do you know?"

"I was there, remember? I'm the one who found it next to Tommee's body. Actually, my dog did."

"So Tommee was about to sing."

I nodded. "It looks as if that was a recent development. From what I can tell, he changed his mind right before he was murdered. His fiancée, Barbara, knew all about it. In fact, she was so upset that Tommee was turning state's evidence that she told one of her friends she was going to kill him."

"If that was true," Wade said thoughtfully, "if he really was going public with this, his fiancée wouldn't have been the only one who'd be upset. Some very important people had a great deal to lose. Tommee managed to make a lot of friends, but if he decided to blow the lid off this, he would have made just as many enemies."

"So there were a lot of people who would have wanted him dead."

"Precisely. As I told you before, Dr. Popper, the best advice I can give you is to let this thing go. Not only are you treading on dangerous ground; the chances of you figuring out who's responsible for Tommee's murder are very slim."

Wade's caution only frustrated me further. Instead of getting closer to learning who had wanted Tommee Frack dead, it turned out there were too many to count.

And I'd put myself right in the middle of it. The image of the canary feather, a warning planted on the windshield of my car, floated into my mind. My stomach wrenched as the full impact of what everyone had been trying to tell me finally hit me: that getting involved in Tommee Frack's murder could have been the biggest mistake of my life.

Another thought struck me. "Why didn't you tell me this the last time I was here?"

"Before, I thought it would be dangerous for you to know. But at this point, you're in too deep. I figure it's more dangerous for you *not* to know."

"If that's supposed to make me feel better, it didn't work."

"It's supposed to make you be more careful. Don't assume anything, and don't trust anybody. There are a lot of barracudas out there."

I didn't doubt that for a second.

• • •

As I turned into my driveway, the names of all the people who were likely to have wanted Tommee Frack dead buzzed around inside my head like mosquitoes. The half-dozen highly visible, highly connected individuals who'd set him up in business in the first place. Every single person who'd been involved in the ongoing game of give-and-take since it started.

Then there was my original list of suspects. George Babcock, of course, but also the women in Tommee's life.

It was almost too overwhelming to contemplate.

But I forgot all about Tommee as I neared the end of the driveway and was confronted with the pulsing red light of an ambulance.

"Oh, my God!" I cried, fighting off the sick feeling that instantly came over me.

I pulled over just in time to see a paramedic slam the back door of the vehicle shut.

"What happened to Betty?" I demanded, jumping out of my car.

"Who are you?"

"Her friend. I live right over there."

"She was attacked. Looks like somebody broke into her house."

"Is she all right?"

"She was in good enough shape to dial 911."

"Where are you taking her?"

"Port Townsend. Norfolk Hospital."

I watched him leap into the ambulance. I immediately got back into my own car and headed toward my cottage.

My head was spinning as I raced inside. Stay calm, I told myself. You've got to think.

As I opened the door, Max and Lou pounced.

"Not now, guys," I told them urgently. "We don't have time."

I made a beeline for the phone. The red light was blinking.

A message from Betty? I wondered. A plea for help—and I wasn't here?

I pressed "Play."

"*You—have—one—message.*"

As the tape rewound, Prometheus launched into his usual tirade. "Damn you, *awk!*"

"Quiet!" I pleaded.

"*Awk!* Jesus H. Christmas!"

I turned up the volume.

"Hey, Jess. It's me, Jimmy. I'm on duty right now, but I thought I'd stop over this evening and take you for that ride I promised. Probably about eight, if that's okay. Hope I catch you in. Later!"

So it hadn't been Betty who called, only Jimmy. I dialed Nick.

"Come on, Nick, answer . . . Nick? It's Jessie. Betty's on her way to Norfolk Hospital. They're bringing her in an ambulance right now."

"Oh, my God. Stroke? Heart attack?"

"Worse," I croaked. "Someone came into her house and assaulted her. Betty's hurt, Nick."

As I raced to the hospital, I felt as if I was in one of those awful dreams, the kind in which you're desperately hurrying and everything around you is moving in slow motion. Every traffic light was red, and there seemed to be an unbelievable number of cars on the road.

When I finally made it to the hospital, I dashed inside. I had to remind myself that I wasn't the only person who was under stress as I stepped out of the way of people in wheelchairs and young couples carrying newborn babies.

I careened down the hall blindly, still managing to hold it together. But as soon as I spotted a familiar face, I lost it.

"Oh, Nick! This is so horrible!"

"She's a fighter, Jess. And they think she'll be fine."

"You talked to her doctor?"

"Yes. He said her injuries aren't bad. It's more the shock of what happened that he's worried about."

I sank into one of the plastic chairs lining the hallway. "What *did* happen?"

"Apparently somebody broke into her—"

"They didn't have to break in. She keeps the back door unlocked during the day. Remember when I barged in on the two of you? Anybody could have walked in."

"However he got inside, he wasn't there to steal anything. Or, from the looks of things, even to hurt her very badly."

"What's left?" I asked, even though I knew the answer.

"He must have been trying to scare her." He swallowed. "Or somebody else."

"Like me," I groaned. "This is all my fault."

"Jess, you could never have anticipated that something like this would happen."

"I should have known Betty was going to become more enmeshed in this, that the creepy phone call was just the beginning." I lowered my voice. "Nick, I found out what Tommee Frack was involved in."

I related my entire conversation with Wade Moscowitz. When I'd finished, Nick murmured, "This is worse than we ever imagined, Jess. More complicated, too. Now we know there are a lot of people who would have loved to keep Tommee Frack from 'singing.' Powerful people, too. Which explains why somebody's been trying to scare you away since the beginning."

"All these 'warnings,' even before this," I mused. "The phone call and the break-in and and the feather and being followed by that Jeep—"

"I almost forgot! I finally heard back from my contact at the DMV. He traced the license plate."

"And—?"

"You're not going to believe this, but there's a black Jeep Cherokee with the New York State license plate BLD-0917 registered under the name Vincent Pascucci."

I blinked. "Officer Pascucci? Jimmy's partner? *He's* the one who's been following me?"

"Excuse me." A nurse carrying a clipboard poked her head out of a doorway. "Are you here with Elizabeth Vandervoort?"

Nick and I both jumped to our feet.

"Is she all right?" I demanded.

"She'll be just fine. You can see her now, if you like. She's a little doped up, but she can manage a quick visit. It'll be good for her to know you're here."

As we walked through the Emergency Room, passing a row of beds separated by curtains, Nick took my hand.

"You all right?" he asked gently.

"I'll feel better after I see for myself that she's okay."

Betty's eyes were closed. She seemed very fragile and very small. No glittery eye shadow illuminated her tired-looking eyes, and the pale green fabric of her hospital gown made her skin look ghostly white.

"Betty?" I said softly.

She opened her eyes. I let go of Nick's hand and took hers. "You look great," I assured her, only lying a little. "How do you feel?"

"Like someone who's been banged on the head with a bowling ball." She forced a little smile. "But they tell me the damage was minimal. According to that nice doctor who was just in here, I should be tap dancing again in no time. What's even more important is that I'll be fine by January."

"January?" I repeated.

"For my trip to Tahiti, of course!"

"So that's where you decided to go."

"I couldn't resist the thought of those men in loincloths with the palm fronds." For a brief moment, the familiar twinkle lit up her eyes.

"Do you know what happened?" Nick asked somberly.

"I was arranging flowers on that table I keep in the front parlor, the one with all the picture frames and knickknacks. The next thing I knew, someone shoved me. I fell across the arm of the couch and hit my head against the edge of the table, which is probably why I feel like I just drank a whole bottle of champagne all by myself."

"That's the drugs. They gave you something for the pain."

"Got a huge gash in my side, too, where I smacked into the corner of the table. Guess I won't be wearing my bikini on *this* vacation."

"You didn't hear anyone?" I asked.

"No. It wasn't until he came up right behind me and I saw him in the mirror that I was even aware that anyone else was in the house."

"You saw him?" Nick and I exclaimed in unison.

"Well . . . not exactly. I keep a small mirror in a silver frame on the table, stuck in with all the photographs, and I caught just a glimpse of him as he came up behind me."

"What did you see?" I demanded.

"Just his shoulder and chest. But I know he was tall. Towered above me, in fact."

Tall. Towering. Those didn't sound like words that described stubby Officer Pascucci.

"Are you sure, Betty?" I wondered if the incident had left her confused.

"Positive."

"But you said yourself the mirror was tiny."

"A mirror's a mirror, Jessica. They don't lie."

"But—"

The nurse reappeared and reached for the curtain hanging above the bed. "I'm going to have to ask you folks to leave now," she said firmly. "We're taking her up to her room now. I think she's had enough excitement for one day."

"She's going to be all right, though, isn't she?" I asked anxiously.

"Sure she is. We just want her here overnight so we can keep an eye on her." She winked at Betty. "I know the type. Stronger than an ox."

Betty laughed softly. "Jessica already knows what a tough cookie I am."

I squeezed her hand gently. "Take good care of yourself, will you?"

"I'll be out of here in no time." She squeezed my hand back. "And you and Nick will come pick me up when they release me, right?"

"Yes, Betty. Nick and I will come. Together."

Nick and I headed out of the ER, this time walking a couple of feet apart.

"I think she'll be fine," he said.

I only nodded. This was all my fault. And even though I'd wreaked havoc with the life of one of my best friends, I had nothing to show for it. As far as the investigation was concerned, I'd come up completely empty-handed. Although I thought I knew *why* Tommee had been murdered, I still didn't know who'd killed him.

When we reached the exit, Nick said, "Want to get something to eat?"

"Thanks, but I've got to get home. I've got other plans."

"Oh." He sounded hurt. "I figured you'd enjoy the company. That you wouldn't want to be alone tonight."

"Actually, a friend of mine is taking me out."

"Don't tell me. Our man in blue."

I was in no mood to play verbal volleyball with Nick. "His name is Jimmy."

"You're going out with him? After what Betty said?"

"Surely you're not referring to the fact that she claims the person who assaulted her was tall!"

"That doesn't make you nervous?"

"You're joking, right?"

"But that Jimmy Nolan guy is tall and he works with Pascucci," Nick insisted. "Doesn't that give you second thoughts about getting in a car with him alone?"

"Aside from the fact that Jimmy is one of the nicest guys I've ever met, he's a cop! Who could be safer?"

"Pascucci's a cop, too, remember? You don't know anything about this guy, Jess. For all you know, *he* could have murdered Tommee Frack!"

"Right." I infused my voice with as much sarcasm

as I could. "Now *there's* a likely scenario. Next you're going to tell me he's the one who stole my notebook."

"What are you talking about?"

"The notebook I used to write down every piece of information and evidence I had. All my conversations, phone numbers and addresses, everything you told me about Frack and his murder. . . . It's missing."

"You mean missing as in *misplaced*? Or missing as in someone deliberately took it?"

"All I know is that this morning, I realized it had vanished. And the thought occurred to me that maybe whoever broke in last night took it."

"Jessie, this is getting—"

"For heaven's sake, I probably just left it somewhere! Or the dogs ate it. At this point, I don't know what's real and what's simply the product of my imagination. But one thing I do know is that Jimmy had nothing to do with any of it."

"Listen to me," he argued. "I've got a lot more experience than you. The main reason people get murdered is that they foolishly trust another person. They figure he's someone he's not—and they don't find out they're wrong until it's too late."

Maybe Nick was a little jealous, and maybe he had a right to be. But trying to tie Jimmy Nolan into the bizarre events of the past few weeks was absurd. Especially if the core of his argument was the fact that, unlike Pascucci, he happened to be taller than five foot six.

"Take Frack," Nick persisted. "Don't you think he opened his door to his murderer without giving it a second thought? Aren't you convinced that whoever killed him was somebody he knew, somebody he had no inkling was dangerous?"

"Goodbye, Nick," I said firmly. "I really have to go."

"May I ask where Prince Charming is taking you?"

"Not that it's any of your business, but we're going for a ride."

He sighed. "In that case, have fun."

"Don't worry," I retorted. "I always do."

Chapter 18

"People who keep dogs are cowards who haven't
got the guts to bite people themselves."
                                    —August Strindberg

Just as he'd promised, Jimmy showed up promptly
at eight. Punctuality was something I liked in
a man.

Politeness, too. I was tickled that he held the car
door open for me as we embarked on our little ad-
venture.

"Hop in, young lady, and get ready for a once-in-a-
lifetime experience. I guarantee this will be an
evening unlike any other you've ever had."

"You'd better deliver," I teased. "I'm counting on
you."

By this point, I was actually looking forward to
that ride in either the James Dean car or the pink con-
vertible. I desperately needed the chance to do something mindless and fun. My only regret was that Nick

wouldn't be there to see me cruising around town with Jimmy.

As we rode along Cross Country Road, I decided to relax. The events of the long, difficult day still swam in my head, but I wanted to forget, at least for a while.

I was almost at that point when Jimmy slammed on the brakes, pitching me forward so hard my seat belt cut into me. He was leaning on the horn, its angry bleating accompanying the ear-splitting sound of tire rubber screeching against pavement.

"Oh, my God!" I cried. I watched in horror as we narrowly missed crashing into the back fender of a car that had just run a red light and shot in front of us.

"Jesus H. Christmas!" Jimmy yelled. "What an asshole!"

"Wow! That was close!"

"You okay?"

"I'm fine, thanks to your reflexes."

Aside from my frantically pounding heart, the only casualty appeared to be the heel of my left foot. The sudden lurching of the car had sent something flying out from under the seat, hitting me with what felt like a sharp edge. I reached down to pick it up.

My notebook.

I stared at it.

"Oh, yeah, that's yours," Jimmy said. "I forgot to mention that you left it in my car the other night."

He glanced over at me, smiling.

"Thanks," I said, smiling back.

But I was thinking, *That's impossible . . . isn't it?*

I struggled to recall the last time I'd seen my notebook . . . Monday evening, right after I'd found the feather on my windshield. As soon as I came home and found Jimmy's message on my answering machine, I'd sat on the couch and recorded everything I'd learned that day at the Athertons' and Pomonok Properties and Jonathan Havemeyer's office.

Afterward, I'd gone out with Jimmy. There was no way I'd brought my notebook along. Not when I clearly remembered ordering myself to take the night off from Tommee Frack.

I started to feel cold.

Is it possible that Jimmy's the one who broke into my house? To take my notebook?

A fog of panic was clouding my brain. *Think!* I commanded. I replayed every word I'd said on our date at Wellington's. I'd shown him the notebook. I'd told him it contained everything I needed to figure out who killed Tommee. He'd said that solving the case was just a question of me going through all the information I'd gathered and piecing it together.

Prometheus. A few hours earlier, when I'd rushed into the house after learning that Betty had been attacked, he'd squawked, "Jesus H. Christmas." The odd expletive that Jimmy used, especially when he was under stress.

At the time, I'd been too distracted to pay attention to my parrot's new phrase. But thinking back, I was positive I'd never heard Jimmy use it inside the cottage.

Which meant the only way the bird could have heard the quirky expression "Jesus H. Christmas" was if it had popped out while Jimmy was prowling around inside my house, looking for the notebook.

It was all starting to add up. I pictured the chair,

left at an awkward angle as if somebody had tripped over a rug—or a cat—and bumped into it. Banging into it unexpectedly would have prompted Jimmy to yell the first thing that came to mind—the same scenario that had made him blurt it out that night at Wellington's.

And then I remembered something else Jimmy had said that evening at the bar. He told me that wherever you go, you take something with you and you leave something behind.

He'd left something behind, all right. An expression I'd never heard anyone else but him use.

The sick feeling got worse as Jimmy drove farther along Cross Country Road, bringing us closer to the quiet, out-of-the-way industrial area where he kept his beloved old cars.

Could he possibly be dangerous? I wondered, my head spinning. He certainly fits Betty's description of her tall assailant . . . But what about Pascucci? Nick's friend traced the car that's been following me to *him*.

Jimmy could have borrowed it, I reasoned. After all, they were friends. Or were they both involved in the Tommee Frack homicide . . . ?

I jumped when Jimmy said, "Speaking of your notebook, you still poking around the murder?"

"Not really." I tried to use the same casual tone. "I decided to leave it to the police, just like you said."

Another thought struck me. I opened my notebook to the first page, pretending I was just flipping through it as a nervous gesture.

There it was, just as I remembered. Back at the beginning, Nick had given me a list of vehicles that the residents of Brewster's Neck reported having spotted in their neighborhood in the hours just before Tommee's murder. I'd written, *Other neighbors, UPS truck, FedEx truck, police car* . . .

Police car. It could have been Jimmy. Of course, it could very well have been Pascucci.

But it *could* have been Jimmy.

"Yeah, you're better off leaving the whole thing alone," he said. "I read about Frack in your notebook—all about that whole payoff thing he was involved in and the fact that he was about to sing . . . The guy was really bad news. No wonder he got iced."

"Right," I croaked.

The air in the car was stifling. *He knows all about Tommee—but there's no way he read about it in my notebook,* I thought. *I didn't find out about the payoff scheme and Tommee's decision to turn state's evidence until* after *the book disappeared.*

Suddenly, all the pieces clicked together. And the picture they formed wasn't merely clear: it was absolutely horrifying.

I glanced over at Jimmy, wondering how I could possibly have been so wrong about him. For the first time, I noticed how tightly he was gripping the steering wheel.

And then I focused on his right hand, my heart skipping a beat as I zoomed in on it.

A Band-Aid stretched across his knuckles.

I immediately experienced a sinking feeling in my stomach. I had a pretty good idea of how he'd gotten hurt—and how he'd reacted when it happened.

Struggling to hide the fact that my hands were trembling, I slipped my cell phone out of my purse.

"Who are you calling?" Jimmy asked, glancing over at me.

"Just a friend. She's in the hospital and I promised to check up on her."

I dialed the familiar number.

Answer, I pleaded silently. *Please, please pick up.*

When I heard the voice at the other end say, "Hello," I repressed a shudder of relief.

"Hi, Betty. It's me. Jessie."

"This isn't Betty. It's Nick."

"Yes, Betty, I know. It's good to hear your voice, too. You're sounding much better."

"What's going on, Jess?"

"I just wanted to tell you I found my notebook. Remember I told you I lost it?"

"I'm listening."

"You'll never guess where it turned up. In Jimmy Nolan's car! Remember, the police officer I've been seeing? I'm with him right now."

"Jess, are you telling me that cop is the one who broke into your house?"

"You're absolutely right, Betty. And what you said about him before was completely true." I chuckled, although it sounded woefully thin in the darkness of Jimmy's car. "You're such a good judge of character!"

"My God, Jess. Where are you?"

"Oh, yes, he's a very interesting guy," I babbled on. "He collects classic cars. Right now, he's taking me to the place where he garages them."

"Damn! Where are the cars, Jess? What's the garage's address?"

"It's an industrial area, near a plumbing supply place—"

"Hey, you gonna be on that phone all night?" It was the first time I'd ever heard Jimmy sound cross. "I'm getting lonely over here."

"Do you know anything else about the location, Jess? Think. The number on the building? The name of the street?"

"I guess that's about it, Betty," I said. "Talk to you soon."

Overwhelming fear crept over me as Jimmy turned down a quiet street I recognized all too well. We would be at the garage in seconds. And even though I'd gotten through to Nick, I hadn't known enough about where "there" was to tell him how to find me.

"So who's your friend?" Jimmy asked. "It sounds as if she likes me."

In the dimly lit car, surrounded by a pitch-black night, the smile that had once looked charmingly boyish now looked sinister.

"My next-door neighbor. Believe it or not, she was attacked, right in her own house."

"Gee, that's too bad." He sounded sincere. His ability to act like someone other than who he really was sent a chill through me. "Do they know who did it?"

"No," I replied. "No idea. Probably just a random thing."

"You think so? Maybe it was something else."

"What do you mean?"

"I don't know. Maybe it was because you've been poking around into this murder. You know, like maybe somebody was sending you a warning."

My mouth was dry as I said, "I doubt it."

"If I were you, my neighbor being attacked would

scare me away from having anything to do with Tommee Frack."

"I told you I've already decided to leave that
alone."

"*Right.*"

The tone of his voice made it all too clear he didn't
believe me. Was it possible that my worst fears were
correct? Was his real motive in bringing me here
tonight putting a stop to my snooping, once and for
all?

I was on the verge of panic by the time we pulled
into the small lot beside the garage that housed
Jimmy's two classic cars. We were completely alone
out here, and it was so dark I could barely see.

If I ran, there was nowhere to go.

"Come on inside," Jimmy said, opening his car
door.

I knew I had no choice.

As we walked toward the building, he took my
arm—something he'd never done before. He opened
the door and half-led, half-pushed me inside.

Jimmy didn't waste any time. "Pick your poison.
The T-bird or the Spyder?"

"You know, Jimmy," I said, trying desperately to
keep my voice from cracking, "I'm suddenly not feeling very well. It's that same headache I got the other
night . . . I think I should just go home."

"I'm afraid that's not possible."

"We can do this some other time. But tonight just
isn't—"

He grabbed me by the arm. "You must think I'm
pretty stupid. Don't you get it? *I'm on to you!* I read
what you wrote in that notebook! All those people

you've been talking to . . . You were *this close* to figuring out who Frack really was—and why he ended up
dead."

"Please let go of me, Jimmy. I don't know anything! All I heard were rumors and—"

"That guy you talked to—what was his name,
Wade? *He* knew." He wrenched me even closer. "You
went back to talk to him again, didn't you?" he
hissed. "And I bet he told you all about Frack."

"You're wrong! I never had any intention of trying
to find out anything more! I decided to forget the
whole thing. It's just too complicated and—"

"Bullshit! You're *lying*!" His mouth twisted into an
ugly sneer. "You were *never* gonna give up! Even having the people who are close to you get hurt isn't
enough to stop you. I figured maybe seeing that old
lady lying in the hospital would be enough to get you
to back down. But I was wrong, wasn't I? Maybe I
really *am* stupid, because it took me this long to figure
out that nothing's gonna change your mind. But your
notebook spelled it all out for me. Getting hold of it
was worth it—even though your stupid dog bit me
while I was looking for it. Jesus H. Christmas, that little bastard is out of control!"

Max. So my hunch about the Band-Aid on Jimmy's
hand had been correct. The "Jesus H. Christmas"
Prometheus had mimicked was courtesy of my terrier's overly anxious jaws.

"You just wouldn't let it go," Jimmy went on in the
same jeering tone. "And you were almost at the point
of running off to the newspapers or the D.A.'s office
or whatever it took to blow this whole thing wide
open, weren't you?"

"Jimmy, no! I—"

"You're just like Frack. He had a big mouth, too. He was about to screw things up for everybody. And in the process, take down a lot of good people while he got off scot-free. We knew what was going on . . . the way he was suddenly best pals with the D.A.'s office. Even though the police commissioner and the rest of the department did so much for him, he still didn't appreciate what he had. He was about to turn them all in, the bastard, every single person who helped make him who he was.

"Some people don't know when to leave well enough alone. Which is why somebody else finally decides it's time they were out of the picture."

He yanked me closer to the Spyder and reached for the passenger-side door. "Get in."

I was frozen. There was no doubt in my mind that if I got into that car, I would never get out.

"Get *in*!"

I tried to pull away, but his grip was too powerful. He pushed me down, trying to force me into the car.

"Yeow!" I screeched as my head smashed against the hard metal edge of the car roof.

For a few seconds, I saw stars. And then I fought back.

I'd never hit anyone in my life. But I curled my right hand into a tight fist and punched Jimmy Nolan in the face with all the force I could muster.

I guess I socked him pretty hard, because he reeled backward, releasing his grip on me.

"*Jesus H.—!*" he yelled, covering his face with his hands. "You broke my fuckin' *nose*!"

I darted away, desperately looking for something—*anything*—to use as a weapon. My eyes lit on the tools that hung from hooks along one wall. Dashing over, I grabbed the first one that looked capable of doing some damage: a heavy wrench, over a foot long. Turning, I raised it above my head and charged toward Jimmy, energized by a dark line running down his chin that could only be blood.

Before I realized what was happening, he'd reached up and wrested the wrench away from me. "We need something better than this," he said, his voice calm but his eyes wild. "Fortunately, I got just the right tool for the job."

I jerked my head around, frantically searching for another weapon. But he grabbed me again, this time by the hair. I did my best to punch and kick as he dragged me back toward the car. The sound of his cold laughter increased my frustration.

I was suddenly hit with the chilling realization that he was *enjoying* this.

"Look, Jimmy, we've got to talk." I tried to sound calm, but fear made my voice waver. "I promise not to say a word to anybody. Just let me go, and—"

"It's not that simple," he said icily. "I work for people who expect me to fulfill certain duties. And letting canaries fly away is not one of them."

He grasped me by the neck with his free hand. From the back of my mind floated the image of the delicate yellow bird I'd found lying near Tommee Frack, his head snapped off as if whoever was responsible had no sense that it was a living being . . .

"See, with Frack, I was just taking care of business," he went on. "Somebody hires me to do something, I do it. Especially when the order comes from Harned."

"Lieutenant Harned?" I gasped, truly stunned. "*Harned* ordered Frack's murder?"

"Him and a bunch of other guys in the department, all the way up to the commissioner. With Harned in charge of the investigation, we knew there was no way any of us would be implicated. And it was a cinch, since Frack knew me and trusted me. We were pals. Bringing him here, to this garage, was a piece of cake. At that point, finishing him off was easy. The whole thing was planned out smoothly, from start to finish. We were even smart enough not to use a gun, since the bullet could be traced. The canary . . . that was my own personal touch. Harned wasn't thrilled when he first heard about it, but just like everything else, he took care of it. The dead bird disappeared before the newspapers ever got wind of it. 'The perfect crime,' just like I said . . . at least, until *you* starting butting in."

He tightened his fingers, digging into my windpipe and cutting off even more air. For the second time that night, flashes of light popped in front of me.

When I started making horrible choking sounds, he let go. I was relieved—but only for a second. Still holding onto me by my hair, he leaned over and stuck his free arm under the driver's seat of the Spyder. I watched him fumble around. When he withdrew his hand, even in the dim light I could see it was wrapped around a ball-peen hammer.

I'd seen them before, of course. They were common enough. And perfect for everyday jobs—like banging out a sports car's crumpled fender. But I'd never thought much about the fact that they mainly consisted of a metal sphere about 3 centimeters in diameter.

"I had a nice spot on the North Shore all picked out for you," he told me. "I figured I'd make things pleasant on your last night out. But I guess we'd better just end this here and now."

As I watched Jimmy raise the hammer high above his head, I felt as if everything was moving in slow motion. I knew exactly what was about to happen.

A feeling I'd never experienced before rushed over me. It rose from somewhere deep in my gut, an instinct I hadn't known I possessed. I suddenly understood the behavior I'd witnessed in so many animals in my care who felt threatened. Gentle house cats and docile lap dogs—including my Max—morphed into snarling, savage beasts who were prepared to do whatever it took to survive.

When I twisted my head around, the arm Jimmy was using to hold my hair was only a few inches away. I lunged forward and sank my teeth into his flesh.

"*Shit!*" he cried. "Jesus H.—"

And then an explosion of sound jolted through me.

Jimmy crumpled, and the hammer clattered against the concrete floor. I watched in horror as a dark blotch appeared on his shirt, near his left shoulder. Instinctively I jerked my head up to see if any more bullets were about to fly.

The man standing in the doorway lowered his arm. But he kept his fingers curled around his gun and his eyes on the man sprawled on the floor.

I blinked as I realized who it was. Officer Vincent

Pascucci walked over to Jimmy. Ignoring me, he knelt to check for a pulse.

"Is he dead?" I croaked.

He didn't answer. Instead, he slid his gun back in the holster, then pulled out his radio and barked, "We got a man down. Send an ambulance to six twenty-nine Front Street in Westfield right away. Hey, Maria? Send backup, too."

Jimmy let out a groan. Pascucci crouched next to him.

"Is he going to make it?" I asked in a hoarse whisper.

"He'll make it." Without taking his eyes off Jimmy, he asked, "What about you? You hurt?"

"I'm okay." My knees felt weak and my whole body was shaking. "Just scared. And very glad you got here when you did."

"Yeah, well, those few seconds you bought by biting the bastard probably saved your life. You got good instincts."

"Thanks." Once again, I thought of Max. "I learned from a master."

"Jessie?"

I whirled around and saw a man standing in the doorway, his face twisted with fear.

"Nick!"

"Are you all right?"

"I'm fine—thanks to very good police work."

He came over and took me in his arms. "Thank God you're—" He couldn't finish.

"Thank God for cell phones." I slumped against him, suddenly exhausted.

When we pulled apart, Officer Pascucci fixed his

dark eyes on mine. "Didn't anybody ever tell you to steer clear of murder investigations? Not to mention murderers?"

I glanced at Nick before replying. "Maybe once or twice."

Pascucci scowled. "When I saw you at the funeral, I got a bad feeling about what you were up to. I checked it out and found I was right. Driving around, asking people questions . . . dangerous stuff."

I nodded. Staring at the limp body lying in front of me, watching the patch of blood near Jimmy's shoulder grow larger, I wasn't about to disagree.

"*You're* the one who's been following me in your Jeep," I realized. "And you made that phone call to Betty and left that canary feather on my windshield . . . You were trying to scare me away."

"Too bad you can't take a hint."

"But tonight . . . how did you know—?"

"Nick got in touch with me after you called him, and I told him where Jimmy keeps his cars. Then I got over here as fast as I could. See, I've been here before, plenty of times." He gestured toward the Spyder. "I even helped put in a new carburetor. That was a while ago, before I figured out what Jimmy was into—and how he was getting the money for all these fancy cars."

"Working for Frack?" I asked.

"Making cash deliveries—and making a few extra bucks on the side for his trouble. That was bad enough. But then Jimmy started bragging about how he was gonna buy himself a '66 Mustang—and the next thing I knew, Frack turned up dead." He shook his head grimly. "I suspected he might have been involved, but I didn't want to believe it. I mean, dirty money is one thing. Murder is something else entirely."

Jimmy let out a another groan. When he moved his arm, I saw the muscles of Pascucci's face tighten.

"Jesus *fucking* H. Christmas!" Jimmy growled. "You shot me, you bastard!"

"You're under arrest for the murder of Tommee Frack," Pascucci replied coldly. "Internal Affairs and the District Attorney are on the way. Anything you do or say may be used against you in a court of law. You have the right to consult an attorney . . ."

A siren wailed. The lights of the approaching ambulance pulsed red through the grimy windows, as bright as fireworks in the dark, starless night. Even more reassuring was the sound of slamming car doors, a sign that more cops had arrived on the scene.

As I gave my statement, I watched a pair of paramedics ease Jimmy onto a stretcher. Once I finished, I couldn't resist moving closer.

"How could you do it, Jimmy?" I demanded in a hoarse voice. "How could you kill a man in cold blood?"

"I did what I was paid to do." Jimmy looked up at me, his face expressionless. "It's like I told you, Jess. To me, it's just a job."

• • •

Never before had the lights of Cross Country Road, the streetlights and the traffic lights and the brightly lit parking lots of the Home Depot and the Old Navy, seemed so welcoming. My throat ached from Jimmy's merciless grip, my arm was throbbing, and a huge bump was growing on my forehead where I'd banged it against the car roof. But I couldn't remember having ever felt happier to be alive.

Nick cast me a wary glance from over on the driver's side. "I hope you learned something tonight."

"I certainly did. I learned not to go to a dark, isolated parking garage with a man until at least the fifth date."

"Didn't you learn anything about the dangers of flirting with strangers?"

"What do you mean, 'strangers'?" I demanded, stung. "Every man you meet for the first time is a stranger. Unless he's your best friend's brother or . . . or your cousin's roommate or something. Even *you* were a stranger the first time I met you."

"You know what I mean." Nick was using that exasperated tone of voice that absolutely drove me up the wall. "When you started in on Nolan, you didn't know a thing about him."

"First of all, I didn't 'start in on him.' I just happened to find him a teensy bit attractive. Second of all, he was a *cop*, for heaven's sake! How much more upstanding could a person be?"

"That's the whole point, Jess. People aren't always what they seem."

"But—you know what? Just take me home," I told him.

We drove in silence for a few blocks. I was trying to muster up the courage to say what I was thinking, which was that I wondered if maybe it was time for me to stop being so guarded.

I'd known all along I was taking a tremendous risk by getting involved with Tommee Frack's murder, but

I hadn't let it stop me. As a result, I'd come close to getting killed tonight.

But I'd survived.

Maybe I could survive taking other risks, too.

"Hey, Nick?"

"What, Jess?"

"I'm absolutely crazy about you."

"It just so happens I'm absolutely crazy about you, too."

He pulled over to the side of the road.

"You know I love you, Jessie," he said gently. "I've never stopped."

"I've never stopped loving you, either, Nick. I was just afraid."

"Then we'll take it slower."

"I'm sorry I hurt you in Hawaii," I said in a hoarse voice.

"You coming back to me here at home makes up for it."

"We really should talk about it one of these days."

"Okay. But right now, there's something more important we have to do."

"What?"

He gave me a look that absolutely melted me. "Kiss."

We did.

About the Author

CYNTHIA BAXTER is a native of Long Island, New York. She currently resides on the North Shore, where she is at work on the next *Reigning Cats and Dogs* mystery, *Putting on the Dog,* which Bantam will publish in fall 2004.

If you enjoyed
Dead Canaries Don't Sing . . .

Dear Reader,

A locked door, an anonymous note, an unidentified footprint . . . there's something irresistible about the unknown.

Ever since I was a little girl, I loved to read. And there were three elements of a story I always found utterly enthralling: a mystery, a spirited heroine (Pippi Longstocking was an early role model), and, as I neared adolescence, a little bit of romance.

Now that I'm grown up—and own a computer— I'm lucky enough to be spinning my own tales filled the three intriguing elements that first hooked me on reading. By making my heroine a veterinarian, I've been able to add a fourth passion of mine: animals.

So, I invite you to come along with me and enjoy the thrill of those locked doors and mysterious footprints, and the antics of Max, Lou, Cat, Prometheus, and all the other characters who are part of the story. I hope you have as much fun stepping into Jessie and Nick's world as I had creating it.

Fondly,

Cynthia Baxter

Read on for a preview of the next
***Reigning Cats & Dogs* mystery**

Putting on the Dog

coming in September 2004 from Bantam Books. . . .

"All men are intrinsically rascals, and I am only sorry that, not being a dog, I can't bite them."

—Lord Byron

Damn you, Marcus Scruggs!" I grumbled, leaning closer to the windshield of my van and peering through the sheeting rain. "Be honest, guys: am I totally nuts?"

Max and Lou, scrambling around on the seat beside me, didn't offer an opinion about my sanity. They were too busy acting like unruly preschoolers, wrestling as they vied for the space nearest the window. It was a close contest. Lou, my one-eyed Dalmatian, had longer legs. But Max, being a terrier, was infinitely more determined.

I sighed. Somehow, this wasn't the way I'd pictured my arrival in the Bromptons, a cluster of posh seaside communities famous for their palatial summer estates, four-star restaurants featuring twelve dollar desserts, and spectacular white-sanded beaches. For decades, the Bromptons had been known as the summer playground of movie stars, rock legends, writers, and artists. So it hadn't been difficult for Marcus Scruggs, a fellow Long Island veterinarian, to sell me on the idea of standing in for him at a charity dog show, answering pet owners' questions at the "Ask-the-Vet" booth.

But in the pouring rain, the area's main east-west route, Sunset Highway, looked like Main Street in a ghost town. Few cars crawled along the puddle-strewn thoroughfare, and fewer yet stood parked outside the pool supply shops and imported tile boutiques lining the edge.

Gritting my teeth, I veered around a body of water only slightly smaller than Lake Superior. Marcus had given me detailed directions for getting to the estate of someone named Wiener, the man who'd volunteered to put me up during the week-long event. I'd followed his directions to the letter, but I still couldn't find Darby Lane. Of course, not being able to make out the street signs through the pouring rain didn't help.

I clamped down on the brake when I spotted a yellow-and-white striped awning, a sure sign that I was approaching a farm stand. *Somebody* around here had to know where the Wiener estate was. I made a sharp turn, sending Max and Lou collapsing against each other in a heap.

"You guys okay?" I asked.

I didn't need an answer. By the time I pulled into a space, the two of them were already climbing all over each other again, making little yelping sounds and occasionally nipping each other playfully in the butt. I was glad somebody was having fun.

I stared out at the rain morosely, wondering why I hadn't brought along an umbrella. With a loud sigh of resignation, I opened the door of my van.

"Stay!" I instructed my two canines. They paused in their shenanigans, both shooting me surprised looks that said they wouldn't even have *considered* venturing out in weather like this.

"You guys are much too smart," I muttered. "You make the humans do all the dirty work."

I picked my way across a parking lot that was quickly turning into mud. I'd made a few Sunday morning emergency calls in my usual work ensemble, but before corralling Max and Lou into my 26-foot van and embarking on the drive to the East End, I'd changed into an outfit I felt better suited my destination. I'd donned a pale blue silk blouse and black rayon trousers, the finest that Bloomingdale's clearance rack had to offer. I only hoped the drops of rain that were turning them from solid colors into polka-dots wouldn't have a lasting effect.

"Excuse me!" I called to the clerk standing behind the vegetable displays, protected from the rain by the awning.

"Be with you in a minute." She turned her attention back to her customer, a woman who'd had the good sense to bring an umbrella *and* wear a slicker.

I glanced around frantically, looking for some friendly local who might be willing to help. And then I let out a screech.

Before I knew what was happening, I was blasted with water. It was as if someone—someone not very nice—had suddenly turned a hose on me.

"Wha-a-a...!" I sputtered.

I stood frozen to the spot, gradually realizing that the front of my silk shirt was splotched with huge, grimy wet spots, while my stylishly loose pants clung damply to my thighs. My dark blond hair felt plastered around my head, no doubt giving me the distinctive look of a sea otter.

I blinked a few times, struggling to get the water out of my eyes. As soon as I did, I saw that a low-slung sports car the same color as the ripe tomatoes on display had just squealed into a parking space less than five feet in front of me.

I just stared as the door of the Ferrari opened. The driver was dressed in torn jeans and a T-shirt. A Dodgers baseball cap was pulled down low over his eyes. With his shaggy hair and a sorry attempt at a beard, he looked like he'd stolen the car, not earned it.

I plunked myself right in front of him.

He peered up at me over his shades. "Gee, did I do that?"

"No, I'm on my way to a wet T-shirt contest," I shot back. "I thought accessorizing with mud would be a nice touch."

"Hey, I'm really sorry. I hope you'll let me pay the dry cleaning bill."

"That's the least you can do. But if you don't mind, I'd rather not discuss this in the pouring rain."

"Okay." He climbed out of the car, grabbed my hand, and pulled me after him. I would have protested except for the fact that he actually seemed to know where he was going.

I was so busy following him that I didn't pay much attention to the Mercedes that had just driven up beside us, or the wiry man in tight jeans and a black silk shirt who jumped out.

The Ferrari driver led me through the farm stand's side entrance, bringing us into a small room. It contained a few shelves lined with household basics like mango chutney and wasabi rice crackers.

He turned to me. "How much do you think is fair? To get your clothes cleaned, I mean."

"Isn't there something else I deserve?"

His expression tightened. "Don't tell me you're planning to hit me up for pain and suffering! Look, if you're going to start screaming about your lawyer—"

I tossed my head indignantly. "Actually, I was looking for an apology. Or is that too much to expect from somebody who drives like this was the Indy 500—"

Suddenly, the man I'd seen get out of the Mercedes appeared in the doorway, holding an impressively large camera. He immediately started snapping pictures, one after another.

I was so startled I didn't know what to think. But the Ferrari driver appeared to have figured it out immediately.

"Get the hell out of here!" he yelled. "You people are leeches—and you're the worst, Barnett! Can't I even go shopping for food without you harassing me?"

The Ferrari driver turned his back on the photographer. "Look, I'm getting out of here," he told me. "Funny, but I've suddenly lost my appetite." He reached into his pocket, took out a wad of bills, and pulled off two twenties. "Here. And I really am sorry."

He thrust the cash into my hand and dashed out. The man with the camera took off after him.

I stood frozen, struggling to make sense of what I'd just witnessed. I was still trying to figure it out when the clerk who'd blown me off earlier came over, snaking her way between the aisles.

"Did you get his autograph?" she asked, her eyes glittering excitedly.

"Who?"

"Shawn Elliot, of course!"

"That was him? In the Ferrari?"

She looked at me as if I'd just climbed out of a U.F.O. "You didn't recognize him?"

I shook my head. I knew who he was, of course. So did every other red-blooded woman between the ages of twelve and a hundred and twelve, at least if she'd been to the movies in the past five years.

"He didn't look the way he does in the movies," I told the clerk with a sheepish shrug.

She nodded knowingly. "He does that on purpose. When he's out here, I mean. You know, grow a beard, dress all grungy...act like he's a regular person."

"How do you know all this?"

"I read it in the *Stargazer*," she replied, looking smug. "Besides, that's exactly what I intend to do. After I get discovered, I mean." She leaned closer. "I'm not really a clerk, you know. I'm an actress, waiting for my big break."

I sighed. I'd been in the Bromptons for less than twenty minutes. Famous actors who drove Ferraris and wore ratty jeans, photographers who leaped out from behind the cucumbers, cashiers who were really movie stars in disguise...it was more than I could handle.

I was beginning to wonder how I'd ever get through the next few days.

．　．　．

As I climbed back into my van, Max and Lou predictably acted as if I'd been away on a Himalayan trek, instead of spending ten minutes getting directions and getting soaked.

"Hey, Maxie-Max. Come here, Louie-Lou." I patiently allowed my canines to slobber over me. As usual, Max got the best seat in the house, my lap. His four paws dug into my thighs like cleats.

"Okay, guys," I finally said, shooing them over to their side of the front seat and shifting my van into gear. "Let's try this again."

I headed out of the parking lot and a few minutes later I slowed down to read a road sign that suddenly emerged from the gray mist.

"Yes!" I breathed when I saw it read "Darby Lane." I had no idea if the clerk at the farm stand was any good at acting, but she'd turned out to be great at directions. Thanks to her, I'd finally found the Wiener estate.

Unfortunately, a wrought iron fence that looked like a leftover from Leavenworth separated me from it.

"Damn!" I muttered.

Through the rain splashing across my windshield, I could see something white clinging to the big lock smack in the middle of the gate. By that point, even the prospect of standing in the unrelenting downpour no longer fazed me, so I got out and retrieved the soggy piece of paper.

"'Gate is locked,'" I read aloud. "Now *there's* a useful bit of information. '*Use side entrance. Come to the house for the guesthouse key. Thanks.*'"

Sure enough, the side entrance was open. As I drove along the curving driveway, I spotted a small building nestled in the trees in the back corner of the sprawling grounds. The guesthouse, no doubt. It looked like a cottage out of a fairy tale, the kind of place the Seven Dwarves had lived in.

The main house was an entirely different story. I hadn't seen anything that grand since my high school trip to Paris, which included a day at Versailles—

white columns, dramatic marble steps, and enough square footage to spark a revolution.

I parked in the driveway, gave Max and Lou the usual warning about behaving themselves or else, and tromped across the lawn. I rang the bell, suddenly self-conscious. Not only was I covered with muddy streaks; the see-through effect of my wet clothing really did make me look like a competitor in a wet T-shirt contest.

Given the formal look of the house, I didn't expect Mr. Wiener to have much of a sense of humor. As I heard someone inside unlock the front door, I prepared an apology.

I never got to use it.

"It's *you*!" I gasped.

Standing on the other side of the doorway was the man who was responsible for my appearance in the first place—the person the clerk had insisted was Shawn Elliot.

"I guess I could say the same." He didn't look particularly happy to see me. "You haven't had second thoughts about calling your lawyer, have you?"

It took me a few seconds to figure out what he meant. "Oh, *that*. No, I don't even have a lawyer."

"Good. You'd be surprised how many people think meeting up with somebody a little bit famous means their big pay day."

A little bit famous? My eyes drifted past him to the huge movie posters that decorated the entryway. Each one advertised a different Shawn Elliot blockbuster, box office hits that had made him the fantasy love object of a large percentage of the world's female population.

He just stood there, looking at me expectantly.

"I read the note," I said. "About the key to the cottage?"

He frowned. "Are you associated with Dr. Scruggs?"

"Didn't anyone tell you? Marcus—Dr. Scruggs—isn't going to be the veterinarian at the dog show. I am."

He just blinked.

"I'm Jessica Popper. *Dr.* Jessica Popper."

"Oh, boy." Shawn shook his head. "Now I feel *completely* ridiculous."

"It's all right. If I could just have the key—"

"Please, come in. At this point, I'd consider it a personal favor."

I only hesitated for a moment before following him into the house. I figured that just getting inside would make me feel more like a human being and less like a water mammal. Instead, the air-conditioning combined with my sopping wet discounted designer outfit made me so cold I started to shake.

Shawn noticed immediately. "We have to get you out of those wet clothes."

"I'm fine. As soon as I get the key, I'll —"

"There's a guest room at the top of those stairs with a pool robe hanging behind the door. Why don't you put it on? You must be so uncomfortable."

The chance to put on something dry was hard to turn down. I climbed up to the second floor and, just as he'd promised, found a bedroom at the top of the stairs. It looked like something out of a design magazine, a perfectly-coordinated medley of soothing earth tones and rich, textured fabrics that made me want to curl up and go to sleep.

Instead, I closed the door and began unbuttoning my blouse. Immediately, something felt wrong. Maybe I was simply a little overwhelmed by all the bizarre events of the day, but I had the distinct feeling I was being watched.

I kept glancing around the room as I slipped out of my shirt and pants, then pulled on the white terry-cloth robe I found on a hook. It was as thick as shag carpeting, monogrammed with a swirling "S. E." on the pocket. As I did, I could have sworn I felt somebody's eyes on me. I was even convinced I could hear breathing. But there was no one in sight.

It wasn't until I opened the door to go downstairs that I discovered I'd been right all along. The Peeping Tom who had watched the entire strip show slunk out of his hiding place under the bed, then tried to slip past me without getting caught.

But I was too smart for a bulldog.

"Oh, no, you don't." I grabbed him by his collar. "Think you're pretty smart, do you?"

"Is that Rufus?" Shawn yelled up from the first floor. "Damn! I don't know how he does it, but every time a woman's getting undressed around here, he manages to get a front row seat."

"Is that true, you rascal?" I demanded.

Rufus just looked at me, as innocent as could be. But I was certain I saw a twinkle in the jowly beast's deep brown eyes before he toddled off, lumbering down the stairs toward the safety of his master's side.

"Is anybody else lurking under beds or in dark corners?" I descended the staircase, carrying my wet clothes in a bundle so I wouldn't drip on the expensive-looking carpeting. "Like maybe Mr. Wiener?"

"I'm afraid you're looking at him."

"Excuse me?"

"Wiener is my real name. Shawn Elliot Wiener. But when I started acting, I was advised to drop the last part." He grimaced. "Think about it. Can you imagine somebody named Wiener doing a love scene in a movie?"

"I see your point," I said as I followed him into what looked like a den. "By the way, thanks for letting me use your guesthouse."

Shawn shrugged. "It's the least I can do for such a good cause. I've been a strong supporter of the SPCA for a long time.

"Besides," he added, "I figured it might help Rufus win a blue ribbon. Not that he couldn't do it on his own. Right, boy?"

He crouched down in front of the animal at his feet, as squat and sturdy as a footstool, and scratched his neck vigorously.

"*Wuzza, wuzza, wuzza,*" he said in a funny low voice that was almost a growl. "Who's the best boy in the world? Who's the *best boy?*"

I had to admit, it was pretty endearing—not only to me, but also to the fifty pound lump of dog. Rufus lay with his four short legs splayed out on the Oriental carpet, grunting and wheezing and obviously in a state of ecstasy. Shawn looked pretty happy, too. I suspected this was a side of the Hollywood heartthrob that few people ever got to see.

"I guess you can tell I'm pretty crazy about this guy." Shawn glanced up at me, his cheeks flushed. "He's one of the few individuals I know who likes me for myself."

"Or else because you fill his food bowl every night."

He laughed. "At least I know he's not just kissing up to me because he wants to impress his friends with the fact that he knows a real live Hollywood actor.

And he never nags me about introducing him to some casting director."

"Maybe he should. He's got real star quality."

"You think?" He beamed proudly. "I guess I don't have it in me to be a pushy stage father. I'd rather protect my loved ones from the heartbreaks of this business. So for now, Rufus is destined to remain just another ordinary house pet."

"Except when it comes to the dog show."

"Hey, every parent has to show off some time. Maybe I don't want Rufus's name in lights, but that doesn't mean I don't want him to be appreciated for the glorious creature he truly is."

Much to the bulldog's dismay, Shawn stopped scratching and stood up. "I don't suppose you have any pull, do you?"

"Me? Naw. I'm just the hired help."

"Too bad. It'd be fun trying to get you on my good side."

Now *my* cheeks were flushed. I was sure of it. How could I not be, when Shawn Elliot was flashing me the boyish grin that, along with his startlingly blue eyes, had gotten him voted "America's Sexiest Man" three years running in *T.V. Guide*'s annual poll?

I quickly tried to come up with some other topic of conversation.

"By the way," I asked, "who was that obnoxious man taking all those pictures of you at the farm stand?"

"That idiot? Devon Barnett."

The expression on my face must have reflected my confusion.

"You've never heard of him?"

I shook my head.

"Probably because you have too much sense to read those ridiculous supermarket tabloids."

"You mean those rags at the check-out counters with headlines like 'Hundred-Year-Old Woman Gives Birth to Kittens?'

"Exactly. Or 'Shawn Elliot Assaults Animal Doctor with $300,000 Car.'"

My eyes grew as big as headlights. "Is that how much your car cost?"

I didn't get an answer.

"Devon Barnett is one of the sleaziest celebrity photographers that ever lived," Shawn went on. "Here, let me show you some of his handiwork."

He reached into a desk drawer and pulled out a stack of newspaper clippings. They were all the front pages of supermarket tabloids. I leafed through them, noting that each one sported accusatory headlines. Underneath, there was invariably a photograph that was just as incriminating.

"But don't all those photographers do pretty much the same thing?"

"Up to a point. But Devon Barnett is the absolute worst. He has no sense of fair play, no notion of what it means to respect other people's boundaries. Here, look at this one."

He leafed through the pile. The photograph he pulled out showed Shawn scowling at a group of crazed fans huddled at the bottom of some steps, frantically thrusting pens and paper in his face.

"Shawn Elliot: 'I Have No Time For Foolish Fans!'" the headline read.

"Do you know where that was taken?" he asked.

I shook my head.

"No, of course not. That's the whole point. The

answer is, outside a funeral home. I was coming out of my father's wake, for God's sake."

"I think I'm beginning to understand," I told him.

"It's not just that Barnett captures people at their very worst moments and then twists them into something they're not," Shawn continued. "What's even more despicable is the fact that he'll stop at nothing to get a photo. One time I was really sick. I'd been in seclusion for almost two weeks. All kinds of rumors were springing up, and somehow, Barnett got hold of my private number. He called me and told me he'd just hit Rufus with his car, right in front of my house. I raced outside, half crazed. Rufus was perfectly fine, of course. But Barnett got exactly what he wanted: a picture of me looking like a madman, running across the lawn in my underwear."

I took a moment to appreciate the fact that I wasn't famous or important. I hadn't realized what an invasion of privacy it was, having someone devote his entire life to capturing your worst moments on film so they could be plastered over every newsstand and supermarket check-out in the country.

Rufus picked that moment to waddle over to Shawn and nudge him. I guess he'd decided it was his turn to be the focus of his master's attention again.

Which made me remember I had some canine lovables of my own.

"My dogs!" I cried. "I mean, I have two of them, a Westie and a Dalmatian, and right now they're probably wondering if I've deserted them forever. If I could just get the key to the guesthouse—"

"Sorry. I know I got carried away. But I can't help it. Just thinking about that Barnett character makes my blood boil."

He got the key, then walked me to the door.

"Keep that robe as long as you need it. Make yourself comfortable, and let me know if you need anything."

"I'm sure I'll be fine," I told him.

"And remember, it's just me and Rufus, all alone in this big house," Shawn said. He hit me again with that grin. "Don't be a stranger, okay?"